cage of ICE and ECHOES

PAM GODWIN

Visit my website at pamgodwin.com

The books in the **FROZEN FATE** trilogy
are not stand-alones.

They must be read in order.
Hills of Shivers and Shadows #1
Cage of Ice and Echoes #2
Heart of Frost and Scars #3
Rise of Ink and Smoke (Spin-off)

Hills of Shivers and Shadows
Links and Content Warning

"Better the illusions that exalt us than
ten thousand truths."
Alexander Pushkin

frankie

ONE

In the quiet of my heart, where death whispers, I tread softly, carrying the weight of Wolfson's absence.

A week has passed without him. A deep, black void. Cold. Painful. Never-ending.

Like the polar night.

Like our empty bellies.

Somewhere north of the Arctic Circle, I stand at the frosted window of our cabin, watching snowflakes dance.

Our cabin.

My prison for over four months. Longer for Leonid and Kodiak. They've been trapped here since childhood.

With Denver and Wolf gone, it's our cabin now. A cage of ice with frozen pipes, dwindling pantries, and echoes of the dead.

A permanent chill lives on my skin, my goosebumps

the size of cherries. But it's a welcome distraction from the ache within.

The heavy weight in my arms, Wolf's saxophone case, holds memories etched in brass and melody. A relic of a tortured soul taken too soon. His haunting music used to fill these walls as vibrant and inimitable as the northern lights.

Now there's just silence. A silence so swollen it chokes.

I feel guilty wearing his coat when he died in the bloodstained ruins of mine. I feel guilty loving his brothers when I couldn't love him the way he wanted. I feel guilty taking a breath when I couldn't stop him from taking his life.

I need you with me. We can finally be together.

He didn't want to die alone.

Part of me, a dark, dangerous shadow, knows it would be easier to join him. To let the cold embrace me, to close my eyes and imagine it's Wolf's arms around me one last time.

I shake off the thought, my survival instinct still too strong. Even stronger is my love for his brothers. I would never do that to them, would never hurt them more than they're already hurting.

The tread of boots drifts from the basement stairs, heralding Leo's approach.

In the caress of candlelight, he emerges, a silhouette of sorrow, cradling a box laden with ghosts of the past. Within lie the remnants of innocence—clothes he and Kody wore as children—and the identities of women lost to this place. Among them, his mother.

My eyes, always on the brink of tears, look away.

Sensing my turmoil, he sets down the box, eases the case from my grip, and lowers it to the floor with reverent gentleness. His hands, red from the cold yet steady and firm, find my shoulders, anchoring me.

Our foreheads meet, resting together in a communion of pain.

"Breathe." His voice is my lighthouse in the fog. "Again."

Our lungs empty in unison, our breaths a coil of vapor.

"Want to talk about it?" His fingers dig in, massaging tense joints.

Wolf lives in my head in fragments, in flashes. Eyes that once held galaxies of mischief, now stilled. Hugs that once thawed the harshest winter, now phantoms. His punch lines and pet names, now lost to the wind.

Wolf.

My Wolf.

He left this world because it hurt him irreparably. From the moment he was born, it brutalized him, molested him, starved him of love, and ripped him apart.

No use talking about it. It won't bring him back.

"We need to move forward." I bury my hands in the fur of Leo's coat. "I don't want to cry anymore."

Understanding shines in his mismatched eyes. "I miss you. Your smile. Your body. Your warmth."

I sleep between him and Kody every night, swaddled in masculine heat. But that's not what he means. He misses our intimacy. Our profound connection through sex. We haven't been together like that in two weeks.

Days consumed by the relentless pursuit of sustenance and solutions leave no room for baser needs.

Nights, while tangled together in a pretzel of limbs, offer no comfort for longing hearts, only the stark reminder that every calorie must be conserved. Anything beyond tender whispers of love is a luxury we cannot afford.

"I miss you, too." I hold my lips to his, soaking in his affection. "So much."

Frustration sharpens his breath.

"This is temporary." He steps away to collect the box.

"Forever awaits." Whatever that means, however long it takes, I'm here for it.

I grip the handle of the saxophone case.

He snuffs out the candles. Then, hand in hand, we step outside, braving the maw of a howling blizzard.

Snow crunches under our boots. Icy air bites at our cheeks. The short trek to the workshop isn't quick, thanks to the brutal, unrelenting wind. When we finally step inside and slam the repaired door on the storm, it feels like I traded one tomb for another.

Not enough candlelight to chase away the shadows. No heat source to cut through the cold. We're out of coal and firewood, and the power system remains inoperable.

I'm afraid. Afraid of the isolation that gnaws as fiercely as the hunger. Afraid of the hope we put into a plane we don't know how to fly. Afraid of a future devoid of Wolf.

He told us we would die before the thaw. I didn't believe him.

But now...

We don't talk about it. Instead, we tackle each day like the beginning of a great quest. A fresh start to a new life. In that vein, we've made it our mission to salvage pieces of our existence and stow them in the bush plane that promises escape.

I've been gathering Wolf's belongings with a

desperate fervor, things like his purple housecoat, dried-up sharpies, sketchbooks, hand-drawn illustration of the cockpit, and saxophone. I fear something irreplaceable might be accidentally destroyed as we break apart the cabin, bit by bit, burning its pieces to keep the fire going in the hearth.

We have months before we can attempt a takeoff. Loading the plane now might be getting ahead of ourselves. But it fuels our will to survive. Keeps the embers of our future alight in the darkness.

As I follow Leo through the frigid workshop, we pass the generator room, still haunted by Denver's death, and emerge into the rear garage. Here, amidst shivery candlelight, the plane sits dormant.

Crouched beneath one of the wings, Kody lifts his head, and those coal-black eyes run me through.

A week's worth of tension strangles the air between us. Even from across the garage, I sense his unease. I feel it in the bones of my soul.

Breaking eye contact, I breeze past him, still angry enough to hold a grudge.

Serves him right for his secrecy and stonewalling, plotting with the devil behind my back, and gambling his life. All of that *after* he yelled at me for confronting the very monster he was conspiring with.

I don't blame him for Denver's death. That burden is mine alone. But I'm not ready to forgive him for the rest. I need him to understand that our relationship won't work without honesty, communication, and togetherness.

Leo helps me into the plane's cargo hold, a silent witness to my conflict with his brother. He's aware of the unresolved issues between us, but in matters of survival, it's not a priority.

We add our collection of memories to a crate in the plane, which already contains Kody's vodka recipes, Monty's slippers, and my scrapbook, full of journal entries and hair samples, including the strands I plucked from Denver's hairbrush.

If death finds us here, or if the skies claim us while we're airborne, I hope the secrets Denver took to the grave will be unraveled by those who discover our remains.

Questions about Denver's past haunt me day and night. What compelled him to move to this unsurvivable place and descend into madness? Had he always been a kidnapping, raping psychopath?

How are Leo, Kody, and Wolf—who were raised by Denver after he abducted their mothers—related to him and one another by blood? What about the unknown brother of Denver and Monty? Why did Monty never mention having siblings? What did Monty take from Denver to provoke him to take me in return? Are the five women before me connected to Monty, too?

Am I still Monty's wife, or has he let me go? Did he look for me or accept the clues Denver left behind, believing I willingly left him?

The unknowns are a labyrinth with no end, and the answers may forever elude us.

Unless we can decipher Denver's cryptic final words.

Beneath its wings lie the answers you seek in a cage of ice and echoes.

Obsessed, we've written this riddle everywhere—on the plane, our skin, the walls, the floors. Kody has been meticulously removing panels from the wings of the Turbo Beaver, searching for clues.

The phrase *Beneath its wings* taunts us. If not inside

the wings, could it mean beneath the ground the plane rests upon? In the impenetrable permafrost?

The machinery required to build this place is long gone, ruling out anything hidden below. Denver didn't have the tools to bury things under the workshop. It sits on a pad of gravel.

Leo kisses me on the forehead, a brief comfort in the cold, before hopping out and joining Kody.

I settle into the pilot's seat, dwarfed by the daunting instrument panel, and rest my gloved hands on the U-shaped wheel. The complexity of the controls, blank screens, gauges, dials, and knobs—it's all so utilitarian. Intimidating. Alien. Built like a tank.

To fly this without piloting experience, simulators, an aircraft manual, or instruction is a terrifying prospect.

Impossible, Wolf would say.

But we have no choice.

When the time comes, we'll have to learn through trial and error, which in aviation can be unforgiving.

Running my fingers over the screen before me, I wonder about its purpose. Could it be navigation?

"Hey." I pop my head out the open door. "If we can power this up, we might have GPS. Maybe comms, too."

"Working on that, love." Leo's timbre, smooth as silk, drifts from behind the plane.

I catch sight of Kody, our gazes clashing as he scowls in his beautiful, broody way.

My heart aches with love for him, a love so intense it infuriates me. Turning away, I face the windshield and focus on bigger problems. Like the frostbite burning my nose. And the missing key to the plane. And the gnawing hunger.

We need answers. Solutions.

Leo, with his technical aptitude and knack for tinkering, believes he can bypass the plane's ignition and manipulate the electrical system. He's trying to do something similar with the cabin's disabled power.

The cabin is his priority.

If he restores the electricity, the pipes would unfreeze. We would have lights. Movies to pass the time. Running water.

Oh, God, to have a hot shower again.

Given his skill at building and repairing machines in this godforsaken place, I have faith in him. But Denver was calculating. He kept all knowledge about the plane and hydroelectric generator safely guarded because it gave him leverage over his sons.

Extinguishing the candle beside me, I climb out and scan the garage for Leo.

"He's in there." Kody nods at the generator room.

A shiver spikes through me.

I can still feel the pipe in my hand and the crunch of Denver's face caving in, turning into pulp beneath my bloodthirsty strikes.

Tools clang within the chamber, followed by a string of curses. Leo's back at it, determined to undo whatever Denver did to the power system.

In the meantime, we need heat and better lighting in the garage if we're going to continue spending every waking moment in here.

Hoss has three coal stoves. One in the kitchen and the other two in this building. Two weeks ago, Leo and Wolf mined a sled full of coal from an interior basin. But the snow machine didn't return. It lies broken and silent, miles from our doorstep along the icy river.

"We need that coal." I breathe into my cupped hands, trying to generate warmth. "How do we get it back to Hoss?"

"Leo's the mechanic." Kody takes a step closer to me, his voice thick, full of gravel. "When he's ready to venture out again, we'll work out the logistics."

Like who goes and who stays.

They don't want me to leave the cabin in this weather. They also don't want me here by myself. With only three of us left, it'll be interesting to see how they work through that dilemma.

"How long are you going to avoid me?" He watches me steadily, tracking every twitch like a damn stalker.

"I'm not avoiding you."

With deliberate slowness, he narrows the gap between us, backing me against the airplane's tail. No part of him touches me, but his heat invades, licking my body, top to bottom, front and back. It's electric. Powerful. Maddening.

Rather than shrink away, I stand taller, lift on my tiptoes, and raise my chin.

I'm still a head shorter, a fraction of his size. Even now, after he's lost so much weight.

For six weeks, we've been rationing, and the toll on his physique is concerning. He and Leo both. Yet his height remains imposing, towering, like an unclimbable mountain.

Despite my stubborn anger, I find myself fighting a different impulse—the desire to caress his cheek, his square-cut jaw, the rustic texture of his stubble, and the firm pillow of his pouty lips.

"What about the pemmican?" I fist my hands at my sides. "When will we retrieve that?"

The cans in the cupboard are diminishing, their labels a blur through my desperate tears. The thought of starving to death, especially when we have high-protein pemmican at their hunting cabin, is unbearable.

"That's a thirty-mile hike." His low, growly tone nettles my goosebumped skin. "Impossible in this storm."

"How long until the storm passes?"

"A few days." He leans in, his teeth bared like knives. "Or a few months."

In a moment of weakness, I'm ensnared by the dark landscape of his black-brown eyes and bold, masculine features. Made by God and raised by the devil, he's a formidable force of nature, devastatingly handsome, looming over me, stealing all my air.

"Back off." I grind my molars.

"Make me." He licks his lips, itching for a fight.

If he keeps looking at me like that, he'll get one.

"Where are the rest of the candles?" My lungs pant, the heat between our mouths hot enough to melt the permafrost. "We're burning through the supply in the cabin."

"That's all we have left."

"So we're to spend the winter in darkness?"

"Scared?"

"Fuck you."

Kody, with his stalking and his secrets and his superior hunter's instincts, can strike fear in the heart of anyone. But he doesn't scare me. He makes me burn. And pisses me off.

"Let's address something we *can* resolve." His dark eyebrows slash over black eyes. "Like your attitude."

"My attitude?" The implication penetrates, invading my veins like Denver's needles.

"Yeah. Time for it to go."

My temper snaps, and I slam my hands against the solid wall of his chest. He doesn't budge, doesn't give me an inch. Just steady heat and an unwavering glare.

"Which part should go?" I shove again. "My emotions? The tears in my voice? The distrust in my gut? The hurt in my heart?"

"What about *my* hurt?" He roars. "I lost my brother! A huge gutting part of my soul!"

"I lost him, too." My sinuses steam, his grief prying me open, exposing the deep, yawning void where Wolf's essence lingers, where he dwells, unforgotten, ever near.

Shadows stir behind Kody, and he spins, thrusting a finger at the intruder.

"No!" He bellows at Leo. "This doesn't concern you."

"You're cornering my girl, snarling in her face." His footsteps advance. "I'm about to send you through the goddamn wall."

If I don't intervene, he'll do exactly that, spilling blood and wasting precious calories.

"Leo." My breath fogs in the boiling space between me and his brother. "I have things to say to him. Let me say them."

"Not like this. Not with his face that close to yours."

"Yes. Exactly like this." I stretch up on my toes, meeting Kody stare for stare. "You said Denver took years off your life when he looked at me. Imagine how I felt when I found you in that cage with him, naked, restrained, and yelling at me to get out. You broke my heart. Broke my trust. Broke everything inside me. I don't know how to recover from that. I lost my mind. Lost my humanity. I almost lost *you*." Tears well, and I swat them away. "So when you say this is an *attitude* problem, I say that's a goddamn shortcut to thinking."

Slowly, he reaches out and strokes a thumb across my wet cheek. He loves my tears as much as he hates them.

"You got what you wanted?" I smack his hand away.

"Yeah." His jaw tightens. "Got my fighter. Knew she was in there, hurting, holding it all in instead of letting me have it." He releases a clouded breath. "Need you to hit me over the head with it. The anger, the tears, the words—I want all of it."

An honest request on demanding lips.

He's not asking for forgiveness but a chance to earn back my trust.

I find Leo's stony gaze a few paces away. He looks entirely too invested in this conversation, angry and conflicted, with his braids coming loose and his chest heaving like he just outran a bear.

"Kody made that bargain for you." He flexes his hands. "But you have every right to be angry. I'm angry, too. We agreed to make decisions together, and he went behind our backs." His throat bobs, his voice rough. "But he did it for you because...we do terrible things for love."

A hollow sensation hits my stomach. "That's what Wolf said the night he made the devil's bargain. I couldn't stop him from going through with it, and he never recovered."

Kody's eyes go wide. "Frankie, no."

"If he hadn't made that bargain, he would still be here. He would still be alive. I'm certain of it. And I keep thinking, what if I hadn't broken into the workshop in time to stop Denver with you? What if Denver had hurt you the way he hurt Wolf? Would you have followed Wolf off the cliff? Would I have lost you, too?" Heartache shatters my voice. "I know you endured Denver's pain before, but do you really think you could've survived it again? After everything you've been through? Everything you sacrificed? The kin punishments, the women who died before me, the months you slept on the couch, trying to stay away from me—you did it all so you would never have to surrender to him like that again. So tell me the truth, Kodiak. Would you have survived a winter in his bed?"

His expression empties, the cords going taut in his neck.

"I didn't think so." I drop back on my heels, exhaustion setting in.

"Better me than you." His posture, stiff and unyielding, seems to grow taller. "Not going to change my mind on that."

I get it. I had the same justification when I sold my soul to the devil.

We deceive and manipulate those we love, out of noble intentions or for our own misguided hearts. Love endures because of one true and constant element. Forgiveness.

"There will be no more secrets between us." I find his hand and twine our fingers. "Not one. That means no more lone ranger mentality. Every decision will be made collectively with everyone's agreement."

"I swear it." Conviction etches his granite face.

"No matter how bad it gets." Leo nods.

A chilling promise.

The darkest nights are yet to unfold, and the price of our survival might be higher than any of us dare to imagine

leonid

TWO

A week later, I discover a sickening revelation.

"Holy fuck." Crouched in the utility room off the kitchen, I drop my head in my hands and bellow, "Kody!"

The heavy thud of boots echoes through the cabin, the wood bones groaning under his strides.

"What?" He braces his arms on either side of the doorframe, looking as wrung out as I feel.

It's late, long after our usual bedtime, but I knew he was still in the armory, changing the cables on his crossbow.

As I rise to my feet, frustration gets the better of me, and I kick a box of electronics toward him. "Look at this!"

He sifts through the parts, his interest guttering like a dying flame. "It's a box of junk."

"They're circuit boards." I open the furnace door

and grip a nest of wires in the lower housing. "These wires should be connected to one of those boards."

"Does this mean…?" He dives back into the box with renewed vigor as if the boards hold the answer to everything.

One of them probably does.

"Denver removed the circuit board and left the box for us to find." A bitter taste fills my mouth.

"Another sick game."

"Without a doubt."

"Fuck." He pinches the bridge of his nose and groans. "So whatever he did to the power…You're saying it was never going to be fixed in the generator room where we caged him?"

Where Kody removed his clothes and intended to surrender his body in exchange for electricity.

"So it seems." I grit my teeth.

The realization sits between us, laden with the gravity of our choices and their unforgiving consequences.

Denver's cooperation was a lost cause from the start.

Who knows if Denver would've actually gone through with his end of the deal if Frankie hadn't intervened? And who cares? The cost was too fucking high.

"Can you fix it?" He pushes the box back to me, his gaze intense, challenging.

"I'm not an electrician."

"You built the dirt bike and repair every machine that breaks—"

"Engines, yes. Circuit boards, no."

"What's the difference?"

"You fucking serious?"

"What's going on?" Frankie squeezes in past Kody,

her presence a soft, welcoming warmth in the cold, cramped space. Wearing a fur pelt like a robe, she holds a flame of light in a tin can. "Did you get the water heater converted?"

I'm reminded of my original task, another problem I haven't solved.

In the past twenty years, the pipes froze twice that I remember, and both times, Denver switched the plumbing to wood-heated hot water. The backup system only works for the primary bathroom, which sits on the other side of this wall. That's all we need if I can figure out how to do it.

"Not yet, but I found this." I show her the wires and box of circuit boards. "This is how he disabled the power.

As I explain my assumptions about the missing control panel, her sexy little mouth forms an *O.*

"Where's an electrician when you need one?" She blows out a breath, making the flame dance in her hands. "There are too many wires. Even if we try every combination on every circuit board, it will take time and resources we don't have. We don't even know if the correct board is here. The box could be a decoy. I hate to say this, but I think we need to forget the generator. It's a dead end."

I arch a brow at Kody.

"Come to bed." She extinguishes the candle on the floor and ducks out, expecting us to follow.

Of course, we do. We would follow her to the ends of the earth if we weren't already standing on the edge.

"What is that you're holding?" I catch up with her, eyeing the flickering can that lights our way.

"I solved the candle problem."

"What candle problem?"

"We ran out."

I knew we would eventually run low, but I've been too consumed with the generator to register much else.

She leads us to the bedroom that once belonged to Denver. It's our room now, empty as it is.

Kody dismantled all the furniture for firewood. Not much remains in the rest of the cabin, either. We'll be tearing wood walls off the surrounding buildings next. Everything that's nailed and not nailed down will be used as fuel.

Except the books in the library. We're not desperate enough to burn those yet.

As Kody heads to the hearth to stoke the fire and prepare the bathwater, I take in the project Frankie's been working on.

"Oil." She follows my gaze to the jugs that line the far wall. "Cooking oil, mineral oil, paraffin oil, inedible animal fats, basically anything I could find to burn."

"How does it work?" I examine one of the many tin cans in a nearby crate.

"I thought you knew." A rare grin glows in her green eyes. "I read about it in one of your survival books." She grabs a spool of gauze from the supplies and twists it into a six-inch rope. "Fill the cans with oil, punch a hole through the lid, and the gauze works as a wick. There's a little more to it, but I worked out the kinks. According to the book, we should get a hundred hours out of each one."

She must've collected every empty can in Hoss. Since Denver didn't make our last supply run, we have months of recycling piled up. Months of soup cans sitting amongst our garbage. It must've taken her days to sift through all of it.

I'm fucking impressed.

"You've been busy." My stomach lifts, feeling a little

less hollow.

"You're working so hard on the power problem, and when Kody isn't chopping wood and rebuilding his strength with the crossbow, he's out there trying to solve Denver's riddle. So I thought…" She shrugs. "I could at least fix one problem. I mean, it's not a life-or-death problem, but you can't work in the dark and—"

"Come here."

She walks straight into my arms, and just like that, I'm home. Settled. Whole. Maybe not complete—without my little brother, there will always be a missing component—but complete enough in this new life we're fighting for. Together. No matter where we land or how painful the journey, as long as I'm with her and Kody, I'm where I'm meant to be.

"You did good." I curl a finger beneath her chin and lift her stunning, rosy-cheeked face. "Thank you."

"Wish I could do more." She blinks rapidly—her attempt to stifle tears. "I feel useless so much of the time, like dead weight. Too weak to do heavy labor. Too limited in my skills to hunt or hot-wire a plane. I've been tearing the cabin apart, searching for the key to the plane, but I don't have the strength to remove the flooring and—"

"Stop right there." My touch becomes a firm grip on her jaw. "Where would we be if you hadn't fixed Kody's hand? Or his leg? We sure as fuck don't know how to administer a blood transfusion. Without you, he would've died that night. We have a long winter ahead of us. We're bound to get more injuries."

"I hope the hell not."

"Well, I'm feeling a lot better about it, knowing we have our own personal trauma nurse. It's an invaluable skill in a place like this. Fixing people is critically more important than fixing snow machines." I raise my voice. "Am I right, Kody?"

"Spot on." He lumbers past us, hauling buckets of water from the hearth to the bathroom. "Let's go, ladies."

"Tell me you understand." I put my face in hers, tempted to kiss that pout off her lips.

"Yeah. I hear you. Thank you for always being so...blunt."

"Water's ready." I give her a nudge toward the bathroom, one she doesn't need.

Nightly baths are her thing. If left to our own devices, Kody and I wouldn't bother with it. Too impractical in these conditions.

But after sleeping between us and complaining about armpits, she made bath time a rule.

For the record, we don't like rules. However, Kody and I are learning to make exceptions for her.

In the bathroom, he's already stripped down to his boxers, standing in the empty bathtub, illuminated by candlelight.

Buckets of fire-heated water line the edge. Clean laundry hangs around the perimeter. We wash what we can in the tub. Another miserable chore we could've avoided if only I'd built that steel door quicker. If I'd finished it even one day sooner, I could've caged Denver before he tampered with the power.

I have a lot of fucking regrets.

Kody removes his boxers while Frankie and I hastily shed our clothes. Nothing sexy about it. The subzero temperatures attack exposed skin like scathing needles.

I lift her into the tub and follow her in. Out of habit or maybe instinct, the three of us lower to our knees and crowd together, seeking body heat. Then Kody starts pouring.

The water is barely warm by the time it hits our bodies. We pass the soap, each of us focusing on our own hygiene, clinically scrubbing and rinsing, hurrying it along, wishing it was over.

It's a humbling exercise. Makes me vulnerable in ways I've never been vulnerable. I can't remember the last time I was this scrawny. Maybe when I was a boy? Maybe not even then.

Frankie and Kody aren't faring any better. I can see every sharp bone in their thin frames, every hollow dip where flesh used to be. They both wear the unsolved riddle scribbled on their arms in the black ink of Wolf's last sharpie.

I turn away, but her hand lands on my shoulder, guiding me to face her, wordlessly asking me to let her look.

Denying her feels wrong. So I hold still while she inspects every inch of my deteriorating physique. She does this every night, probing and prodding, feeling my abdomen, checking my breathing, looking for bruising, abnormal swelling, or...I don't know. What is she afraid she'll find?

As much as I hate this, I also treasure it. These uncomfortably intimate moments peel away our shields, divest us of our egos, and bare us to one another on a level most people never experience. We've been reduced to half-starved, physically weak, brutally exposed, feral creatures in survival mode. Impossible to hide from one another when we're like this.

But there's no judgment. No shame. No secrets between us.

It's liberating.

Soul-binding.

"You're dehydrated." She lightly slaps my face, her tone scolding. "Water is the one thing we have in abundance. Drink more of it."

Okay, maybe there's *some* judgment.

"Yes, ma'am." My lips twitch. "Any other concerns?"

"Is that a trick question?" She releases a shivery breath and turns to give Kody the same treatment.

Even with our guards down, they're still tense around each other, still hanging onto unsettled feelings.

I don't like it.

If this were about sex, I'd have a different opinion about the strain between them. But sex has nothing to do with this.

We're a unit, the three of us. When part of that unit is broken, it affects all of us.

"We finished here?" He climbs out before she answers.

"Kody." She holds out her hand, offering an olive branch.

He ignores it. Makes a grunting sound. Loosens a breath. Then he reaches for her waist and lifts her out, plastering her against his chest.

I wait for her to push away, to wriggle to be put down. But she never does what I expect her to do.

As I step out and drag on my clothes, her limbs instinctively wrap around his torso. Like she belongs there.

She buries her face in his neck, and his hands slide up her back to tangle in her hair.

Guess they're resolving shit.

If he gets a hard-on, I don't know what I'll do. The impulse to rip her out of his arms is a fire in my gut.

But it's dimmed by a stronger need.

The need to erase those dark shadows from her eyes.

Hers *and* his.

Grabbing a clean blanket, I drape it around them and give his shoulder a shove. "Go warm up by the fire. I'll bring your clothes."

He meets my gaze, his expression thoughtful, questioning, maybe even dumbfounded. It's a fleeting hesitation before he whisks her off into the bedroom.

I grab three pairs of wool socks, boxers for him, and an oversized shirt for her.

The transition between the bathroom and bedroom is a jolt to the system, like walking out of a freezer and into an oven.

That's how it feels to me, anyway. For anyone who didn't grow up here, I imagine it feels exactly like what it is. The Arctic.

Kody spent the past week boarding up the windows, caulking all the leaky cracks, and insulating the bedroom until it's airtight. With the hearth roaring and our shared body heat, the cold won't penetrate us while we sleep.

He and Frankie lie on the mattress beside the fire, huddled beneath eighty-thousand blankets. She holds up the edge of the pile, waiting for me to join them.

I climb in with their clothes and help her dress beneath the covers. Once we're in our socks and settled on our sides, exhaustion hits me from all directions.

Without proper nutrition, I don't have the endurance to keep up with this place. I know Kody feels the same. I see it in his bloodshot eyes.

When Denver was alive, tasks like heat and trash and roof maintenance just *happened* without our time and attention.

Thank God we have Frankie. Contrary to what she thinks, she's a fast learner and a hard worker. But without Denver and Wolf, we're down two experienced sets of hands, and I feel that in every achy bone in my body.

Inching closer to her sweet backside, I give into the pull of sleep.

Until she flops to her back and starts drumming her fingers on her abdomen.

"What's wrong?" My eyes pop open and collide with Kody's above her head.

"In the spirit of honesty…" She purses her lips. "Is there anything either one of you wants to tell me?"

That's a loaded question if I've ever heard one.

"Uh…" I scratch my jaw. "Nothing comes to mind."

"Can you be more specific?" Kody glowers.

"Yeah." She props up on her elbows, compelling us to do the same. "Which one of you ejaculated on me?"

"Excuse me?" My breath seizes as I flick my gaze between her and Kody. "If you're referring to that night in the workshop—"

"No, before that. When I first arrived here and slept alone in Kody's room, I woke covered in semen."

My pulse thunders, and my mind races as I regard my conniving, broody brother, studying his reaction.

His stone-cold expression gives nothing away.

Guilty as fuck.

I open my mouth to accuse him, but he beats me to it.

"It was me." In a flash, he angles over her and catches me by the wrist.

Even malnourished, the bastard still has a ruthless grip.

"I'm going to tell her what she wants to know," he growls, "and when I'm finished, you and I aren't going to fight about it."

"Leo isn't going to do anything." Flattened on the

mattress beneath him, she pushes against his weight. "I'm already yours. *Both* of yours. There's no need for any of us to feel territorial. Tell him I'm right, Leo."

When I let loose a growl, she looks at me with fear in her eyes.

Dammit. I can't stand it. There are so many things for her to fear right now. I don't want to be one of them.

"Fine." The heat in that word evaporates on my tongue like steam as I yank my arm away. "No fighting."

Kody returns to his side of the mattress and gives her his confession.

"I sneaked in every night while you slept. Sometimes, just to watch you. Other times..." He clears his voice, wets his lips. "I caught urges, feelings I couldn't shake. You're so fucking pretty. Never seen anything like you. Better than any image I could conjure in my head. Touching myself felt natural. I know it was wrong, marking you the way I did, but that felt natural, too. Nothing demeaning or disrespectful in the way I felt. I didn't molest you. I would never do that without your consent."

My feelings are all over the place. I understand why he did it. She arouses those same urges in me. But jerking off on her? That's bullshit.

I restrain my reaction, waiting to see how she responds.

"I knew it." Lying on her back, she stares at the ceiling and chews her lip. "Remember when I asked you if you watched me sleep? I fucking knew it was you."

He wasn't supposed to be looking at her like that. Or thinking about her. Or wanting her. We had a pact. But I won't call him out on it because I'm just as guilty. Hell, while I was telling my brothers to stay away from her, I was pinning her against walls and shoving my tongue down her throat.

"How many times?" I look him square in the eyes.

"Twice." He holds my glare, unapologetically stony.

"Nope." She squints. "I remember three times."

He turns his attention back to her, his expression softening. "Four, actually."

My temper pounds at me like a second heart. I whip off the blankets, letting the chill rush in to cool my raging blood.

"Oh, my God." She heaves. Her cheeks flush. Then…"Kody Strakh, you are sick!" She lunges at him, her stern tone belied by the too-light swats she gives his chest. "What the hell is wrong with you?"

Rolling on top of him, she lands on his hips, straddles his waist, and continues to scold him while fighting laughter. "You masturbated on me four times! And you were never going to tell me!"

"I was going to, I swear." Biting back a grin, he blocks her slapping hands. "Just waiting for the right time."

"The right time to tell me you're a pervert? How about the morning after? Or maybe the night you ejaculated on my face? That would've been a good time." Perched on his hips, she crosses her arms. "We need to talk about that, too. That night in the workshop."

"No, we don't." I shift to my back and drape an arm across my forehead, trying to school my breathing.

"I know you're tired and angry, so the conversation can wait." Her tone hardens. "But we *will* talk about it."

I close my eyes as my fingers, teeth, legs, every damn part of me clenches.

"Hey." The mattress jostles, signaling her approach. "Don't hide from us."

"I'm not."

Her hands slide across my arm, dragging it away from my face. I open my eyes and find hers inches away, huge and green, searching, digging, prying me open.

"I don't know how to do this." She cups my jaw. "This love. The three of us sharing it. I'm blundering through it, but I've learned to let my senses and my past tell me what's right and true. *This* is right and true. Us. I know the sharing part isn't easy. The best things are never ever easy. You can wish it away, but I'm fighting for it. With every drop of blood in my body, I'm not giving up on us. Because this right here, the three of us..." She grips each of our hands, pulling them onto her lap. "This is the only good thing we have. The only thing that matters. If one of you disagrees, you better speak up." Her cheeks bounce. "So I can change your mind."

This woman.

She's so fucking adorable. I forget I should be mad.

"Love that look in your eyes," Kody murmurs.

"Which one?" She lowers to her belly, releasing our hands to prop up her chin.

"The one that promises total annihilation to anything and anyone in your way."

"Oh." She dips her head, peering at us from beneath her lashes. "I get a little crazy when I set my mind to something. Fair warning...I've never wanted anything as much as I want this."

"Your crazy is irresistible." I catch her around the waist and drag her against me, squeezing her so tightly I'd have to break my ribs to pull her any deeper.

She lets out a little gasp but doesn't complain.

Kody shifts closer, pressing against her back,

trapping her in. The sigh she gives him sounds so weightless, so full of contentment, it melts any lingering tension from my muscles.

I'm viscerally aware of which parts of him touch her—his chest against her back, a hand on her hip, an arm folded beneath her head, his nose in her hair, both legs tangled around hers—but I don't hate it.

Between him and me, she has double the protection. Double the warmth. Double the emotional and physical support to survive the months ahead.

If something happens to me, she won't be alone.

But the sharing part? That's what makes me feel unhinged.

You can wish it away, but I'm fighting for it.

I'm trying to process what it means to be in a relationship, let alone a relationship with her *and* my brother. I'm trying to accept it even as everything inside me rebels against it.

Hell, I watched him come on her face. I let it happen, and the world didn't end.

But the thought of them sneaking off together, fucking like animals, and falling deeper and deeper in love? Where do I fit into that? What if she loves him more? What if she chooses him?

Choosing. Sharing. Neither option is ideal. But for now, I'm content just to hold her while she sleeps, to hold them both and keep them safe, exactly where they're supposed to be.

THREE

When we were kids, we spent a lot of mornings on this porch, drinking coffee and oat milk and watching the sun crest the eastern edge of the hills.

With the first glow of light after a month of polar nights, we would sit beneath the overhang, huddled in our blankets, exhaling white clouds of poignant relief.

Like now.

The horizon subtly shifts in color, moving from deep, persistent blacks and blues into softer, warmer hues. The landscape emerges from the darkness, donning a gown of snow and ice, shimmering in lavender and gold.

It's a visual spectacle that carries emotional weight. From dark to light, from despair to hope, it mirrors the dreams of our childhood, only now our hearts crave adult things, and the stakes are so much higher.

I've never been this hungry. Hungry for food.

Hungry for answers. Hungry for the woman on my lap. Hungry for a future with her beyond these hills.

Hunger has a way of motivating a man.

"The skies are clearing." I glance at Leo, who is sprawled in the chair beside us. "We might have a reprieve from the storm."

"Maybe." He passes Frankie a steaming mug of black coffee and rests a gloved hand on her leg. "I'll get that water heater converted today. Then, weather permitting, I'll hike to the snow machine at first light tomorrow."

He claims he has the parts to fix it, can get it purring in under an hour, and return the same day. Still...

"You're not going alone." I sip my coffee, savoring the roasted flavor, the smokiness of a campfire, knowing the taste will be a distant memory when we run out in a few weeks.

"I'm going with him," Frankie says as if we've already put it to a vote.

Leo's gaze meets mine, a storm of its own brewing in his eyes. Like me, he's torn. To leave her alone is unthinkable. She either goes with him or remains under my watchful guard.

Sending him out there alone when a blizzard can sweep him away without warning is a fool's errand. Sending him with someone who can staunch bleeding, set broken bones, and treat hypothermia is the only sensible choice.

But my protective instincts howl at the idea.

She's too small. Too invaluable. Too intertwined around my heart.

The easy answer is we stick together and all go. Except the snow machine can only carry two people. I would have to walk back, an undertaking I wouldn't blink at if I had proper nutrition.

"I can hear your brains grinding." She twists on my lap, her eyes flitting between us. "Put your misogynist, old-fashioned caveman shit away and give me one logical reason why I shouldn't go."

Every argument I possess is rooted in a primal urge to shield her from harm.

"You could freeze to death." Leo drums his fingers on his knee.

"So could you." She pokes his nose. "What else you got?"

"You have spaghetti arms." He sucks his lip between his teeth, his eyes flirting.

"Hold this." She hands me her mug and jumps into the space between his spread legs, leaning over him. "They may be spaghetti-ish, but they can still hold a grudge...or throw a right hook. Care for a demonstration?"

"Sign me up." A low, horny rumble does weird things to his voice, making my eyes roll.

She seems to like it, though, given the heavy way her lashes flutter. I'd rather watch her send an uppercut across his dumb face, but we don't always get what we want.

Another low murmur rumbles past my ears. This time, it emanates from somewhere deeper, as if vibrating from the very earth.

Or the heavens above.

That sound is not coming from my brother.

"You hear that?" I'm on my feet, flying across the porch to the railing.

In the distance, high above the icy hills, a small silhouette glints against the purple sky, creating a brief flash the size of a sparkling star.

This is no star.

The sound, muffled by distance and the thick, cold air, is human-made. The object moves steadily, leaving a faint trail of condensation in its wake.

I'm startled by the sight of it, utterly gobsmacked, my reaction delayed and steeped in denial.

Leo sprints past me, down the stairs, and along the path to the hills, yelling and waving his arms.

"A plane." Frankie's burst of excitement at my side snaps me out of my daze. "Here? This close to Hoss? What are the odds?"

"Zero." I grip the railing with white knuckles.

As the plane's journey across the sky takes it farther and farther away, I know there isn't a chance in hell anyone on board can see my desperate brother running through the tundra.

Hoss is veiled in the shadows of the hills. No lights glow in the windows. No SOS fires burn on the property. Even if the cabin is spotted from the sky, there's no indication of human life here, let alone human life in duress.

"They don't see us." She slips under my arm and hugs my waist, her voice hollow. "It's too dark. We're too far away."

"Yeah." I cup the back of her head, pulling her tightly against me. "Maybe they'll come back."

Leo, barely a dot in the tundra, no longer chases the hope in the sky. He must be spitting mad, punching the air, his eyes wild, and lips curled in a snarl. Good thing he has to walk all the way back. It'll give him time to cool off.

"Want to help me build some trenches?" I tug on the thick, red braid in her hair.

"Trenches?" She stares up at me, the devastation on her face morphing into confusion before dawning with realization. "To build a SOS signal?"

"Sure. What do you say?"

She clutches the rabbit-fur ear flaps of my hat with both hands and pulls, bringing my head to her level. When my mouth is within reach, she kisses me, hard and deep, with a passion that sets my blood on fire.

I eat her up, giving her my tongue, my heat, and my hope.

If, by some miracle, that plane returns, I'll make damn sure they see us.

kodiak

FOUR

We work through the day and long into the night, carving our plea into a canvas of untouched snow. Every shovelful weighs as heavy as the dark sky on our shoulders. Each movement, a war against the dropping temperatures, saps our strength and paints exhaustion in the hollows of our eyes.

Fatigue isn't just a side effect. It's a living, breathing opponent, infiltrating our bones and slowing our joints with calorie-deficient cruelty.

Frankie battles alongside us, her spirit far livelier than her body. The relentless cold seems to claw at her more fiercely, chattering her teeth and fucking with her coordination. She pushes herself too hard, and I worry she'll pass out.

"Frankie," I growl for the hundredth time. "Take a break."

"You take a break."

I don't know how all that stubbornness fits into such a small package.

While she helps me dig the waist-deep trenches, Leo hauls materials from the cabin and other buildings. To maximize the visibility, we're filling the ruts with dark-colored debris, anything Leo can find that won't be used as firewood.

Barrels, metal shelving, steel siding, trash, recyclables, ashes from the hearths, tarps, drapes, mattresses, old motor oil, paint, and wood stain—most of it is environmentally unfriendly, but it's all we have to darken the trenches and make the letters stand out.

"Think of it like this." She stabs her shovel into the snow and stumbles to remain upright. "We're enjoying this beautiful, otherworldly view." She motions at the northern lights above the hills. "And getting exercise in the process. We're better off than city folks in cold climates."

"How do you figure?" Leo tosses an old tire into the curve of a trench that stretches as long as the bush plane.

"Well, we aren't shoveling dirty snow off a driveway while inhaling the fumes from a neighbor's car as it warms up. We don't have to drive on icy roads with thousands of commuters distracted by their phones. There are no snowplows throwing salt-treated slush onto our boots or traffic jams or noise pollution..." She sways.

The shovel tips out of her grasp, and she tumbles with it, face-planting in the trench.

My heart stills in my chest.

"Fuck." I forge through the snow, stomping away the distance, and sweep her into my arms. "Frankie?"

She laughs, but it sounds like a sob as she buries her face in my coat. "I'll never be strong enough."

"Shut up." I hitch her up my chest until our noses touch. "You're the hardiest woman I've ever met, and I've met a lot of women. At least four."

"Funny." She groans. "Put me down."

I'd rather die.

Leo storms toward us, the stark white of his eyes shining brighter than the moon. Yanking off his glove, he touches her face and captures her hooded gaze. "You're done."

Too weak to argue, she hangs limply in the cradle of my hold.

He stares at her, rapidly blinking as if trying to keep his eyes open. Yeah, he's done, too.

"Take her inside. I'll finish up." I transfer her into his arms.

She weighs less than air, this fragile beauty of human endurance. She should've hung up her shovel hours ago, but that's not how she's built.

"Are you sure?" He studies me.

"Yep. I have hours left in me."

"Watch your back." He surveys the hills, the shadowed valleys, and the crossbow strapped to my spine. "She's not patching you up tonight."

"Not true," she mumbles into his neck.

A crooked grin pulls the corner of his mouth, but it quickly falls away as he rescans the surrounding darkness.

Searching for wolves.

This time of year, the scarcity of prey forces them from the hills to hunt elsewhere. They'll start circling Hoss, if they're not already.

With my injuries fully healed, I can take on the whole pack. We need meat.

But where do we draw the line? A week ago, we fed

Denver's corpse to those beasts. Imagining his flesh in their teeth doesn't exactly whet my appetite. It turns my fucking stomach.

"I'll keep an eye out." Bending over the woman in his arms, I press a kiss to her forehead.

Frowning, he tucks her closer and carries her off to the cabin. Once they're safely inside, I return to my task.

As the night presses on, he comes out multiple times to help, but I send him back inside to watch over our girl.

Under the Alaskan sky, I labor without stopping, growing more lightheaded by the second and cold in a way that has nothing to do with the climate. But I'm determined to finish.

A beautiful woman waits for me in the cabin, keeping my spot warm beside her on the bed. Soon, my spot will be between her legs where she's soft and sweet and smells like cherries, primed for my teeth.

The thought keeps me going until I lose sensation in my arms. A low buzz circulates through me. My knees hitch, and my stomach feels weird. I probably just need a break. And food.

Definitely need to eat.

I step back and examine my progress.

Three dark letters, each thirty feet in length, carved into the moonlit snow.

SOS.

Save our souls.

Almost finished. Just a few more loads of debris and—

I feel it, the moment my body gives up. The limits of my strength hit my muscles, turning everything into meltwater. My knees sink to the ground, then my hands, my chest. Debilitation floods sinew and bone, softening every living part of me. It's not the cold or the exertion. I'm used to those things.

It's the lack of food.

I ate two meals but not nearly enough calories to fuel the day's activity.

Digging my elbows into the snow, I try to crawl toward the cabin, but my limbs are too sluggish, too heavy. I'm so fucking tired, it tugs on my eyelids and blackens my vision.

Oh, fuck. Not good.

As consciousness tries to abandon me, I hear approaching steps and pray they belong to boots, not paws. Tracking the sound, I cling to awareness with every beat of my heart.

Stay awake. Stay awake.

My fingers fumble for the crossbow on my back, but my fine motor control is gone. I can't release the straps, can't even pry my eyes open. Removing one of my knives proves impossible.

I try to shout, but my voice sounds muffled, echoing in the hinterland of my mind.

All I want is sleep. With a pillow of snow under my cheek and the howling song of wolves in my ears, I surrender to the darkness.

Until something slams into my side, shooting unholy pain through my ribs. I yowl in agony, but the sound is drowned out by gunfire.

Directly above my head.

"Get up!" Leo kicks me again, my shoulder this time, and fires at something behind me.

Blurry silhouettes. Pounding headache. Wooziness. Why is my face in the snow?

"Jesus Christ." He shoots off another round. Then his hands are on me, hauling me off the ground. "As stubborn as she is. If I don't kill you both by the end of winter, it'll be a fucking miracle."

He drags me like a slaughtered carcass across the tundra, stopping every few feet to spray bullets at the shadows.

"Frankie!" More gunfire. Then he's pulling me again. "Get your fucking ass inside!"

"I can...wah...walk." My tongue doesn't feel right, sticking to my lips like dry ice.

"Can't even talk." He halts, letting my body crumple against something hard.

Stairs?

The thunder of gunfire reverberates through me. Spent shell casings plink off my back as I reach for the next step up, knowing I need to climb.

What's wrong with my reflexes?

I dig my knee into another stair, pushing, rising, slipping, then...

Oblivion.

The next thing I register is the orange glow of a fire, heat on my skin, and farther away, hushed voices.

"No," Frankie whispers harshly. "If we don't do this, there will be worse effects than low blood pressure and unconsciousness."

"Worse than death?" Leo snarls.

"Yeah. Much worse. If you hadn't found him when you did, he would've been eaten alive by wolves. There's more going on here than the wasting of fat and muscle beneath our skin."

"Like what?" His whisper lowers, cracking with fear. "What are you looking for when we bathe every night?"

A long pause. Long enough for my vision to adjust to the darkened doorway of the bedroom and the silhouettes filling it.

Leo towers over her, leaning in as he always does,

trying to intimidate her. But she holds her ground, with her chin jutted out and her hands on her hips, radiating attitude.

When she finally speaks, it's in her no-nonsense professional tone. "I'm looking for skin atrophy, hair loss, dehydration, significant weight loss, slow heart rate, low body temperature, anemia, osteomalacia."

"Osteo-*what?*" His nostrils pulse.

"Rickets. Tenderness in the bones, muscle cramps, thickening of ankles and wrists, bowlegs, bending spine..." She sighs. "All symptoms of marasmus. I also check for kwashiorkor, which causes depleted muscle mass but retention of subcutaneous fat." She smacks his stomach, making him flinch. "Distended abdomen, fluid retention in the legs and feet, irritability, and fatigue." Her gaze slides to me, and her eyes widen. "You're awake."

"Do I have kwaa-shee-or whatever you said?" I ask.

"No." She rushes to me and kneels at my side, her rosy face brightening my view. "How do you feel?"

"I'm...fine?" I lift my arm and realize it's attached to an IV. Panicked, I follow the tubing to a clear bag that hangs nearby. "What happened? Did wolves attack?"

"No, no! Shhh." She strokes my face, instantly calming me. "You blacked out."

"Why the fuck would I do that?"

"Low heart rate, overexertion, dehydration, hypotension, hypothermia, hypoglycemia, severe protein-deficiency..." She throws a glare at Leo over her shoulder. "Shall I keep going?"

I caress the satiny curve of her neck, bringing her attention back to me. "Am I going to die?"

"Not today, handsome."

"What were you arguing about?"

"We need to increase our daily rations." Her features tighten, bracing for an argument. "I recommend that we dip into our meat reserves, rebuild our strength, and retrieve that pemmican as soon as possible."

"We?" I exchange a look with Leo.

He leans against the hearth behind her, one arm tightly folded across his chest as he chews on his thumbnail.

"You and me." She puts her face in mine, blocking my view of everything else.

"You want to increase our rations *then* retrieve the pemmican?" I tuck a fiery lock of hair behind her ear. "Shouldn't those steps be reversed?"

"No. We need energy to retrieve more energy."

"This is your professional advice?"

"Yes. If we don't fix your nutrition, your immune system will be compromised, making you prone to infection and illness. It will lead to hypovolemic shock, cirrhosis of the liver, atrophy of the pancreas, heart failure, starvation, *then* death." Another glare at Leo.

My chest constricts. "Got any good news, doc?"

"I'm not a doctor, and yes. You're still breathing. No signs of marasmus or kwashiorkor. And..." She winks. "You finished the SOS signal."

I did?

My pulse spikes. "Did the plane return?"

"Not yet." She turns her attention to the IV in my arm. "I gave you fluids for dehydration. Looks like I can remove—"

Gripping the tube, I yank it from my arm.

"Kody!" She sits back on her heels with an exasperated huff.

"You've been here twenty-seven years," I say to Leo, pushing to my feet. "Never seen a plane, right?"

"Right."

Cold air prickles my skin, and I glance down, completely nude. "Did you bathe me?"

"Yep." She crosses her arms. "Gave you a rectal exam, too."

My ass clenches. "You into that?"

"Depends."

"On?"

"If you're into that." She bites her lip.

I can feel that sexy little nibble on my cock.

"The plane." Leo throws a pair of jeans at my face. "It was a high-performance aircraft. Expensive."

"Trophy hunters?" I shove my legs into the pants and dig a thermal shirt from a nearby pile.

"That's my assumption." He runs a hand through his hair. "Maybe a snowstorm rerouted their usual flight path and forced them over our hills."

Polar bear trophy hunting is a popular pastime for rich, bored city folks. They charter fancy aircraft, making tracking much easier and faster than hunting by dog sled or on foot.

Lazy fucks. And wasteful. In Inuit traditions, hunters treat the polar bears with respect, before and after death. Killing for fun isn't in harmony with tradition.

But money talks, and wealthy assholes cough it up for the thrill of danger and adventure.

"The plane was headed north, likely to the coast." I shove on my boots and lace them up. "It'll return to whatever city it came from when the hunt ends. Maybe it'll take the same route back."

"Where are you going?" Frankie grips my arm. "You've been in bed for two days and—"

"Two days?" My stomach plummets.

"Yeah. You need to eat before you pass out again." She thrusts her implacable chin and punches my chest for good measure. "Right now."

"Don't boss me, woman."

"Someone needs to." She turns toward the door.

I smack her backside on the way out, making her yelp.

Leo stiffens, glowering, seconds from blowing steam from his ears.

"Lighten up." I clap a hand around his neck.

He turns even more rigid beneath my grip.

"Hey." Softening my tone, I step into his space and bow my head with his. "Thank you for coming for me. I owe you my life."

"You owe me nothing." His tension melts away with his exhale. "Wish I'd killed a wolf or two."

"Yes, but...if we ate the wolf that ate Denver, does that make us cannibals?"

"Fucking hell, man." He stares at me like I've lost my mind. "What the fuck is wrong with you?"

"It's an honest question."

"One I never want to think about again." He strides to the door, shaking his head. "Keep that shit to yourself."

I follow him out. "Can't believe I was out for two days. What did I miss?"

"Frankie's undivided attention. You worried her." He veers into the kitchen and pauses at the island. "We were both worried."

A swallow sticks in my throat. "I put us behind schedule."

"We don't have a schedule. But now that you're up, I'll convert that water tank."

"Not until you eat." Frankie emerges from the pantry, holding a package of cured caribou meat we've been saving. "Sit. Both of you."

We sit on the only two stools we haven't chopped into firewood.

"Now listen up." She measures the meat on three plates, adds some canned vegetables from the greenhouse, and pushes the dishes toward us. "We're going to eat more, drink more water, increase our energy levels, retrieve the snow machine…"

Leo drops his head in his hands, probably fighting the urge to argue her first point.

"Once we're strong enough," she goes on, "we're going to have sex."

His head pops up. I stop breathing.

"Oh, good. You're listening." With a grin, she bends forward, setting her elbows on the counter. "I'm not kidding about the sex. I miss it with you." She looks at Leo then turns to me. "And I want it with you. I'll wait until we have our strength back. But just so we're clear, when you're both ready, I am, too."

I'm hard. Instantly. Prematurely.

A glance at Leo tells me he's hard, too. Hardheaded. Hardfisted. Hard-set against sharing her.

He'll get there. I may not be able to convince him, but she will.

"In the meantime…" She chews on a strip of meat, watching us. "We're going to solve the riddle, get the plane running, make the trek to the hunting cabin, and get the pemmican. Maybe even shoot a few wolves on the way. What do you say?"

"I miss it with you, too." Leo reaches across the counter and captures her hand.

Her entire body melts.

Every day, her face grows thinner, sharper, making her eyes appear too big. But goddamn, she's still stunning. Especially when she looks at him like that. Like she would die for him.

She shifts those too-big eyes to me, and a different emotion transforms her expression.

Want.

Never has a woman looked at me like that, but my body recognizes it, understands it instinctively. This tension between us isn't just about earning back her trust. It's carnal in nature. Primordial. Sexual. We have things to work out. Physical things that need to be addressed and soon.

"I'm going to keep searching for the key to the plane." She collects her plate, taking it with her as she leaves the kitchen.

I watch her go, my eyes glued to the way her leggings mold to her delicate form. Leo stares, too. Stares at the same ass I'm staring at. It's impossible to look away. There's something there. Something magnetic and potent about her, pulling everything and everyone into her orbit.

"It's cute how she thinks she's in charge." I'm still staring, spellbound, long after she vanishes from view.

"Yeah." He hasn't looked away, either. "Cute is one way to put it."

frankie

FIVE

Trapped in a cabin that holds the whispers of our despair and the heat of our intertwined bodies, we exist in a limbo of ice and shadows.

Will the plane return and see our signal?

Will we solve the riddle and escape on our own?

Which will come first? Salvation or starvation?

Hunger occupies most of the space in my mind. It goes beyond the stabbing pangs, fatigue, and depletion of muscle and fat. The psychological impact cuts deeply and incessantly. Depression, anxiety, hallucinations, and preoccupation with food...God help me, eating is all I think about. I think about what I ate last, what I'll eat next, how it will smell, what the taste and texture will feel like on my tongue. It's agonizing.

None of us complain openly, but oftentimes, I'll find Leo or Kody in the pantry, holding a pouch of grains or a can of soup, staring at the promise of it, fantasizing about devouring it when no one is looking.

It's easy to let our fixation on food spread its roots and consume our minds like a parasite. That's why I convinced them to increase our rations.

It was the right call. After two days of extra calories, we already feel stronger, physically and mentally. Still hungry but we can't completely forgo our rationing.

Adding to our improved spirits is Leo's victory with the water tank. He successfully converted it to a wood-heated system, and though it only works for the primary bathroom, it makes cooking and bathing an absolute luxury.

"You're a miracle worker." I stand under the warm spray, my cheeks overflowing with my smile.

To conserve hot water, we still bathe together. With a gorgeous man before me and another behind, it's a slice of paradise in the unforgiving Arctic. Here, in their embrace, I have the entire world wrapped around me. Because my entire world is them.

I'm bound by heartstrings to two souls, brothers in name, family in blood, rivals in love, united in their resolve to protect one thing.

Me.

I may not be strong enough to protect them the same way, but I'll do whatever it takes to keep them healthy and return the light to their eyes.

As the water paints trails of happiness upon my skin, I sigh, sinking into Leo's strong arms.

"We need a good night's sleep." He palms my butt, giving it a squeeze. "I'll double-check our packs and join you in bed."

The weather has abated. No blizzards or snowfall in days, leaving an ominous calm in its wake. We need to take advantage of it and retrieve the snow machine.

Leo and I will leave before dawn.

As he exits the bathroom, I turn to Kody, his gaze as dark as the storm-ridden skies. Always hovering. Always watching.

I touch his face, take him into both hands, and run my thumbs across his bristly jaw.

He wants to go with us, and I don't want to leave him behind, but the snow machine can only carry two. Besides, someone should be here if the plane returns.

No need to voice our wishes. They entwine like the steam that rises around us, mingling with our breaths.

Even here, beneath the heavy aroma of iron-rich groundwater, his scent overpowers. That allure he has, the essence that makes him so impossibly attractive and irresistible, drapes his tall, shadowed frame like magic.

"Keep looking at me like that," he rasps, "and I'll sink my teeth into you."

"Promise?"

In the next breath, his hungry mouth crashes over mine. I open for him, licking his tongue and threading my fingers through his hair. His lips, soft and dewy, taste like the sweet mint of toothpaste, as he plasters me against the shower wall with his long, hard body.

Hard and dark and wild, he's a tempest of arousal. The hardest part of him, usually kept contained, now glides against my stomach, pulsing, rubbing, leaking from the tip, and wanting in.

The want is staggering.

This is a different kind of starving, an ache so deep and vast it stretches beyond our bellies and burns through our veins. The press of his teeth against my jugular consumes me, drawing me closer, a seduction that calls to the very core of my being.

His touch, his kiss, his bite—all of it is a promise of safety.

"Leo's right." That hot mouth travels down my neck, traces my collarbone, and laps at my nipple. "You need to sleep and conserve your energy." He steps back, robbing me of those sinful lips. "Tomorrow will be a long day."

I groan. "I don't care."

Not with his hand clenched around the thick steel of his cock, denying me, denying us both profound pleasure. Our connection, wet and waiting, thrives here, creating its own steam.

"I'll be waiting." He traces a finger along the seam of my lips. "Waiting for you. Keeping our fire alive."

The next morning, he pulls me into a rib-cracking hug and whispers the same promise. It fuels my determination to return, not just for survival, but for love.

He and Leo exchange a similar embrace, their breaths fogging in the cold air.

Stepping off the porch, I look skyward. We all do. The horizon appears brighter this morning, more glowy in its pastel hues. But there's no plane. No distant rumble of an engine.

As the wind shrieks its mournful dirge, the reality of our predicament scrapes at my insides.

If we don't return, Kody will survive on the remaining food until the thaw. But he'll be alone. Alone with a plane he can't fly. Alone with a grief he may never overcome.

I glance over my shoulder and find his stony gaze locked on mine. "We're coming back."

Hands in his pockets, he lowers his chin in a nod.

My chest stings. I don't want to go.

Leo strides toward me and clasps my hand as he passes, pulling me along. His sidelong glance and severe expression tell me he knows my mind. He understands my hesitation.

It's not safe out here. The skies could open and unleash a blizzard when we're miles from shelter. Wolves could pounce from the shadows and tear us apart before we fire a bullet. We could break a leg on the ice. The river could steal our supplies. We could succumb to the cold and lose our sense of direction.

If we got separated, I may never find my way back.

The world beyond Hoss is a realm where the moon reigns and the sun dares not linger. The cold is a beast that gnaws at my bones and seeks to pry apart my flesh with frostbitten claws.

I'm wrapped in layers upon layers, yet they seem as flimsy as gauze against the relentless chill. The snowshoes help navigate the deep drifts but require strenuous movement.

Strenuous for me, anyway.

It's a long day of hiking where time loses all meaning. The only measure of progress is the slow, steady rhythm of our footsteps against the snow.

For miles, I follow him, the man whose heart beats in a rhythm I long to call my own. He moves with a purpose, a determination that I find both exhausting and exhilarating. There's a lupine grace in his steps, a harmony with the elements that I struggle to emulate.

He carries his rifle with an ease that speaks of familiarity and readiness. I carry mine on its shoulder sling to avoid shooting off a toe.

Every now and then, he stops, scanning the horizon for signs of danger. I can't help but admire the way his eyes narrow with focus, the way his body tenses, ready to spring into action.

The broad expanse of his back, the shifting of muscles beneath his fur coat, he's built for this, drawing from an endless reserve of strength. Watching him, knowing he slows his gait for me, I'm filled with a warmth that defies the brutal wind.

He's more than just a man I love. He's my guardian, my guide, and my assurance that we'll survive.

We haven't spoken for hours, but I'm acutely aware of his every twitch and glance as he leads me through the darkness of midday. With the hills behind us, I know we're hiking south, miles downstream from Hoss.

To our left, the river hems us in. I can't see it, but the moment I hear it, I'm overwhelmed with thoughts of Wolf.

Will we find him washed up on the shore? Are pieces of his clothes tangled amid the rocks? Are his bones picked clean by predators?

I have distant pinpricks of hope, too, like maybe he survived the fall and found a cave. Maybe he's living off fish and river water.

But there are no fish, and that fall…

It wasn't survivable.

As we approach the cliff's edge, I feel so heavy, anchored by a sadness that knows no bounds.

One glance at Leo, and I know he's thinking about Wolf, too. Eyes glassy, he sniffs, drags the back of a gloved hand beneath his nose, and stares out beyond the treacherous ledge and into the abyss below.

A blanket of obsidian swallows everything except the faint glimmer of stars overhead. What is he looking at?

"Leo?"

He stiffens, straightens, and pins me with a sideways glare. "You love him?"

My breath freezes before me, a swirling cloud of the life that stubbornly clings within me.

Kody. He's asking if I love Kody.

"Yes." My teeth chatter, my trembling uncontrollable.

"And you love me?"

"You know I do."

He turns to me fully and grips my shoulders, putting his frost-covered face in mine. "Then you will live. Hear me? You'll survive for him and for me. No matter what happens, you'll put your life first."

"You're scaring me."

"Good. I need you to be aware and alert. Because if you fall..." He glances at the slope behind him and returns to me. "I won't survive it."

"You mean I won't survive it."

"No, love. My life begins and ends with you. You're my forever." He touches his brow to mine and whispers under his breath, "Please, God."

"Are you praying?"

"To whomever will listen."

"Okay." I swallow. "So this is the dangerous part you were talking about?"

"Yeah. We passed the snow machine a half mile back. Down there." He motions at the river below. "The incline behind me is the only way down, but it's not safe. It's steep and icy with no handholds."

"How did you get the snow machine down there?"

"Very carefully. Listen, I've made this climb a hundred times, and I need you to do exactly as I say. The traction pattern from my snowshoes will score the ice, providing added grip for yours. Step where I step. Walk on the sides of your feet to create a ledge in the slope. And hold my hand all the way down. I won't let go, Frankie. You will *not* fall."

"Why not just tie a rope around me?"

"Because if I fall, I'll take you with me."

"Then I'll tell you the same thing. You will *not* fall."

"Yes, ma'am."

My heart races with a flux of adrenaline and deep affection. "Lead the way."

He flashes his teeth in a grim smile and takes my hand.

And down we go.

I trust in his strength, his skills, and above all, in the love that leads us into the gorge. As long as he's with me, I believe in our survival.

Slowly, carefully, I match my footholds with his, trying my best not to be a burden. Ahead of me, he moves with a confidence that negates his fears, his silhouette gliding along the cliff face as if resistant to the pull of gravity.

There are dangers hidden everywhere in the beauty of this frozen hell—crevasses that yawn open like the maws of giants, ready to swallow us whole, and thin ice that threatens to crack beneath our weight, plunging us into the icy depths below.

Every step is a gamble, each breath a defiance against the frozen air. Yet I find a perverse thrill in this dance with death. To be here, with the man whose hand I hold in mine, is to be alive in a way that the safety of civilization could never offer.

His gaze is everywhere, all at once—on our feet, the cliff, the river below. Every time I slip or lose my balance, his mouth forms a lipless slash, hoisting up an expression stark with terror.

"I love you." I squeeze his hand.

He scowls, apparently not in the mood for my assurances.

The wind howls like a banshee, whipping snow at our goggles, trying to blind us and sweep us off the narrow path. But he leads on, unerringly finding the best places to step, his hand a constant support for my fumbling, ungraceful descent.

By the time we reach the bottom, my legs have lost all strength. I collapse on my rear, laughing at myself.

He kneels at my side and shoves up his foggy goggles, scanning me from head to toe, looking bewildered.

"Go ahead and say it." I remove my goggles, too. "Tell me I have spaghetti legs."

A pinch of amusement dimples the corner of his mouth. "You didn't fall to your death."

"Neither did you."

"I'd sell my soul for spaghetti right now."

"With spicy tomato sauce."

"And huge, juicy meatballs."

"Mmm." My mouth waters. "Too bad we're never selling our souls again. Not even for spaghetti."

"Indeed." Kissing my icy lips, he pulls the pack off my back and removes his own. "Let's take a quick lunch break."

My pack carries the medical supplies and half of our food. His holds the rest, including the heavy stuff, like the weapons, ammo, and tools to repair the snow machine.

The busted hunk of metal lies half a mile upriver. If we're lucky, he'll have it running within an hour or two, and we'll be on our way back to Kody.

Rocky walls rise into the darkness on both sides, forming a river gorge, trapping us in. The deep current rushes by, carrying chunks of ice and little else.

No sign of Wolf. No tracks in the snow.

For a moment, I let myself believe he made it to the hunting cabin, and he's there now, eating the pemmican. I would give all the food in the world to have him back.

"The worst part of the trek is over, right?" I accept my portion of cured meat, shoving it into my mouth.

"Right." He squints at the pitch-black sky.

I follow his gaze. "What?"

"No stars." He stands abruptly, swinging on his pack. "The wind is picking up."

As if to punctuate his point, strands of hair escape his hat and lash his harsh jawline.

He lowers his goggles and meets my gaze. "We need to hurry."

frankie

SIX

"A storm?" I can't see anything in the drench of darkness overhead.

I guess that's Leo's point.

The stars, visible the last time I looked up, are now completely obscured. Whatever is coming must be moving fast. As if we need another adversary threatening to turn our journey into a fight for survival.

"Could just be heavy cloud cover." He holds up a hand, watching a fresh gust of sleet coat his glove. "Or not."

My nerves go to hell as he helps me into my backpack.

Then we're off, each step along the icy river a battle against the spitting wind. He doesn't make it far before stopping at an opening in the cliff wall.

A cave.

"We use this as a landmark to find the trail to the

top." He crouches, gesturing for me to join him.

I do, wiping snowflakes from my goggles.

Curiously, his hand runs over the rock face in a strange sort of veneration.

Aren't we in a hurry?

Then I see it.

A butterfly engraved upon the wall at the cave's mouth.

"Wolf carved this." Expression drawn, he traces the outline of wings spread wide, each one spanning the length of his hand.

With every heartbeat, I feel Wolf's absence, endlessly deep. I know Leo does, too, especially in the familiar spaces they once shared.

My chest aches for all that he was and all that we've lost. I'll carry that devastation forever.

"Why a butterfly?" I ask.

"Arctic Blue butterflies flourish here in the summer, nectaring on the primrose that grows in the riverbed."

"Are they truly blue?"

"As blue as Wolf's eyes."

"That's such a rare color in nature."

"So was Wolf." He rises to his full height, the snow raging around him, indifferent to our pain. "If we get separated, if something happens—"

"I won't leave you."

"Frankie." He flexes his jaw. "Pay attention."

"Fine. I'm listening."

"Look for Wolf's butterfly. The cave is deep and provides good shelter. We've slept there many times. If you find your way to the cave, you'll find your way to Hoss. Take the trail to the top and follow the river all the way back. Understand?"

The ice beneath my feet cracks.

I would never leave him, but that's not what he

wants to hear. "I understand."

"Let's go."

And so, we press on through the increasingly turbulent snowfall, lost in our thoughts.

I keep my ears perked for the howls of wolves, watching for predatory eyes glinting in the shadows. We could be walking right into their territory, but I trust Leo implicitly. He would protect me with his life, standing between me and any threat without a second thought.

Doesn't mean I'll let my guard down. I'm so focused on the dangers that could be lurking on every side that I don't realize he stopped until I slam into his back.

He spins toward me, eyes wide.

"What's wrong?"

"Beneath its wings..." His gaze drifts over my shoulder. "Lies the answers..."

"You figured it out?"

"Beneath its wings," he repeats.

"The butterfly?"

In a cage of ice and echoes.

"The cave," we say at the same time.

"Holy fuck." He shakes his head. "It can't be that easy."

"Easy? Which part of this is easy?"

"I don't know. If he meant the cave, why did he say *cage*?"

"He was in an actual cage when he said it. Why didn't he just tell us where he hid the answers? Or better yet, why hide them at all? Why force you to make a dangerous trek for coal when he could've restored the power? He was a fucking psychopath. That's why."

"He came here a lot, usually in the summer with Wolf. But I was just here less than two weeks ago. In that fucking cave. I didn't see anything, so I'm struggling to believe that's the answer."

"Is it a big cave?"

"Yeah. A lot of tunnels. And ice."

"And echoes?"

"Right. It seems too obvious. Like another trick." He pivots in the direction of the snow machine.

It sits somewhere along the river, ensnared by the frozen landscape, awaiting revival. It's our only hope for a fast return, our only way to outrun the approaching storm.

"We don't have time for a goddamn scavenger hunt." He stares up at the sky, his face quickly submerged in snow before he wipes it away.

"Can we wait out the storm in the cave? Spend the night there?"

"What if the blizzard last days? Or weeks? We can't risk being snowed in. The trail to the top could become impassable, and we only have two days of food."

"This is the only opportunity, Leo. If the answer to the power system is in that cave, we don't need the coal."

"We need the snow machine to get back."

"Do you need my help repairing it?"

"I'm not leaving you here, Frankie."

Our caloric intake is too low to make a second trip back here. Kody and I still need to hike to the hunting cabin and retrieve the pemmican.

This investigation must happen now.

"I'll be right here in the cave." I point behind me. "I have a gun and a lantern. I'll search for the answers while you fix the snow machine. We'll be back at the cabin before the blizzard hits."

"No."

Goddamn, he's hardheaded.

"Splitting up the tasks is our best option." I clench my teeth. "If Kody were here instead of me, you would do it exactly that way, no hesitation. Put some damn trust in me!"

"Fuck!" He paces in a tight circle, pulling on his hat. "Fuck!"

He knows I'm right, and man, he doesn't like it.

Overprotective brute.

In the next breath, he's in my face, grabbing the back of my head and hauling me close.

The man can find my mouth in the direst moments, in the dark, in the blistering cold, in an arctic snowstorm with the sky falling down around us.

Sleet melts between our lips as he kisses me, jaws open, tongues sliding, breaths heating. He eats me alive, pouring all his fears, hopes, and trust into our connection.

With a tormented snarl, he comes up for air, barking orders.

"Keep the rifle at the ready at all times." He takes my gun and swaps it with his. "You have three rounds."

"What are you doing?"

"Arming you with *my* rifle. It's the deadliest one we own, designed to kill large, dangerous game."

"You're overreacting."

I don't feel comfortable taking his gun, but he shoots me a look that makes me wither.

"Three rounds, love. If you aim true, you'll only need one." He adjusts my goggles, clearing the lenses. "It has a mean kick when you fire. Be ready for it."

"Okay."

"It'll knock you on your ass."

"I'll be ready."

"There's a sharp drop just beyond the entrance of

the cave. Watch your footing. Stay alert. Don't leave that cave until I return. Promise me."

"I promise."

He stares for an unnerving second, his face stark behind the goggles. "When I tell you I love you, it isn't out of habit or because I think you need to hear it. I say it to remind the world that you're irreplaceable, and it will suffer my eternal goddamn wrath if anything happens to you."

"Savage." My stomach swoops.

"That's how I love you."

"With eternal goddamn wrath." I grin.

"Forever."

"I know."

"I'll hurry." Another kiss, quick and unhappy, and he steps back.

Before he can change his mind, I race to the cave and skid into the entrance, still in his sight. He hasn't moved, watching through the flurry, ensuring I made it.

My fierce protector in this brutal land.

"Be safe," I shout over the wind and enter the mouth of the cave.

Whoa, that's a sharp descent. I slide all the way down, wheeling my arms and somehow staying upright as the sudden plunge into darkness swallows me whole.

I remove my goggles, grab the small lantern, and light the wick, its glow a feeble defense against the pressing gloom.

The first thing that strikes me is the bottomless silence, broken only by the sorrowful drip of meltwater and the distant echo of the river behind me. The air, so crisp and cold, carries a purity found only in pristine environments, untouched by human presence.

My breath forms clouds, drifting upward, mingling with the cave's frigid exhale.

The walls, ceiling, and floor are sheathed in ice, varying in color from the purest white to the deepest shades of blue. The hues shift and change with the cave's curvature and the light's angle, generating a multifaceted spectacle.

Icicles hang from above like crystalline chandeliers. Stalagmites and stalactites of ice rise and descend in frozen mimicry of their limestone counterparts.

Despite the beauty, a chilling sense of danger trickles from every shadowed crevice.

Am I alone? Bears, wolves—they're out there, or *in* here, masters of a domain where I'm the intruder.

The rifle slung over my shoulder is a cold comfort, its weight a reminder that, without Leo, a bullet may be the only thing standing between life and death.

If bears hibernate in this cave, he would've told me, right?

I push deeper, lantern held high, casting long, wandering shadows. The ground, layered in permafrost and accumulated snow, crunches softly underfoot. In some areas, transparent ice reveals the depths below, offering a glimpse into the deep, frozen tiers of history encapsulated within.

The cave narrows, forcing me to squeeze through gaps that scrape at my coat and tug at my hair. My heart races, pounding against my ribs like it wants out. Every rustle, every shift of ice sets it fluttering like a caged butterfly desperate for the sky.

Beneath its wings lies the answers you seek in a cage of ice and echoes.

The words play over in my mind as I creep deeper, no longer able to hear the river.

"Beneath its wings..." I scan the glacial walls, searching for...what? A literal cage? A chamber of echoes? Something encased in ice? Maybe the lost ark? Or the deathly hallows? My thoughts run rampant with possibilities, each more fantastical than the last.

A fully charged satellite phone would be life-changing. Or a treasure trove of canned food.

Knowing Denver, it's probably a frozen corpse trapped in a coffin of ice. Hopefully not his elusive unnamed brother.

The walls stand silent, guardians of the answers I seek, their surfaces glinting like blue and white jewels.

The lantern's glow, dim and faltering, becomes my sole lifeline through the cavern's depths. As the light filters through cracks and openings, it scatters, creating an ethereal glow that illuminates the surroundings with a soft, diffuse luminosity, revealing intricate patterns from air bubbles trapped eons ago to delicate frostwork that adorns the surfaces.

Despite the thick gloves, my hands are achingly numb as I probe crevices and underhangs, tearing at the frozen veil that separates me from the answers.

Distanced from time and weather, I don't know what's happening outside or how long I've been gone. I keep moving, combing through the maze, my steps echoing off the ice. The symbolism isn't lost on me.

The cold bites at my flesh. Shadows twist around me, specters conjured by my flickering light, their forms melding with the ice, playing tricks on my eyes.

Frustration mounts with each passing moment, each dead end. The riddle that once seemed within reach now feels like it's slipping through my frozen fingers.

"Beneath its wings..." I repeat it again and again as if the cave might answer back.

My resolve wavers. The edge of despair gnaws at my spirit.

Where could it be? What am I missing?

I peer closer at the rounded walls, the tunnels shaped by external temperatures, the flow of meltwater, and the overarching effects of climate change.

Nothing.

There's nothing here.

As I start to turn back, my light catches something, a formation unlike the rest. A crevice, hidden beneath an overhang shaped uncannily like the outstretched wings of a bird.

My heart surges with a renewed pulse of adrenaline. That has to be it, the shape too symbolic to be coincidence.

Shivering, not just from the chill but from excitement, I inch closer. The ice around the opening is thick, a barrier formed by the slow tears of the cave. My fingers scrape against it, the effort sending stabs of pain through my numb extremities.

I dig, clawing with a desperation born of fear that this might lead to nothing.

Ice chips away under the assault of my determination, each fragment a tiny victory. The aperture yields slowly, grudgingly, as if reluctant to relinquish its secret.

Removing the gloves makes it easier. And more painful.

Until my fingers brush against something that doesn't belong.

Not ice, not rock, but something man-made. Frozen rubber? Plastic? The shock of it cuts through the fog of exhaustion.

Whatever it is, it's entombed in a small, icy cage formed by the dripping water over countless years.

With trembling hands, I pull and scratch and slowly pick away its frozen shackles. Each small piece revealed sends a shiver of triumph and dread through me.

What secrets does this mystery hold? What truths, frozen in time, await their exhuming? The weight of the moment presses down on me. Solving the riddle holds the promise of answers and, perhaps, the key to restoring the power.

Maybe there's a journal. One that will unlock the unknowns about how Leo and Kody are related, how Monty is connected to this, and the identity of his other brother.

At last, I remove enough ice to reveal a heavy-duty dry bag. Within the transparent material lies a book.

My fingernails tear to the quick in my haste to pry open the thick, frozen plastic. I wipe blood on my snow pants and reach inside.

Thin binding. Old, flimsy pages. My pulse goes berserk as I force myself to slow down and remove it carefully.

The cover boasts the image of a Turbo Beaver bush plane.

The flight manual.

I don't believe it. If this is a sick joke, my heart won't survive it.

Too stiff and frozen, the pages won't turn. My hands have no feeling.

Breathe, Frankie. Calm down.

At last, I crack open a section of the book, revealing a diagram of the fuel system. I bring it to my mouth and huff hot breaths until the paper softens enough to flip to another page.

More diagrams, illustrations of gauges, descriptions, and explanations on the electrical switch panel, the flight control system, take-off power time limit, the throttle lever, engine stuff...Oh, my God, this is pure fucking gold, promising the sky to those daring enough to claim it.

Why would Denver leave this here? If he didn't want us to find it, why not destroy it?

When he uttered the riddle, he knew he wouldn't live. Some part of him must've wanted to give his boys a chance to survive. I don't know how to process that, but I'll take it.

I clutch the manual to my chest. Time is a luxury I don't have, with the storm's breath already frosting the air outside, turning black into white, life into death. I have to get back to Leo, to share this sliver of hope, this promise of flight.

But there's something else in the bag.

I shove my hand inside, curling frostbitten fingers around a small, smooth object. Artificial. Metal or hard plastic.

A thumb drive.

Why? What could be on it? Bank records? Passwords or keys in the outside world? Answers to our questions? To Denver's history? To every mystery his sons never hoped to solve?

Right now, it's as useful as a stone, without power, without purpose.

But the manual...That's our salvation, our freedom. With it, we can do more than survive. We can escape, soar above the hills that threaten to bury us here.

Gently, I return the treasures to the waterproof bag and stow it in my pack. As I work the gloves back on, the lantern's flame starts to gutter.

"No, no, no. Don't you dare—"

The light burns out, dousing the cave in darkness.

"Shit!" I try with no avail to relight it.

Out of oil.

Just my luck.

Into the pack it goes, freeing my hands to hold the rifle.

The return journey through the labyrinthine tunnels feels like a descent into madness. Shadows cling to my heels, whispering their deadly threats, my heart a frenzied drumbeat, echoing the frantic need to see Leo again, to meld my lips with his in a kiss that will silence all doubts, to prove to him he was right to trust me with this quest.

Beneath the wings of the cave, I found one of our answers—not in a cage of ice and echoes, but in the pages of a manual that could very well be our wings to safety.

Guided by the ghostly sighs of the wind, I navigate the stygian darkness. The cave's mouth calls to me with the voice of the storm beyond, a cry of the roaring river and keening gales.

Are we too late? Is the trail to the top already impassable?

I reach the bottom of the slope that leads to the entrance. Beyond the threshold is nothing but a flurry of blinding white.

Leo's words echo in my mind, a plea to wait inside, a forced promise.

What if that promise becomes our enemy? What if he's stuck? What if he's hurt?

No, he's too strong. Too smart. Too invincible.

Hope flickers dimly, fueled by the fragile wish to find him waiting just outside, beyond the curtain of snow and wind.

If I go out there, I'll know. Maybe I'll hear the sound of the snow machine as it approaches.

Heart heavy with worry, I ascend the treacherous

slope, my snowshoes biting into the ice with each laborious step, until I stand on the brink of oblivion, swallowed by the ferocious whiteout.

Visibility is a cruel joke, the world reduced to a blur of arctic fury. Powerful gusts try to topple me over as I inch closer to the river. Stinging ice plasters to my exposed lips and works its way under my goggles.

Where is he?

The storm mocks me, its frigid fingers smacking my flesh, daring me to venture farther in search of him.

I should turn back and wait. But for how long?

How far did he go? A mere half-mile? Is it a straight shot? Did the blizzard obscure the path, leaving only a maze of white and danger?

Panic creeps in as I hesitate, torn between the urge to retreat to shelter and the drive to press on.

The deeper fear spurs me forward, the terror of what lies ahead with Leo alone against this raging tempest.

Each step is an eternity. A calorie-sucking, unbearably cold, impossible eternity. Five steps. Ten steps. Too late, I realize the stupidity of this decision.

I need to go back.

As I start to turn, a strange noise tingles through me.

Huffing.

Grunting.

Then a vibrating sound cleaves the wind.

A growl, inhuman and terrifying, a harbinger of death.

I spin, my stomach bottoming out. Through the sheets of snow, a nightmare takes shape.

A grizzly bear.

A behemoth of muscle and bared fangs emerges

from the storm thirty yards away, its gaze locking with mine.

My soul leaves my body. My blood drains to my boots. Fear paralyzes me, rooting me to the spot, a deadly indecision.

I should've stayed in the cave, and now it's out of reach, somewhere behind the thing that wants to eat me.

To run is to invite death, yet in my hands lies the power to stop it. The rifle trembles with my trembling pulse.

Three rounds, love. If you aim true, you'll only need one.

Ice coats my gloves and numbs my fingers, rendering them clumsy and unresponsive, a poor match for the rifle's demanding trigger.

The bear doesn't care. It charges, and the pressure to act tightens a fist around my throat.

Leveling my aim, I fire, and holy fuck, I'm not ready.

The explosive boom, the violent recoil, it's an unforgiving punch against my shoulder, sending me careening backward as if a wild creature struggles against my hold.

The bullet misses, and the terror of my situation crystallizes, threatening to bring me to my knees.

It's not just a physical failure but a psychological blow, stripping away the thin veneer of control and leaving raw, unmitigated panic.

I can't do this.

With the beast barreling toward me, each second stretches into infinity, warping time under the strain of my imminent death.

Two rounds left.

I eject the shell. Chamber the next. Adjust my grip, the act of pulling the trigger complicated by the bulky gloves and the shockwave of fear ricocheting through my system.

I'm going to die.

My second shot is a *fuck you* in the face of the storm, a bullet of hope that falters, hitting a front leg.

The grizzly continues its relentless advance, slowed, limping, but undeterred.

A juggernaut of rage, hunger, and undying strength.

I open the bolt and chamber the last round.

My shoulder throbs as I dig the butt of the rifle deep into bruised muscle. Steadying my sights, I fire.

Hit!

I stumble back, and the bear stumbles, too, roaring as it crashes onto its chest and skids across the ice. But I'm already turning, fleeing into the blizzard.

Sprinting, heart pounding, lungs panting, I muster every ounce of energy left to distance myself from that thing.

Then I hear it.

That vicious, harrowing growl, crashing down my spine. The thunder of enraged footfalls, stomping, gaining speed, shaking the ground. The sound of chaos unfolding.

Don't look back. Don't look back.

I glance over my shoulder and scream.

SEVEN

The bitter cold stings my face as I tear through the blizzard, the snow machine's engine reverberating through the gorge. Every gust hits me like whiplash, the snow pelting my goggles relentlessly, obscuring my vision.

I push forward, faster, my heart racing with urgency.

Frankie.

The mere thought of her waiting in that cave, alone in this brutal weather, sends a shiver down my spine.

It took me too long to repair the machine, and I can't shake the worry gnawing at me, the fear that something could've happened to her.

She promised to stay put, but anything could've gone wrong.

Like her inability to follow orders.

The river beside me thrashes and roars like a beast

unleashed, guiding me back to the cave. I try not to think about Wolf falling into that deathtrap, the rapids pulling him under, slamming him against rocks and jagged ice.

My throat burns, and I slam a door on those thoughts.

Snowdrifts pile higher, erasing my earlier trail, and the heavy sled of coal behind me drags, slowing my progress. I curse under my breath, willing the machine to move faster.

The storm intensifies, biting through every layer of clothing, sinking deep into my bones, burning my fingers, and chilling my soul. The very air wants to freeze the life out of me, making it hard to think, to breathe.

I should be close. But how will I know? I can't see shit. Did I pass the entrance? I could really use Kody's sharp hearing and superhuman tracking senses right now.

Wait. What was that?

I strain my hearing until it sounds again. A sharp, high-pitched scream, and another, cutting through the howling wind.

Panic grips my chest. It can't be...Frankie?

No, she wouldn't venture out in this weather. Would she?

I kill the engine and tilt my head, listening, searching for any sign of her.

Movement up ahead.

A streak of color.

Red. Fiery red hair contrasts starkly against the white flurry as she runs toward me with desperation etched into every line of her face.

My heart lurches at the sight of her.

She screams again, and the chilling sound rips open

my chest, releasing all the air from my lungs. Crippling fear crashes through me, akin to the horror and helplessness of watching Wolf jump off the cliff.

As she sprints toward me, I feel like I'm unraveling, losing my balance, barely able to stay on the snow machine. I can't see the danger, but I know what lurks in this land. In the darkness, in the heavy shower of snow, it can't be good.

I leap off the snow machine, rifle in hand, ready to face whatever threatens my entire fucking world.

"Frankie!" I bolt toward her, waving an arm.

She sees me but doesn't slow.

The next second, a raging giant explodes into view behind her.

Fucking God.

A massive grizzly, wounded and enraged, limps after her with terrifying speed. An inexorable force that crushes everything in its way.

A predator in pursuit of its prey.

Over my cold, dead body.

I level the rifle, my hands trembling with adrenaline, trying to steady my shot.

Fuck! Too far away.

My blood runs cold as I charge forward, losing precious seconds as I try to get within range. I've never felt terror like this before, the horror of knowing I might not reach her in time.

Weaving and leaping, she dodges obstacles in her path. She's so close but still too far from me. The bear gains on her, its claws swiping out, snagging her hair.

"Run, run, run!" My heart hammers, my gut a sickening knot of fear, as I urge my legs faster, aiming the rifle and shouting words of encouragement, of warning.

As I try to get a shot, my hands shake violently despite my efforts to steady them. I trip over rocks, slide across ice. The blizzard swirls around us, obscuring my vision.

Squinting through the blowing snow, I lock onto the target—the bear, lumbering ever closer. But with each passing second, my dread grows. My certainty wavers.

The wind threatens to knock me off balance, to send my shot veering off course.

What if I miss? What if I hit her instead?

With death looming on all sides, it feels like the universe is conspiring against us.

I can't lose her. I won't survive without her.

My finger tightens on the trigger, hesitating. She's in the path of the bullet, and the fucking bear is right on her heels.

"Frankie!" I'm running again, gritting my teeth and willing my hands to still, to find their mark.

Never in my life have I run *toward* a bear. This is madness. It's suicide.

"Turn back!" she screams, her eyes locking onto mine, filled with a ferocity that pierces through the storm. "Run away, Leo!"

Never. As long as I'm alive, I'll fight, for her, for us.

I change course, veering toward the river and risking the thin ice to get the angle I need. The ground slides and shifts beneath my feet as I make a wide circuit.

She sees what I'm doing and swerves toward the cliff, out of my way, running her beautiful heart out.

With a steadying breath, I adjust my grip, my focus narrowing to a razor-sharp point. She's so close now, so close to safety. I won't let her down.

As I take aim, heart pounding in my throat, I pray to

whatever gods may be listening—for the strength, for the accuracy, to save the woman I love.

The cold digs deeper, slowing my movements, clouding my thoughts.

I blink, focus, and the instant she's out of firing range, I shoot.

One bullet isn't enough. Not with this gun. Not with this bear.

I keep firing, round after round, slowing it, maiming it, but not stopping it. I reload, running closer, slipping on the ice, the glacial water slamming against my thighs, trying to pull me under.

Still, I continue firing until finally, the bear lies still in the snow.

Slowly, I approach it, gulping for air. Five feet away, I send a final bullet between its eyes, a guarantee it will never threaten her again.

She races toward me with tears streaking her goggles, her breath coming in ragged sobs.

"Are you hurt?" I lower the gun and haul her into my arms, gathering her close.

"No. I'm just shaken up."

"Shhh." I squeeze her harder as if I could protect her from reliving the nightmare of a near-death confrontation with a grizzly.

But I can't. No one walks away from something like that unchanged.

I nearly lost her. If I had arrived one minute later...

She's my life. Her safety is my duty, my number one priority, and I failed.

"You're okay," I whisper repeatedly, my voice hoarse with emotion.

She clings to me, quaking violently, her heartbeat echoing mine. I kiss her head and inhale her feminine scent, letting it calm the wildness inside me.

As we stand there, surrounded by the raging threat of another adversary, I know we won't make it out of this gorge anytime soon.

But we won't starve. The fallen bear provides the promise of life. Food, precious and vital, now lies at our feet.

I have a million questions about the attack and her search for answers, but I ask the only one that matters. "Where's the cave, love?"

"Five minutes that way?" She points behind her. "I think? It's not far."

"We'll shelter there until the storm passes." I lower my pack beside the bear and remove the heavy-duty ratchet straps. "We need to hurry."

"What are you...?" She stares at the beast, her eyes widening with realization. "Oh, my God. We have food."

"That's right." I grin, sharing in her excitement. "Can you grab the snow machine?"

Nodding, she reloads the rifle—*smart woman*—and races off as I secure our prize in the straps.

Hope, bright and warm, fills me to the brim. Bears don't often wander out of hibernation in the winter. This one was probably hungry, drowsy, and confused. That, combined with the bullets she put in the front leg and flank, slowed it down enough for her to outrun it.

I've seen bears emerge early but never in this area. Had I known it was a possibility, I would've never agreed to let her out of my sight.

I can't find it in me to be mad. This is a blessing. A miracle. This full-grown, six-hundred-pound, muscled female will fill our bellies for a month.

"Thank you." I sink my hands into the thick fur and bow my head. "You saved us, old girl. I won't squander this gift."

The purr of the snow machine sounds behind me as I tighten the final strap.

A few minutes later, with the bear attached to the sled and dragging behind us, we make the slow journey to the cave.

I check the trail to the top, and just as I thought, the conditions are too dangerous to attempt the steep climb. We're stuck here indefinitely.

The cave entrance provides enough shelter to stow the machine and its bounty. We have hours of work ahead of us, but the instant we're safely beneath the overhang beyond the reach of the storm, I turn to her with questions in my eyes.

"I found it." She lowers her pack to the ground and removes a dry bag, offering it to me.

Found what? I watch her, searching her face for clues.

"Open it." She bites her lip.

"Is this what I think it is?" My chest lifts as I remove a book from the bag and pore through the pages. "This...Holy fuck, Frankie. This is..."

"Freedom."

Unblinking, I stare at the diagrams of levers and gauges in disbelief. "We're getting out of here."

"Yeah."

"You did it!" Whooping with laughter, I grab her around the waist and swing her into my arms. "You fucking did it!"

"I didn't do anything. You're the one who will be decoding all that stuff and flying us out of here." Smiling, she pushes at my chest and stretches her toes toward the ground. "Better put that away before something happens to it."

"Yes, ma'am." I smack a kiss on her lips and return the manual to the bag. "What's this?"

Something catches my eye at the bottom, and I reach in, removing a thumb drive.

My mind swims, and apprehension trickles in as I conjure endless ways Denver can still fuck with us.

"I don't want to know what's on this." My fingers clench around the casing.

"Don't break it." She plucks it from my grip and drops it in the bag. "Might be important."

"Might be a trick. More twisted discoveries about our fucked-up history."

"We won't know until we have a computer or something with power to read it."

"This is everything? A flight manual and thumb drive?"

"Yeah, but we can check again." She squints at the slope that descends into the cave. "Since we're staying in there, I'll show you where I found it. Maybe I missed something."

"Not likely. The manual is more than I hoped for, but..."

"The key to restoring the electricity would've been the cherry on top." She glances at the dry bag. "I wouldn't put it past him to put instructions for the power system on a thumb drive that requires power. I'm expecting that, actually. It will no longer matter after we freeze through the winter."

"I'll keep you warm." I lower my brow to hers.

"I'm counting on it."

leonid

EIGHT

Over the next several hours, Frankie helps me field-dress the bear. We dump the unusable parts in the river, tie the organs and meat in tarps on the sled, and haul enough coal and river water into the cave to keep us sustained for a few days.

By the time we finish, we're bone-tired and covered in blood.

After we remove our snowshoes, she sets up our double sleeping bag, and I start a fire in the stone pit I've used many times through the years.

Doesn't take long to coax a blaze strong enough to chase away the chill in our small alcove. We shed our outerwear, heat the water, and roast our dinner.

As we wash our skin and clean our teeth, I can't help but marvel at her beauty.

Her delicate bone structure, sculpted by the harshness of this unforgiving land, shimmers in the light. Long strands of hair cascade down her back like trails of fire, swaying with her movements as she scrubs away the remnants of a very long day.

Green eyes, vibrant and alive, reflect the flickering glow of flames with a mesmerizing intensity. They hold a depth that speaks of the challenges she's faced, the trials endured, and the hardships still to come. Yet there's resilience in her gaze, a stubbornness that refuses to be broken by the brutal realities of our existence.

A swell of gratitude washes over me as I watch her work. Grateful that she's by my side, that she survived the day. Each stroke of her hand, each drop of water mingled with blood, attests to her courage and determination.

Despite the savage storm that surrounds us on all sides, there's a warmth in her presence that fills me with hope. Hope for tomorrow, hope for a future where we can leave this treacherous place behind and build a life together.

But for now, at this moment, I'm simply grateful she's here, beside me, her beauty a glimmering orb of light in a cold, dark cave.

As the smoky scent of meat saturates the air, my mouth salivates. She smells it, too, pausing to stare at the sizzling slab with longing.

"Here." I tear off a piece and hold it to her lips. "Blow."

She clutches my wrist as if I might pull it away and frees a soft breath, cooling down the morsel. As I slide it into her mouth, I feel her groaning satisfaction in every cell of my body.

Providing for her, putting that radiant smile on her face, it satiates a deep, fundamental need. She would call me a caveman for that, and maybe I am. My lips twitch as I glance at my surroundings.

"You better eat." Humming, she slips another strip between her lips. "Why are you smiling?"

"You're beautiful."

Soft warmth suffuses her expression. Drifting closer, she lifts a bite of meat to my mouth, and I suck it from her fingers, licking her slender digits.

Fuck, that's good. The rich, gamy flavor sweeps over my taste buds, making my eyes roll back into my head.

Cooking it over the fire adds a charred exterior while retaining moisture inside. I've never eaten anything this appetizing.

"Delicious, isn't it?" She pops another savory treat in my mouth. "Tastes like beef but with its own unique flavor profile."

Bear meat is usually tougher and more fibrous, but not tonight.

Tonight, it's a gourmet meal, a luxurious delicacy that melts in the mouth.

The experience of tasting it after being hungry for so long probably intensifies its flavor, making it seem more satisfying and nourishing than it actually is.

I don't care. The joy in her eyes shines so brightly it illuminates the cave, penetrates my chest, and settles into the notch at the base of my spine.

We eat our fill, taking turns feeding each other and grinning through every bite, licking our fingers, licking each other's fingers. We're a pair of gluttonous, hedonistic animals until every juicy piece is picked clean from the bone.

The visceral warmth and protein the meal provides is so comforting it's overwhelming. Together, we lie back on the sleeping bag, rubbing our bellies and moaning between bouts of laughter, drunk on our fullness.

"We shouldn't have done that." She angles her face toward mine, swiping her tongue across grease-slicked lips. "Our digestive systems need to readjust after going so long without. We're probably going to puke."

"No regrets." I clasp her hand, lacing our fingers. "I love seeing you happy."

Beyond the physical relief, there's an integral, emotional significance in experiencing this with her. The meal signifies survival, resourcefulness, and overcoming extreme adversity.

The act of taking down a bear, preparing it, and finally eating it feels deeply symbolic. It's an ego stroke, for sure. But my emotions run the gamut from gratitude and relief to awe and respect for the bear that provided our sustenance.

"Come on." I crawl beneath the blankets of our makeshift bed and pull her in after me.

With the fire blazing in a bed of coal, our bellies stuffed, and my beautiful girl tucked safely into the cradle of my body, I release my first contented sigh in weeks.

"Do you think there are more bears out there?" she whispers.

"They're asleep, deep in their caves. Strange that one roused early. Not unheard of but..." Guilt stabs my chest. "I should've—"

"Don't say it." She flips over to face me, pressing her palms to my cheeks. "Don't you dare apologize. I forced that decision on you, and when we return to the cabin, to Kody, we'll be carrying not just the coal but the bear's meat and the promise of escape, of a future beyond this frozen prison."

"I almost lost you." I touch her face, mapping her sweet, angelic features. "I regret—"

"No. I was taken from my house, my husband, and my career. Should I regret that?" Her hand moves to my jaw and squeezes. "I fell in love in an endless night, in the heart of hell, where evil reigned. I lost my baby. We lost Wolf. But we found each other. No regrets, got it?"

"Give me your mouth."

She leans up, closing her lips over mine, and the moment of remorse is gone. She's alive and safe. With the coal, bear meat, pemmican, and flight manual, it's enough to keep her that way.

We're going to make it off the ground. After that? Well, I need to learn how to fly and land a plane.

"I feel bad." She threads her hand through my hair. "My pants are bursting from overeating, and Kody is alone, counting his ration of beans and worrying himself sick because we haven't returned. He's probably imagining the worst, and in two days, he'll think we've run out of food."

"Kody is the toughest bastard I know. He doesn't worry. He understands the numerous ways we can be delayed out here. He can probably see the blizzard on the horizon if it hasn't already reached him. He also knows you're in safe hands. He trusts me to protect you."

"Do you trust him? With me?"

"Absolutely."

"Good." She nestles closer against my chest. "Maybe that plane came back, and they'll be waiting for us when we return."

This woman. I wish I had her optimism. She's an unsinkable buoy, no matter how rough it gets.

"Kody should be here," she says, "feasting and snuggling with us. I miss him."

"I know." I try to push down the rising jealousy.

"Does that bother you?"

I pause, struggling to find the right words. "I would be lying if I said no."

It bothers me more than I care to admit. It isn't just about sharing her with my brother. It's about sharing so much of her that he'll steal her away.

I know I need to get over that. After all, he makes her happy. We both do. Yet, deep down, I can't shake the possessiveness.

Maybe it's because I can't imagine loving two women. She's it for me. My forever. I will never want another, even if she stops wanting me.

Perhaps another part of it stems from my twisted history with Gretchen. My first and only relationship was forced on me, butchering me with scars that run far deeper than the one on my stomach. It robbed me of control, leaving me broken and wounded. The memory of it still haunts, making me cling to the need for dominance in every aspect of my life.

Unlike me, Kody doesn't carry the weight of such baggage. Frankie is his first female connection. First love. First kiss. First sexual encounter. She represents tenderness and benevolence, untainted by the shadows of the past. Despite his broody, rough exterior, my brother is innocent at heart. And eager. Of course, he is.

Because Frankie...she's utterly perfect, the complete package, drawing us both in with her warm eyes and easy affection. It's no wonder Kody is captivated by her.

But for me, it's a constant battle between wanting her happiness and struggling with my own.

"I'm trying." I stroke her silky hair. "My past with Gretchen made me jaded. But that's just an excuse. I'm an asshole with control issues. You deserve someone who is open and willing to share like Kody—"

"Stop right there." She lifts on an elbow. "You're

wrong. Except the part about being an asshole with control issues. But so is every alpha male on the planet. You have nothing on Monty."

"Fucking great." I grind my molars.

"Point is...alpha men don't share. Kody's willingness to do so is shocking. Mark my words, the moment we get out of here and enter society, his stance on that will change."

"What do you mean?"

"When another man smiles at me at work or approaches me in a park, what will Kody do?"

"He'll break the fucker's face."

"Yeah." She sighs. "Then you'll jump into the brawl and both go to jail for assault. We'll work through an adjustment period to get you two acclimated to rules and social norms."

"Nah. If a man goes near you, we'll still break his face." I take in her exasperated expression. "What's the problem?"

"The problem is I don't want you to escape this prison only to end up in another. Listen, Kody loves you and trusts you. He would never share me with someone who isn't you. I don't want that, either. I don't even know how to manage two lovers. Never even considered such a thing. I'm as new to this as you are." She edges closer, brushing her nose against mine. "I know what you're feeling, Leo. I can't fathom the thought of sharing you with another woman. Even if I had a sister, I couldn't do it, no matter how much I loved her. The idea makes me murderous. What I'm asking from you is selfish and unexplored and could blow up in our faces and shatter our souls."

Her admission loosens the tightness in my chest. I don't know why, but her words give me permission to frame it in a different light, to study it from another perspective.

She's right about sharing her with an outsider. Under no circumstances would Kody and I be okay with that. But keeping her between us? That's safe. It's right.

The three of us are connected in a rare and unbreakable relationship. We find our strength in one another, in the promise of a dawn beyond the darkness, a spring beyond the winter. Three hearts, entwined by circumstance, bound by necessity, and fueled by love, beat as one against every threat we face.

"If this is what you want..." I kiss her lips. "I won't fight it."

"Leo—"

"I'm not finished." I taste her mouth again, lingering, savoring her breath. "The three of us...it's the only thing that makes sense. But I'm going to fuck up."

"Me, too."

"How do we do this?"

"We're already doing it." She peers at me through her lashes. "There's no one-size-fits-all approach, but I think the basics apply. Trust your instincts. Set clear boundaries. Communicate openly. Manage jealousy. And have lots and lots of sex."

"How much sex are we talking?"

"At least ten times a day. Probably more."

Rock hard. I'm instantly, painfully, impossibly hard.

It's been too long. Bathing with her, sharing her bed, breathing her air, watching her walk, hearing her voice, staring into her eyes, and *not* fucking her?

Torture.

But not unbearable.

Nothing is unbearable when I'm with her.

The way she looks right now, like she didn't just

spend the past twelve hours on her feet in the ruthless Alaskan wind, I want nothing more than to devour her.

I shouldn't be getting worked up, but it's her. She's so tempting and sweet, and I've been carrying the taste of her mouth on my tongue all day. I'm desperate for more.

But first, I need to address something she probably hopes I've overlooked.

"You broke a promise today." Keeping my gaze on hers, I curl a hand around her hipbone and hold it still.

"Hmm?"

"You swore you would remain in the cave. Did the bear chase you out?"

"Not exactly."

"There are no signs of bears in these tunnels. Did it venture in here?"

"It could have."

"But it didn't."

If she followed my order, the bear would've lumbered by without detecting her. Maybe it would've encountered me instead. Maybe not. I won't lecture her about disobeying me. She learned a hard lesson. But I will drive home my point another way.

"Roll to your hands and knees." I push to a sitting position, thrumming with anticipation. "Time for your punishment."

The only part of her that moves is her eyes as they thin into sexy slits.

I remind myself that only a few months ago, she gave me that same look when I tossed her a knife and told her to cut her wrists.

Shame burns through me like lightning.

I will never deserve her, and if I thought she wasn't into this or me, I would back down from that stink eye she's giving me. But when she told me Kody reddened her ass in the tundra, she confessed she loved it.

That, I need to see for myself.

With warp speed, I flip her over onto hands and knees. She gasps, starts to pull away, but I catch her by the waist and yank her leggings and underwear off, baring her stunning backside.

Fuck me, what a view. The lush curves, porcelain skin, and the hot little crack that runs down, down, down...

Even in the low light, I see her desire dripping from her pretty pink cunt.

On my knees behind her, I jerk her against my groin, my hands dwarfing her hips, her ribs. Jesus, she's tiny. So fucking breakable. But as I trace the sinuous line of her spine and soft hills of her ass, I'm in awe at how something so small can contain so much power.

This delicate creature owns me, and damn if I don't crave her claws.

She directs her eyes over her shoulder and opens them wide, their depths greener and brighter than springtime, blooming through melting snow.

"Beg, Frankie." I brush a knuckle, light as a breeze, along her seeping slit. "Beg for your punishment."

She shakes her head.

"No?" I unzip, shove down my pants, and fist my erection, lazily stroking.

Her teeth scrape her bottom lip.

Wordlessly, but with a burning glare that hitches her breath, I run my hand from root to tip and back again. She shudders, curling her toes in the bedding beneath her.

I've never wanted anything as obsessively as I want her. I've been starving for weeks. Not just for food. I'm famished for *her.*

My hunger leaks from my crown, easing the glide of my hand.

"Leo." Her breath quickens as she watches with heavy-lidded eyes.

"Beg." Inching closer, I swipe the tip of my cock across her ass and down the backs of her thighs, leaving shiny trails of precome. "Let me hear you."

"Fuck me." She rocks back, trying to grind up on me.

"Not yet." I smack my erection on her butt, once, twice, aching to impale her. Then I rest it there, on the rise of her ass, rubbing it slowly. With my hands. With the valley of her cleft. I let her feel the heat of it, the throbbing hardness. "Feel what you do to me?"

"Please, Leo." She arches her spine, angling her slick flesh upward in invitation.

I groan at the sight, jerking myself harder. Christ, I want to press my face in her and eat and eat until all I taste is the sweet tang of her cream on my lips for days.

"Killing me." I palm her warm cheeks and caress down to her pussy, massaging the opening. "Use your words."

"Do it." She claps lust-tinged eyes on mine. "Spank me before I change my mind."

Biting back a grin, I strike her hard enough to sting my palm.

"Fuck!" Her yelp echoes through the cave and tumbles into a moan.

"That's my girl." I match her sound with another smack that steals her balance.

Catching her by the hip, I adjust her stance and give her three more ruthless swats that have her trembling and panting and dropping her head.

She doesn't just love the burn of my hand. She

melts into it, so damn relaxed she's about to fall over.

I'm going to fuck her so thoroughly that she passes out.

Lowering her to the ground, I position her on her side with her back to my chest. Then I make love to her with my fingers, rolling her clit and worshiping her frilly, velvet folds until she's shattering around me and dripping down my wrist.

"There you go." I lick her neck, her jawline, the graceful shell of her ear, and bend over her to stare into her smoldering eyes. "So goddamn beautiful."

"You're an animal." Her cheeks twitch. "Lick me again."

Gladly, I drag my tongue across her lips and down her throat to her breasts. Ticklish, she squeals and squirms. That smile. I slide two fingers into it, pumping gently, relishing the suction of her bowed lips.

Until she bites down. Growling, I yank my hand away. Playtime's over. I want inside her so badly it consumes me.

With a quick shift, I kick off my pants and angle my hips right up against her backside.

She parts her legs. Wriggles that ass.

Slowly, teasingly, I enter her from behind. Inch by inch, her tight heat steals my vision and empties my lungs.

"Jesus Christ." Shaking from the intensity, I moan loudly and sink to the root.

It's too much and not enough, everywhere, instantaneously. The squeeze of her body, the contractions along my cock, it's heaven and hell, tightening and releasing and driving me to insanity.

With digging thrusts, I deepen my strokes, stretching her, making room, taking up all the space inside her.

"So good." Trembling, clenching, she's already primed, ready to come again. "Oh, God, Leo."

I wrap a hand around her throat, gripping, groaning, fucking into her with deliberately drawn-out motions.

My lips on her jaw, our bodies tangled and rocking, her hand reaching back to claw at my ass—this is us. Fire and ice. Raw and organic. Our love grows from the earth, rooting in the dead of winter and awakening like seeds in the thaw.

She cries out, her release spilling over me, soaking my cock, and trickling over my balls. Her thighs quiver as I slide my hand from her throat to her pussy, cupping where we're joined. I ease my fingers into her and stretch them alongside my length, rubbing her inner walls, rubbing myself, making her tight channel all the more tight.

I pulse within her as her cunt contracts, our rhythm timed with the gallop of our hearts. There's nothing sexier.

"Yes!" She moves her hips, shuddering against me, riding the double penetration of my fingers and cock.

"More." I know I should stop, should let her sleep, but I can't get enough.

She gives it to me, climaxing again, hard and fast.

Dipping my head to her neck, I exhale hot breath against her shivering skin. Still moving inside her, languorously, dreamily. Gently making love long into the night. Falling in and out of sleep with my cock buried deep and her tits in my hands.

I lose count of how many times I fill her with my seed. It leaks from her, from where we're still connected, making me feel dizzy and fuzzy and heavy with pleasure. Like only she can.

Moaning through a languid orgasm, she finally passes out in my arms. My dick is sore and softening, but I want to stay. Withdrawing from her is out of the question.

With our hips tucked tightly together, I bury my face in her neck, and sleep the best sleep of my life, in a cave, in a blizzard, inside my whole world.

monty

NINE

The harsh wind cuts through my coat as I stand at the railing, staring out at the Gulf of Alaska. The waves crash against the hull of my yacht, a token of my wealth and power, yet utterly useless in finding the only thing that matters.

My missing wife.

It's been 143 agonizing days since she quit me, leaving behind a void in my heart that grows deeper with each passing moment.

I should move on.

God knows I've tried.

But no one compares to her. There isn't a woman alive who can rival Frankie's natural beauty, ball-busting ferocity, and faithful devotion to those she loves. Not even close.

I should be at the office, running my global empire, but instead, I spend every waking hour on my yacht, which serves as a mobile command center in my obsessive search for her.

As it glides through the braying waters of the Gulf, I pore over marked-up maps with locations yet to be explored. Every island, every inlet, every remote corner of the Pacific Northwest is meticulously scrutinized, my team of experts working tirelessly to unravel the mystery of her disappearance.

My hunt isn't limited to the physical landscape. I'm also combing through the depths of my memories, searching for any overlooked detail or forgotten conversation that might shed light on her whereabouts. Every argument, whispered confession, and moment of tenderness shared between us is dissected and analyzed as I strive to understand where she went.

Despite her justification for not wanting to be found, I should've located her by now. How has she evaded the resources I put into this five-month-long pursuit?

It doesn't make sense. None of this makes sense. If she simply ran, she would've left a trail, a clue, something.

Yet she vanished without a trace.

I'm not even thinking about how I will win her back. At this point, I just need some fucking proof of life.

I've enlisted the help of every contact, government agency, and connection I possess.

Private bush planes scour the Interior from Whittier to Utqiagvik. The Coast Guard District 17 sweeps forty-seven-thousand miles of shoreline throughout Alaska and the Arctic. The ABI is working diligently with all police agencies, maintaining an intrastate network of communication about her whereabouts.

My team of private investigators cast a countrywide net, utilizing facial recognition and public security cameras, leaving no stone unturned.

Somehow, she's eluded thousands of resources.

Wilson, head of my private investigative team, checks in daily. His team leader, Sirena, remains at my side to manage the local operation.

Every day, it's the same. No sightings, no clues, nothing to indicate where Frankie might have gone or what could have happened to her. It's as if she vaporized into the mist, leaving me to wonder if she ever truly existed at all.

The night she left, the security system in our mansion didn't detect breaches. No alarms sounded, and the motion detectors outside failed to register movement. She cut the power to them after our employees left for the day.

No one witnessed her departure.

No evidence of foul play or assistance from an outside party, either.

She docked her boat in our slip in Sitka and...what? Walked away on foot?

It's inconceivable.

She's always been resourceful, but to leave me in the dark like this? Without a phone call or a message or any sign of life? That's not her. She's too kindhearted. Thoughtful. Compassionate. Even for the asshole who broke her heart.

The Frankie I know would've found an untraceable way to tell me she's okay. Especially in her condition.

She would be six months into her pregnancy now.

I clutch at the railing, feeling the weight of despair pressing down on me. She left behind her phone, her wedding ring, but took clothing and documents necessary for survival.

Effectively severing all ties to me.

Fine. I get it. But where did she go after she docked her boat?

Search parties have covered every inch of the Sitka Sound, assuring me she didn't fall into the dark depths that night and drown.

But something happened. I feel it in my bones.

Across the deck, Sirena emerges from the companionway, her seductive gaze instantly latching onto mine.

Christ.

When Wilson agreed to provide a local team of investigators to assist in my search, I was pleased. Then I met the team leader.

Sirena is stunning, with her long, flowing, dark hair and piercing blue eyes that seem to hold the secrets of the ocean depths. Her unrestrained, flirtatious personality provides levity to my otherwise sour mood. Her intelligence and efficiency have been invaluable in managing the details during this tumultuous time. And her elegant body...

I catch myself stealing glances at her, admiring the graceful curve of her neck, the way the sunlight soaks into her golden complexion. Her presence is a comforting distraction from my relentless ache for Frankie.

Too comforting.

It's a dangerous game, one that threatens to betray the vows I made to my wife.

Again.

My affair with Aubrey sickens my stomach. It was a moment of weakness, born of loneliness and rage. I was so fucking angry with Frankie when she left. I couldn't stop picturing her in her happy new life, carrying our baby, and sleeping with other men.

I went to a dark place, drank too much, and fucked my office manager, which only served to deepen the pit of despair that separates me from my irreplaceable wife.

My infidelity cost Aubrey her job. I couldn't look at her without feeling sick. So I let her go.

Then Sirena showed up.

She makes her way to me, hips swaying and mouth curving into a red-painted smile, shooting a jolt of electricity through my gloomy fog.

"Quite the view, isn't it?" Her voice, low and sultry, strokes between my legs.

"Indeed." I tear my gaze away, setting it on the horizon. "But I find that the true beauty lies in the eyes of the beholder."

"Smooth, as always." She giggles softly, a melodious sound. "But I have to admit, it's hard to compete with the splendor of nature."

Frankie, gloriously nude and spread out before me, is the splendor of nature. I miss the authentic perfection of her body, her subtle curves without augmentation or surgeries, her natural red hair, and makeup-free ivory skin.

Fuck, I just...miss her.

"Nature may have its charms," I murmur, "but there's something undeniably captivating about the human form."

"You do have a way with words." Her laughter swirls with the wind, the salty tang of the sea.

She reaches out to brush a lock of hair from my face, her fingers lingering, stirring a conflicting surge of hunger within me.

We've spent too much time together, too many days

at sea in close proximity, and too many nights in the cabins below with only a thin wall between us. Her glances and touches grow bolder. In the midst of my anguish, it's a temptation I find difficult to resist.

It would be so fucking easy. She wants me, and eventually she'll throw herself at me.

She's not the first, nor will she be the last. The world is full of eager admirers drawn to my wealth, my dominance, and the magnetic pull of my presence.

I've fucked them all.

Despite the countless opportunities that present themselves, each encounter only serves to magnify the emptiness gnawing at my soul. The hollow ache of loneliness, like a persistent shadow, follows me wherever I go, a constant reminder of Frankie's absence.

It's a cruel irony to be surrounded by adoration and desire yet feel utterly alone. Sirena, with her beauty and charm, is a fleeting distraction, a temporary salve for the wounds that refuse to heal.

But she's not the one I want.

I want the woman who turned me down a dozen times, who wouldn't give me the time of day or fuck me on our first date. I want the only one who never chased me, who made me work for her attention for a goddamn year, the only one I pursued and wooed and crawled on my knees to win.

I'm haunted by the ghost of the woman who left me.

So while the tantalizing prospect of fucking Sirena over this railing whispers seductively in my mind, I know that to give in would be to betray the one person who truly holds my heart.

I already betrayed her once, and the guilt festers like an incurable STD.

"I know you have a lot on your mind." She leans

into my side, her breath warm against my neck. "I can make you forget everything but the present moment."

"As tempting as that may be..." With a tight smile, I step back, yanking away from her touch. "My heart belongs to my wife."

"I know." Her expression softens, a flicker of understanding in her eyes. "But you are..." She looks me up and down and sighs. "Fucking gorgeous. A girl can dream, can't she?"

"She can." I turn back to the maps on the credenza behind me. "We're here to find Frankie. She's the only dream I want."

"Right. Of course." She straightens, blinks, and assumes the role she came here to do, joining me to peer at the maps. "It would help if you told me why we're headed to this particular island."

I'm not accustomed to explaining myself. With more money than God, I get what I want, when I want it.

But this...this will require a little transparency. And a lot of delicacy.

I pace the deck, my footsteps echoing with the words I haven't spoken in years.

"My father, an oligarch whose wealth and power knew no bounds, presided over the largest construction company in the Pacific Northwest."

"An oligarch?" She arches a stenciled brow. "Like from Russia?"

"Yes. I was born there. My parents moved to Alaska when I was a baby."

What I won't tell her is that my mother was pregnant with my brother, and the construction company was just a facade for the obscene billions of dollars my family hid away in offshore accounts, every cent tainted by corruption and deceit.

My family's history is littered with secrets too dark to bear.

"Why did they leave Russia?" She leans a hip against the credenza.

"Business conflicts."

They feared for their lives. My parents often whispered about threats from criminal organizations, political rivals, and powerful government entities. My father, Rurik Strakh, was embroiled in legal disputes and perceived as a tyrant in Russia. No doubt he earned that claim. He didn't play by the rules. He was ruthless, lawless, and power-hungry.

"My parents died in a plane crash."

She grimaces. "I'm sorry."

"It was many years ago."

By then, I had already cut ties with them, shedding my given name like a snake shedding its skin. My brother's death caused the rift between my parents and me. I needed to be free of them, determined to forge a new path, with a new name, to build my own legacy disconnected from the contamination of theirs.

For years, I buried the memories of my parents and brother. I kept my secrets hidden from everyone, even my most trusted confidants.

Even my wife.

I went as far as implementing a prenuptial agreement, so the poison of my inheritance couldn't touch her.

But now, faced with the possibility of never seeing her again, I find myself confronting the skeletons of my past.

Has she uncovered my family's crimes? Did I whisper gruesome secrets in my sleep? Leave a confidential document or email unguarded? Reveal something during our conversations?

If she somehow learned where I grew up and what I buried there, she may have felt compelled to check it out, to see it with her own eyes.

It's a long shot, I know, but desperation has a way of sharpening one's instincts, and I can't shake the feeling that there's more to her disappearance.

So I set a course for Kodiak Island, the yacht slicing through the waves with steadfast purpose. If I want Sirena's help, I need to give her a valid reason for this detour.

Pausing at the railing, I return my attention to the woman whose eyes cling to mine with persistent longing.

Temptation.

I steel myself against it, the siren song of her lust, and focus on the only thing worth fighting for. Until Frankie is back in my arms, I'll endure the torment of loneliness.

"I inherited my family's construction company and my childhood home on Kodiak Island. I failed to mention its existence to Frankie, but maybe she discovered it. No one lives at the estate. A few times a year, I send people to tend to it, but it's otherwise abandoned."

It's the priciest property in the 49th state, sitting atop a scenic cliff overlooking Settlers Cove. It's so big and tucked away that my private island in Sitka could fit in one of its inlets. With private beaches, rugged coastlines, pristine acreage, and spectacular ocean views, it would be easy to hide there.

Exactly why my parents chose that location.

I could send a search party, but I know that island like the back of my hand. An island fraught with depraved memories, a reminder of the life I left behind when I severed ties with my family.

If she's there, hiding in the carnage of my past, I need to be the one to find her.

For Frankie's sake, I'll follow this path to its conclusion, no matter where it may lead, even if my sins come crashing down around us.

"Okay." Sirena nods and turns back to the maps. "We'll start with the estate. Do you have a layout of the property?"

"Yes. Here." As I shuffle through documents and maps, my resolve grows stronger, fueled by the unwavering belief that one day, I'll hold Frankie in my arms once more.

I'm tired of waiting. Tired of the uncertainty, the doubt, the gnawing ache of not knowing. I need her. More than anything.

Every shadow holds a secret, every shiver of wind an echo of her name. I'll search every inch of Kodiak Island, every hidden cave and secluded cove, hoping against hope to find some sign of her.

I won't rest until she's back by my side, where she belongs.

frankie

TEN

The blizzard traps us in the cave for five days. With nothing to do but wait, I lie on the sleeping bag, soak up the warmth of the fire, and watch Leo stalk in and out, doing whatever hardworking Alaskan men do.

I would help him, but I've been banned from going outside. I've also been accused of *getting in the way*.

Fighting the control freak on this only makes him surlier and more agitated. So he's on his own.

There's not much to do beyond hauling in food, water, and coal. But the man can't sit still. I think he harbors some insatiable, driving need to provide for me. Like, he gets off on it.

He's out there right now, working on the trail to the top of the cliff. The snowfall stopped, but the incline remains impassable. He's building a roped path that will help me safely scale the ice.

But that doesn't help the snow machine.

He has a plan, and I trust him. I just wish I could do more.

Something stirs in the tunnel beyond the firelight. I tense, jackknifing into a sitting position and grabbing the loaded rifle.

Please, don't be a bear.

Eyes straining, I listen with my heart in my mouth.

Footsteps. Graceful yet determined. As confident as a predator. But I know that gait well.

Not a bear.

A lion.

He prowls out of the darkness, carrying a bag of coal and a smoldering smile.

"Good girl." He nods at the gun and sets down his haul.

"One of these times, I'm going to shoot you." I lower the rifle and snuggle back into the bedding. "How's the trail?"

"It's ready. We'll leave in the morning."

"Let's go now."

"Tired of me already?"

Tired of sharing a cave with him? Feeding him? Whispering against his lips? Kissing? Cuddling? Sitting on his face? Riding his cock for hours every night?

I'm living my best life. It's as if we stepped through a rip in reality and found a private frozen bubble where time and pain don't exist. Here, it's just Leo and me and endless, lazy pleasure.

But there are moments of clarity when guilt sneaks in, reminding me that a vital part of us is waiting alone in a dark, cold cabin.

I've never missed technology like I do in these moments. The desperate need to send a text, make a call, deliver Morse code, anything to let Kody know we're alive and safe...It's killing me slowly.

"I'll never tire of you." I squint at him. "But if we don't leave, Kody will. He'll risk his life to go searching for us."

"No, he won't."

"He thinks we haven't eaten in days."

"He knows we can survive on melted snow for two months. When Wolf and I were delayed on our last outing, was Kody worried then?"

"No. He was too busy making bargains with the devil behind my back."

"Frankie," he scolds.

"Fine. He's pragmatic, but under that hard exterior is a man who loves deeply, and the only two people he has left in the world are missing. He's feeling that right now."

"I know." He removes his snowshoes and crouches beside the fire. "But his practical side rules his actions. He'll stay put and wait it out." His eyes lift to mine, flaring with a bright spark. "The sun peeked over the horizon today. I felt it on my face for a few minutes."

"Really?"

"Yeah. There's still a long way to go, but we have a fighting chance. We'll win this battle with winter."

If only until we get the plane in the sky. If we can't do that, we'll face more winters, more eternal nights.

No sense dwelling on that.

"Since we're leaving tomorrow," I say, "you need all the rest you can get tonight."

"That an order?" His beautiful mouth twitches, those mismatched eyes doing fluttery things to my insides.

"I'll beg."

"Yes, you will."

Smug, overbearing jackass.

If I told him all the things I love about him, his jackassery would make the list.

But his protectiveness would be at the top. Even when it's excessive and snarly, I still love it.

Then his dick. That long bulging vein that runs along it when he's hard, the freckle at the base, and the heavy sac beneath...My God, he's well-endowed and can maintain an erection for hours.

His hair would be a runner-up. The braids and knots holding back those thick, brown locks give ruggedly masculine Viking vibes. *Delicious.*

And his eyes. How can I forget that unique pairing of gold and blue? It's like staring at the sun in a cerulean sky.

Oh, and his undying compulsion to take care of me. I never needed that in my life. Not until him. Now I can't live without it.

When I think about those early days, about the hostility and tension between us, I don't hate it. The bad parts had to happen so we could find our way here, to each other, to help us appreciate and treasure our hard-won love.

I'll never take him for granted.

My hungry lion, my possessive Viking, my hot-headed lover, and coming soon...my cocky pilot.

He strips down to his snug thermal pants, his sculpted chest glistening in the amber light. An unholy vision of strength and beauty, even after working on the trail all day.

Strands of hair escape his knotted braids and hang in wild waves around his face, adding to his battle-ready allure. After weeks of strife and starvation, his body remains hard and chiseled, only it's sharper now. Leaner. Honed like a blade.

As he prepares our dinner, I marvel at the way his

hands deftly tend to the fire, the flex of muscle beneath his skin. The scar on his abdomen twists with his movements, reminding me of all he's suffered.

Lost in my fixation, I realize I've been staring at him for what feels like hours. I could gaze upon him for eternity and never tire of his presence.

As if sensing my eyes, he looks up, a soft smile playing at the corners of his full lips.

Everything else fades away.

Without a word, he rises from his crouch and joins me on the sleeping bag. Pulling me onto his lap, he holds me close and nuzzles my neck.

The warmth of his love envelops me like a blanket. In his arms, I find solace, safety, and something I never dared to believe in. A mated soul.

The fire sizzles and pops, casting shadows on the walls. I close my eyes and breathe in his scent. Not the musky mechanic aroma that usually clings to him, but the drugging fragrance of snow and testosterone.

I press my nose against his carved chest and fall asleep, endlessly grateful that he's here.

The next morning, I forget all about those soft, cozy feelings.

As I stand at the top of the icy trail, my pulse races, thudding loudly in my ears.

"This isn't going to work!" I scream, my fists clenching at my sides.

The shy, uncertain sun offers a teasing peek of light as Leo maneuvers the snow machine into position at the bottom of the slope.

Climbing up here was cake. With my hand on the rope railing he built and his strong arm supporting my back, I reached the top without any missteps.

But this...

This is not the plan I envisioned.

He attached a daisy chain of ratchet straps to the front of the machine. The other end anchors to a stake at the top of the cliff.

The plan? He wants me to engage the ratchet mechanism and tighten the line as he drives up the steep incline.

With a full sled of coal and meat dragging behind him.

As if the straps will keep him from slipping and falling to his death.

I kick at the stake.

Ow! Fuck, that hurts!

Okay, it's buried in solid ice, but still...

He's crazy. Absolutely insane.

Every fiber of my being screams that this will end badly. The trail is treacherous, a narrow path up several stories of rock and ice, with the abyss yawning beside it, waiting to swallow anyone who falls off.

Him.

It's going to swallow him.

He shouts something over the roar of the engine, gesturing for me to get ready.

"I don't want any part of this!" I shout back, wildly waving my arms.

He lowers his goggles and revs the engine.

Fuck me.

My hands tremble as I reach for the ratchet, my eyes locked on his form as he hits the gas and begins the ascent.

Immediately, the snow machine slips and slides backward with too much slack in the line.

My shriek echoes off the icy walls, my heart plunging to my stomach.

I'm already fucking up.

He skids to a stop and stares up at the doomed path, *at me,* his eyes unreadable behind the goggles.

If he doesn't trust me with this, I don't blame him.

But in the space between us, there's no accusation. There's only love as my stomach squirms with dread.

I can't lose him.

He looks pensive, his jaw clenched tight, the rest of his body relaxed.

Maybe he finally realized this is a terrible idea.

Nope. He's ready to go again, adjusting his stance and hitting the gas.

Goddammit.

I grip the ratchet mechanism, rapidly locking and tightening the cogwheel, trying to prevent the strap from loosening with the vibrations and movement of the machine.

Far below, he wrestles with the steering, his eyebrows clenched in concentration. As he inches upward, I struggle to keep the line taut, my hands sweating in the gloves despite the freezing temperatures.

Every moment feels like an eternity as the engine splutters and strains, the sound reverberating through the gorge.

But he's climbing.

Inch by agonizing inch, his relentless determination shines through. Slowly, miraculously, he fights his way up the incline, his muscles pumping with effort.

My lungs seize every time he teeters too close to the edge. The ski runners barely fit on the path, and each thrust upward has them precariously balancing on the icy slope.

One tiny slip...

He accelerates. The machine lurches, but instead of

advancing, the front end lifts dangerously high.

"Leo, no!" Panic locks up my limbs, making them too heavy and sluggish as I fight to tighten the line and force the skis to the ground.

The snow machine hovers at an angle, its nose reaching for the sky, threatening to flip backward and send Leo hurtling into the river below.

He fights to regain control, throwing his weight into it. I don't have enough strength to crank the ratchet and level him out.

The straps strain, creaking, fraying, threatening to snap.

I'm losing him.

My blood pounds, pounds, pounds, rushing between my ears. My throat closes, the airway so tight I can't breathe.

This is terror. Crippling, soul-sucking, hellborn terror.

With a roar, Leo shoves his body forward, and the snow machine slams back down with a bone-jarring thud, sending a spray of snow into the air.

The straps hold.

Adrenaline crashes through me, and I drop to my knees, trembling and sick.

He grits his teeth, his fists clenched around the handles. When he meets my eyes, I see the resolve in his.

He's halfway up the slope. No turning back.

Fuck.

So he presses on, and the mishaps continue. Each jolt, slip, and wheelie takes years off my life. My breath comes in ragged gasps as I helplessly watch the man I love hang in the balance. It's an unending nightmare, unfolding before my eyes, each moment more terrifying than the last.

Through it all, he remains stoic, dauntless, his willpower unwavering in the face of death.

After what feels like a thousand lifetimes, he finally reaches the top, the snow machine lurching onto solid ground with a triumphant roar, not a piece of meat or chunk of coal lost in its journey.

Weak-kneed and shaking, I rush forward and throw my arms around him in a rib-cracking embrace. Tears sting my eyes as I bury my face in his chest, overwhelmed with relief.

"I thought..." My voice chokes. "I thought I was going to lose you."

"I'm here." He hauls me closer, his chest rising and falling with exertion, his hug a vise of indomitable strength. "I'll always come back to you."

"Damn straight. Because you are *never* pulling that stunt again."

"No argument there." He laughs.

"Let's go home." I push back my shoulders.

"Home?"

"Kody. He's our home."

He inclines his head in a slow nod, and in the reflection of snowlight, his eyes thaw, cradling a rare gentleness that smooths the years creasing the corners.

"To home, then." He lifts me onto the snow machine and straddles the space between my legs.

And we're off.

Riding across the arctic tundra on the back of a snow machine with him is an experience of extremes.

I love the intimacy of it, the melding of our bodies. With my arms banded around his hard abs and his heat pressed firmly against me, he's a barrier between me and the endless white expanse.

He takes the reins confidently, guiding us through

the dangerous darkness with a grace that belies the peril. I place my life in his hands, surrendering to the thrill of trust and love that burns through me.

But the cold. It's deep and invasive. A gnawing, sucking, draining pain that siphons the strength from every muscle and joint.

The shivering is fucking relentless. The wind lashes us like an icy hurricane, the terrain a minefield of bumps and dips, each one jarring my bones and bruising every bit of flesh that already aches with a dull, persistent throb.

It's a brutal test of endurance that lasts hours, pushing me to my limits and demanding its toll.

We stop periodically to refuel, not just the machine but ourselves. As he unstraps the gas container and fills the tank, I stretch my stiff legs, trying to get blood flowing and to chase away the frostbite that digs in with frozen talons.

After a fleeting visit from the sun this morning, the polar night returned with a vengeance. Daytime darkness makes the cold so much colder, each breath a sharp intake that smothers my lungs with frost.

It's a miserable contrast to the warmth I crave. I'm tempted to be the girl who sits in the back seat and asks repeatedly, "Are we there yet? Are we there yet?"

I can't, even if I wanted to. Mounted behind him, with the roar of the engine and wind tearing past us, I can't voice my complaints, see his expression, or look into his eyes for comfort.

Despite the discomfort, the pain, and the cold, there's nowhere else I'd rather be. With each mile we cover, it's a journey of us.

Us against the wild.

He maintains a steady clip all the way back. Eventually, the snow machine bucks forward with a sudden surge of speed, and I straighten against him, my hackles bristling with alarm.

The hills stretch out before us like sleeping giants. If they're that close, so is the cabin.

And the wolves.

The wind howls across the snowdrifts, drowning out any approaching sound. I can't see in the dark. A critical disadvantage to the snarling beasts that prowl this land.

I reach for the rifle strapped to my back, squinting, straining, trying to interpret Leo's stiff posture and his urgent need to double our speed.

In the distance, maybe a mile away, a huge, smudgy silhouette takes shape.

Desolate and ominous, the cabin emerges, seemingly darker than the shadows surrounding it.

And closer, only a few hundred yards from our speeding approach, looms its brooding overseer.

Warmth blooms in my chest.

Kody stands on the crest of a slope, his jet-black hair caught in a fervent tango with the wind. Cloaked in furs and holding a crossbow, he's the quintessence of the untamed Alaskan wilderness.

Despite the distance, I feel the weight of his gaze, intense and feral. He's been waiting for us, fearing for our safety, just as I expected.

I can't help the grin that splits my face, knowing the news we carry will light up his world. We have meat and coal and, the most thrilling of all, the flight manual.

The thought of kissing the scowl from his beautiful, pouty lips makes my heart race.

The snow machine growls between my legs, pounding with the heartbeat of a steel stallion as we fly across the tundra. The urge to leap off and run to Kody overwhelms my senses, a reckless impulse that Leo, ever vigilant, quickly stifles by clamping a hand on my thigh.

His touch is a silent command, one that I begrudgingly obey.

As we draw closer, every cell of my body tunes into Kody.

He doesn't move, his stillness not a sign of indifference, but a demonstration of his patience and stoic nature. A trait that once scared me. Now it draws me in.

Leo brings the machine to a crashing halt, and without a moment's hesitation, I leap from it because, unlike Kody, I'm not one to hold back.

"I missed you." I collide with his unmoving bulk, wrap him up in a hug, and shower his scowly, scruffy face with kisses. A kiss for every day we were separated. "We have so much to tell you."

He catches my mouth with his, sealing our lips together and lapping at my tongue until we're both breathing hard.

When he leans back, a maelstrom churns in his eyes, turbulent and suspicious, as they dart back and forth between mine. Then they lower, scanning me up and down, looking for something.

Something he thought he lost forever.

"I'm healthy. Unharmed." I touch his clenched jaw, drawing his attention back to my face. "We're both good."

He grips my shoulders and backs me against the snow machine.

What is he doing? Why isn't he talking? Did a week of isolation steal his voice?

His hand sweeps to my neck, his fingers twisting in my knotted hair, holding me in place as he surveys his brother.

Emotion creeps into his black eyes, slowly, subtly. If I didn't know him, I wouldn't notice it. But it's there, his relief softening his face and relaxing his shoulders.

His free hand catches Leo by the nape, and he pulls us both against him. As he holds us tight, we melt together, the tension of the past week sluicing away.

"Christ, it's good to have you back." All the worry and anger and love in the world bleeds into Kody's voice.

Then he releases us, tosses me over his shoulder, and charges off toward the cabin.

I guess he's going to carry me back? Not the most comfortable way to go, but sensing that he needs this, I loosen my limbs and hang like a sack of coal.

Behind us, the engine roars to life, and Leo catches up. Rather than zooming ahead, he keeps pace beside us all the way back.

Together.

frankie

The crackle of the fire and the low hum of male voices float around me in a calming harmonic of warmth. After reacquainting myself with the luxuries of a hot shower, I'm back where I belong, nestled between Leo and Kody.

Our shared bed by the hearth cocoons us in furs, my head resting on Kody's lap. Leo's arms encircle my legs, his chin a gentle weight on my hip.

A week in an arctic blizzard clawed itself upon my body, but with my limbs entwined with theirs, my aches and pains fade into oblivion.

In a deep, velvety cadence, Leo recounts our confrontation with the grizzly and the storm that tried to claim us. His words vividly portray the terror that gripped him when he saw me running for my life.

But the way he tells it inaccurately shifts the hero's cape to my shoulders.

"You should've seen her." He kisses my hip bone, his hand lazily caressing my thigh. "Tearing through the whiteout, bold and unstoppable, leaving that bear eating her dust."

"All lies," I mumble, half-asleep. "Leo's the brave one, always jumping into danger, or in this case, sprinting toward it. Me? I was just losing my mind, screaming my head off, and peeing my pants."

Kody's reaction is immediate and intense, his rugged features hardening, his lip curling, baring clenched teeth. From the way his grip on me tightens, there's no mistaking the surge of protectiveness.

"Don't even joke about it." His eyes, usually so commanding, flare with a rare glimpse of fear. "The thought of you being that close to a grizzly..."

"Hey." I lean up and place a soft, lingering kiss on hard, growly lips. Then I pull back just enough to whisper with a playful smile, "Guess we need to be better prepared for our hike to the hunting cabin, huh? You, me, and a bear-proof plan. How about we make a pact? If we encounter another beast, we'll be brave together. Or run together. Whichever comes first."

He grunts, his hand absently playing with my hair.

I've never heard him laugh. Not sure he knows how. A man cruelly shaped by abuse and raised in the wild doesn't express emotion in normal ways.

But I can read the glint in his eyes. I saw it when he hunted me down in the tundra. I notice it when we bathe together every night, and I feel it now.

Happiness, love, hunger—it all rolls into a spark in the dark. That's how he laughs. With stars in his black bear eyes.

The conversation shifts, turning toward the flight manual and the enigma of the thumb drive. Speculation bounces between them, a potluck of possibilities, as they debate why Denver chose that hiding spot, when he placed the dry bag there, and how Wolf's butterfly engraving might've inspired the riddle.

"He thought up that riddle long before we put him in a cage." Leo yawns through a slow, contented stretch and presses closer to me.

"Maybe." Kody rests his head on the wall, breathing deeply. "Impossible to guess what he was thinking or planning. To be honest, I don't want to know."

As they delve into the mysteries left by Denver, their tones shift, laden with curiosity and unanswered questions.

I fight the pull of sleep, trying to listen to them, to be part of this moment.

"What do you think is on the thumb drive?" Leo inches closer, nuzzling his nose in the dip of my waist, the heat of his body wrapped around me.

"The truth, hopefully." Kody caresses my ear, my jaw, his voice a calm counterpoint to Leo's burning intensity. "Maybe it's the key to everything. Denver's secrets, our past, maybe even access to his fortune."

"Wouldn't that be something?" In my drowsiness, my mind swirls, imagining the unimaginable. "If it were all there, every question answered with just a click…"

"He would never be that generous," Leo scoffs. "It's probably videos. Disgusting recordings of us as children. Of his abuse."

"Did he…?" My stomach sinks. Deep down, I've always wondered. "Did he record you?"

"We don't know. But it wasn't his style." Kody spirals a strand of my hair around his finger. "If the riddle is true, the thumb drive is exactly what he claimed. Answers."

Their conversation turns technical as they open the

flight manual and pore over every illustration and instruction.

"This lever." Leo leans over me, pointing. "It controls the flaps. Critical for reducing speed for landing."

"If we pull it twice, will it dispense vodka?" Kody turns the page. "I'd rather not be sober when we start defying gravity."

"There will be no in-flight cocktail service for the pilots." I scan the next diagram, intimidated by all the lines and tick marks. "What is that?"

"The artificial horizon." Leo quickly reads about it, his tone eager. "It shows the aircraft's orientation relative to the Earth. See the pitch and roll here? Without that, we're flying blind."

"Just to clarify…" Kody tips his head at Leo. "You're flying this thing, not me, right?"

"Yes. But we're all going to learn. If something happens to me—"

"Nothing is going to happen to you." I brush a braid from his face, hooking it behind his ear. "But I'll gladly be a co-pilot."

They smile at my offer, their expressions softening.

"This diagram explains the engine controls." Leo studies it, chewing on the inside of his cheek. "We need to understand every part of this inside and out."

"These gauges—fuel, altitude, airspeed—are straightforward. Everything we need to operate the plane is here." Kody's silken baritone, always so steady, instills confidence even in the face of the unknown.

"Don't forget the emergency procedures." I shut my eyes, resting them. "We need those, too."

A hand strokes my hair. Another slides down my leg, lulling me to sleep.

The discussion continues in a haze of technical

jargon and shared resolve, delving into the intricacies of aviation. Each page of the manual is meticulously examined and discussed.

I drift between wakefulness and dreams, their hushed voices a comforting lullaby.

As the night deepens, their focus meanders to our next obstacle, the retrieval of the pemmican. Despite my heavy exhaustion and mental fog, I feel the shift in the air, the tentacles of urgency pulling me fully awake.

"The bear meat will feed us for a month." Leo lightly kisses my arm, my bare shoulder. "Longer if we ration."

"We can't wait too long." Kody readjusts my head to rest in the crook between his bicep and chest as he slides into a more comfortable position on his back. "The weather won't wait for us, and we can't risk getting snowed in until the thaw. You know how unpredictable it is this time of year. We need to be smart, plan carefully."

Leo's agreement is silent, a shared understanding that speaks volumes.

In the firelight of their pause, he moves up to spoon me from behind, resting his head beside Kody's.

They can have the pillow. I'm perfectly content using their biceps.

As they talk above me, their exchange, a seamless flow of understanding and productive debate, underscores the depth of their bond—a connection forged in mutual suffering, unbreakable and essential.

"How much fuel is left for the snow machine?" Kody sniffs my scalp, his hand roving my hip.

"Not much." Leo's shoulders rise and fall. "Not enough to drive it thirty miles to the cabin."

"I figured. Do we have enough jet fuel for the

plane?"

"No idea."

My eyes fly open. I hadn't even considered that.

"Denver would've kept enough on hand to fly a direct path to wherever he went for supplies." Kody scratches his stubble. "But we need extra. For our practice runs. For any rerouting and backtracking we might do. We don't know where we are or how far the nearest town is."

"I can run some numbers. The manual has fuel consumption rates—gallons per hour—at specific conditions." Leo thumbs through the pages. "I just need our estimated distance and payload. That's how Denver calculated how much fuel to carry to reach whatever city he visited."

"A port," I interject. "In the Prince William Sound."

Two hard bodies stiffen against me.

"How do you know?" Leo shoots up on an elbow.

"When he abducted me, he transported me on a yacht for several days. Kept me below in a cabin." I roll to my back to say this part to their eyes. "I couldn't see outside, but I screamed a lot. Called for help. It pissed him off. Right before he docked, he threatened to toss my lifeless body into the Prince William Sound."

Kody's hand forms a fist on my abdomen, his voice pitch-black. "Where did he take you from there?"

I'm ready to steal his angry lips and end this conversation. But that won't save us.

"I don't know. He tranquilized me right after that threat. When I woke, I was in a crate on the plane, not far from Hoss." My chest constricts in memory. "He must've put me in the crate while still on the yacht. He had several crates of fish with him."

"I remember." Leo flares his nostrils.

"Any witnesses would've assumed my crate was

filled with fish, too. I guess that's how he transported me undetected from the yacht to the plane. But he must've had help."

Leo's breathing accelerates as Kody asks, "How long does a tranquilizer take to wear off?"

"Depends. After he died, I went through his kidnapping kit in the closet. I don't know which cocktail he used on me or how much he injected, but he was in possession of some highly potent shit. Any of it can keep someone my size down for six hours or longer."

"Let's do some math." Leo pulls the manual closer and flips through the pages until he finds what he's looking for. "What are the port cities around the Prince William Sound?"

"Valdez, Whittier, Cordova..." I wrack my brain, trying to recall the health clinics and doctors in the area. "Chenega Bay and Tatitlek."

"And the northernmost city in Alaska?"

"Utqiagvik." My forehead furrows. "I thought everyone in Alaska knew that."

Leo raises a brow. "There are three things Denver refused to teach us."

"Okay. So that was aviation, the cabin's power system, and...? Geography?"

"*Alaskan* geography." Kody idly traces circles around my belly button. "We have no maps or books or any information about the geography of the state."

"He implied we live in Alaska." Leo's mouth trails my cheek to my ear, distracting me. "But he never confirmed it. How do we know this isn't Russia or Canada? We don't have maps of those places, either." He returns to the manual, reading through the text. "Cruising speed is approximately 161 miles per hour, and maximum flight range is six hundred miles with a heavy payload. With a lighter load and optimal conditions, that range can be extended." He looks at me expectantly.

"That rules out Russia." I shrug. "The flight distance between the Prince William Sound and the northern coast of Alaska is over seven hundred miles. Farther to Russia. But the Northwest Territories in Canada are closer. We could be there, I guess. Except..." Rubbing my tired head, I sift through what I know about the landscape. "There's a mountain range that extends from west to east across northern Alaska. The Brooks Range. I think our hills are part of that range."

"Are there river gorges in that mountain range?" Kody asks.

"I know of the Koyukuk and the Anaktuvuk, but there are others that remain unfrozen year-round."

Geological and hydrological conditions, including warm springs and rapid currents, prevent some of the rivers from freezing completely, even during the harsh Arctic winters.

"We can estimate our location." Leo's bicolored eyes gleam in the glowing flames. "What's the distance from the Prince William Sound to the Brooks Range?"

"Maybe five hundred miles?"

"How confident are you about that?"

"When I did my residency program in Anchorage, I treated people with life-threatening injuries from all over, including the North Slope Borough. When they were transported by life flight or military Black Hawk helicopters, I knew where they were coming from and how long it would take to arrive. I have a pretty good feel for the distances between the coasts and the mountains."

"Good girl." Leo drums his fingers, silently moves

his lips, and stares at nothing, lost in thought. Then his eyes find mine. "Three hours and fifteen minutes."

"Huh?"

"That's the time it takes the Turbo Beaver to fly from the Prince William Sound to the mountain range."

I blink. "You just calculated that in your head?"

He grins.

"That's some Sherlock-level deduction." I shake my head. "Next you'll tell me the airspeed velocity of an unladen swallow."

"Nah. But I can tell you the speed that you swallow."

"Nice." I laugh. "Let's not forget, you swallowed first."

"Hm." His voice drops. "I might need a reminder."

"What the hell are you two talking about?" Kody's brows knit.

I clear my throat, unsure of what to say without making things awkward.

Leo has no reservations. "She snowballed me."

Kody's mouth forms a brutal slash, the only hint of tension in his otherwise impassive face.

Does he know what snowballing is? I'm about to ask until I glance at his lap.

Good God.

I mean, I know the man is hung. I'm reminded every night when we bathe. But I rarely see him hard. He usually conceals that from me.

Not right now. Nope. I'm staring at a full-blown flagpole in his briefs.

I look up, and our gazes fuse in a moment of raw, unfiltered truth.

He wants to fuck me. He's been more than patient, and his restraint is reaching its end. He's going to be inside me soon, and when he is, he'll be feral, with his teeth in my flesh and his monster cock ripping me open from end to end.

Sweet Jesus, I want that. I want *him*. The thought burns in my eyes and throbs like a heartbeat between my legs.

"Seriously?" Leo tosses a blanket over Kody's lap. "A fucking boner, man? I'm your brother."

"She's not."

"Thank God for that." I bite my lip.

"Can we focus here?" Leo scowls. "Let's say the tranquilizer gave Denver a four-hour window."

"Why four?" I blink.

"If it takes six hours to wear off, he would plan for four hours to minimize risk."

"I hate that you knew him that well."

"Me, too." He clenches his teeth. "After he drugged you, he had to dock the yacht and move the crates. If the flight to Hoss is over three hours, he had less than an hour to get you on that plane and in the air. Anything over a fifteen-minute drive would've been too far and too risky to transport a kidnapped woman. Especially the missing wife of a billionaire."

"I wasn't missing. Monty thinks I left him."

He shoots me a look that shuts down further talk of my husband. "If my calculations are correct, Denver kept the Turbo Beaver near the Prince William Sound."

"Even if we knew which port, how does that help?" I blow out a breath. "We don't know which yacht is his."

"We can ask around."

"Okay, but why do we need it? If we reach a town with people and law enforcement, we won't be alone anymore. We can find someone to help us."

"They'll do that?" Bewilderment twitches in Kody's features. "No one knows us. Why would they help?"

Oh, Kody. He's so self-reliant and fearless that I

sometimes forget he's never left these hills. I wouldn't call him naive. He's more experienced and educated than the acquaintances I had in Sitka. But his cloistered life casts a shade on the intricacies of society.

"Not all people are evil. Most are inherently good." I consider that statement and shake my head. "No, that's not true. People suck, but the social norm is to be polite. On the surface. As long as you don't threaten their identity and goals, they'll do what's expected and offer help."

Jesus. I'm describing civilized humans like they're a different species than Leo and Kody. But in many ways, they are.

"That's fucked up," Leo says. "Why would anyone pretend to be something they're not? It's dishonest."

I don't have an answer for that.

Kody picks at a fraying thread in the blanket. "Denver told us our entire lives that no one lives within hundreds of miles of Hoss. What's the likelihood of encountering a populated area before we run out of fuel?"

"Not likely." I make a face. "If we're in the Brooks Range, our best bet is to fly south and look for Fairbanks."

"That's where you were born." Kody looks at Leo.

He blinks. "Is that our only option?"

Anchorage, Wasilla, and Palmer have hospitals, but they're all farther south.

I nod.

"You were wearing a headset when you arrived on the plane." Leo studies me. "Did you hear Denver talking to anyone over the comms?"

"No. We were out of communication range when I woke."

"If the comms work, we should be able to contact an air traffic control tower as we approach civilization. Maybe someone can guide us through the landing."

My insides thrum with nerves. I dread the landing the most. I don't care how much we study the flight manual. It won't teach us how to put a plane on the ground without crashing it into smithereens.

"We're getting ahead of ourselves." Leo closes the book and sets it aside. "First we need to survive the winter. To do that, we need the pemmican."

"Since we can't take the snow machine..." Kody sighs heavily. "Frankie and I will be walking thirty miles there and carrying it all back."

"Frankie won't be going anywhere until she's rested." Leo touches his lips to my head, always putting me before everything else.

No one argues. Not even me.

My eyelids droop beneath the weight of a hundred polar nights. I don't have the energy for another hike in the snow. Not tomorrow. Maybe not this week.

"You guys made that trip in three weeks." I swallow, pushing down memories of what Wolf and I endured during that time. "Since we're not stopping to hunt or make pemmican, we should be able to do it in half the time, right?"

"No, love." Leo sweeps a hand up my arm and into my hair, his breath heating my scalp. "Now that it's winter, the terrain is exceedingly more difficult. In snowshoes, you're looking at an average pace of one mile per hour, accounting for icy slopes and the need for breaks to avoid fatigue and cold-related injuries. Best guess, it'll take thirty hours to cover thirty miles. That doesn't include prolonged rest periods, setting up camp, or any unforeseen delays such as bad weather or difficult navigation."

Fuck.

As they discuss the logistics of the hike, I silently fret over my ability to survive it. Trepidation builds in my chest, and my rib cage feels too small to contain it.

It's not just the journey ahead that troubles me. I also worry about the cold months that will follow, the escape, the landing, and most of all, finding our place in a world that has remained so far beyond our reach. A world full of regulations, legal systems, technology, people, social interaction, consumerism, media exposure, and...other women. So many women, so many options. How will Leo and Kody mentally and emotionally adjust to it all?

How will *I* adjust?

The one constant I can count on is their indestructible bond. A bond I've been privileged to become a part of.

Despite their differences—Leo's possessiveness and fierce need to protect what's his and Kody's quiet strength, a shield against every enemy we face—they're two halves of a whole, each complementing the other, always on the same side, never apart, no matter how many levels of hell they walk through.

As the fire burns low, its embers glowing softly in the darkness, their voices become the soundtrack to my thoughts.

I wonder at the paths that have led us here, to this moment of unity. How many times did I tell them I was too broken to love again, too scorned to trust another man, too fucked-up to try?

When I learned about Monty's affair, I swore off the male population for good. To protect myself, I vowed never to be that vulnerable or susceptible to heartbreak again. No more romance. No more relationships.

How quickly they made a liar out of me.

The depth that I have fallen terrifies me. They have more power over my emotional well-being than Monty ever did. If I lose them, or if they hurt me, I won't recover this time.

"I love you both," I whisper. "We'll face whatever comes, together."

Their response, a tightening knot of masculine arms and legs, wraps around me, forming the warmest, coziest hammock. In their embrace, I find not just safety but a sense of belonging that I've searched for all my life.

With my arm draped over Kody's waist, he presses closer, trapping me against the immovable wall of Leo's solid frame. They're so sturdy, so comforting, erasing my anxiety over everything we have to do in the coming days.

Our bodies melt and fit together like pieces of a jigsaw, my breasts flush with Kody's chest and my backside slotted against Leo's groin.

The complex chemistry we ignore during the day spills out in the night, connecting all our matching parts and fusing us into a singular unit.

Kody guides my leg around his hip, and Leo holds my neck, his other arm bent to cushion my head, joining us in a position that's made for sex.

It's inevitable. No words needed, not with our bodies slowly rocking and our hands wandering.

I glance up at Kody's dark eyes, his pupils blown with lust.

"Please." I don't know what I'm asking. I really don't care.

I'm theirs.

Theirs to tease, to touch, to kiss, to fuck. Whatever they want, I'll bend.

I'll beg.

"In case you didn't know, you're both hard." I rotate my hips between their pulsing erections. "I'm right here. Do something about it."

frankie

TWELVE

"Do something?" Leo's silky braids tickle my shoulder as he lowers his head. "What do you suggest?"

I release a sharp exhale at the sudden heat of his lips on my neck, the wicked caress of his tongue tasting my skin.

"This." I tilt my head, giving him better access. "This is a good start."

How far will he take it with Kody here? Given the smolder in Kody's eyes, he doesn't intend to sit on the sidelines and watch this time.

Leo grips the neckline of my oversized shirt and yanks it down my arms, baring my breasts. Cold air stiffens my nipples to hard points, drawing two pairs of eyes.

No one moves as they stare with scalding intensity. My lungs ache for air. My flesh prickles with goosebumps.

Then their gazes lift, connecting above me,

speaking a language I can't hear. A private language of eye contact and expressions known only to them, a means of communication between brothers who grew up under the reign of a psychopath.

In the next breath, Kody pushes me to my back, and Leo swoops in, covering my breast with his hot mouth and sucking hard.

Holy.

Fuck.

My spine arches, and my jaw opens with a gasp. Before I can shut it, a long, rough finger presses down on my tongue.

My eyes flash to Kody.

Oh, it's on.

With a slow grin, I close my lips around his assertive digit and suck it like a pro.

His features freeze as if carved in ice.

And Leo...he's on the move, sliding down my body, his mouth trailing wet kisses along my quivering belly.

With a snarl, Kody pumps his finger, swirling it around my lips and dipping back in, showing me how he would fuck my face. Slow at first. Then faster, harsher, riding the edge of control.

I tongue the length from tip to knuckle, swallowing him to the back of my throat. He groans. The growly, rumbling sound is so fucking erotic that I can't stop myself from biting down.

A piercing hiss slips through his teeth as he yanks his hand free and grabs my throat, applying pressure.

I go still, trembling with anticipation.

Leo's lips lift from my hip.

Oh, shit.

Is my brawler about to start brawling?

As I swing out an arm to stop Leo, Kody captures my mouth in a savage, teeth-clashing kiss that sends me spinning into the cosmos.

He comes at me like a bear, all fangs and claws and voracious strength. The hand on my throat loosens enough to allow air, but my God, his dominance hits just right. His tongue controls mine, hunting and licking with a predatory hunger.

His kiss takes feral to another level. I can't tell if he's tasting his next meal or offering benediction for it. Whatever this is, his intensity threatens my very existence.

Lord help me, I'm here for it. His tongue is my communion, and I'll eagerly spread my legs to feel it part me from ass to clit…Oh, God. The man knows how to *lick.*

Leo's mouth returns with purpose, teasing along the waistband of my sweatpants.

He's allowing this with his brother? For how long?

Blindly, I reach for him, tangling my fingers in the twisted knot holding back his hair.

"Please." I whimper against Kody's plundering kiss.

I've completely lost my mind.

"What do you want?" Prowling up my body, Leo skims warm breath from my waist to my breast. His stubble tickles as he flicks his tongue around my nipple.

My pussy throbs from all the attention it's *not* receiving.

Kody breaks his kiss to run his tongue over my cheek.

He's…he's actually *licking* me—my face, my neck, my mouth. His entire body moves with the strokes of his tongue, surging against me, thrusting his raging erection, full-on humping me like an animal.

"Frankie…" Leo's weight, now pressing in and trapping one of my legs, feels like a torment and a promise, teasing the very core of my being. "I asked you a question."

I try to reposition, to move his hips into the space between my thighs. I just need some friction.

More than that, I need them to fuck me senseless.

He bites my tit, his teeth ruthlessly catching my nipple, demanding my focus.

"Fuck!" I can't think with two men teasing so many nerve endings at once. "I forgot the question."

"Tell me what I should do about this." His tone holds a lethal edge.

"This?"

"You, me, Kody." He separates each word with taunting nips on my breast. "Us."

Kody's erotic tongue swirls around my earlobe, screwing with my concentration.

Overstimulated and soaked, I'm nothing but sensation. "You should both fuck me. Quickly. Before I die."

"Too bad." Leo sits back, removing his mouth, his touch, and his beautiful heat.

"Prick." I narrow my eyes, ready to call him out on his jealousy.

"Does he look like he wants to stop?" Kody sweeps red hair behind my shoulders, his lips brushing my ear. "He's as hard as I am. But no one's having sex tonight. You've burned through your calories for the day—"

His palm clamps over my mouth, stopping my argument.

I claw at his hand, trying to escape the muzzle.

In a blink, he pins my arm above me, buries his nose in my armpit, and inhales loudly. "Christ, I can smell you. Your goddamn pheromones make me *ache*."

My armpit? No. That can't be sexy.

Except it is. The ravishing steam of his breath, the

vibrating sound of his groan, the sensual motion of his hips as he humps me and scents me...*Holy hell.*

With his hand still trapping my mouth, another glance passes between him and Leo, a conversation I have no hope of interpreting.

Leo looks conflicted, tangled in a barrage of possessiveness and hunger. I don't know which part of him will win, but he's making a gallant effort to work through it. For me.

They settle on something, a truce of some sort. Instead of throwing his fists, Leo rests them on his thighs, closes his eyes, and inhales slowly.

Kody readjusts to sit with his back to the wall. Then he hauls me onto his lap.

Not a sleeping position.

Confused, I catch Leo's gaze. Deep in those blue and gold eyes, I glimpse a flicker that I trust. Whatever happens next, he'll be in control from start to finish.

Looming over me, he grips my sweatpants, his intent clear.

Perched in the *V* of Kody's powerful legs, I raise and lower my rear, letting Leo strip me bare from the waist down.

"What are we doing?" I reach back to touch Kody's soft black hair. "I thought you said no sex."

"There's one thing Leo and I will always agree on. Your happiness." Kody seductively licks my jaw. "Spread your legs."

A thin sheen of sweat forms on my skin, bubbling from the burn of desire building inside me.

My legs fall open.

Kody's cock jerks against my rear. Leo swallows, his eyes stark, fixed on my exposed pussy.

Overheated, I shed my shirt and lean back on

Kody's chest. Stark nude. More than ready.

An invisible leash snaps as Kody's hands fly over me, gripping my throat, kneading my breasts, rubbing, pinching, grabbing, bruising.

Then he reaches between my legs.

Leo captures his wrist, stopping those fingers from penetrating.

The room falls still, save for the pop of embers in the hearth.

"Leo." I know he's struggling, but he can't start and stop this at will. "Please, don't—"

"Shut up, Frankie." Holding Kody's arm, he guides it up my body and places Kody's hand on my breast. "This isn't a race, man. Take your time. Warm her up. Never go straight for the holy land. Not until she begs."

Oh.

He's teaching him.

"You're doing great." I nuzzle my nose against Kody's rigid, scruffy jaw.

He grunts.

An excited grunt. A hungry, heart-racing, can't-catch-his-breath grunt. My new favorite sound.

His palms flatten over my abdomen, circling, exploring, and climbing higher to trace the undersides of my breasts. I melt beneath the reverent caresses, tracking the path of his hands.

A long red scar covers one, jagged and ugly from my stitches. Calluses roughen his fingers from the crossbow. More scars lash his knuckles. But his touch feels like velour. So plush and smooth for such a hard, brutal man.

Leo captures my thighs, opening me wider as he bends forward and fills his lungs with my scent, his nose a hairsbreadth from my dripping flesh.

With a grip on my throat, Kody turns my head and

rubs his cheek against mine, nosing me, sniffing me, scraping his teeth against my skin, conjuring images of an apex predator, wolfish and primal, protecting his pack.

Soon, his nuzzling turns into deep, wild kisses that deplete my lungs and scramble my brain.

"Oh, God." I tremble. I whimper. I lift my hips and shamelessly hump the air. "I need...I need more. Please, keep going."

"There she is." Leo sucks on my inner thigh and nods at Kody.

Kody doesn't hesitate. Gliding a hand between my legs, he sinks two fingers into my soaked cunt.

And freezes.

"What's wrong?" I twist my neck and find his eyes squeezed shut.

"You're so..." He expels a shaky breath. "Hot. Wet. Too fucking small." His eyes open, colliding with mine. "There's no way I'll—"

"You'll fit." I kiss his chiseled cheek, shuddering with the need to come. "Curl your fingers."

His brows crash together, and I feel a twitch inside me. Barely.

"You won't hurt me." Panting, I widen my legs. "Harder."

"Like this." Leo slowly eases his fingers inside me, alongside Kody's.

God.

Jesus.

Yes.

Leo sucks the tender skin on my thighs, marking me with hickeys as his fingers thrust in tandem with Kody's.

I cry out, overflowing with delirious pleasure.

Kody cups my throat and covers my cheek with sultry kisses as his other hand works my pussy, following Leo's rhythm, filling me, stretching me, massaging my inner walls.

"Fuck, I'm close." I feel Leo guiding Kody's thumb, showing him my clit, how to tease it, rub it, and get me off. "You guys are ruining me. It's fucking incredible. Don't stop, don't stop, don't stop—"

A shower of sparks explodes through my body and shimmers across my vision. I thrash atop Kody's chest, grinding against the fingers inside me as Kody's tongue fucks my mouth.

Wave after powerful wave, the orgasm grips me, breaks me, lighting me up from the inside out.

Kody stiffens beneath me. His breath cuts off. His mouth falls away, and I moan with realization.

He's coming with me.

As his thick cock pulses against my backside and releases in his briefs, I clutch his hair and hold his face against my neck, twitching through the remnants of ecstasy.

Leo's unreadable gaze captures mine.

He and his brother just fingered me. At the same time. Is that weird? Reprehensible?

It doesn't feel wrong.

It feels fated and soulful and pure. There's nothing more tragically beautiful and honest than the three of us together.

Slowly, Leo withdraws his fingers from my body and brings them to his mouth. Without looking away, he sucks them clean, thoroughly, diabolically.

Deliciously fitting for a temperamental savage.

Quirking my lips, I crook a finger.

On hands and knees, he crawls up my love-bitten thighs, slides against my breasts, and forces me back onto Kody's heaving chest. When his mouth greets mine, it's with a devastating kiss that makes me forget my name and turns me into a bottomless pool of want.

His pajama pants ride so low on his hips it's easy to plunge a hand inside and free his thick, swollen cock.

"Frankie." He groans against my mouth and shifts his hips out of reach. "This isn't about me."

"Why not?"

Kody puts his mouth to my ear. "He went along with this to relax you, to make you happy."

"What's the point if we're not all relaxed and happy?" I capture Leo's erection again, stroking the hot, velvety length and whispering into his kiss, "I love to feel you throb as you come. That makes me happy."

A trapped breath bursts past his lips as he yields, flexes his hips, and thrusts into my fist.

It doesn't take long. Mere seconds of focused stroking. With his forehead against mine and his arms braced on either side of Kody and me, he fucks my hand and chases his release.

Amid the woodsy, snow-frosted scent of his skin, I detect another irresistible smell. The clean, alkaline aroma of come hits the air and spurts across my stomach.

He roars through his climax, wrapping a hand around my fist and violently milking himself until the very last drop.

With loud gulps of air, he tries to catch his breath, his cock still hard and pulsing in our hands. When I let go, he wipes the sticky tip across my stomach, spreading his mess, smearing it in.

"Filthy." I lick my lips.

He closes in and licks them, too, kissing me languorously, rubbing my tongue with his, pillaging, desolating. His hand runs up my thigh as Kody's slide around my ribs to palm my breasts.

I'm lost in the heat of the body beneath me and the depths of the multicolored gaze above me. The cold isolation around us has no bearing when the warmth of our love pounds through my veins.

With so much at stake and no guarantees for survival, this may be the worst possible time of our lives. But we have each other's backs, no matter how tough it gets. As long as we seize these moments, our small glimmers of peace in the dark, we'll find our way out.

"We're going to clean up." With a kiss on my nose, Leo climbs to his feet and straightens his pants. "Stay there."

Kody clasps my waist and sets me away. When I cling to him, refusing to give up my Kody-shaped heating pad, he flips me onto my side and slaps my ass.

I laugh through a yelp and tiredly sink into the mattress.

They vanish into the bathroom, their voices soft and muffled.

What are they doing in there? Standing side by side at the sink, washing their dicks and talking about...? What could they be discussing during such an intimate task?

Then again, it can't be more intimate than what the three of us just shared.

Lazily, I lift my thigh and smile at the hickeys peppering my skin. If I had a short skirt and somewhere to go, I would show off the marks with pride.

How will our unconventional relationship be received in the public eye? Two brothers sharing one woman? Will we be lambasted and shunned?

I don't give a fuck what people think about me. But

I'll cut a bitch for talking shit on my guys.

Their conversation ebbs and flows in the bathroom and follows them back to me. As Kody presses a warm, damp cloth between my legs and cleans my come-streaked stomach, Leo towers over us.

What a striking image he makes.

Sculpted arms folded above a scarred abdomen. Shoulder-length hair pulled back in a braided knot. Stern features chiseled in brutality. Exotic eyes glinting in the firelight. The man looks like an honest-to-gods Viking king of the North, holding a position of authority over his merciless army.

There's no smile on those cruel lips. No hint of softness in his deadly aura. He watches Kody wipe away the mess he made with a hardened expression, as if one wrong move will entice his violent, possessive side.

When Kody finishes, they bundle me up in the sharp curves of their shirtless bodies, enveloping me like a blanket.

A blanket of muscle and masculine heat.

Their discussion continues, shifting from practical plans to dreams about the future, each word building a life beyond the hills of shivers and shadows.

Leo's strategy to own a private airport, Kody's vision for manufacturing vodka, and my ability to work in any hospital in the country—their blueprint for our life together sounds so obtainable, so utterly perfect.

As I drift on the edge of sleep, I realize that this, a life with Leo and Kody, has always been my fate. We're more than survivors. We're a family.

In the heart of a relentless winter, with our bodies entangled beside the fire, our survival entwines like the twisted limbs of ancient pines. Every battle, every blizzard, has led us to discover a strength within ourselves and in one another.

As much as I dread the hike to the hunting cabin, I know that it, too, will make us stronger.

"We'll take our time and do it right," Kody murmurs, his voice growing groggy. "The wilderness is unforgiving. We have to respect its power."

Leo nods. "We've overcome worse. We'll do it again."

They circle back to more planning, detailing the specifics of our departure, the supplies we'll need, and the route we'll take.

As sleep finally claims me, I find a profound peace, swaddled in the love of the two men who have become my forever.

kodiak

THIRTEEN

Three days dissolve in a whirlwind of hurried preparations. Our urgency to outrun the next blizzard fills the confines of our cabin with thickening tension.

We move around one another with restless energy, our actions fueled by the need to be ready, to leave nothing to chance. Yet beneath it all, dread lingers, an unspoken fear of what can happen along thirty miles in the heart of an arctic winter.

The morning of our departure arrives with quiet reluctance. The workshop, once a frigid mausoleum of unfinished projects and frozen breaths, now maintains a bearable temperature, thanks to the coal that Leo and Frankie recovered.

Our packs are heavy with provisions, each item a preventive measure against the unknown. The thought of the pemmican waiting in the hunting cabin, potentially ravaged by animals, adds another pound of uncertainty to our already burdened shoulders.

I've made this hike countless times, but never this time of year. And never with Frankie. So I took our preparations to an excessive level.

I doubled, even tripled, our supplies of matches, bullets, and arrows, knowing the devastating consequence of a fire that won't light or a weapon that can't shoot. Each item was carefully waterproofed against the pervasive damp that seeps into everything.

The weight of our packs became a secondary concern to the assurance that we would have enough to survive. I packed extra bear meat, more than we need, just to ensure Frankie would have enough energy to sustain her through the demanding hike.

The thought of her going hungry, of her body succumbing to the cold because of a lack of nutrition, spurred me to add just one more piece of meat, one more pouch of nuts.

Even the clothing we wear was subjected to my over-preparation. I checked and double-checked the insulation, waterproofing, and stitching, making sure Frankie's gear would offer her the utmost protection against the vicious wind. If she's shivering in the cold, or if frostbite claims her fingers or toes, that's on me. I won't fucking allow it.

So I made lists. Checked them numerous times. Still, I'm not ready.

Have I forgotten something? Missed a vital detail?

If it were just Leo and me, we would already be on our way. But traveling with Frankie? It changes everything.

With her, I have zero tolerance for error.

In the glow of her ingenious tin lights, we linger at the door in the workshop, the time for saying goodbye hanging heavy among us.

A sense of foreboding mingles with the warmth from the coal stove, creating an atmosphere thick with emotion.

Leo breaks the silence first, his voice rough. "Take care of each other out there."

His mercurial eyes linger on her, tinged with uncharacteristic vulnerability.

We share the same mind, he and I. A mind that spins with strategies and contingencies, each one centered around a single, unyielding priority.

Keeping Frankie safe.

Our love for her transcends the bounds of romance. It's a fierce, protective force that drives us to extremes. Every step we take, every decision made, is filtered through this lens to the point of obsession.

In the nights leading up to our departure, with our woman asleep between us, Leo and I lay awake, going over every detail, ensuring nothing had been overlooked.

We became students of survival, poring over books and manuals, gleaning every tip, every trick to keep her alive. We went over the route a thousand times, recalling landmarks and potential shelters, should a blizzard overtake us. We argued about what-ifs, each scenario darker than the last, but we planned for them all the same.

Her medical training is invaluable. She already saved my life once. But if she becomes critically injured or unconscious, she can't save herself.

So I practiced and rehearsed first aid, familiarizing myself with treatments for frostbite, hypothermia, and injuries from animal attacks. My mind is a catalog of survival techniques, each one earmarked for a possible future where her safety is threatened.

We weighed the merits of Leo going with us but decided against it. Someone needs to maintain the SOS signal when it snows. If that plane returns, we need someone here. There's so much to do before the thaw. He needs to memorize the flight manual until he can recite it in his sleep. He also needs to hot-wire the plane. We never found the key.

She thinks we're crazy, claiming that all our planning is over the top, the product of overactive imaginations. But out there, in the unforgiving Arctic, there's a fine line between caution and recklessness, between survival and demise. Every extra bullet, every additional ounce of food, every redundant piece of gear is a parachute to keep her safe.

I'll spend the rest of my life planning, preparing, and protecting her with a single-minded focus. Her safety is my responsibility, my burden, and my honor. I will do everything to ensure she returns from this journey unscathed.

Leo knows this. He trusts me with her life.

Stepping forward, he wraps his arms around me, his hug firm, the grip of a brother who's seen too much, lost too much.

"Keep her safe, Kody." A command sheathed in a plea.

I nod, the weight of his trust settling on my shoulders. "Always."

Then it's Frankie's turn, her eyes shimmering with unshed tears as she faces him. The distance between them closes in a heartbeat, the rest of the world disappearing as she reaches up, her hands framing his face.

"We'll come back to you." A fierce whisper.

He pulls her into a tight embrace, his response too low for my ears. A private exchange that I pretend not to see. My heart twists at the intimacy of it. My stomach tightens with envy.

I don't begrudge them or feel resentful, but I covet their familiarity, their closeness. I know Leo fucked her in that cave for five days. When they returned, his entire demeanor was calmer, lighter, *glowing.*

Not that I blame him. But I hate that I don't know her in that way. It slithers into every thought and taunts me while I sleep.

I've waited months. Suffered her justified anger. Tried to earn back her trust. Bided my time.

When I think about how she was the one to kill Denver, I want to punch something. Like my own face.

I'll never be a good man, but goddammit, I won't stop trying to be a better one for her.

Still, my patience is fraying. I'm fucking starved for her.

While I'm not looking forward to this thirty-mile hike, I'm secretly, selfishly eager to have her alone for a month without my brother.

I haven't stopped thinking about the shocking, squeezing heat of her cunt around my fingers. To sink my cock in that lush, slippery paradise...it's unfathomable.

My dick swells in anticipation, and I have to mentally calm myself down. We have a long journey ahead. Weeks of walking, surviving, protecting her with my life, all the while keeping my senses on constant alert.

I can't lose focus. No matter how beautiful she is or how alone we are, I won't let my guard down.

Their whispering goodbyes melt into open-mouth kissing. It's tender and desperate, filled with a reluctance to separate, a promise to reunite, and all the emotions in between.

I should look away, but I don't. We're together in this. Together in all things.

The kiss ends, but their foreheads remain connected as silent tears fall down her cheeks.

When they finally part, there's a lingering touch, a longing look, each of them carrying the gravity of this moment, the fear of finality, the hope of forever.

It's heart-wrenching to watch. I hate seeing vulnerability on my brother's face, but it pales in comparison to the grit and determination that defines our existence.

She heaves on her pack and treads to the door.

I insisted she carry the lighter pack, redistributing the weight so that I bear the brunt of our supplies. My back will pay for it, but the pain is inconsequential compared to the peace of mind it'll bring, knowing I've lightened her load even by a little.

As I turn to follow her, Leo grabs my arm and puts his strange, unmatched eyes right in front of mine.

His mouth opens, but nothing comes out.

I know what he's holding back, the demands that burn in his throat.

Don't touch her. Don't fuck her. Don't steal her. She's mine.

His unspoken commands hit my chest and bounce off.

I twist my arm from his grip and grab his head with both hands. "She's ours. That doesn't mean she's a possession, a toy to pass back and forth. She's ours in a partnership. She doesn't divide us. She multiplies us." I bow my forehead to his, my voice hushed. "Claiming her is our vow to stand by her and cherish her. It leaves no room for jealousy, only pleasure. No space for division, only unity. We're building a future with her, a life without boundaries, where we can thrive, share, grow, and fuck. The three of us together? We're an unstoppable force. I know you know that. You want it. I see it on your damn face. But it scares you. Fuck man, it scares me, too. Doesn't change the fact that she's ours. That means I will never take her from you. She loves you as much as I do. She's ours, and I'm bringing her back."

I lower my arms and scrub a hand over my mouth, stunned by how much just spilled from it.

He stares, blank-faced and mute.

"Say something, fuckhead," I huff.

A muscle twitches in his cheek, another at the corner of his eye. Then he blinks.

"I think…" He sets his hands on his hips. "That was the most words you've ever strung together at one time. Who are you, and what have you done with my brother?"

"Did you hear anything I said?" My nostrils flare.

"Yeah." He nods, scuffs his boot on the floor, and nods again. "I'm taking it to heart." He leans in and squeezes my neck. "Especially the part about you bringing her back."

"I swear it, Leo."

"Okay, then." He sniffs and steps back.

We turn toward the door and find Frankie watching us with tears in her eyes. She quickly spins away, pressing the heels of her gloved hands to her face.

Beautiful and compassionate. A deadly combination. She has no idea how alluring she is for men like us. Our need to protect and provide for her is impossible to resist.

"Ready?" I prowl toward her, prepared to carry her if she needs that.

She doesn't.

Straightening her backbone, she opens the door.

With a final wave, we step into the cold, leaving Leo standing alone in the doorway.

"I hate this part." She adjusts the straps of her pack and trudges through the snow.

"Which part?"

"Leaving. Leaving you, leaving him, it never gets easier."

The miles ahead loom menacingly, but the promise of return, of reunion, gives credence to my response. "This is the last time."

"What do you mean?"

"After this, the three of us never have to separate again."

She considers that, squinting at her shuffling snowshoes. "I hope you're right."

Through hell and high water, I'll make damn sure I am.

As quickly as a breath, the light of dawn comes and goes. In the return of darkness, we walk in silence.

The sharp morning air slaps our exposed cheeks and follows us like an uninvited companion. At least it's not snowing. That mercy allows us to forgo the goggles.

The moment the cabin fades from view behind us, my senses sharpen, every nerve attuned to every possible danger and the precious cargo I've vowed to protect.

I position myself slightly ahead, setting a pace that's brisk yet mindful of the physical demands on her. My eyes constantly scan the horizon, the snow-laden tundra, and the dense clusters of rocks that sporadically break the monotony of the white landscape. Every shadow, every change in the wind, is a potential threat, and I'm the barricade between that threat and her.

Despite the physical exertion of plowing through the snow, which at times reaches up to our knees, my mind never wanders from its primary task. As she focuses on maintaining her footing, I watch for signs of predators—wolves that see us as intruders or a bear displaced from hibernation.

As we approach a section where the snow appears packed enough to support our weight, I test it first. Offering her a hand to help her across, ensuring she doesn't break through into a hidden crevasse beneath.

My crossbow never leaves my grip, its weight a comfort and a reminder to remain focused. She carries a rifle strapped over her shoulder. I know she's competent in its use and always aware of its presence, frequently adjusting the sling and checking the safety.

I love the way she moves. Even in the snowshoes, she walks with a determined grace, her vigilance an echo of my own, though tempered with an innate temerity that I find fascinating.

"You know," she says after a mile of silence, "for someone who speaks in grunts, you're pretty loud with your thoughts."

I glance at her, the corners of my mouth twitching in what could be a smile.

"Hm," I grunt, true to form.

She laughs, a sound too bright for the sunless sky. "What are you watching for? Wolves or bears?"

"Anything that sees us as a meal. I've fought every form of dangerous beast out here. I'd rather not do it again."

She nods, her gaze on the dark horizon. "When I first arrived, I thought the biggest threat was you."

"Why?" My eyebrows shoot to my hairline.

"Well, let's see. You glowered and grunted and

didn't use words. You separated yourself from everyone, looking ten kinds of pissed off. You weren't just physically distant from the others. You had this whole moody, detached vibe." She waves her arms around, talking with her hands. "This murky, underworld air about you. All muscle and mystery. Totally unapproachable. Unquestionably lethal. I thought you were the scary one. The dark one. When I saw you the first time, leaning against the wall in the kitchen, I couldn't breathe. Denver said not to worry. It would take you some time to warm up. Then Wolf started choking on a laugh like it was a private joke, and I was the punchline."

Wolf.

Sometimes, I forget he's gone. Then, like a sucker punch out of nowhere, his absence hits me in the chest, knocks the wind out of me, and burns my fucking eyes.

"I miss his laugh." She swallows and looks away. "Even when I *was* the punchline."

I should say something, soothe her with words, but I don't have any. So I give her the response I'm good at.

I grunt.

She sucks in a breath that turns into a half-hiccup, half-laugh. "You're ridiculous."

"Says no one ever."

"Seriously, Kody." She weaves closer, bumping my arm with her shoulder. "If we run into a bear, would you just give it one of your looks?"

"No." I shoot her a look, not the one she's suggesting. "I would protect us with my crossbow. Not a goddamn look."

"I know that. I've seen you in action. But I'm not kidding. You would scare off the bear if you glared at it the way you glared at me that day in the kitchen. I mean, you scared me off for weeks."

"I'm sorry." My chest pinches. "I won't make excuses for that. I was an ass and—"

"Stop it. I forgave you a long time ago. And given the circumstances, no apologies are needed." She sighs. "I'm so glad we're past that. Getting to know you guys was the hardest and best thing I've ever done."

An inner fire unfurls inside me, radiating like a hearth.

For all the pain and trauma that Denver inflicted on us, he made up for it in one gloriously sinister action.

He gave us Frankie.

FOURTEEN

As the day wears on, the conversation flows between Frankie's playful jabs and my staccato of grunts, an exchange that somehow bridges the gap between our contrasting personalities. Despite my long silences, her confrontational warmth slowly pulls me out of my clunky shell.

My vigilance never wanes, but her incessant probing and challenging keeps the silence from returning.

I watch her closely for signs of exhaustion or the onset of cold injuries. When her steps falter, I suggest breaks, framing them as necessary for my own well-being, though my primary concern is for her.

During these brief rests, I study her face for frostbite, the telltale white patches on exposed skin. I demand she eat and stay hydrated, even when the subzero temperatures make the idea of consuming anything unappealing.

After an eternally long day, our relentless march through the snow takes its toll.

Our conversation becomes sparse, conserved like the energy we need to keep going. But I'm always listening to her voice, alert to any change that might indicate distress or discomfort.

I'm so in tune with the rhythm of her lilt that I instantly notice when she starts masking her fatigue with a forced tone.

She's done for the day.

"We'll camp here." I break trail and select a site that offers some shelter from the wind.

I erect the tent with practiced efficiency, securing each stake against the erratic gales. Inside, I combine our sleeping bags to maximize warmth, insisting she takes the spot farthest from the entrance.

There's little I can do about the cold. Burning a fire isn't possible unless we find a cave. We'll sleep in our boots and coats. If hers aren't warm enough, I'll give her mine.

Huddled together in the tent, we eat quickly. Fatigue visibly engulfs her fragile body, her eyelids drooping at half-mast. She struggles to keep them open, each blink growing heavier and longer.

I feel it, too, my bones completely drained of energy, every muscle screaming for rest.

But as she starts to fall onto the bedding, I stop her. "You need to pee."

She glances at the tent flap and grimaces. "Nope."

"You haven't emptied your bladder all day."

"My bladder and I appreciate your concern, but my girly parts are boycotting the cold."

"So...you're not going to pee for a month?"

"I'll wait until we reach the hunting cabin."

"That's two weeks away, and there's no indoor plumbing."

Her eyes go round, fully awake now. "We have to go outside?"

"Same as here."

"Well, shit." She draws in a shaky breath. "Then I guess I'm holding it for a month."

My back aches. My head hurts, and I can't keep the cold from sharpening my voice. "Frankie..."

"When you say my name in that tone, you offend not only me but my grandfather."

"Your...grandfather?"

"My father's father. I inherited his name. Never met him, but if Frankie Trevis were alive, he would not appreciate your snarling, young man."

"Trevis? Is that your given name? Before you married?"

"Sure is, and it'll be my name again when I become unmarried." She drops her chin, mumbling, "If I'm not already."

Leo or I could make her ours by law. We could give her our name.

Frankie Strakh.

The notion hits me with the force of a physical blow.

In all my fantasies, I never dreamed of passing along that surname. A name that was forced onto me by the monster who stole my childhood.

I don't know what my birth certificate shows. Kodiak Knowles? Or my biological father's name, whoever he is?

Do I even care?

Strakh is all I know, and it means something that Leo and Wolf share that name, too. I wouldn't change it. To honor Wolf, I would pass it on. To Frankie. To our children...

Children.

Another dream I never dared to have. It scares me to even hope.

Right now, it's not even a possibility. She takes her pill every night. Never forgets.

If she were free and safe from starvation, I wonder how that might change. Frankie, pregnant with our child, could be a good thing.

It could be a wonderful thing.

I unzip the tent flap, bracing myself against the blast of icy air. "Let's go."

With a jolt, she scrambles away.

I don't know where she's trying to go, but I have her draped over my shoulder before she can sink those kitten claws in my face.

"It's not healthy to hold it in. Could lead to an infection." I carry her out, the wind slicing through our layers. "You don't want that, especially out here."

"It's not healthy to get frostbite on your vagina, either." She wriggles in my hold, her movements slow and weak. "I can't believe you're making me do this. Stop. Put me down. I'll fucking walk."

There's no fight in her voice. She doesn't need to be a nurse to know I'm right.

The blustery night drenches us in a darkness that swirls with the aurora's green ribbons. I carry her a short distance from the tent, crouch in the snow, and set her on her feet between my legs.

"Strip. Squat. Pee." I reach beneath the hem of her coat and find the zip on her snow pants. "We'll do it quick."

"*We* aren't doing anything." She makes a shooing motion. "Give me space."

"Space? Too late for that, woman. We shower together every night. You helped me piss when I was injured. I've had my fingers knuckle-deep inside you. You and I are joined so tightly not a whisper of air can slip between us."

The way she stares at me, I don't know whether to protect my groin or bend her over my knee.

She leans in, putting her face in mine. But instead of a kick, she delivers a kiss. A sweet cherry-frosted kiss on my gaping mouth.

"I love you, Kodiak." Her gloved hands adjust my hat around my ears, her breath clouding with mine. "But if my vagina freezes off, we're looking at a long celibate future together."

"Nothing's freezing off. Here." I widen the spread of my thighs and dig a hole in the snow between my boots. "Squat over this. I've got you."

With a sigh, she gives me her back, shoves down her pants, and lowers her gorgeous bare ass to the ground.

Gripping her waist, I support her slight weight over the hole and try to give her as much privacy as the position will allow.

The wind pounds against us, stripping away all warmth, all comfort, but it's not life-threatening in the short time this will take.

"You're beautiful," I say at her ear, my body folded around her to shield her from the wind.

The awkwardness of the situation is undeniable, but out here, survival trumps modesty.

Once she's done, I help her cover her exposed skin. Then I set her away from the hole and take my turn.

As I piss, her arms come around me from behind, and she hugs me with her whole body. Maybe she's seeking warmth, but it feels like an apology, a thank you, and something else.

This is what it feels like to be loved by a woman.

I have nothing to compare it to. Brotherly love is all I know, and that's...not this. With Leo, it's an obligation of support, strong and certain, a cohesion so hard we can't be separated.

But Frankie's love is satiny. It's tender and fluid and warm with affection. It must be earned. Protected. Appreciated. Whatever she's doing, it's transforming me, making me a little softer and a lot more complete.

I show her a gentleness I've never extended to anyone else, and I find I'm a better man for it.

We return to the cramped confines of our tent. The cold seeps through the thin fabric as we wrap ourselves in the sleeping bag, seeking warmth in layers and proximity.

Shifting and reaching, we come together as close as humanly possible, chest to chest, her tiny frame curled up against the mantle of mine.

"I'm sorry for making you go out there." I brush my nose along hers.

"I'm sorry for being difficult. I..." She groans. "I just really don't like the cold."

"You may have mentioned that a time or two."

"I like this, though." She combs her fingers through my short beard, brushing away ice crystals.

I started growing it out a few days ago in preparation for this hike. "It's a barrier against the cold."

"How's that working for you?" She plucks out a chunk of ice and holds it up, her eyes glittering in the dark.

"Have I told you how beautiful you are?"

"You have. Just a few minutes ago, actually. While I

was peeing in a snow hole. The timing wasn't great."

She wings up a brow. "Did I pee on your boots?"

"Do I care?"

"You should. It's only the first day. Given my luck, I'll start my period while we're out here."

"I packed provisions for that."

"Stop!" She laughs. "You did not!"

"Why is that funny? You said it could happen anytime, and I don't want you to be uncomfortable."

"Oh, man, you're..." She strokes my face, my hair, and returns to my mouth, tracing a finger along my lips. "You're ruining me."

I feel her touch everywhere, deep beneath my skin, like a balm on the wounds inside that never healed. Every moment with her is another stitch, another bandage, closing up my damaged parts.

"You're healing me." I tighten my arms around her.

"How are you real?" She slides her hands beneath my fur collar, caressing the skin on my neck. "Men like you don't exist."

"No?"

"Nope. You're one of a kind. I want to put you in my coat. Can I do that? I need to feel you against me while I sleep."

Her coat belonged to Wolf. Definitely not big enough for both of us. But my coat?

I open the clasps on the front of my furs and tuck her inside, right up against my chest. The heavenly sound she makes raises my body temperature by several degrees.

"Much better." She rests her face against my throat, tangles her legs around mine, and within minutes, she's asleep.

I lie awake, listening to the sound of her steady

breathing.

My vigilance doesn't end with the zip of a tent flap. It's a constant, unwavering commitment to guard her against the threats of the night, the unseen dangers that prowl beyond the thin walls of our shelter.

But I do rest my eyes, taking short naps and waking quickly at the slightest sound.

She sleeps just as fitfully, her face turned up toward mine, her lips so close that when she sighs, I taste her sweet breath on my tongue.

The zipper on her coat hangs open a few inches, exposing the silky skin of her throat.

I want to sink my teeth there and leave my marks like the ones Leo left on her thighs.

I want to hold her in my arms just like this the entire time we're gone.

I want to consume her attention and make her blood pound with every look, the same way she does to me.

I want all this while my brother waits in the cabin. It's only fair. He had her for months to himself.

When our mission is complete, I want to return her to him and show him how she's ours, how the three of us fit together in love and intimacy and every way possible.

Warmth spreads from my chest to my stomach and gathers between my legs. I fist my hands in the bedding to keep from touching her, from starting something I can't finish in an ice-cold tent.

The road ahead will be the longest twenty-two miles of my life.

I pace the chilly, silent corridors of my childhood home, feeling the onus of this dead end bearing down upon me.

The estate, an oligarch's sanctuary nestled in the remote wilderness of Kodiak Island, feels like a crypt.

Not much has changed in that respect.

It's been two weeks since I set foot in this place, driven by desperation. But with each passing day, impatience gnaws at me. Failure drags at my bones.

I'm Monty Novak, for fuck's sake. The wealthiest man in Alaska with a global empire at his fingertips. A man who bends the world to his will.

Yet here, in this mansion of long-buried secrets, I'm merely a man tormented by the absence of his other half.

Under my supervision, my investigative team launched an exhaustive search of the abandoned estate and pristine acreage, delving into hidden caves, tracing the rugged coastlines and inlets, and scouring every inch of dirt for a sign of Frankie.

We've turned up nothing.

She isn't here.

Never was.

My team arrived at this conclusion days ago.

The mystery of her disappearance remains as impenetrable as the dense forests surrounding us. Yet I can't bring myself to leave. I'm missing something. Overlooking some vital clue.

I pause at the last door in the corridor and step into my father's office, a room stripped of its corruption long ago when I removed every financial document and confidential file after my parents' deaths.

The emptiness of the cabinets and drawers reflects the void within me.

I stride through the vacuous space, running a finger along bare surfaces. My frustration morphs into exhaustion. Pacing turns into denial, denial to fury, until a solid paperweight flies from my grasp and crashes against the wall.

But instead of embedding itself in the sheetrock, it blows right through it and keeps going, bouncing into the recess beyond, revealing a deep, hollow chamber.

What. The. Fuck?

My pulse races as I approach the hole, my hands curling into fists.

There's something there. Something deliberately hidden from me. Why?

Overwhelming betrayal consumes me, fueling the force of my punch. I unleash another and another. The drywall crumbles beneath my strikes, a physical manifestation of my relationship with Rurik Strakh.

What else did my father keep from me?

Punch.
Why didn't he trust me?
Punch.
Why didn't he love me?
Punch.
Dust clouds the air with each blow, driving me faster, harder. I pound away sections of gypsum and clay, breaking the skin on my knuckles and unveiling another layer of secrets that have lain dormant for twenty-five years.

At last, the wall gives way to the cavity within. My heart hammers as I reach inside, the dim light catching on objects unfamiliar yet deeply personal.

With shaking hands, I sift through the debris, touching photographs, a book, a wooden box, a velvet pouch. No doubt incriminating relics of my father's past.

As I lift them from their tomb, there's a menacing weight to them, a sense of evil I know too well.

These aren't just trinkets but artifacts of a sadistic life left behind.

In the box rests a row of Soviet military medals. Stolen off dead bodies? Trophies of my father's victims?

The velvet pouch holds a collection of rare, pre-revolutionary Russian coins, their edges worn by time and history. Blood money? Payment of blackmail to my father?

A stack of faded photographs captures moments of his reign in a homeland I don't remember. My scowling father in suits and tuxedos. Shaking hands with powerful figures more corrupt than him. Standing with others I don't recognize.

I don't fucking care. I'm looking for my wife, not trying to exhume my family's skeletons.

Tossing aside the photos, I examine the most perplexing item of all. A well-worn, leather-bound copy of Pushkin's poems, its pages dog-eared from frequent visits.

I hold it in my palm, feeling the weight of my father's madness. Why was this sealed in a wall? It looks ancient. Probably priceless. But Rurik Strakh wasn't a romantic. He was a vicious monster with more blood on his hands than in his entire body.

Perhaps, within the pages, amid these mementos of his life, lies a clue, a key to unlocking something significant. The book could be a cipher, the photographs a missing link in history or an answer to unsolved mysteries.

None of this will bring Frankie home.

Still, I can't ignore the discovery. These aren't merely items. They're fragments of my heritage, carried across continents and seas, too integral to be forsaken.

The thought urges me to search deeper, to look beyond the surface.

What was my father trying to protect? *Or forget?* Is there more to my family's story? Is their past finally catching up to me?

Most importantly, do their crimes—and my part in them—have anything to do with Frankie's disappearance?

I can't see how. But the questions swirl in my mind, each one opening doors to answers I'm not ready to uncover.

As I stand amidst the debris of the wall I shattered, a shadow creeps along the edges of my mind.

These items, hidden away so carefully, speak of deception.

My father didn't want me to find this.

If such a place existed without my knowledge, what

other hidden compartments does this house conceal?

I send a text to the leader of my investigative team.

Within minutes, the click of Sirena's heels reverberate through the hallway, announcing her approach.

As she steps into the room, her scent hits me instantly—a natural, honeyed, distinctly feminine fragrance. Not the artificial kind, but something deeply womanly and organic, stirring the baser parts of me I've neglected for months.

She heads toward me with a sway in her hips, commanding yet softened with a grace that seduces.

Her black hair, long legs, and golden complexion sharply contrast my feisty, little sunburn-prone redhead. Sirena is a beautiful woman, but she's not Frankie.

Her gaze tracks me with longing.

That is a problem.

While her desire centers on me, mine is complicated. I miss affection. I ache to be touched. I love the attention of women almost as much as I love to spoil them, worship them, fuck them...

Goddammit, I'm lonely. Sex is my outlet for stress. Frankie used to say it was my love language. I fucking need it.

I need my goddamn wife.

Pushing aside my turmoil, I update Sirena on what I found.

She listens intently. She's good at that, hanging on my every word without interrupting. Frankie would've questioned me a dozen times before I finished the briefing.

Christ, she was frustrating. But if I got her back, I wouldn't trade her irritating quirks. Not for Sirena's respectful silence. Not for anything in the world.

Sirena reaches up and brushes drywall dust from my suit jacket, her touch lingering on the open collar of my button-up shirt.

Until she notices my hands, the blood drying on my knuckles.

Without a word, she strides into the attached bathroom and returns with a damp towel.

"Allow me." She clasps my wrist.

I let her, holding still, barely breathing, as she cleans the cuts with efficiency.

Like a nurse.

Another reminder. Another stab in the gut.

"Don't touch me again." I pull away, putting several steps between us. "This stops now. I'm not interested. I will not fuck you. Are we clear?"

"Yes." She straightens her shoulders, her eyes glinting.

"Tell your team to dismantle the estate. Seek out every false wall, floorboard, and crawl space."

"Monty..." Her voice, a euphony of professionalism with an undercurrent of something fragile, caresses along the line of concern. "The perimeter's been thoroughly searched. No stone left unturned."

"Yet you didn't find this." I pull my hand from hers, motioning at the hole in the wall.

Her eyes linger on mine a moment too long before she nods. "I'll have the team double down."

"Thank you." I lean against the desk, crossing my legs at the ankles. "I don't know what we're looking for, but any clue, any secret passage might lead us to my wife."

Her smile flickers, a brief spark of something. Jealousy? "We'll comb the estate, every inch. For you...I would scour the ends of the earth." She steps closer.

"I'm here for you."

"Not for me." I stop her with a look. "For *her*."

"Of course." Her gaze holds mine.

"You're dismissed."

Her smile slips. Then quickly returns.

As she turns to leave, I collect the photographs and the book of Pushkin's poems. "Sirena."

"Yes?"

"I want these analyzed. They may hold a clue or a secret code. Could be a waste of time."

"Consider it done."

As she takes the items, I say, "If you discover anything—"

"Discretion is my job, sir. I'll bring all information to you directly."

"Good."

Rurik and Asya Strakh fled to this secluded island to escape the threats on their lives. They built this estate as a fortress, raised my brother and me here, and kept their criminal identities a secret until they died.

What else might they have hidden from the world? From me?

As the days bleed into each other, my childhood home transforms into a maze of gutted passageways and broken floors, every hollow wall a potential clue, every loose board a possible lead. We tear the place apart so completely that it becomes unrecognizable.

Each night, I lie in a bed that's not my own and watch videos of Frankie on my phone. With a hand around my throbbing dick, I beat it ruthlessly. After I come, I start again. Another video, another torment, another unsatisfying release.

This isn't pleasure.

It's punishment.

Punishment for not finding her.

Punishment for cheating on her.

Punishment for losing her in the first place.

If she knew the degree to which I stalked her, the level of my obsession, she would never come back.

I have dozens of recordings, all without her knowledge, videos and pictures of her flawless body in various stages of undress, sometimes when she showered, other times while she slept.

Even now, a video streams of her wearing nothing but a thong as she lingers in our closet, choosing something to wear. She thought I was asleep, not angling my phone and intruding on her privacy.

If idolizing my wife makes me a pervert, I don't give a fuck. I would do it again.

In the loneliness of the night, these recordings are what keep me anchored.

Another week passes. A week of anguish and fruitless searching.

It's time to let Sirena go, return to the yacht, and continue the investigation on my own.

As I plan to do exactly that, a breakthrough shatters my resolve.

The discovery comes unexpectedly with a text on my phone.

Sirena: I'm in the wine cellar. Come quickly.

monty

SIXTEEN

Excitement rushes through me, alive and visceral, as I pocket my phone and run.

What did Sirena find?

Yesterday, she began to explore parts of the estate previously deemed irrelevant, impenetrable spaces enclosed in stone, untouched by the chaos of our search.

Heart pounding, I bound down the dusty stairs and descend beneath the earth.

"Over here." Her voice drifts from behind rows of aged bottles and forgotten vintages.

As I round the corner of the wine cellar, she waves me over.

"There's a closet." She steps back, making room for me in the narrow space. "Lots of shelves. They're all empty but one. We didn't remove anything. I sent the team away, just in case..."

In case I find something incriminating.

The air swirls with dust as I squeeze behind a wall of wine.

Hidden behind a false panel in the wine rack lies a chamber so cleverly disguised that it blends seamlessly with the surrounding stone.

Inside, carefully preserved against the damp and the dark, waits a fireproof safe with a keypad lock.

The set of my jaw, the tension in my shoulders, every inch of me is strung tight as I remove the box. The sleek keypad gleams under the flickering light, each button a gatekeeper to the unknown.

One by one, I input the codes known only to me and my father, a series of numbers and combinations, each carrying the burden of past confidences.

When I reach the date of my brother's death, my fingers hesitate. A chill brushes my spine. The digits fall like a hammer, each press a stab of accusation.

The safe clicks open, the sound reverberating against stone, unlocking more than just a metal door.

The moment hangs, suspended between the shadows of the past and hope for the future.

Sirena backs away, giving me privacy.

My hands steady as I reach inside, withdrawing a cache of documents. The papers rustle, a whisper in the silence, promising answers or perhaps more questions.

Each breath is a battle, every heartbeat a drum of war, as I unfold the first secret.

Blue paper. White lines. Before computers, this is how architects created building drawings.

If this is the blueprint for this estate, it's too little, too late.

But as I study it more closely, I don't recognize the floor plan. The design is a two-story log cabin built on massive pilings that anchor into permafrost.

With a cellar.

That's insane. The ground freezes and thaws every year over permafrost, making it an active layer. No one builds beneath it.

Except Rurik Strakh.

He was an architectural mastermind, top of his class at university. He owned the largest construction company in Russia and here in Alaska.

But that's not how he accumulated his obscene wealth.

The craftsmanship and sophistication detailed in this blueprint is unmistakably that of my father, his genius evident in the lines and annotations that pepper the pages.

The question is...did he build this? Where? For what purpose?

Maybe he wanted a safe house in the event that his enemies discovered his fortress here?

More blueprints accompany it, designs for solar panels on the roof, dual chimneys, coal stoves, a water tank that switches between electricity and wood heat, and...

What is this?

A hydroelectric generator?

My eyes scan the mechanics, the complexity. It's a rural, single-family power system that feeds off a nearby river. The concept is brilliant and innovative, promising self-sufficiency.

This is the work of my brother.

Denver was a genius with an engineer's brain. Years ahead of his time, he conceptualized and designed machines that ran on alternative power. Before he died, his dream was to harness free energy for everyday use.

My stomach knots.

All of this reeks of an off-grid refuge, hidden from the prying eyes of the world.

If it wasn't built, the blueprints wouldn't be here. Maybe I'm wrong. Maybe my father died before he completed it, and the structure is sitting in a remote corner of the world, half-finished and forgotten.

But I don't think so.

When I cleaned out his office, it was filled with unfinished projects.

He hid this one in a stonewall behind the wine cellar for a reason.

Setting the blueprints aside, I search the other documents for locations, maps, points of reference, anything that may indicate where this cabin was built.

Instead, I find flight logs.

Meticulously recorded, they trace a pattern of movement for a Turbo Beaver, chronicling a series of journeys to and from Whittier. Each entry includes the tail number, checkpoint, hours of operation, and arrival and departure dates. No destination. No pilot information.

I flip to the end.

The log ceases twenty-five years ago. A few months before my parents' deaths.

Whittier.

Blood roars in my ears.

My parents died in their private plane—a luxury Gulfstream—on their way home from Whittier. To this day, I don't know why they visited that small port town or how the engine malfunctioned, causing the freak accident.

After an intense, unsuccessful investigation, I left it alone and moved on.

These flight logs, marked by the name Alvis

Duncan, may be a key to unlocking the mystery of their visit to Whittier.

Alvis Duncan.

Never heard of him, but it shouldn't be hard to track him down.

"Sirena." I turn to her with a surge of excitement.

As she strolls forward, I'm quickly tempered by a stark realization.

This discovery, while significant, doesn't draw us closer to Frankie. If anything, it opens a new avenue of inquiry. The off-grid cabin, the plans, the flights—they weave a narrative separate from her disappearance, a divergence from our primary goal.

Regardless, one thing is certain.

"We leave tomorrow." I breeze past her, heading toward the stairs.

"Okay." She follows, huffing. "Are you going to tell me what we found? Or where we're going?"

My breath quickens, caught in indecision.

Alvis Duncan, a name never mentioned or documented in all my dealings with my father, merits exploration. But not at the expense of our current quest.

At the top of the stairs, I pause, staring at the documents in my hand. "These are blueprints for an off-grid cabin. Probably a safe house for my parents."

"Another clue. This could be it, Monty. It could lead us to her." She smiles. "Well done, us."

"Well done, you."

She doesn't know that this discovery saved her job. It shows her determination, her ability to accomplish anything I demand.

I need her at my side, despite her infatuation with me.

"So where's the cabin?" She angles around my arm,

trying to peek at the blueprints. "Where are we going?"

"Sirena..." With a heavy heart, I acknowledge the need to compartmentalize our efforts. "This discovery, while momentous, cannot distract us from finding Frankie."

"But I thought—"

"I didn't know about the cabin's existence until now. That means Frankie doesn't know, either."

The question of why these documents were hidden so deeply, of what my parents were involved in that necessitated such secrecy, compels me to hand over the flight logs.

"Alvis Duncan." I point at the signature. "Find this man, see what he knows, but keep it separate. Our priority remains on my wife."

"Understood." She reads through the logs, fully absorbed, given her robotic response. "I'll handle the investigation discreetly and find out what Alvis knows without losing focus on Frankie. You have my word."

She flips through the pages. There must be a hundred flights listed over ten years.

As she reaches the end, a few slips of paper fall out, fluttering to the floor.

Two photographs.

One of them lands face up, and a pair of chilling gray eyes stare up at me.

Eyes I hoped never to see again.

I slam my shoe down on it. Too late.

"Who is that?" Sirena squats, tugging on the corner, trying to slide it into view. "Looks like Brad Pitt."

A sickening wave of nausea swarms in my gut. I press my weight into my foot, holding the photo in place.

I burned every picture, document, and mention of Denver's existence. I erased him from this house, from my memories, from the goddamn planet, yet there he is, glaring a hole through the bottom of my shoe.

"If you're withholding information..." She releases her grip on the photo, staring up at me. "I can't help you."

"He has nothing to do with my wife."

"Who is he?"

"My brother."

"Why is this the first time I'm hearing about a brother?" Her eyebrow curves upward. "Any other siblings I don't know about?"

"Just the one."

"Where is he?"

"Dead."

Leave it alone, Sirena. This is not a hole you want to go down.

Gone is the woman who wants to fuck me. The team leader of my investigative team plucks the second photo off the floor and straightens to her full height, glancing at it before meeting the full force of my glare.

"Give me the photo." I hold out my hand.

She tucks it behind her back. "How did he die?"

"I don't know." I shake my hand with impatience.

"Liar."

My nostrils pulse on a harsh exhale. "His death has no bearing on this investigation."

"Are you sure?"

"Positive."

She considers that. Then passes me the second photo. "Who is this woman?"

My heart stops, careening to a sudden, hard death that sends me stumbling into the doorframe and gripping it for support.

It's her.

The girl who haunted my teenage years stares back at me, captured in a moment of unguarded beauty.

Fucking hell, it's been years. Decades.

Yet I remember her like it was yesterday.

In the photo, she stands alone against the black backdrop of her bedroom window. Her long hair cascades like a dark waterfall, framing a face that embodies the essence of the North. Resilient, captivating, utterly gorgeous.

Her eyes, vast and deeply brown, hold the depth of the night sky, sparkling with the light of a thousand stars that seem to pierce through the faded ink of the photo.

Memories crash in, unbidden. She was the daughter of our live-in maid, three years younger than me, her daily life intertwined with ours, yet always a world apart.

Our age gap...

Three years is nothing compared to the twenty years between me and my wife. But back then? When I was sixteen?

She was forbidden.

Didn't stop the intensity of my crush, or how her laughter filled the corridors of our frigid, imposing home with warmth and life. I wasn't alone in my admiration.

Denver was obsessed with her, too. Once she invaded his filthy mind with her irresistible innocence, he was hooked like an addict, which set the stage for a rivalry that simmered until his death.

Our competition for her attention was ruthless.

And futile.

She remained achingly too young and unattainable.

The rivalry with my brother, the intense emotions she evoked, the threats my father made against us if we touched her—everything rushes back like a punch in the heart.

I stare at the photo, remembering that yellow dress, the way it hugged her curves and exposed her cleavage.

The emblem of my first fierce yearning.

Her Inuit heritage, pronounced in the striking contours of her face, draws me into a gaze that feels both familiar and ineffably mysterious.

She must've been sixteen when this was taken, still living in this house after I went off to college.

After Denver's death.

Finding her photo now, amid my father's secrets, provokes a deep, possessive snarl in the back of my throat.

"Monty?" Sirena reaches out, her touch hovering. "Who is she?"

"Kaya Knowles." I step back and swipe the photo of Denver off the floor.

A brief glance at his face sends a shiver down my spine. His eyes whisper of intention, of secrets so depraved I can't look at them.

I pocket the photos, rubbing my head. "What is the date of the first flight in those logs?"

Sirena checks the documents and rattles off a time frame that rules out Denver's involvement. He couldn't have been on those flights because he died a year prior.

But Kaya? She was still around. When her mother died from a heart condition, my father took her in, provided her schooling, and gave her a job among his staff.

None of this explains why photos of Denver and Kaya were tucked inside the logs. My father didn't do anything without calculation and purpose.

"Kaya grew up here." I meet Sirena's patient gaze.

"Her mother was our maid. They were part of our family."

"Where is Kaya now?"

"No idea. She moved on when my parents died."

"You grew up with her but never looked into her whereabouts?"

"I was wrapped up in the investigation of the plane crash. She left in the middle of that. Never reached out to me. Never even told me she was leaving. She was in her early twenties. Beautiful and ambitious. I think she was ready to get out of here and start a new life on her own. I didn't blame her. Didn't even know where to look for her. So I let her go."

"Do you find it strange that photos of her and your brother were buried in a wall with blueprints and flight logs?"

"Of course, it's fucking strange. But none of this has a goddamn thing to do with my missing wife."

The pieces are falling everywhere, but the picture they form is unclear.

"Do you want me to find Kaya Knowles?" She tips her head.

Tempting. So fucking tempting.

"Fine." I expel a breath. "While you're investigating Alvis Duncan, look for her, too. But—"

"Keep it separate from Frankie. Got it."

"Tomorrow, we'll return to the yacht and resume our search along coastlines. Prepare the team."

I'm ready to put this place behind me.

kodiak

SEVENTEEN

For two weeks, we walk with the shadows, hunched beneath a sky that weeps snowflakes as sharp as shards of glass. The tundra threatens to swallow us with each step, and exhaustion clings like a second skin.

No matter how many breaks we take, I can't shake off this fatigue. Frankie doesn't complain, but the journey has been immensely hard on her.

She moves with a sluggishness that wasn't there before. Every mile seems to cost her more than the last, her snowshoes dragging against the thick blanket of white.

There's a slump to her shoulders beneath the pack. The skin around her eyes pulls tight, and perhaps the most telling is her silence. Her voice, when she does speak, lacks emotion and animation.

I stopped forcing her to rest. My concern only makes her more agitated and miserable.

But every night, she crawls into my arms and laces our legs together, seeking my comfort and body heat.

Every day, we wake before dawn and push forward, our eyes fixed on the horizon, longing for a glimpse of the cabin.

We're close.

The landscape subtly shifts beneath our weary feet, and the air feels different, not warmer, but less biting. The snow begins to relent in places, exposing patches of frozen earth, hardy shrubs, and animal tracks. Rabbits. Foxes. Moose. Specks of life that signal how far south we've traveled.

The most heartening sight is the gradual appearance of a frozen stream, a guidepost paved in the landscape that runs all the way to the cabin. In the summer, it babbles and rushes with life, but now it lies in hibernation.

"Look." I veer toward the icy path. "The stream means we're close. We'll reach the cabin by the end of the day."

"Thank you, Jesus."

My veins shimmer with anticipation. My circulation buzzes with a renewed energy, quickening my pace.

Tonight, we'll have a safe shelter, a fire, and deep, restful sleep.

My lips squirm, making uncomfortable movements. She studies me with an odd look. "Is that a smile?"

"No."

"It totally is. Aren't you just a little ray of sunshine?"

I shake my head. She laughs, and we trudge through the snow in silence, our breaths forming clouds of mist.

Every few minutes, I glance at her, her face partially obscured by loose strands of red hair.

The way she makes me feel, it's the sweetest agony,

the most exquisite pain.

The thought of anything happening to her under my watch weighs heavier than the pack on my back.

I love her, and that has redefined every aspect of my life.

The tundra is my home, my teacher, and my jailer, but as I walk beside her, I find myself dreaming of a different future. A future where the desolate wilderness is replaced by the chaos of civilization.

Breaking the silence, I venture into the unknown. "What's it like...living in a town? Among other people?"

"It's different." A tired sigh escapes her lips. "There's noise, a lot of it. And people, everywhere. But there's a sense of belonging, too. You can find community, friends, those who care about you outside of survival."

I nod, trying to imagine such a world. "It must be overwhelming to always have people around."

"It can be. But you find your spaces, your peace. There's beauty in solitude, but there's beauty in connection, too. In a town, you learn to balance both."

"The transition..." I don't know how to put my concerns into words. "Going from this..."

"From isolation to over-stimulation? Yeah. That won't be easy." Her gaze softens, understanding. "It'll be a shock, at first. The pace, the noise, the sheer number of people. But you'll adapt. You'll find the things you love about it. The convenience of stores. The easy access to food, music, and different cultures. The joy of going to the bathroom without freezing off your dick. But you'll also miss the quiet, the connection to nature. It's a trade-off."

The thought of such a drastic change makes me uneasy. I'm good at this life, where success is defined by hard work and resilience. But out there? In a city? What am I? Who am I?

I don't want to be a disappointment. The fear of failing, of fumbling, of fucking up, crawls into my voice. "What if I can't adapt?"

She stops, turning to face me, her eyes earnest. "Then we adapt together. We find our way, like we always do. But I need you to promise me something."

I grunt.

She snorts. Then her expression sobers. "Don't lose yourself in the change. Remember who you are and hold on to that."

"I don't know how to be anything else but this."

"Cool. Because I'm kind of obsessed with this." She waves a hand over my body, making my cock twitch. "You and Leo, exactly as you are, can take on anything, including a new life."

As we resume our journey, her words echo in my thoughts, a mix of warnings and promises, fears and dreams. The prospect of leaving behind a lifetime of isolation for the bustling life of a world I've only ever known through books and stories…it's daunting.

But the promise of a new life with her? I'm grabbing hold of that with both fucking hands.

The final stretch is a monumental effort, but our pace carries an undercurrent of urgency, a desperate need to find shelter.

When the hunting cabin finally emerges on the dark horizon, we slow to a stop.

"We made it." Her eyes, wide with disbelief, regard the modest shadow.

It's a simple structure, solitary and stoic against the harsh landscape, made of weathered wood that has stood the test of many winters. There's no plumbing. No windows. Just one room that serves as my haven during hunting season.

The best part? It has a hearth and an abundant supply of firewood and heavy fur pelts that Denver hauled in years ago. We'll be able to dry our wet clothes and thaw our frozen limbs.

From this distance, it's a faint outline. But I find myself scanning the ground for boot tracks and scenting the air for wood smoke.

Beside me, she remains motionless, her eyes sweeping over the tiny shape and its surroundings with a fervor that matches mine.

Unspoken questions hover between us.

Could Wolf have survived? Did he find refuge here?

As we draw closer, my entire body is sensitized to pick up on any signs of him—depressions in the snow that might suggest the presence of waste holes, discarded animal bones or scraps from meals, worn paths left by repeated trips between the cabin and the stream.

But the snow appears uniformly unmarked, and the chimney stands cold and silent against the night sky.

The absence of human presence adds to the growing anxiousness between us. We linger at the threshold of the cabin, the door sealed and offering no sound.

"No signs of bears." I remove my gloves, my throat thick. "The pemmican should be safe."

That's why we're here, but neither of us is focused on that.

Trembling fingers caress the chilled tips of mine.

I squeeze her hand and reach for the door with my other, hesitating. The possibility that Wolf might be inside, alive and waiting, is a hope so powerful it's paralyzing.

Hope is a treacherous bitch.

It crushes, darling.

She watches me, her expression a mirror of my rising disquiet.

With a deep breath, I push the door open, the creak of its hinges cutting through the silence like a verdict.

The interior greets us with darkness, dusty and untouched. The hearth is cold, the wood stacked neatly beside it, exactly how I left it.

The crushing emptiness squeezes around us, thinning the air, making it hard to breathe.

Her pack drops to the floor, and she shuffles away, giving me her back. Her shoulders tremble, and quietly, almost imperceptibly, she begins to cry.

The sound of her sobs, muffled by the thick wool of her gloves, is gutting.

I'm on her in three strides, my heart cracking at the sight of her anguish. It's an instinct, as natural as breathing, to protect her from this pain, to shield her from it.

Gathering her into my arms, I hold her tightly, trying to absorb her suffering, to take it all upon myself.

"He can't be gone, Kody. He can't."

He is. He's gone, and he's never coming back.

But what solace can the truth offer against the raw, gaping wound of loss?

"If only I'd given him more." She collapses into me as quiet tears shake her frame. "Had I been enough, the partner he needed, he would be here—"

"Stop." I kiss her face, her lips, her wet cheeks, and stare into her watery eyes. "Hear me, woman. You're more than enough. You were the best thing in his life. His decision to give up has nothing to do with your worth. His fate was frozen the moment he killed his mother. He never came back from that."

"I know, but I hate it. For him, for you and Leo. I hate this pain so much."

"I'm here. Not going anywhere."

I feel the depth of my loss in the soundless release of her sobs. It's a hot, twisting clench that never lets go.

My mind races, searching for something, anything, to ease her sorrow. But there are no words, no actions that can heal this.

Time, maybe. But Wolf left a deep, enduring mark on us. If I ever see him again, in this life or the next, I'm going to beat his fucking ass.

For now, I do the only thing I can. I sit with her in the dark, holding her through a grief that consumes us both.

When her sniffles give way to sleep, I know the pain hasn't left. It's merely settled. But together, we'll carry it, sharing the burden as we've shared every challenge since our paths converged.

Tucking her against me, I strike a match and light the fire.

In the warmth of the crackling flames, I build a nest of fur pelts, strip us down to our thermal underclothes, and settle us into bed.

Through it all, she doesn't wake, and that suits me just fine. I'm ready to join her.

The cabin, though empty without Wolf, offers a bounty of pemmican and sanctuary from the night. With a heavy beam securing the door, nothing is getting in. Not the howling wind or the predators or the obstacles that await us tomorrow.

Not tonight.

frankie

EIGHTEEN

An unsettling sound stirs me from sleep. I open my eyes to the glitter of dying embers in the hearth, the soft luster barely illuminating the room.

But it's not the cold that chills me.

I'm alone.

Panicked and disoriented, I'm transported to another cabin and a different morning, waking without Wolf and finding him on the cliff.

"Kody!" I shoot upward, heaving, wildly scanning the single-room cabin.

Fear sends my heart into a gallop, then pushes it faster when I spot him.

A sharp outline cut against the wooden walls, huddled in a corner, facing away, clad only in underwear, and rocking back and forth.

A protective alarm shrieks through me.

In the low light, I tiptoe forward, straining my eyes

to examine his nude back, the muscles rippling beneath a map of old, chaotic trauma. Overlapping wounds, too numerous to count, render years of suffering and human malice. The patterns are random, vicious, the work of various implements of torture.

The work of Denver.

"Kody?"

He doesn't react, his body rocked by tremors and whatever memory he's lost in.

My stomach churns as I approach, my legs sore and unsteady.

A sheen of sweat covers his skin. His shoulders hike around his ears, his chin to his chest, his entire frame tensed in a posture of defense. He looks so small, so vulnerable, like a child who's known nothing but pain.

Such a stark contrast to the strong, feral Alaskan man I've come to know and love.

It brings tears to my eyes, but my medical training kicks in, overriding my emotions.

Does he have PTSD? Was it a nightmare? Did my breakdown last night trigger this?

Drawing closer, I assess his physical state, checking for any sign of self-harm, any indication of a nightmare so severe it may have resulted in bodily injury.

He appears unharmed...on the surface.

Slowly, I lower myself to the floor beside him. "Kody?"

He lifts his head, eyes wide, haunted, staring right through me.

As if staring at a ghost.

"Are you okay?" I reach out tentatively, my hand hovering over his shoulder, unsure. "Kody? What happened?"

No response. No indication that he even hears me.

"You can tell me." I lace my fingers together on my

lap to keep from touching him. "Or we can sit in silence until you feel better. Whatever you need."

He blinks slowly, his gaze gradually clearing, focusing on me.

"Nightmare." A hoarse whisper. "I was back there...in that cage with Denver. He never stopped..."

"He's dead," I say too forcibly and try to gentle my tone. "He can't hurt you anymore. You're safe here, with me."

"Safe?" His expression twists into sudden, violent rage. "I'm weak!"

His bellow sends me careening backward. Not out of fear. He would never hurt me. But my shock at his outburst knocks me off balance.

"Kody, you're not—"

"I just stood there while you fought him, shot him, beat him with your bare hands. I. Did. Nothing."

"You were restrained—"

"On my own order, my own fucking stupidity! I put you in that situation. A situation that endangered your life and forced you to kill him. It should've been me, Frankie. It should've been *me* protecting *you*!"

"You went to him *because* you were protecting me. You protect me every fucking day. You're not alone in this. We protect each other. Leo, too. It's what we do."

"I wanted to be your savior." He pulls at his hair and resumes rocking. "It should've been me."

He's breaking my heart.

I don't know what to do. I can treat physical wounds, but healing the scars of such deep emotional trauma is uncharted territory for me.

All I can do is give him my unwavering support and a safe space to confront his demons.

"The nightmare felt so real." He covers his face with

both hands, scrubbing, breathing heavily. "Except you didn't show up, and he kept going. He hurt me over and over, and I couldn't stop him because I wasn't a grown man. I was just a boy. A weak, helpless little boy."

Tears well in my eyes, every part of me aching for the child who endured so much alone.

"I'm here." I brush my fingers along his stiff jaw. "You're no longer small or helpless. That boy overcame unspeakable horror, fought the worst monster imaginable, and grew into a strong, dependable, compassionate man. You *are* my savior, Kodiak."

"But you slew the monster."

"We both did. You were the brave one who went in there alone with a plan. All I did was follow and react, recklessly and emotionally, like I always do."

He turns to me, the transformation immediate and startling. His dark features take on a stoniness, a determination that forges him anew right before my eyes.

"It will never happen again." His gravelly growl vibrates the air between us. "I'll fight for you, protect you. I'll be your shield, your blade, your goddamn army."

"And my stalker."

"That, too."

"Okay. Now that we have that sorted, what do you need? Food?" I twist, scanning the dark, barren space. "How about some frozen pemmican? Or a sponge bath? Maybe a nap?"

"You. I only need you." He grabs my neck and hauls me against him, stealing my breath with his mouth.

His kiss is more than a collision of lips. It's a storm. A vicious thunderbolt of fury, charged with loss and love and every battle in between.

Burying his hands in my hair, he holds onto me as if

I'm the anchor in his cruel, turbulent world. His teeth capture my lower lip, sinking, claiming, a fervent assertion of his nature.

Then he tongues the punctures and fiercely stares into my eyes. "I love you."

He's not the first man to give me those words, but he's the first to declare them like a vow.

A vow stronger than a legal contract, more sacred than a religious oath, and longer lasting than a marriage.

A vow that engraves itself on my headstone.

"My soul is yours." I swing a leg over his lap and straddle him. "Now kiss me again."

My Lycan prince might be cold and deadly, but never with me. As his lips seal with mine, it begins with a gentle urgency, a touch so soft and meaningful it whispers of a lifetime of longing.

He tucks me against his chest and rises to his feet. The room spins, and in a heartbeat, I'm lying on a bed of furs beneath his weight, his heat, and his impenetrable hardness.

He's insurmountable everywhere. But there's an excessively large part of him, rigid and heavy, pressing between my legs. The part he's never given me. Never given to anyone.

The thought jolts lightning along my spine, crackles across my skin, and sizzles through my blood. I want to be his first and his only. That's the electricity.

He plants a hand beside my head and cups my throat with the other, his hips grinding with intention.

Then he gives me a kiss that erases all others. It's a kiss that transcends time and space, where two souls merge and mate in pure bliss.

Our eyes lock, and in that glance, a thousand

unspoken words pass between us, a dialogue of desire, trust, and deep, abiding connection.

Our lips slide in a slow, intoxicating caress of intimacy. Our tongues swirl in a delicate exploration that deepens with every breath. Our teeth catch and release in veneration of every heartbreak and joy, every moment of finding and losing.

The universe fades into the ether, leaving only two beings in existence, wrapped in a sanctuary of healing wounds and endless tomorrows.

This.

This is the greatest kiss of all time.

It robs us of air and fills us with new energy, turning us into wild, desperate creatures. Fingers in hair, mouths gasping and consuming, he uses his grip on my neck to angle my head and thrust his tongue deeper, working me toward the edge of rapture.

He doesn't need to touch my body. I can come simply from this kiss.

"Kody." I moan, running a hand down the scarred line of his back, tracing the muscle there. "Please."

For months, this hunger simmered between us, burning my skin and broiling my organs. Without the arctic chill, I wouldn't have survived it.

But now the flames of our impending joining lash against me, igniting an inferno.

He shifts down my body, dragging lethal teeth over my breasts and clamping them around a nipple. "I'm going to quench my thirst between your thighs."

"Not until I quench mine first." I give his face a nice, firm push.

Because he's twice my size, I throw all my strength into the shove that rolls him onto his back.

Wide-eyed, he stares up at me, his hard-packed abs flexing with the force of his breaths.

And his cock. That enormous, imposing extension of his masculinity stretches the fabric of his briefs, demanding to be freed.

I oblige, wrestling his underwear down powerful legs.

Holy mother, there it is, looming before me, a beast in its own right, with its own head, its own weight, and its own thudding heartbeat. It jumps and swells in my hands, refusing to be contained.

How will it ever fit in my mouth?

One way to find out.

Shaking with need, I lower my head.

"Wait." He grabs my hair. "I want you naked when you do this. I'll start a fire."

"No need." Pushing up, I slide out of my top and shove down my pants. "We are the fire."

"Damn right." He braces himself on his elbows, watching, waiting, his cock straining, ready to be sucked.

For the first time in his life.

I licked the tip once and made him come. But now?

I'm going to blow his fucking mind.

With his sinful body stark naked and laid out before me, I soak him in. First, with my eyes. Then my hands.

Then with my kiss-stung lips.

He groans and writhes beneath my assault, flexing his hips against the air. Whispers of musk tease my tongue, his delicious, earthly essence of wildfire and berries a potent aphrodisiac.

As I work my way toward his erection, his exhales snarl from him.

With a wicked grin, I lick a path around his heavy sac and follow the ropes of muscle that run down his thighs, then back again, nipping at his clenched abdomen, his granite chest.

"Stop teasing me, woman." His voice is guttural, roughened with want.

I meet his eyes, and my mouth goes dry.

He's huffing, panting, his eyes dark and wild, his hands fisting the fur blankets, and his body...my God, his beautiful body in all its rippling golden flesh and scarred power.

Desire pierces me, rushes down my spine, and slides liquid warmth low in my belly, tightening, tightening...

This foreplay is its own hell. He's endured enough.

I grip the massive girth of his cock, stretch my jaw, and feed the fat head into my mouth.

A rough groan tears from his throat.

My skin tingles. My fingers curl and pump, and my tongue glides, tasting and licking from tip to base.

Need surges through me. A single-minded determination to make him roar.

I want to take all of him, but there's no way. He's too long, too thick. One thrust would break my jaw.

As I work him toward the back of my throat, he can't hold still. His hips piston. His hands grab and pull, and his chest heaves through the loudest breaths I've ever heard from him.

Such a powerful, needful, sensual animal.

With teeth bared and predatory eyes aglow in the dark, he's *my* animal.

I whimper as he finally hits my throat. He quickly withdraws, but I suck him back in, swallowing, humming, and finally making him roar.

Not an orgasmic roar. The man is fighting back his release.

Considering he's a virgin, I didn't think he would last this long.

I should've known better.

Evidently, stamina runs in the family.

All at once, his hands capture my waist, lifting me over him, turning me, and positioning my pussy directly over his mouth.

As I wrap my lips around his cock, he holds my legs open, widening them around his face until I'm fully, gapingly exposed.

A hot stroke of breath caresses my cunt, followed by the long, firm slide of his tongue.

"Uhhnngh!" I choke on his dick, jaw aching, nipples throbbing, hips bucking, and eyes squeezed shut.

There is nothing, absolutely nothing that compares to the sensation of Kodiak Strakh lapping between my legs.

His pace quickens, his tongue plunging deep, as his hands roam my body, worshiping my breasts, my thighs, my clit.

When his tongue finds a rhythm, circling that pulsing bundle of nerves, I'm so lost in the sensations that I forget my task.

Until a large, rough hand slams down on my ass, making me yelp.

"Suck me, woman." He thrusts his hips like a male possessed.

This is what I crave. I want him demanding, dominating, taking away all thought, and turning me into a quivering puddle of pleasure.

"More." I swallow his monster cock, fitting half of it into my mouth and down my throat.

"I'll drink from you until the day I die." His husky growl vibrates up my back, prickling my nape and tingling my scalp. "Vodka never tasted this good."

That's a pretty high compliment from a man who

loves vodka more than people.

My body rocks against him, the pressure within building around his impaling tongue. Then his fingers join in, rubbing my inner walls and producing a deep, violent clenching between my legs. So close, so close...

"You need to come." He pulls me tighter against his open mouth and licks mercilessly, grunting. "Now."

Pleasure bursts, powering through me like a bomb going off.

His hand flies to the base of his cock, squeezing and stroking, as I suck as much as I can fit past my lips. I'm still coming on his face when he exhales sharply, groans painfully, and explodes down my throat.

The force of his release floods my mouth and snatches the air from my lungs. I swallow and gulp, and it keeps coming in powerful, salty jets. I may have choked. I definitely made a drooling mess down my chin, but I don't care.

I'm floating in a dreamy place, enveloped in his dark, manly scent, warm and safe against his body, and shimmering with unfathomable sensation. I never want to leave.

A drop of seed trickles down the length of his twitching cock. I lick it away while his tongue flicks out, licking me.

We're both slick with sweat, our chests rising and falling as we reclaim our breaths and reposition.

As I twist around and fit myself against his side, he looks...different. Sated yet unreadable.

"What's wrong?" I kiss his nipple and rest my chin there.

"I've never..." He blows out a breath. "I've never felt more like myself than I do now."

I grin. "How does that feel?"

"Free."

Oh, Kody. My beautiful, complicated, broody man.

I settle against him, head on his shoulder, basking in the lazy passage of his fingers through my hair. When his hand ceases its movement, I glance up to find him in the grasp of sleep.

After two weeks of hiking, maintaining a constant vigilance over me, and his nightmare this morning, he needs to sleep for a year. But we only have a day or two. Just long enough to rest and recharge before making the exhausting trip back.

I doze off with him, fully expecting to sleep all day.

But three hours later, he's up, dressed, fed, and ready to take on the world.

"I saw moose tracks a short distance from here." He pulls on his gloves.

If he can hunt one of those beasts without getting hurt, I'm all for it. By the time we return to Leo, we'll be out of bear meat. I'd rather not live on pemmican for the remainder of winter.

He tosses my gear at my feet.

I guess I'm going with him.

frankie

NINETEEN

"How much longer before the thaw?" I pull on my snowshoes, my pulse drumming with nerves and anticipation.

"Two months, give or take." Kody straps a quiver of arrows onto his back.

"Are you sure you want me to go with you? Won't I scare away the moose? I mean, stealth isn't exactly my thing."

"I'm not letting you out of my sight."

A thrill shivers through me. I've always wanted to watch him hunt, to see him in action. I'll just stand on the sidelines and try not to drool.

"What?" He tips his head.

"Huh?"

"You're staring."

"Can you blame me? Look at you. You're sexy as hell."

He glances down at himself, layered in thermals, insulated pants, heavy boots, and a fur parka that screams rugged mountain man. The scowl beneath his rustic beard and the crossbow in his grip take his dangerous aura to another level.

"See what I mean?" I bite my lip.

He shakes his head. "This gear ensures I remain warm and dry for the long stalks and waits during the hunt."

"Never mind." I rise to my feet, wearing similar clothing.

So why do I feel like an overstuffed penguin? Is it the waddle?

I step toward him, short steps with short legs, rocking side to side.

Yep. Definitely the waddle.

I'll never understand how he and Leo move so gracefully beneath all this gear.

He watches me with an arched brow.

"Stop looking so hot." I scoff. "Let's go."

With a sparkle of laughter in his eyes, he opens the door and leads the way.

I have no idea where we're going or what we're looking for, but he seems to have no trouble scenting or tracking or doing whatever stalkers do to pick up the trail.

His confidence in navigating the terrain is infectious, his protectiveness a constant reassurance. He moves with such certainty, his steps deliberate and sure. I trust in his knowledge of the land and find myself relaxing enough to let my mind wander.

"Who named you?" I grip his offered hand and let him help me scale a slope.

"I don't know. Watch your step."

As the ground levels out, I look around at the stark

beauty of pristine white. "What am I watching for?"

"We're standing on a lake. It stretches from this hill to that one." He points. "It's frozen right now, hidden beneath all the snow."

"Really?" I scrape my snowshoe against the hard-packed ice. "It won't break?"

"Not this time of year." He lifts his face to the dark sky. Scenting the air? Listening for cracking ice? "It's too cold. But I've never traveled here this deep in winter, so I only have Denver's word on it. Just...don't leave my side. Step where I step. Understood?"

"Got it."

"The moose went that way." He gestures toward the farthest hill and sets off in that direction on silent feet. "It's a male. Should be a big one. And aggressive."

"How do you know?"

"The size of the hooves." He points at a scuff mark in the snow. "I found scratches on the cabin from antlers. Also, bulls travel alone. And I hear it. The grunts and bellows in the distance."

"Right." I haven't heard or seen a thing.

And that's why I'm a nurse, not a moose hunter.

As he follows the tracks across the snow-laden lake, my thoughts circle back to the meanings of names.

"Who named your brothers?"

"No idea." He casts me a sidelong glance. "Why?"

"Hear me out. Denver and Monty are brothers. Denver and *Montgomery*. Both refer to well-known U.S. cities. Leo and Wolf refer to animals. Wolf was born here. Leo arrived when he was three, but he could've arrived with a different name."

"You think Denver changed his name to Leonid?" He surveys the horizon, expelling white clouds from full, pouty lips.

"Yeah, I think he could've named Wolf and Leo." I release an exhale. "Then there's you."

"My name also refers to an animal. But my mother..."

"What about her?"

"The address on her license is Barrow, Alaska."

"It's not called Barrow anymore. The name changed to Utqiagvik."

"I know." He halts, his brown eyes ensnaring mine. "But that's not where she's from."

"It's not?"

"No. For some reason, Denver wanted me to know that she grew up in Port Lions, Alaska, wherever that is."

Ice creeps across my scalp.

"Kody..." I brush my fingers against his. "Port Lions is a town on Kodiak Island."

Surprise flickers across his face before he clears it.

"So she named me after an island." He starts walking again.

"Did she?" I hurry to catch up. "Or did your father?"

"I don't have a father. What are you getting at?"

"There's too much coincidence here. I mean, you and Leo have names connected to your mother's address. Makes me think she's the link. What do you know about Kaya Knowles?"

"I know what you know. Her address, her age, how she died, her Inuit heritage...that's it."

"According to the birth date on her driver's license, she was twenty-one when she had you and twenty-three when Denver took her. When she died. She was so young. I'm sorry. It's just...when I first started putting all this together, I was convinced that you were Denver's missing brother."

His nostrils flare.

"Denver, Montgomery, and Kodiak," I go on, "all locations. But Denver and Monty are twenty-five, twenty-six years older than you. I think Denver is your biological father."

"Why me? Why not Leo or Wolf?"

"I don't know. Do you think Leo was named after Port Lions? Did Denver go there before you were born, get your mother pregnant, then hunt her down two years later in Utqiagvik? Looking for you?"

"He said he took me because he hated me. Hated me with every breath. Doesn't sound like a father who's desperate to unite with his child."

"No, but maybe Kaya rejected him. Scorned him. He said he hated you until he couldn't. Until he loved you most of all."

He pulls in a slow breath and releases it on a snarl. "You're reading too much into this."

"You can't deny the correlation between your names."

"What about Wolf? I bet there's a U.S. city with his name."

"Not in Kodiak Island. I just wish I knew how you are all related. It's driving me crazy." I stare up at the starless sky. "Did you know that Kodiak bears are a subspecies of the brown bear, and they live exclusively on the islands in the Kodiak Archipelago where your—?"

He stops abruptly, his back stiff as a board, his eyes fixed on the shadows stretching ahead.

My heartbeat thunders in my ears.

Shifting his gaze to mine, he holds a finger to his lips then slowly extends it toward the horizon.

My eyes thin, focusing on the darkness, searching for movement. Then a shape materializes. At first, it looks like branches suspended in mid-air. But no, those are antlers.

Holy shit, it's a moose, massive and stately, and it's staring right at us. If it charges, we have nowhere to go, nowhere to hide, nothing but vast, uninterrupted tundra.

Prowling forward, Kody doesn't share my fear as he lifts his crossbow and loads a bolt without making a sound.

I stare at my snowshoes. One waddling step, one unstealthy crunch, will ricochet like a bullet, alerting the entire Arctic of our presence.

No thanks. I'll stay right here and watch my beautiful man do his thing.

Several yards away, he slows, peers back, and gestures me forward.

I shake my head.

He gives me a look. Not just any look. *The look.*

I grit my teeth and lift my foot.

Be soft like snow. Light as a feather.

As I slowly ease into the first step, a faint, almost inaudible whisper tiptoes through the silence. Like the tentative creak of a door hinge.

Did I do that?

"Wait!" He thrusts up a hand, the moose forgotten, his face paling into stark horror. "Don't mo—"

A loud, sudden fracture cleaves through the air and detonates into a series of sharp, echoing snaps. The thunder of cracking ice grows louder and more frantic, spreading like glass shattering under stress.

The noise reverberates through the frozen landscape.

Then it stops.

My lungs pant so violently it doubles me over. But I don't dare move my feet.

He doesn't, either.

Knees bent, wide stance, and crossbow slung over his back, he stares at me from too far away.

Three strides would put me safely in his arms.

One stride might send me through the ice.

"Kody?"

"Shh." His eyes sweep over the surrounding snow, his jaw clicking so hard I worry he might break his teeth.

With each second, the tension in the air thickens as if the very atmosphere holds its breath, bracing for the worst.

There are no visible cracks around us. Nothing moves beneath our feet.

He meets my eyes. "Stay still. I'll come to you."

Before he moves a muscle, the surface of the lake gives way, the crust of snow and ice collapsing beneath my feet.

One moment I'm on solid ground, and the next, I'm plunging into the icy clutches of the lake.

"Frankie!"

The shock of the frigid water swallows his roar and takes my breath away. Its chilling grip yanks me under, and the weight of my gear drags me down deeper.

Panic flares, and a wild, desperate instinct takes over. My limbs fight the pull of the water, but my movements are sluggish, the cold so fucking sharp it's paralyzing. My body temperature drops rapidly, dangerously, making every attempt to swim to the surface feel like I'm battling through mud.

At last, my hands brush something solid. My head hits it next.

The frozen surface.

I'm trapped.

Trapped in the dark beneath a layer of ice.

I bang my fists and kick my legs, my lungs burning for air. My eyes, my ears, my chest, everything burns.

Terror spikes through my heart.

I think of Kody, just moments before, the look of absolute horror on his face.

He's still up there. Safe. He didn't fall in. But the guilt and fear that must be surging through him...I can't bear the thought. It pierces through the cold, driving me to fight harder, clawing and kicking. But I can't find the break in the ice.

My lungs are failing. I'm out of air.

Out of time.

This is the end. I won't make it out of this frozen tomb alive.

kodiak

TWENTY

A moment of distraction, a split second where my attention fixates on the moose, and a frozen lake that I mentally marked as safe—the cumulation of my oversights shatters in a heart-stopping instant.

Her feet breaking through the crust, her startled cry as she plunges, her body engulfed by the dark water beneath, and the terrible silence that follows.

It breaks me. Slays me. Cuts my legs out from under me as I scream, "Frannnnnnkie!"

Everything freezes—the wind, the shadows, my blood, my breath.

Everything but the cracks of ice splintering beneath my knees.

Fear chokes me, its icy claws holding me immobile. I need to reach her, but one wrong move will drag me down. If I join her, I can't save her.

My mind races, thoughts fragmented by terror and

desperation. Every instinct bellows to rush to her, but the ice above her sloshes and creaks, so dangerously thin, a trap waiting to claim another victim.

I drop to my stomach, spreading my weight as I inch forward, eyes glued to the dark hole. The cracking sounds continue, sinister and threatening, punching my heart into overdrive.

"Frankie!" My voice is raw, shredded from shouting her name.

There's no answer, only the cruel, hollow echo of my panic.

Pulse hammering, I reach the crumbling edge of the hole and peer into the cold, dark water.

I see nothing but my terror staring back at me.

Without hesitation, I stab an arm into the freezing abyss, my fingers instantly numb yet desperately reaching, searching for her. The cold shocks my entire system, crawling up to my shoulder and slamming into my chest.

The temperature of the water is lethal, and she's completely submerged in it.

Time is a predator. Every second matters. Every breath I take is one she loses.

How many seconds does she have left?

Fuck this. I'm going in after her.

Then, I feel it. A piece of clothing, slick and elusive between my fingers. I grab hold, refusing to let go, and pull with all the strength that despair lends me.

She emerges from the water, limp and terrifyingly still. I haul her onto the firmer surface behind me, my movements fueled by adrenaline and sheer terror.

The ice beneath us groans, a cracking, taunting threat, and she's not breathing.

Fuck, fuck, fuck!

Quickly, I drag her away from the hole to a patch of

snow-covered ground. There, I set her down, her skin pale and lips tinged blue, the sight ripping out my heart.

No pulse.

No breath.

"C'mon, Frankie." My voice breaks as I start CPR, pressing down on her chest, rhythmic and forceful, in sync with my pounding blood.

I tilt her head back and breathe for her, trying to push life back into her lungs, into her soul.

My beard rubs her beautiful face raw, turning it red. My hands have lost all feeling, hanging like ice blocks, utterly useless, but I don't stop, can't stop.

"Please, Frankie. Don't you dare fucking leave me." I sob between compressions, unraveling, prepared to die with her. "Fight, goddammit. Come back to me!"

Nothing.

"Fuuuuuck!" My head drops back, and I roar, screaming with helpless agony, my face frozen with tears.

Then I set my shoulders, refocus my efforts, and begin anew.

Nothing else exists—no ice, no cold, no pain. Just a fierce, endless drive to see her smile again.

I lose track of time between counting compressions and checking for signs of life. Each time I put my ear to her chest, I hear nothing.

Until there's something.

A cough.

I jerk back, frozen, not trusting the sound.

She splutters. Chokes. Then a gasp of air so sweet it shakes my foundation and reshapes my entire being.

Her eyes flutter open, confusion glistening in their depths.

"Oh, thank fuck." I haul her into my arms, ripping open my coat and wrapping her in my warmth. "Thank fucking Christ. Stay with me."

She's alive. She's breathing. But she's not safe. Not with the threat of hypothermia hanging over her.

Instinct takes over, primitive and urgent, propelling me to my feet. With her limp body, soaked and heavy with ice water, against my chest, I sprint toward the cabin, each step a battle against time.

The arctic air lashes against us as I push my legs faster, desperate to bridge the distance that separates us from warmth and salvation.

As the cabin emerges, I run harder, my lungs on fire. Seconds later, I burst through the door with a force born of raw fear, the impact sending a jarring shock through my tense muscles.

Kicking the door shut, I barricade us against the icy death outside.

The next steps are a blur of frantic action. My hands, numb and clumsy, work to ignite the fire. Sparks catch. Flames lick the air, and soon, the hearth radiates heat.

Turning my attention to Frankie, I peel away her waterlogged clothes, each piece a frozen layer clinging to skin that's alarmingly icy to the touch.

Her lips have taken on a deathly blue hue against the ghostly white of her complexion. Veins weave a glowing web beneath her translucent flesh. Her circulation can't maintain enough warmth in her core.

She stares up at me, unable to speak, seemingly in shock, and that alone sends my heart rate into a frenzy.

I'm losing her.

Her teeth chatter uncontrollably, her breathing terrifyingly shallow, struggling against the cold that constricts her airway.

Every second her skin remains exposed is a second too long.

I quickly strip my clothes and drape my nude body over hers, around her, sharing my warmth, skin to skin, covering us with every blanket and fur pelt in our possession.

She shakes viciously under me, each shiver more violent than the last. Her arms lay limp and unresponsive, heavy with the creeping numbness that threatens to immobilize her permanently.

I'm acutely aware of the gravity of her condition, every symptom a dire warning of the precipice upon which she teeters between life and death.

My body heat is all I can offer her. So I hold her close, trying to will my warmth into her, to stave off the chill that has taken residence inside her.

"I'm so sorry." I squeeze her tighter, my brow against hers, my hot breath falling over her face. "I told you it was safe, and you trusted me. I failed you."

The terrain, deceptively solid under the weight of the recent snowfall, gave way with little warning, betraying her.

I betrayed her.

"I-I-I..." Her eyes find mine, half-closed and glazed, barely conscious. "T-t-tru-sssst y-you."

"Shh." I kiss her brow, her frozen nose, her trembling lips. "Conserve your energy. I've got you."

Her breath, faint and uneven, is the only sound in the cabin, a fragile thread binding her to life.

I whisper encouragement, promises, anything to fight back the silence that tries to envelop us. The fire crackles, spreading its warmth, as I use every shred of my strength and will to ward off the grip of hypothermia.

It's a race against time, against nature itself, and I'm determined to win, to pull her back from the edge with nothing but sheer willpower and the heat of my body.

The blaze in the hearth grows hotter, but it's the warmth between us, the shared fight to stay alive, that will save her.

She. Will. Not. Die.

It's a long night.

My eyes remain open, my hopes quietly murmured into her ear. For hours, she drifts between awareness and unconsciousness, lethargic and unresponsive.

But as the light of dawn filters through the cracks of the cabin, her shivering recedes. Her strength returns just enough for her arms and legs to wrap around me, clinging to me even in sleep.

Slowly, color returns to her skin, her lips recovering their sexy pink glow. Her core temperature appears to have normalized. Still, I refuse to move.

My arms shake in their locked position, my elbows bracketing her head and bracing my weight just enough to trap our body heat without crushing her.

Her lashes fan upward, revealing those deep, stubborn eyes that have become my everything. Lying beneath me, wrapped in my arms, she exhales, close enough that I feel the soft return of her breath against my face.

Proof that we won another battle.

"You stayed." Her voice, barely above a whisper, carries her gratitude and her surprise that I didn't move from my protective position.

"All night," I confirm with a silent vow never to be anywhere else but with her.

A faint attempt at laughter escapes her, but it's laced with weakness. "It must be exhausting...playing my hero all the time."

The idea of being her hero fills me with ridiculous joy, even though deep down, I know it's not about being a hero. It's about being hers—entirely, fiercely, without reservation.

"Watching over you? That's the easy part." I drag my nose through her hair. "Watching you fight, never giving up, that's inspiring and terrifying."

"Just trying to keep you on your toes—literally. Are you planking?" She reaches between us and runs a hand along my engaged abs. "Jesus, Kody. No wonder you have an eight-pack. Come here."

"I'll crush you."

"Yes, please, be my weighted blanket."

Unable to deny her anything, I lower my weight into the cradle of her thighs and release a sigh.

"Thank you." She finds my hand in her hair, squeezing with a strength that refutes her brush with death. "For saving me, for being my warmth in the coldest night."

"Always." I drag my nose along the side of hers. "I'll face down the coldest nights, the deadliest storms, and the nastiest monsters just to see your smile for the rest of my days."

"Well, in that case, you owe me. I've worked up quite an appetite fighting for my life."

"You got it. The best cabin breakfast you've ever had." I glance at the rustic shelves of frozen pemmican that hover over an old, wobbly table. "Just give me a moment to thaw out the kitchen."

"That's not the appetite I'm talking about." She trails a tiny foot up the back of my leg. "You're as hungry as I am."

I'm painfully hard. Can't hide that from her. I've been fighting an erection all night. With her soft, sensual nudity pressed against me, it's a losing battle.

While my physical response to her is instinctive, I possess the self-control not to act on it.

No matter how badly I want her.

Our shared eye contact acknowledges the heat gathering between us, knitting us closer together. It's in these moments—her nestled in my arms, safe and starting to heal—that I feel it most. This undying need to protect her, to make her happy.

And to fuck her so thoroughly and for so long that neither of us can walk for days.

I'm a man with thorny edges and an unapproachable demeanor, but for Frankie, I'll be whatever she needs. Making her smile, ensuring her safety, and providing for her is not just what I do—it's who I am.

And right now, she needs to rest, not a hard, unpracticed cock rutting inside her.

"You need to empty your bladder," I say.

"Already did...the second I fell into the lake."

The lake.

A landscape, usually so familiar, concealed a danger that tried to take her from me forever. I fucked up, and I will never forgive myself.

Self-loathing takes fire in my stomach, and I find myself growling in her face. "You stopped breathing."

"I know." Her voice drops to a husky whisper. "That happens every time I look at you."

"You died."

"I lived." She grips my jaw. "Let it go. Forget this need to be my constant protector and give me what we both want. Be selfish with me. Wreck me. Ruin me. Show me the feral beast I fell in love with."

By the time she utters the last word, I'm thrusting against her, grinding my hips and fisting my hands in her hair.

There's so much life in this woman, and I want to devour it. I want to sink my teeth into her flesh and fill my mouth with the essence of her soul.

I grab her throat, making her gasp. "Open your fucking legs."

kodiak

TWENTY-ONE

The speed with which Frankie spreads her legs for me makes me harder than I've ever been in my life.

With a fist in her hair, I yank her head back and bury my face in the small moons of her breasts, lavishing them, scraping them with my teeth. Christ, I love her nipples, the way they swell and harden against the curl of my tongue.

I should be hydrating her, feeding her, making her rest, but it's too late for that. I spent the night between her naked thighs, and fuck me, I only have so much restraint.

My hands span the entire circumference of her rib cage as I clutch her to me and devour her chest like an animal.

She arches and moans in my grip, such a tiny creature with fierce, unending energy. Scratching and groping, she touches me everywhere. But when her palms skim down my hips and seek out my erection, I capture her arms and trap them above her head.

"Relax," I rasp.

She sighs.

Now where was I?

Biting her round, perky tits, I move from one to the other, then on to her armpits. I ravish the sensitive skin there, inhaling her pheromones and rubbing my face in those sweet hollows under each arm until she's squirming and giggling uncontrollably.

As I return to her nipples, her eyes follow mine, lips parted and panting heavily.

So beautiful. So inconceivably precious.

I frame her stunning face with my hands and kiss her madly, aggressively, unleashing the feral man that makes her so fucking wet.

She lowers her arms, her fingers tiptoeing down my restless, grinding body, on the hunt for my cock again.

Impatient, greedy hellion.

I shift my hips out of her reach. "Hands where I can see them."

Slowly, she flattens them over my mouth, her lips struggling to contain the laughter glinting in her emerald eyes.

I sink my teeth into her fingers.

"Ow!" She yelps with glee and grips my neck. "Why can't I touch you? You never let me near—"

"Because I'll come, woman. Not gonna last the way it is. This first time? It's just a practice run. It doesn't count toward my overall performance."

"You guys and your egos. Just put it in me already."

I grab her throat and pin her to the floor. "I give the orders."

Her eyes glimmer, her voice a strangled whisper. "There you are."

"Here I am." I thrust against her thigh, releasing her neck. "Arms at your sides. Hold onto the bedding."

She obeys, lying back on the furs, softly panting, hands balling in the pelts, and legs falling open.

The sight explodes my heart. Not just my heart. I feel her everywhere, pulsing, igniting, spinning me off balance at the thought of sinking into her warm, tight body.

I sit back on my heels and stare at her openly, intrusively, the way I've always wanted.

Jesus Christ, I have no words. She's a vision. A beautiful, sparkling mirage in a cold, dead place. She doesn't belong here.

But I do. I belong with her.

My hands shake as I run them over the faded hickeys Leo left on her thighs, stroking the toned muscle down to her calves and the arches of her delicate feet.

Her eyes never leave mine as I kiss her knee, then the other. Shifting forward, I drag my tongue across her flat stomach. It quivers beneath my licks. She laughs. Then she whimpers as I taste the dip of her waist.

She threads her fingers through the fur of the bedding, gripping, pulling, obeying my command.

I watch her watch me as I kiss her knuckles, her little fists. I pry them free and lick her fingers before placing them between her legs. Over her glistening pussy.

"Touch yourself." I press my nose there, between her curling digits, deep within her soaked folds, inhaling her intoxicating scent.

Outside, everything is fatal. Everything dies. But in here, with our eyes locked and our souls touching, we're eternal.

I glide my mouth along the sinuous lines of her body, tasting her, marking her, leaving a fresh trail of hickeys for my brother to find.

When I reach her mouth, I part her lips with my tongue. Grip her waist. Sink my fingers into the curves of her ass and grind my cock against the hand between her legs.

"Touch me." I kiss her hungrily, trapping her with my weight, my erection massive and indecent between us.

The instant she holds my dick in her soft hands, my pulse detonates into a violent throbbing. Her grip feels so small around me, her fingers unable to fully close.

Yet she can overpower me with just a few rigorous strokes.

I lift my hips just enough to nudge the tip against her warm, wet opening.

Then I stare into her eyes. "In my dreams, I've already had you a million times over."

"If fate were kinder, if it were a little less frozen, we could've been doing this every day."

"Less frozen?"

"Yeah." She teases her grip along my shaft, making me groan. "If we were stranded on a desert island instead of the middle of the Arctic, we would've spent the past five months lounging in the sun, eating coconuts, and fucking like rabbits." She squeezes the base of my cock. "I'm ready, Kody. Give it to me. Hard and fast. Remember, this is just the practice run. We have all day."

"We have the rest of our lives." I wrap my hand around hers, adjusting the angle, shaking with restraint. "I just want to outlast Leo's first time with you."

"Well, then...two thrusts should do it."

"Really?"

Her eyes sparkle.

"You're teasing me." I nip at her jaw. "Payback is hell."

With a flex of my hips, I push into her an inch. Just enough to watch her eyes widen, to hear her gasp.

Or is that me gasping?

Another inch, and I lose the ability to breathe.

This is what death feels like. No more cold. No more pain. Just pure, red-hot rapture.

Her cunt is an inferno, dripping molten honey. The clamping tightness, the sucking heat, the unholy pleasure—it's better than anything I could imagine. Better than any way I've tried to console myself over the years.

Her breath quivers against my throat, her fingers digging into my flexing ass as I rock my hips in short, assertive strokes, working myself deeper, stretching her, sinking, withdrawing, digging.

Christ, she's clenching, pushing me out.

"Let me in, woman."

"Too big." She whimpers.

"Too fucking small."

I can barely fit halfway, but holy fuck, I've died and gone to heaven. My nerve endings fizzle. My blood roars, and my vision flashes with endless sunrises.

Her sharp nails claw my scarred back, shredding my fucking soul. As damaged as I am, she'll stitch me up and make me whole again.

"Harder." She presses her pelvis against mine. "You won't hurt me."

With an arm braced beside her head and the other hooked under her knee, I widen her thighs and thrust deeper.

"Fuck!" I feel her opening for me, tugging at my

cock, sucking me all the way in.

And that fast, a familiar heat gathers at the base of my spine. My balls tighten. My pulse rushes, and my body takes over, driving me toward the edge.

"Dammit, Frankie. I'm close."

"Come inside me." She holds my gaze, panting with pleasure-stricken tears in her eyes. "I want to watch."

My hips thrust wildly, urgently, hammering with unwavering focus. I fuck her so hard I fear I'll break her from the force of it. But she gives it back just as ferociously, meeting me thrust for thrust with her heels digging into my ass.

My hands find her face, fingers weaving into her hair, pulling her lips to mine. The moment our mouths collide, fire ignites, consuming us in a blaze of desire that swallows all thought, all reason.

Her tongue laps against mine as I angle her head and lick her gasping mouth, breathlessly pouring every unspoken emotion into our wild, messy kisses.

"I'm gonna come." Her head falls back on a moan. "Oh, fuck, Kody."

I shove a thumb past her lips, pressing down on her tongue, handling her roughly, dominating her the way we both love. Then I replace my hand with my mouth and hold her tighter. Kiss her deeper. Fuck her harder. Feel her clenching, swelling, tensing.

"Right now. Come on my fat cock." Circling my hips, I hit a spot.

The right spot.

Eyes leveled on mine, she convulses around me, trembling desperately as an orgasm shatters through her. Wetness splashes with my thrusts, squelching, leaking over my balls.

I slam a hand into the bedding beside her, tunneling in and out, pounding deep and slow, fucking her into the floor.

"Frankie." My groans vent from somewhere deep, ripping past my throat as my mind splinters, my veins burst, and my body releases twenty-five years of repressed voracity.

I erupt with the potency of a volcano, spurting, flooding, filling her with what feels like gallons of come.

My breath whistles past clenched teeth, molten lava sloshing through my circulation. I twitch inside her, my hips still jerking, my cock refusing to calm down.

I want to feel her come again. Want to see her fall apart in every position.

With a growl, I duck my head, bite her lips, and lick the salted sweat from her neck.

The taste of her jumpstarts another hunger. My grip tightens in her hair, demanding her to feel what I feel, to be as lost in this as I am.

Her moan against my lips is all the answer I need, pushing me to deepen the kiss, exploring, claiming, giving, and taking in equal measure.

She's all around me, in the very air, seeping into my pores and reshaping everything inside. Our breaths heave as one, hearts racing in unison. It's a merging of souls, a declaration made without words, a promise of more, of everything.

I'm overwhelmed by her—by her scent, her taste, the feel of her heat sheathing my spent cock. We're a single entity of raw need, profound connection, and an unyielding desire to make this moment last forever.

When we finally surface, gasping for oxygen, our brows rest together, our exhales loud and heavy. The look in her dazed eyes is one of wonder, matched by the storm of emotions raging through me.

This union, this perfect mating, it's not just sex. It's

a fire, an undying flame that burns brightly, lighting up the darkest, coldest corners of our lives.

It's the beginning of everything.

Reluctantly, I withdraw from her body and reach for a nearby canteen of water.

"Drink." I hold it to her swollen lips.

"How was that your first time?" She gulps down the hydrating fluid and passes it back. "Jesus, I'm in trouble. Your sexual energy is in a league of its own."

"That right?"

"Yeah, Kody. That was incredible. Mind-blowing. I'm ready to go again."

"You need to eat." I finish off the canteen, thinking about all the protein I can give her the next time I fuck her throat.

"I need…" She rises to her knees and climbs over me, purring like a kitten. "You."

"The fire is low." I capture her wrist, stopping her from tormenting my eager cock. "You'll get cold."

"I'm burning up." She straddles my raging hard-on, trapping it against my stomach as she leans in. "How can I distract you away from this need to coddle me?"

"You cannot."

Challenge flares in her eyes, and her lips curve in a wicked grin.

Oh, fuck. That look. I'm certain it razed every man in her past.

Straightening, she folds her arms above her head and rocks her hips in a sensual slide. Rubbing her soaked slit along the length of my cock. Stroking me with the sweet flesh of her cunt. Shuddering over me. And grinning.

That diabolical goddamn smile. She's fucking arresting.

"Stop, woman." My hands fly to her hips, my jaw

opening with a soundless gasp. "Have mercy."

"You're not done with me."

"I'll never be done with you."

Damn me to hell.

I grip her thighs and wrench them apart, watching her leak all over me. My heartbeat sprints. My breath comes faster. I try to temper my body's responses to her, to keep things under control, but my God, she's devastating.

With my hands holding her open, I glide my thumbs along the velvety edges of her pussy. The soft, pink, juicy parts, drenched with our combined come. As I knead the hooded bud, she jerks and undulates, riding the underside of my straining erection.

The choking lust in my throat expels on a groan. "Put me in."

Biting her lip, she lifts my hard length from my stomach and angles it toward her entrance. Her fingers, soft and electric, trace the thick veins and broad head before feeding it into the tight clasp of her body.

My head tilts back, jaw clenching, and abdomen tightening beneath her as she slowly lowers, inch by inch, until fully seated.

"Fuck." I throb inside her, the pleasure unbearable. "You feel so fucking good, Frankie."

"You do, too."

When she moves, it's a curl of seductive motion, an erotic roll of her hips as she stares into my eyes, and I feel it—the electric current that crackles between us.

This is more than desire. It's a primal, magnetic pull. A living, ravenous thing that grows with every kiss, every thrust, guiding our movements and aligning us perfectly—where our mouths meet, where our hands intertwine, and where I'm buried so deep as her heat pulses and tightens around me.

Every shared look inflames it further. Every touch sends shockwaves through our connection.

We fuck for hours, pushing the boundaries of our energy and stopping only for quick breaks to hydrate and eat.

I'm lost in the seduction of her body, in the way she matches my intensity, stroke for stroke, the push and pull, the clash of wills and desires that melds us so perfectly together.

This raw, carnal energy is as old as time yet uniquely ours. Every orgasm leaves us reeling, satiated, yet ever hungry and forever altered. Forever entwined.

Late into the night, she collapses on my chest, boneless and panting. I'm so relaxed beneath her, I couldn't move her if I wanted to.

I've never known such peace. Such soul-deep joy.

How often have I sat in this barren, one-room cabin alone, missing my brothers, aching for company, for affection, for anything that might soothe my loneliness?

Every hunting season, from the moment I could shoot a crossbow, has seen me here.

Not once did I imagine losing my virginity in this place.

Now I want to lie here forever, just like this, with Frankie in my arms. Would it be so terrible if we stayed a week? Or even just one more day?

A pinching stab of guilt arrives with the thought.

I know how it feels to sit in that house of ghosts and wait for Frankie and my brother to return to me.

A week felt like a lifetime.

Leo has already endured two weeks of waiting, and it'll take us another two weeks to hike back.

She stirs on my chest. "What about the moose?"

"It got away."

"Oh, no." Her sultry tone doesn't hold a hint of regret. "I kept you from hunting."

"Fuck that. You gave me the best day of my life. When we escape..." I kiss her head, tucking her close. "I'm going to find you the biggest bed in the most luxurious hotel and fuck you until you tire of me."

"I don't need a bed or a hotel. I just need you and Leo. Forever. Because I'll never tire of you."

"Go to sleep. We'll start our journey back to him tomorrow."

kodiak

TWENTY-TWO

Two weeks later, Frankie and I crest an icy slope and stare out at the vast emptiness of the landscape.

As far as the eye can see in every direction, nothing exists but her and me.

My senses, however, tell me differently.

It's an instinct honed by years of navigating this unforgiving terrain. The distinct outline of the jagged ridge to our right, the way the ground slopes gently downward on our left, the slight change in the snow's consistency underfoot, the angle of the wind, the shift in the scents on the breeze—all of this tells me we're nearing familiar territory.

Beside me, she tucks her gloved hand in mine and tilts her beautiful face heavenward, absorbing the pastel shades of blue and pink. "The sky is glowing."

Not with snow or stars or northern lights. It shines with the promise of daylight.

"The days will grow longer going forward."

"And warmer." She smiles, head tipped back, watching the transformation.

As the rare arctic sunlight breaks through the cloud cover, it casts a celestial glow over everything it touches. Frankie is the centerpiece of this natural illumination.

The rays catch in her red hair, setting it ablaze with hues of gold and copper. Her green eyes, vibrant against the snow's glare, sparkle with a luminance that reflects her inner resilience. Her cheeks, kissed by the cold, carry a natural blush that complements her vivid eyes and fiery hair.

Even after an arduous thirty-mile hike through ice and snow, her beauty remains untarnished. She embodies the raw, untouched allure of the Arctic— wild, breathtaking, and utterly authentic.

She's impossibly, unreasonably captivating.

"I wonder if Leo is staring at the sky right now, feeling its warmth." She steals a peek at me.

"You can ask him in a few hours."

"Really? We're that close?"

"Close your eyes and listen."

"Okay." She stands taller, adjusts her pack, and shuts her eyes.

"What do you hear?"

The usual silence of the tundra, broken only by the crunch of our boots and the occasional distant crack of shifting ice, is now punctuated by a soft, consistent whisper in the distance. I have exceptional hearing, but if she focuses hard enough, she'll hear it, too.

Her eyes pop open. "The river."

"Good girl."

Partially frozen over, it's a sound that has guided me back on the darkest nights.

We still have miles to go, but I sense the familiarity

of our surroundings tightening its grip around me, pulling my aching body forward.

As we trek onward, my legs feel leaden. The desire to simply stop, to collapse into the snow, wraps around my bones. My back aches from the burden of our supplies and the added weight of the pemmican. The constant pressure has become as familiar as my heartbeat. And the cold has seeped so deep that no amount of movement will shake it off.

Frankie's ability to keep up astounds me, though her usual brisk pace has been replaced with a plodding stride, and the way she hunches under her pack announces the state of her fatigue.

The closer we get to the cabin, the lighter my chest feels. Not just at the thought of providing her with warmth and rest, but at the anticipation of seeing my brother, of witnessing the relief on his face. I imagine him pacing the empty rooms, casting anxious glances out the windows.

"Leo's probably wondering if we ran away together." I squint at the northern hills, my voice rough with tiredness.

"Because we have so many places to go." She chuckles, gesturing at the nothingness surrounding us. "More likely he's worried we've been eaten by a family of bears."

"Just one bear." I flash my teeth.

"Yeah, I'm wearing his bite marks all over my body."

Despite the cold and exhaustion, my cock stirs. "I won't apologize for that."

"Don't you dare."

We share a look charged with tension and energy. A deep bond has formed between us. We were close before, but this journey, the reliance on each other for morale and survival, and the sex…Goddamn, the sex. The past month has brought us closer than I ever thought possible.

But I haven't been inside her nearly as much as I hoped.

She rode my cock once on the journey back. A quick fuck in the tent with our clothes on. It was so painfully cold. We could barely move from sheer exhaustion, but we needed the connection, the intimacy, to get us through the rest of the trip.

"Leo better have that fire roaring." I envision the warmth that awaits us, the comfort of family. "First thing I'm doing is stripping all this gear and face-planting by the hearth. For a week."

"I'm claiming the first cup of whatever hot drink he's managed to concoct. I hope there's still coffee."

"How about spiked coffee?"

"If only we had alcohol."

"I might have a bottle of vodka stashed away."

"Shut up!" She gasps and shoves me. "You said we ran out!"

"I was saving it." I slow to a stop, cocking my head. "Look."

She follows my gaze to the multitude of tracks stitched into the snow. "What in the world?"

The sheer volume of crisscrossing trails is jaw-dropping. Everywhere we look, the land shows signs of passage. Back and forth, side to side, the area is well-traveled, the snow compacted from countless journeys.

She crouches beside a large impression in the ground. "Is it a migration trail for a herd of animals?"

"No." I sigh. "Just one animal."

"One…?" Her eyes narrow, scanning the tracks, her voice dropping with realization. "Oh, no."

Oh, yes. The well-worn route, made by the repetitive tread of boots and press of the snow machine, reveals precisely how Leo spent his time alone.

He's been here daily, perhaps multiple times each day, keeping watch for us. The numerous grooves and indentations, evidence of hundreds of passes from boots and machinery, show his relentless commitment, his undying vigilance.

His neurotic obsession.

"This hurts my heart." She rises, her gaze raking across the bleak stretch of hills to the North. "I'm surprised he's not here now."

"These are new." I gesture at a fresh path of boot imprints. "He was here this morning."

The older tracks were made by ski runners. The snow machine hasn't been here in a while. He must've run out of fuel.

Yet he kept coming, his constant presence in this spot obvious in the worn snow, the paths beaten down by tireless pacing. In every footprint, I feel his concern, his anticipation, and his unwavering resolve to be here the moment we emerge.

I feel it because I went through the same damn thing when he and Frankie retrieved the coal.

It's a symptom of the bond that tethers us.

As we resume walking, a figure materializes on the horizon, a distinct shape against the white hills.

Leo.

He charges down a path so deeply etched into the snow it might as well be part of the landscape.

Instantly, Frankie's stance shifts from exhaustion to action, a spontaneous release of energy. With an excited squeal that pierces the frosty air, she takes off running.

He quickens his pace, eating up the distance with his long legs, a far more controlled gait than her reckless, full-on sprint. She shrugs off her pack and rifle, dropping them mid-stride, and they meet in a crash of bodies, their embrace a desperate tangle of arms.

I hang back, watching them with a flood of warmth in my chest.

The chill of our surroundings dims in the heat of their reunion, their famished kisses, creating an ephemeral bubble of happiness.

When he lifts his head and finds my eyes, I approach them slowly, soaking in the silent laughter and shared joy emanating from them.

I need to tell him she died on my watch, that I almost broke my promise and didn't bring her back to him.

But not now. Not in this moment of perfect relief as I join their embrace.

His arms envelop me, thawing the cold that settled in my bones and softening the aches from the long journey.

With Frankie trapped between us, I rest my nose in his braided hair. He smells as familiar to me as my own skin. But beneath the usual woodsmoke and mechanic oil, there's something new. I sniff him again.

Jet fuel.

"You started the plane." I lean back, meeting his mismatched eyes. "Did you hot-wire it or find the key?"

"Both, actually." He perches his chin on her head, grinning. "I bypassed the ignition, got it running, and decided to roll it forward a few inches..."

"No." My eyebrows shoot upward.

"Yeah. The key was under one of the tires."

"Beneath its wings..." Frankie stares up at us. "Lie

the answers. So what did he do? Park the plane and physically push it over the key?"

"Yep." He kisses her brow. "The gauges show full fuel, and comms appear to work."

"But we're out of range." Her lips curve down.

"Unless another aircraft flies over." He looks at me. "The other one never returned."

It's been six weeks. It's not coming back.

"How about a hot shower and a meal?" Leo hauls my pack off my back, giving me instant, blissful relief. As he shoulders the weight, his eyes fall on her. "Want a piggyback ride?"

"Nope. I have a few more miles left in me." She bends and stretches her legs. "Kody might need a lift, though."

With a grunt, I snatch her pack off the ground and give her ass a hard swat. "Let's go."

On the hike back, Leo doesn't press us with questions. But she senses his need for answers and fills the silence with every detail of our one-month journey.

She recounts the long, frigid nights we spent huddled in our tent and doesn't hold back on her disdain for outdoor bathroom breaks, which never got easier for her.

She mentions my nightmare, addressing her concerns about it. Then she moves on to the moose I tracked, which led us across the frozen lake.

Leo, usually a ball of tension, walks quietly at her side, his demeanor calm, attentively listening.

It's her retelling of the plunge into the ice-cold lake that brings him to an abrupt stop.

Her voice trembles as she describes the terror of falling through the ice, the bone-chilling cold, and the struggle to reach the surface.

"I remember being trapped under the ice, then...nothing." She shrugs. "There's this huge hole of nothingness in my memory. Not a tunnel. No bright lights. No angels or demons or anything. One minute, I was in the water, and the next, I was lying beneath Kody on solid ground."

Leo's gaze slams into mine, demanding answers.

"Her heart stopped." I run a hand down her arm, holding his stark stare. "I performed CPR."

His reaction shocks me. The brother, who's always quick to anger, remains stoic, his expression thoughtful.

She jumps in, detailing how my prompt intervention brought her back from the brink twice. First from drowning. Then from hypothermia.

There's a new maturity in his silence, a depth to his calm that wasn't there before. He absorbs every word, nodding at times, his face betraying nothing of the turmoil he must feel hearing about her death.

When she finishes, the silence stretches between us.

"I'm glad you're both safe." His gaze lingers on her before shifting to me. "Thank you for bringing her back."

To me.

Those two words hover at the end, but he doesn't say them. With regard to Frankie, there's no more *me* or *mine.*

There's only *us.*

Ours.

He knows I fucked her, and his ability to embrace that without explosion marks a new chapter for us. But I know he has questions, concerns about how he fits in this inexperienced, unexplored dynamic and what it looks like going forward.

As he searches my eyes, I open my expression and let him in. I let him see everything.

My connection with her has evolved and deepened. Sex was just one part of it. I'm certain he noticed the change the second he saw me. I'm not the only one who's grown and matured over the past month. I feel different. Lighter. More complete. He sees it in my eyes, in the set of my shoulders, in the twitch of my lips.

He growls at that but says nothing.

There are things to discuss, details to share, boundaries to establish, but I'll let him initiate that conversation when he's ready.

"You guys are doing the thing again." Frankie resumes walking.

He gives me a final look and catches up with her, entwining their hands. "What thing, love?"

"The silent conversation with your eyes." Keeping her gaze forward, she holds out her other hand for me. "Sometimes I feel like a third wheel in your bromance."

I grip her offered hand, matching their strides. "Every look shared between us whispers your name, woman."

"Mm-hmm." She presses her lips together, but the corners pull upward.

"You're not the third wheel." Leo bends in, laying it on thick. "You're the heart that keeps us breathing."

I narrow my eyes at him. "By breathing, he means panting."

She bursts out laughing.

The final miles feel both interminable and fleeting, each step bringing us closer to the end of our journey. When we finally reach the door of the cabin, I pause, letting the significance of the past month wash over me.

I don't intend to ever return to that hunting cabin, but whenever I think back on it, it will no longer be a place of terrible loneliness in my mind. I'll remember it as a harbor of survival, rebirth, discovery, and love.

Sharing a look with the two people who are my future, we step over the threshold together, ready to face what comes next.

kodiak

TWENTY-THREE

After a hot shower and a hard sleep that feels too long and not long enough, I stir from the warmth of the hearth.

The fire has dwindled to embers, but the residual heat lingers.

Frankie lies nestled against me, her breaths even and calm in sleep. Leo, however, slipped out of our embrace at some point.

I lift my head, but my search is brief. He sits on the floor across the room, back against the wall, legs bent, his gaze fixed on us.

Pushing myself up, I breeze past him with a nod and navigate the cabin's cold, sparse interior toward the armory. Hidden inside one of my old quivers is a bottle of cherry vodka, my last project before our ingredients ran out. Retrieving it feels like unearthing a piece of the past meant for this moment.

Returning to Leo, I join him on the floor and set the bottle between us. We drink in silence, the kind that only brothers who've shared lifetimes of unspoken words can appreciate.

Yet, amid this comfort, the need to clear the air intensifies.

"I missed you." It's a simple truth, as easy to voice as breathing.

His response comes with a half-smile. "We've been apart for longer stretches. Every time you went hunting, it felt like you were gone for months."

"It was different this time. Everything feels more dangerous and desperate."

He nods, his gaze fastened on her. "Everything is changing."

"So are we." I watch the way he studies her peaceful form. "Our relationship has shifted, including our relationship with her, in a positive direction." I tilt my head. "I know this is new, and we're still adjusting, but I'm struggling to read you. What are you thinking?"

"I don't know, man." His voice lowers, a confessional tone creeping in. "While you both were gone, I went through hell. Anger, worry, jealousy—it all got twisted up in my head. Every single day, I thought about setting out after you, following your tracks in the snow."

"But you didn't."

"I made it to that point on the hill every day, the one where you can see for miles. And every day, I stopped myself. I paced back and forth, fighting with everything inside me." A sigh escapes him. "But I calmed down, every time. Because I knew. I knew you would take care of her. You promised me you'd bring her back safe, and despite all the shit snarling in my head, I trust you."

The glow from the dwindling fire casts shadows on

his face, giving his admission a stark intimacy. "So I went back to the cabin, slept on it, and the next day, I'd find myself back at that spot, pacing again. That's why the snow there is so worn down. It became my stopping point, my waiting spot...my boundary I wouldn't cross." He meets my gaze, his eyes clearer now than I've ever seen them. "As the days passed, I grew calmer, more accepting. I reached a point where nothing else mattered but seeing you both return to me. It didn't matter what happened between you out there, how close you became, how often you were fucking her, or if you were stealing her heart away...as long as you came back to me, happy and healthy."

"Leo, I..." My throat tightens. "I didn't steal her heart. I couldn't even if I tried. She fucking loves you."

"Didn't stop me from thinking it." He shrugs, but the tension in his shoulders has lifted. "I told you to bring her back. And you did. That's all I needed."

The simplicity of his statement, the trust he placed in me, adds a new layer to the bond between us.

In the quiet that follows, we sit side by side, passing the vodka and watching over her as she sleeps.

His admission not only reveals the strength of his feelings for her and her happiness but also our faith in each other.

No matter what happens, the three of us are bound by something stronger than circumstance and more powerful than the doubts and fears that might seek to divide us.

"This is fucking good." He tips back the bottle, his throat moving with a deep swallow, and passes it to me. "Might be your best batch yet."

"Thank you." I take another drink, savoring the hints of cherry that Frankie inspired. "Thank you for waiting, for trusting me."

His nod is slow, thoughtful. "How do you see this working? With all of us together?"

I consider his question, the complexities in it. "I don't have the answers. But I know that what we have here, what's left of our family, is stronger because she's part of it. She needs us both as much as we need her."

"And you're okay with sharing...everything?"

"Everything."

He looks back at her, then at me, a sense of resolve settling over him.

Our conversation meanders, questions about the journey, her fall into the lake, and how we'll navigate the future. But underlying every word is our commitment to each other. We drink to that commitment, to the future, uncertain but faced together.

As she begins to stir beneath the blankets, our voices trail off. The way he stares at her, the longing in his eyes is unmistakable, a silent echo of my own feelings.

The sound of a delicate yawn drifts from the bed, followed by her drowsy voice. "Are you drinking without me?"

"She was craving spiked coffee," I say, too low for her to hear. "Any beans left?"

He shakes his head, a small smile breaking through.

Rising to his feet, he sheds his clothes. Then, stark nude and unabashedly hard, he plucks the bottle from my hand, takes a mouthful, but doesn't swallow.

With the confidence befitting a lion, he prowls across the room, climbs over her on the mattress, and pushes aside blankets, garments, everything in his way.

She gives him a sleepy smile and twines her arms around his neck.

He glides her legs around his hips and kisses her, letting the vodka trickle into her mouth. As she laughs and moans, he kisses her deeply and fucks her slowly just like that, one hand in her hair and the other stroking her sensual body.

I lean my head back against the wall, content to watch her sigh and writhe beneath him.

When they climax together, I don't feel like an outsider. My heart is with them, brimming with our combined happiness. It reaffirms my belief that our lives will be like this forever.

The scent of the earth, overwhelming and pungent, invades my senses as I step out of the old pickup truck.

I paid a guy twice the truck's value to borrow it for a couple of hours so that I could drive from one end of buttfuck nowhere to the other.

"Wow...okay." Sirena joins me on the dirt driveway in a snow-frosted field, surrounded by mountains, untouched wilderness, and the icy waters of the Prince William Sound. "It's pretty here."

I hadn't noticed.

The stillness is oppressive, broken only by the wind, which insists on smearing a fine mist across the lenses of my designer sunglasses.

The quaint little port town of Whittier, Alaska, isn't a town. It's a fourteen-story building on a harbor.

With a population of 250, nearly all its residents live under the same roof, which also contains the post office, church, laundromat, health clinic, and general store.

Evidently, one of the few residents who doesn't live in the complex happens to be the person I'm looking for.

Alvis Duncan.

A name buried within the walls of my childhood home, hidden among flight logs, a piece of a puzzle I didn't know I was assembling.

Sirena found him easy enough.

"That it?" I remove my shades and squint at a small airplane hangar perched on the edge of the field where the wilderness begins its reign.

"Yep." She proceeds to the modest house beside it and knocks on the door.

My breath forms clouds in the cold air as I approach the hangar, its open doors beckoning me inside. The wind follows me in, passing through me like a frozen ghost, whispering tales of the past.

The day my parents died, their flight departed from the Whittier airstrip not far from here. I don't know how Alvis Duncan is connected to that. He refused to tell us anything over the phone. The moment Sirena mentioned the flight logs, he disconnected the call.

That alone means he knows something.

With no other option, I'm forced to confront this situation in person, further delaying my search for Frankie.

Inside the hangar, a dismantled bush plane reveals the innards of a mechanic's life. Tools of the trade scatter the space, including a forklift and flatbed truck.

No Turbo Beaver.

Not that I expected to see it here. It's been twenty-five years since the last flight was logged.

I loosen my tie and tug at the cuffs of my sleeves,

distinctly out of place. My expensive shoes shine against the dusty ground, the fabric of my tailored jacket fluttering in the grease-scented breeze.

Wealth is my cloak, shielding me from worlds like this. Yet here I stand, surrounded by simplicity and purpose. It's unfamiliar, this proximity to manual labor and the grit of modest living.

But there are answers here.

My heart races at the thought of uncovering something, anything that could lead me to Frankie. The absence of clues has been crushing. I'm caught in a holding pattern where sleep evades me, and desperation constricts my chest.

With every passing day, the trail goes colder. Staler. Each tick of the clock is a drip of acid on the steel of my resolve, corroding layers of calm.

But as I pace through the hangar, I know she's not the reason I'm here.

My restless steps stir up a cloud of dust that clings to my shoes and takes me deeper into a world far removed from my own. But I'm driven by a need to understand my family's connection to this place.

The tread of footsteps approaches, drawing my focus.

Sirena strides in with a rugged-looking man in his fifties, his face etched with the deep creases of a life spent outdoors. A gray beard drapes over his chest, and his denim overalls struggle to contain his ample belly.

Her investigation into Alvis Duncan's background revealed nothing out of the ordinary. He's lived on this property his entire life, been married for thirty years, and earns his living doing mechanic work on small aircraft.

But he knows something.

"This is my employer, Monty Novak." She motions at me. "Like I said on the phone, we're looking for a missing person, and your name showed up on some old flight logs."

Alvis greets me with a wary look, the kind that's seen too much yet expects more.

"Thank you for meeting with us." I grip his calloused hand in a brief shake.

"Told you I don't know nothing."

I remove two photographs from my breast pocket and hold up the first one. "Do you know this man?"

He glances at the stoic image of my father. "Never met him."

"Look again. This is Rurik Strakh. He died twenty-five years ago."

Glancing away, he mumbles, "I know the name."

"How?"

"You with the police? The FBI?"

"No." My pulse quickens. "Rurik was my father. How do you know him?"

"I don't. But he used to send fancy people dressed like you." He makes a whistling sound. "Must've been thirty years ago when the first man showed up. Said he worked for Rurik Strakh and would pay me good money to keep a log of the comings and goings of his plane."

"A Turbo Beaver." I rattle off the tail number by memory.

"Yeah. That's it."

"Where did it go when it left here? Who was on board?"

"Can't say."

"Can't say or won't say?" My hands twitch to reach out and strangle the answers from him.

His eyes dart to the exit, his breaths growing

shallow, like he's running out of air.

"Won't say," I answer for him.

Rurik Strakh kept some dangerous men on his payroll. Ex-Russian military. Armed escorts. Mobsters. Hitmen.

It's safe to assume these hired guns put the fear of God in poor Alvis Duncan. If Rurik built an off-grid safe house with regular supply runs and staff to maintain it, he wouldn't want anyone to know its location.

So why keep a flight log?

Why involve Alvis at all?

"These men…" I snag his gaze and hold it steady. "If they threatened you to keep your mouth shut, none of that matters now. They no longer work for my father. He's dead. I'm here on unrelated business."

"You're his son. No offense, but I didn't like his fancy, uptight men. And I don't like you much, neither."

My anger crackles, a live wire sparking and snapping as I shove a finger at his chest. "Listen to me, you redneck fuck—"

"Excuse us for a minute." Sirena wedges between us and forces me backward with a loud glare and a hushed voice. "You're not helping. Can you give me a minute with him, please?"

I take a deep breath, attempting to quell the storm.

She plasters on a sweet smile and turns back to Alvis. "We're not investigating you, Mr. Duncan. We're trying to find Monty's missing wife."

His lips purse. "Sorry to hear that."

"You might be able to help us find her." She taps on her phone screen and shows him a photo of Frankie in a cocktail dress. "Have you seen her?"

"No." He peers at the image a little too closely for my liking. "I see why you're trying to find her."

Gritting my teeth, I flip Sirena's phone around so he can't ogle my wife. "Who was the pilot? What was his destination?"

He stares at me, his eyes reflecting the murky depths of my father's grip. Whatever he's hiding, I'm not above beating it out of him.

"What about this woman?" Sirena pulls the crinkling photo of Kaya from my fist.

With one phone call, Sirena was able to locate Alvis Duncan. Finding Kaya proves more challenging.

When Kaya left Kodiak Island twenty-three years ago, she went to Utqiagvik, Alaska, according to state licensing records. But no one in the town remembers her. It's like she vanished into thin air.

Just like Frankie.

Except no one reported Kaya missing. With no living relatives, I was the only person she had left, and I let her go.

Maybe she's not missing. But after a week of digging, Sirena is still at square one, without a single lead on Kaya's whereabouts.

"This is Kaya Knowles." She shows him the photo. "It's a very old picture. She's forty-six now."

"Never seen her." His gaze shifts to me. "You lost this one, too? Maybe they don't want to be found."

This motherfucker is begging for a broken face.

Sensing my rising temper, Sirena presses Kaya's photo against my chest and waits for me to take it. When I snatch it back, she returns to Alvis. "Can you tell us about the men Rurik Strakh sent? What did they want?"

"I kept the flight logs. They collected them, and I got paid for doing it. Easy work." He shrugs. "Then about ten or fifteen years ago, they stopped collecting those logs."

Ten or fifteen years? My father has been dead for twenty.

"Which is it?" I ask. "Ten or fifteen years?"

"Don't know. I got a bad memory." He scratches his beard, studying me. "But I still keep those logs."

My breath stills. "The plane is still coming and going?"

"Look, I don't want any trouble."

"Neither do we." Sirena steps toward him, her demeanor soft and coaxing. "Like Monty said, those men are gone. I know they told you not to share this information, but Monty's wife..." She opens her phone and puts Frankie's picture in his face again. "This sweet, beautiful woman is a nurse. Her name is Frankie Novak, and she's pregnant. Due in the next month or so. We think she's in trouble. She and the baby. So you understand our urgency in finding her."

He examines the photo, looking conflicted. Christ, she almost has him.

"Those logs you're still keeping..." She touches his arm, sidling closer. "Can I just take a peek? It could save their lives, her and the baby."

His silence is deafening, thundering in my ears.

Then, after an agonizing eternity, he blows out a breath and walks toward the door.

I'm about to blow a gasket until he stops at a workbench and opens the top drawer on the right.

"I've been helping a man for twenty-five years," he starts, his voice rough. "A man who lives by his own rules, off-grid, no way to contact the outside world. His only lifeline is that Turbo Beaver. He flies in and out of here, getting supplies. Dependable. Like clockwork. Until he wasn't."

"My father's Turbo Beaver?" I float toward him,

barely breathing, gripped by the story.

"Yes. Same aircraft. It's been completely overhauled over the years with upgrades, a new engine, and modern avionics."

"You did the work on that?"

"That's right. I do all the maintenance while he gathers his supplies. He's got a yacht in Whittier harbor. Takes it to catch fish and visit other port towns. I don't know where he goes, to be honest. But he's always on time. Tells me when he's flying in, when he's returning on the yacht. He was supposed to return before winter, but he missed his last supply run." A furrow of concern creases his brow. "That's not like him. Something's wrong."

A missing bush pilot. Not uncommon. Weather conditions, mechanical failures, wildlife encounters, sickness—there are numerous risks in living off-grid.

But this isn't just any bush pilot. He likely worked for my father, lived at the safe house, and still resides there, maintaining it.

Alvis retrieves a logbook from the drawer, the pages worn and yellowed. As he flips through them, my heart pounds, a sense of foreboding growing with each turn. Then he stops, pointing to an entry. The last one.

Six weeks after Frankie vanished.

My eyes shift up one line, reading and rereading the prior date.

A week before Frankie left.

The pilot wasn't here during her disappearance.

This isn't connected to her. It can't be.

I lean in and scan the page, every detail sharp in the frigid air.

Then I see it.

The name of the pilot.

Denver Strakh.

TWENTY-FIVE

"No." A chill crashes down my spine.

Denver.

My brother.

No, no, no, no.

That's impossible.

Denver died thirty years ago.

Violent tremors shake me, crumbling my entire world.

"How is this possible?" I whisper. "He's dead. My brother is dead."

Memories flood back, a torrent of pain and shame and rage. So much fucking rage.

"Your brother?" Alvis widens his eyes before blinking rapidly. "I don't know about that. But Denver is the man who's been coming here. If he's your brother, you need to find out what happened to him."

I don't believe him. I don't believe any of this.

"What does he look like?" Panic flutters in my chest.

"I have a photo." Sirena reaches into her purse.

"No." I point at her, keeping my eyes on Alvis. "Describe him."

Please, don't say it. Please, don't say it.

"Well, he looks nothing like you." He rubs his balding head. "I mean, he's a handsome fellow like you. But without all the fancy clothes. He reminds me of that one guy."

A cold knot forms in my stomach.

"He was in that one movie. What was the name of it? *Fight* something or other. Oh, what was that actor's name?" He glances around, looking at us for help. Then pauses. Snaps his fingers. "Brad Pitt."

Bile surges in my chest and burns the back of my throat. Sickening waves of nausea slam into me so hard that I double over in pain, stumbling against the workbench, fighting for air.

"Monty?" Sirena hooks an arm around my back and touches a cold hand to my brow. "Are you okay?"

I send her stumbling backward with just a look. Then I aim that furious glare at Alvis. "Where does he live? Where is Denver?"

"I don't know."

"Fuck!" I swing an arm across the workbench, knocking tools and manuals to the floor. "If you're protecting him—"

"I'm going to ask you to leave now." Alvis inches backward, holding up his hands.

"Alvis, you can't protect him. He's a bad man. A fucking monster."

"I've known him for thirty years. Been working for him for twenty. He's been nothing but nice to me." His face turns a deep shade of red, heat radiating from his skin. "He never lost his temper like you just did."

"No. He wouldn't." I scrape a trembling hand over my mouth, fighting the urge to puke. "He's a psychopath."

"Now, I don't believe that."

"Did he tell you he had a brother? What about Rurik Strakh? Did you know he was Denver's father?"

"No. I figured there was some relation with Rurik, same last name and all."

"What about passengers? Does anyone fly with him?"

"Never. He's always alone. He lives alone."

In an off-grid safe house, self-sustained by a hydroelectric generator, that my father must've funded and built for him.

If Denver's alive, he knows I orchestrated his murder.

He knows everything.

A cold sweat beads on my forehead.

He would've come for me or...

Frankie.

No. Oh, God, no. I can't let my mind go there.

"Are you sure he was alone?" I seethe past clenched teeth. "Think carefully. Could he hide someone on board? Stuff a body in the cargo hold inside a box or a bag?"

"No, I..." His brows knit. "I don't believe he's capable of that. He's a gentle man, always so charming and polite."

"See this girl?" I hold up Kaya's photo, my voice breaking. "He molested her when she was eight years old. And she's not the only one. He hurts women. *Children.* Swear to God, Alvis, if you don't tell me how to find him right fucking now—"

"I don't know!" The blood drains from his face,

269

leaving him visibly shaken. "He never told me where he lives. It's up north somewhere."

"North where?"

"Give me a minute." He steps to the workbench and braces a hand on the surface. His other hand removes a handkerchief from his pocket and blots his sweat-slick face. "I think he said it's three hundred miles northeast to his homestead, but he hauls logs in that plane twice a year. He must be farther than that, north of the arctic tree line. At least four hundred miles. But depending on the payload, that Beaver has a six-hundred-mile range."

He could be anywhere in the North Slope Borough or Yukon, Canada. It's such a vast, barren landscape with so many places to hide.

But it's a starting point.

Sirena waits nearby, clutching her phone to her chest, lips parted, eyes round, seemingly in shock.

"Sirena." My voice makes her jump. "Call it in."

"On it." She steps outside, lifting her phone to her ear.

The moment she alerts the authorities, this will hit the media stations.

Richest family in Alaska hides pedophilia crimes for thirty years.

Statewide search for brother of billionaire business mogul Monty Novak. Considered dangerous.

It'll make national news.

It'll ruin me.

I don't fucking care.

Thirty years ago, when I discovered what Denver was, I wanted him incarcerated. At age eighteen, he would've been tried as an adult and put away for the rest of his miserable life.

But my father fought me, told me our family wouldn't survive the media attention. His enemies would find us and slaughter us all.

So we handled it quietly. I convinced him to enlist one of his hitmen, to make it clean and quick.

Denver disappeared a month later. My father assured me it was done, and that was the end of my relationship with my parents.

For ten years, they blamed me for forcing them to murder their son.

They despised me until the day they died.

But Rurik Strakh lied to me.

Rather than removing my depraved brother from the planet, he protected him. He built an off-grid cabin, isolated Denver from the world, or at the very least, kept him on a short leash by monitoring his comings and goings through Alvis Duncan.

He fucking hid this from me.

How often did he visit Denver? Did they spend holidays and vacations together?

Were my parents visiting him the day they died?

My hands fumble for the logbook, flipping through the pages, searching, scouring, my mind spinning, and my chest aching so badly I can't breathe.

There.

The date of their deaths.

Denver was here. Right fucking here in Whittier the day they died.

Did he tinker with the engine and cause their plane to crash? He's capable of that. He has no emotion or compassion yet every bit of the mechanical aptitude to make it look like an accident.

But what would've been the motivation?

"You said you've worked for Denver for twenty-five years." I glance up at the man beside me, who appears to be stunned into silence. "Who flew the Beaver before him?"

"It's always been him. But for the first decade or so, he was just a job, someone I kept tabs on. I reported his flight schedule to your father's men and didn't interact with him. He was young and quiet, kept to himself, didn't ask for nothing."

"When did that change?"

"About twenty-five years ago. He started paying me to gather supplies for him. Hard to find things. Rich folk stuff."

"Like what?"

"Designer outerwear. Crystal dishes. Rare and exotic foods." He heaves a sigh. "If Rurik Strakh died twenty-five years ago, why did his men keep coming? They collected my flight logs for years after. Doesn't make sense."

"They must've been under contract with my father. When the contracts expired, they were no longer indebted to him. Does Denver know about the flight logs?"

"Yeah, he knows. But we've never talked about it."

I wonder if those logs kept him in check, if they kept him from hunting his favorite prey.

Children.

My soul recoils, cornered by unspeakable memories. "What kept him from flying to other towns, other ports?"

"Nothing, I suppose. But the Hobbs meter makes him liable. You know what that is?"

"Yes. Denver and I got our pilot licenses at age seventeen. But the meter can be manipulated, much like an odometer on a car."

"Sure. If he runs the engine without leaving the ground, it puts more time on the clock and makes it look like he went farther than he actually did. But he can't reverse the hours without tampering with the meter itself. I check the mechanism every time he arrives and log the hours." He points at the entries in the logbook. "I would know if the meter was tampered with. It never is. And according to the logged hours, he's never flown that plane longer than four hours in each direction."

"That means he's not flying anywhere but here."

"That's what I reckon."

"That also means he lives four hours from this location."

"Give or take, depending on the payload and the speed he sets. Unless he's letting the engine idle and running up the hours. It's not a reliable gauge to estimate distance."

I leaf through the pages of the logbook, noting that the flights average about five times a year. "Why did you continue to log his flights after my father's men stopped coming for them?"

"You were right about the threats. I got a daughter and grandchildren in Fairbanks. Those men told me to keep the logs until the day I died. If I stopped, they would kill my family. That was the deal."

"And you agreed to it?"

"I was a young, naive man when they first approached me. Offered money when I didn't have any. The threats came later."

The tread of Sirena's footsteps draws our attention to the door.

"Detectives are driving in from Anchorage." She heads straight toward me and rests a hand on my arm. "You doing okay?"

No. I'm far from okay.

Denver is alive.

I'm drowning in a canyon of disbelief, where shadows whisper truths too monstrous to bear, and every beat of my heart is a drum of horror and dread.

I've seen first-hand what Denver is capable of, and he was only eighteen then.

At age forty-eight, what kind of monster has he become?

He has a brilliant mind, understands the mechanics of things, including people. He can outsmart and out-manipulate the sharpest, strongest person. And he does it without mercy or feeling.

There's no limit to the depth of his evil.

If he took Frankie...

I can't let myself grasp the gravity of what that means.

Not here.

Not yet.

Soon, this place will turn into a shitshow, swarming with cops, detectives, and reporters. I need to get as many answers as I can before that happens.

Determination sets in, hardening like the ice beneath my feet.

"You said you did his shopping for twenty-five years?" I slide over a stool and motion for him to sit. "Do you have those shopping lists in writing?"

"I have financial records of every item bought and every penny spent." He lowers onto the seat. "He gave me an unlimited bank account for that."

A bank account can be traced. I share a look with Sirena.

"Start from the beginning." I pace before him, heart racing. "Tell me everything."

monty

leonid

TWENTY-SIX

I crouch beneath the shadow of the bush plane, my fingers stained black with oil and grime, checking the hydraulic lines for leaks, abrasions, or anything that might indicate a weakening system. I've inspected the landing gear more than I can count, but it bears repeating.

Weeks have passed since Kody and Frankie returned with the pemmican. Perhaps a month or longer. In that time, my intimacy with this machine has ascended to another level.

I've dissected its anatomy like a surgeon, familiarizing myself with every nut, joint, and seal.

Using a checklist I compiled from the flight manual, I mark off the equipment as I go so I don't miss a single component. If I encounter something not in the manual, I take it apart, figure it out, and reassemble it.

There isn't a wire, bolt, or piece of this bird that I

haven't touched and learned its purpose.

Every hour beneath these wings solidifies my dream to be a pilot and aviation mechanic, running my own private airport.

But my obsession with this particular plane has nothing to do with my future plans. When I take it off the ground, I'm responsible for the safety of my family. One mistake up there, and I could lose them forever.

I cannot, will not, let that happen.

They're usually in here with me, learning and asking questions. Frankie loves to sit in the cockpit and write in her scrapbook while Kody and I thoroughly inspect every bolt, gasket, and spark plug.

She journals daily, documenting every detail of our lives—the good and bad parts, the struggles and victories, our abominable pasts and our dreams for the future. And the sex. She writes about that, too.

I haven't read any of it. I don't need to relive most of what happened to us, but I understand why she's keeping written records.

When we leave this place, we have a story to tell. Not just ours but that of the victims who died here. The gritty details are all there in the pages of her scrapbook.

When we leave...

That's the question.

Each day, the sun climbs a bit higher and lingers a bit longer. Little by little, the snow retreats, revealing patches of earth that haven't seen the light of day in months.

This morning, I spotted a few tiny buds breaking through the frost-hardened ground. And the air carries the faint, almost forgotten scent of thawing earth.

Winter is slowly releasing its hold on us.

By my estimation, we have another month before the blizzard risk drops enough to get the plane out.

I've powered it up, idled the engine, driven it forward and backward in the confines of the garage. But I haven't taken it off the ground.

The thought races my heart with anticipation.

I've imagined it so many times. The plan is clear in my mind. As soon as the snow melts, I'll roll it onto the tundra and test every theory I've learned. After a few practice takeoffs and landings, I'll load up Kody and Frankie and hit the skies.

Buzzing with the rush of excitement, I tighten a bolt on the landing gear and climb into the cargo hold to finish installing the third seat.

The distant trill of female laughter drifts through the slightly ajar door. It's a welcome interruption, a comfort to know she's nearby.

I secure the passenger seat to the mounting points in the cabin floor and give it a hard shake, testing the installation.

Denver removed the rear seating to accommodate more cargo space. Thankfully, he kept the chairs, and I found this one still in working condition.

As I shorten the straps on the seat harness, picturing Frankie's petite frame, her laughter peaks again, cutting through my concentration. The sound is mesmerizing, warming my chest and pulling at my lips.

The plane can wait.

I hop out and wipe my hands on a rag, curiosity guiding me to the door.

Peeking outside, I find her kneeling in the snow. Bent over a plot of barren earth, she makes a small hole and sprinkles seeds in it.

The very idea of growing anything in this terrain feels like a defiance of nature. That's why we have the greenhouse.

She knows that. She also knows we'll be gone before those seeds yield food.

Maybe this attempt to start a small garden, to coax the soil to life, is an act of hope.

We've been living on pemmican for weeks and rationing for months. Veggies would be a welcome change. Anything sprouting from the cold, stubborn ground would be a welcome change.

Hunting season remains months out of reach. We can't hold out that long.

We've extended our food supply to its limits. With the pemmican we have left, surviving another month will be pushing our luck.

Kody stands a few feet away, loading a bolt in his crossbow. "Give me another target."

"Okay." She twists toward him, scanning the perimeter. "How about that rock? The one with the pointy side?"

He lifts the bow and trains it on a boulder thirty yards away. "Behold, as I, the great and fearless Lord Strakh, take aim at the beast most foul, a vicious Boulderax, known to strike terror into the hearts of the bravest souls."

As he releases the arrow and nails the target, her laughter rings out, vibrant and unconstrained.

Christ, she's beautiful.

"Oh, my God." She erupts in more giggles. "I'm dying. How about that can over there?"

Securing a fresh arrow in the crossbow, he follows her gaze to the recycle bin and takes aim at the can on top. "Watch closely, fair maiden, as I embark on a perilous quest to vanquish the dreaded tin dragon, perched menacingly upon yonder stand, its gaze enough to petrify a lesser man."

He lets the bolt fly, hitting the mark.

"I can't..." She hugs her midsection, cackling hysterically. "I'm going to pee my pants."

I draw my bottom lip between my teeth, biting down on a grin.

My brother is in rare fucking form. Who knew he could be so entertaining?

"One more." He slots a new bolt, his tone serious.

"The compost pile." She wipes tears from her eyes.

"This is it, the moment of truth, where legends are born, and tales of epic battles are woven into the fabric of history, all centered around the mighty clash between man and...well, essentially a rotting pile of shit."

She falls over, howling with laughter before he even releases the shot.

That sound, that infectious, carefree peal of happiness, is something that's been scarce in this place. I can't remember the last time I heard anyone laugh like that. Maybe never.

And Kody...what the fuck? He's actually smiling. Cheeks lifting, teeth showing, eyes shining, full-on smiling. I don't even recognize him.

He catches me staring, and I grin back, shaking my head. It feels weird, sharing such a lighthearted expression with the grumpy bastard. Things are changing, indeed.

A soft, guttural croak overhead pulls my attention skyward as a ptarmigan approaches from the North. Its wings beat through the air with a whooshing whisper, steady and purposeful.

Kody watches it momentarily before readying a new arrow and training it on the bird's path.

If we stewed its meat with herbs, it would be a mouth-watering delicacy after weeks of eating nothing but pemmican.

But a moment of hesitation has him glancing at Frankie.

She's on her feet, lips parted, and huge eyes fixed on the bird with wonderment.

He lowers the bow, the shot forgotten, and stares at her with adoration.

She watches the ptarmigan until it fades from view. Then she sighs, her breath no longer visible in the sunlit air.

Turning back to her garden, she locks eyes with me. "Hey there, gorgeous."

"Hey, yourself." I nod toward the seeds she planted. "You think those will take?"

"They better." She cocks her hip. "If they know what's good for them."

The snowdrifts reach waist-high in most places around the property. But here, where we repeatedly walk between the cabin and the workshop, the snow is worn down and melty.

I kick at the ground, now more slush than ice, watching it slowly reveal the soil beneath. "We'll be trading snow for skies in about a month."

"Just in time to see my garden grow." She shrugs. "Something for the rabbits to munch on."

"The rabbits? We don't feed the critters. They feed us."

"Exactly."

She planted this here as bait?

Damn.

Gorgeous, sassy, and smart as hell. I couldn't love this woman more if I tried.

"I told her those seeds won't sprout there." Kody prowls toward her little patch of dirt. "This time next year, we'll be laughing about it over a real meal somewhere far from here."

He and I exchange another grin just as a snowball flies out of nowhere, smacking him squarely in the face. Stunned, he pauses, blinks away the surprise, and gently clears the icy mush from his vision.

"Talking shit on my garden?" She tosses another snowball back and forth between her hands. "Do it again. I dare you."

"Shit, man." I laugh. "Consider yourself officially challenged to a duel."

With slow, deliberate movements, he sets aside his weapons and removes his fur coat, revealing his bare chest beneath.

Her snowball drops to the ground as he stalks toward her. Then, with a squeal, she takes off running.

I lean a shoulder against the doorjamb, watching her scramble to pack snow into ammunition and duck behind a piling beneath the deck. Her laughter bubbles up as he pretends to search for her, his mock-serious expression adding to the playfulness of their game.

I'm tempted to join them, but my thoughts are consumed with the bush plane.

As they hurl snowballs at each other, I return to the garage, floating on the sound of her joy. Hell, maybe her little garden will grow. Even in the harshest conditions, life finds a way to push through.

And so will we.

Our survival depends on scraping by day to day, but the plane represents a chance at real escape, a flight toward something resembling a future.

With a safety inspection to finish, piloting skills to learn, and a journey to plan, the responsibility sits heavily on my shoulders.

For the next hour, I lose myself in the work and the

satisfaction of my progress, each turn of the wrench, every inspection and adjustment inching closer to our escape.

But at some point, the absence of laughter and playful shouts from outside slices through my focus. I can't hear them at all.

What are they doing?

I have an idea, and my sudden unease over being left out pulls me away from the plane.

Grabbing a towel, I clean my hands on my way to the door and step outside.

Stillness greets me. They're nowhere in sight.

Instinctively, I follow the tracks they left behind like a breadcrumb trail in the snow. The path meanders in every direction before aligning with purpose toward the sauna.

Now that we have coal again, we've been able to use the steam bath. But only occasionally. It's not a practical way to keep warm since it requires so much maintenance and coal.

As I approach the building, the reality of this special occasion tightens my stomach.

He's fucking her in there. That's what I would be doing.

The thought tunnels through me, hot and electric, a restless energy taking hold.

Pausing at the door, I brace an arm on the frame, reluctant to intrude.

We share her, but we haven't *shared* her. Not the way I've seen two men share a woman in porn videos.

Over the past few weeks, he's watched her with me. I've watched her with him. Sometimes we take turns. But our focus is and always will be on her. That's the only way this works.

When we're with her, we draw an invisible line

between us. One accidental brush across that line could resurrect demons, memories of childhood trauma, and battles lost against the devil himself.

Then there's the issue of our blood ties. We don't know if we're brothers by birth, but we're brothers in every way that counts. The very thought of touching Kody in a sexual way makes me sick.

Yet, it's the bond that ties us together, strengthened by tragedy and shared dreams, that propels me into the sauna.

With a single step inside, I can hear her moaning. By the time I strip my clothes, I'm hard as steel.

As I open the interior door, I can't see them through the haze of escaping steam. But I feel her, smell her, taste her in the humid air.

Lowering onto the opposite end of their bench, I relax against the wall and wait for the swirling mist to settle.

Slowly the fog lifts, and there she is, magnificently nude, with her head thrown back, eyes closed, and legs spread wide as she grinds herself on Kody's face.

He grabs her by the hips and buries his tongue, licking, sucking, and flicking over her again and again.

A flush creeps up her neck, betraying the heat igniting beneath her skin. Her lips are red and swollen from how hard she bites them. Or maybe how hard he was biting them.

Either way, she looks stunning.

Her body writhes against his mouth, fluid and hypnotic, as she chases her pleasure.

Leaning back, he spits on her opening and pushes two fingers inside her.

My own fingers twitch, itching to close the distance and join with his as he twists his wrist and strokes her deep.

Her eyes fly open, colliding with mine, as a low, husky moan tumbles from her lips.

He's become adept at navigating her body, building her need, and drawing it out with impressive proficiency.

Her pussy glistens around his fingers. He kisses her there, lapping and biting at her clit until she grabs his hair and pulls his mouth to hers.

My cock juts from between my legs, stiff and aching, but I don't touch it. I can get off just from watching her in the throes of unfiltered passion. The wetness of my excitement leaks glossy strings down my shaft and onto my thigh.

He continues to fuck her with his fingers as he kisses her, breathless. When they come up for air, he presses his face against her neck, working his hand and groaning from the sheer pleasure of touching her.

I hold her gaze through her shuddering release, through the blood rushing in my ears. She cries out. Her head falls back. Her nails dig into his scarred flesh, and her thighs clench around his wrist.

As he fingers her through the orgasm, my cock throbs, thickening further, dripping with the need to explode.

It's weird watching them together but also wildly arousing. I prefer to watch rather than be watched, but I'll have to get used to all of it if we'll be sharing her...forever.

She slowly catches her breath. Then they both turn to me.

"I want you on your hands and knees, sucking me off," I rasp, "while he fucks you from behind."

We did it that way the first time, but it was me doing the fucking.

I have no idea what I'm doing. When we're together like this, I rely on instinct and try to keep my thoughts out of it.

As he flips her into position with her head over my lap, I let my body take over and sink into the seductive, carnal beauty of mutual, consensual fucking.

It's the only time I truly let go.

Gripping her gorgeous hair, I guide her head and feed my length down her throat until she gags.

Kody kneels behind her and unsheathes his teeth, scraping them down her spine, surrendering to his innate savagery. He takes his time, playing with her, drawing it out. When he finally impales her on his mammoth dick, she moans around me, completely filled at both ends.

Christ, I feel that. Her tongue. Her heat. Her beautiful desire. She knows how to suck a cock, hollowing her cheeks and taking me as deeply as she can.

"So fucking good, Frankie." I throw myself into the infinite pleasure of it, into the blissful sounds of three people in love.

The hunger between us, the physical and emotional connection that laces us together, promises this will never end, that we'll always be good together.

We take her from top to bottom, listening to her whimpers and filling her with our come. Then we trade places and take her again.

The smile she gives us afterward? It breaks like dawn upon the endless night, scattering the shadows and thawing frostbitten skin.

I melt with it, with her, pulling her against me and groaning into her warmth. She caresses her body with mine—her lips, her hair, her nipples. She's so soft and lush, gliding over my chest.

"Not finished with you." I tongue her lips and taste her breath.

"Join me in the shower." With a wink, she pushes off me and struts out of the sauna, gloriously nude.

Kody and I share a look.

A million tasks demand attention, yet only one holds true significance.

Everything else can wait until tomorrow.

frankie
TWENTY-SEVEN

One month later, the hills begin to thaw.

Rain and meltwater seep into the soil, carrying away not just the bulk of the snow but the imagined scents and sights of a spring that cannot find its way here.

Instead of the delicate flutter of butterflies on the breeze and the sweet aroma of blueberries ripening under the sun, the tundra rolls out a squelching carpet of cold mud, slush, and dread.

Sweaty, nail-biting dread.

My skin drips with it as Leo maneuvers the Turbo Beaver over the icy muck and attempts the impossible.

"Come on, Leo. You've got this." Kody sits beside me on the front porch steps, elbows braced on spread knees and dark eyes tracking his brother with unwavering focus. "Easy does it. Don't force it."

"I can't watch." I bury my face in his arm as the

knots in my stomach pull tighter. "Tell me when it's over."

He grips my waist and effortlessly lifts me, setting me on his lap. His gaze remains fixed on the plane's movements as he tucks me close to his chest, his heart a grounding rhythm against my ear.

"Nothing's going to happen." His fingers weave through my hair in soothing strokes. "He'll master this like he masters everything else."

"With his fists?"

"Christ, I hope not."

We have one shot at this escape. If he hurts himself or the aircraft, we're fucked.

"All right, Leo. Deep breath. This is it." His concern for his brother and the anxiety lacing his words turn my neck.

Across the field, Leo accelerates. The plane lurches awkwardly, its movements a series of rapid, jerky hops that shake the steel frame.

"Oh, God." My heart can't take it, yet I'm transfixed, unable to look away.

Clutching Kody's shirt, I tense with white knuckles and hold my breath until Leo finally rolls to a safe stop.

Almost immediately, he springs forward again, rounding into a tight circle and setting up for another try.

"Remember the wind. Watch the gauges. Do it just like we talked about." Kody's fingers gently comb through my hair, his focus split between comforting me and cheering on his brother.

Leo's next attempt at lifting off is premature. The Beaver barely grazes the tundra before thumping back down, a misguided leap rather than a flight.

"He's pulling up too soon." The worry in Kody's voice matches my fear.

Again and again, Leo tries. Each endeavor soaks me in ulcer-inducing panic. When he overcorrects, veering dangerously close to the cliff, I strangle on a gasp, my blood pressure sky-high.

"He's not keeping it steady," I say, as if I could do better.

I listened when he explained the basics of aviation, but at the end of the day, I know negative things about flying a plane.

His determination and quick reflexes are unrivaled, but so is his inexperience. The plane wobbles on the edge of out-of-control, a wild beast charging head-first into disaster.

Another run sees the tail swing too aggressively, a near spin that has me standing, ready to race toward him, toward the fiery crash that's bound to happen.

But Kody's hand captures mine, firm and unyielding, holding me back.

"He has to learn, Frankie." He sets me back on his lap and places a reassuring kiss on my cheek, but it does little to calm my unraveling nerves.

"He can't learn if he's dead." I slump into the solid warmth of him, my voice muffled against his sleeve. "The whole reason he's practicing is so we don't crash. But if he crashes while practicing, what's the damn point? He only gets to crash once. If it's going to happen, I'd rather be on that plane with him than out here watching helplessly."

If he wrecks the plane, we're dead, whether we're on it or not.

We're down to our final scraps of food.

We've been rationing our meals for months, each portion calculated and minimal. Hunger has become so familiar that its sharp pangs have dulled to an echo in the background. The pemmican, once overpoweringly gamy and chewy, now tastes like nothing.

We've lost so much weight that our raised bones scrape together every time we touch. And that feels...*normal.*

We've adapted, our bodies and minds conditioned to the constant gnaw of emptiness. We talk about our plans, our hopes for escape, but the conversation about food is conspicuously absent. It's as if we've grown beyond hunger, beyond the physical demands that once dictated our every thought.

But that's about to change.

Our food supplies have run out.

The remaining pieces of pemmican might last two more days, but no more.

"Let's leave today." I straighten on his lap. "Right now."

"No," he growls at my ear. "He needs a better grasp on this before your precious ass leaves the ground."

Leo already said as much.

Their entire lives, they stood on this porch and watched Denver take off and land that bird. They know what it's supposed to look like and sound like, even if they have no memory of flying inside it.

At least Leo's practice runs don't involve reaching the clouds or carving arcs across the sky. He can't waste the fuel doing a complete lift-off. He'll use just enough gas to get a feel for ascending, breaking free from the earth's hold, and touching down. Nothing crazy.

Doesn't stop my heart from slamming against my ribs. Every effort he makes, every bump, skip, and near collision with the ground, sends a fresh wave of anxiety through me. I imagine everything that can go wrong in vivid, terrifying detail, each scenario more gruesome than the last.

He practices for two more days, carving furrows into the landscape while my fingernails carve gouges into my palms.

But his dedication is legendary.

Each morning before dawn, he pores over his notes and makes adjustments in the flight manual, recording his mistakes and replaying maneuvers in his mind. His focus never wavers, his eyes scanning diagrams and instructions with a hunger for knowledge that's insatiable.

Out in the field, he approaches the plane with deep respect, his hands running along the fuselage, familiarizing himself with every curve and line, committing it all to memory.

Every day, I sit beside Kody on the porch as Leo climbs into the cockpit with a quiet, steely resolve that contradicts his hot-tempered nature.

When his takeoffs stagger and slide into rough, bouncy stops, he nods to himself and tries again.

As the sun sets on his final day of practice, casting long shadows across the tundra, he remains in the plane, reviewing the day's lessons, perhaps mentally preparing for the actual flight.

The only one that counts.

We're leaving tomorrow morning.

Or attempting anyway.

After all his practicing, he never achieved a takeoff with any real promise that we'll make it higher than ten feet into the air.

But we're out of time.

The pantry is completely bare. Every shelf. Every cabinet. My garden never sprouted. The rabbits never came. We're on our last bar of pemmican. And he can't use any more jet fuel for drills.

"I'm scared." The words tremble as they leave me, carried on an exhale that feels too shaky, too thin.

"Hey." Kody pulls me against him, his mouth lowering to mine.

Our lips barely touch. Instead of kissing, I breathe love into him, and he breathes steadiness into me, calming the drumbeat beneath my skin.

Until a rumbling roar vibrates the air, yanking our gazes across the tundra.

Leo revs the Turbo Beaver, maneuvering it into position for another run.

"What is he doing?" I climb to my feet.

Kody stands against my back, wrapping his arms around me from behind.

The sound builds, the growl of horsepower and propeller thrust echoing across the landscape, as Leo pilots the plane along the bumpy terrain, gaining speed.

Then something shifts. The plane accelerates, and this time, when it lifts, his adjustments are more subtle. It doesn't immediately fall back to the earth. It hovers, a perfect glide that separates wheels from ground and a gentle touch that reunites them without a jolt, without a mark. Not far, not high, but it's enough to ignite a hot flash of hope in my chest.

"He did it." I sag against Kody, relief washing over me, swamping the residual pounding of my heart.

"He did." He tightens his embrace. "I knew he would."

Leo circles back toward us, the plane bouncing gently along the ground, his face alight with a triumphant grin visible even from a distance.

The Beaver comes to a rest, the engine quieting into a hush that settles across the tundra.

He hops out and prowls toward us, his point made, his confidence buoyed.

We all feel it.

Together, we climb the steps to the deck and sit beneath the overhang, shoulder to shoulder, enveloped in a silence that's thick with a thousand unsaid things.

Tomorrow marks the end of our captivity, the end of an era for Leo and Kody, and for me, an unexpected, full-circle turn onto a new path.

I don't know how long I've been here, but I counted my daily entries in the scrapbook and estimated how many days I didn't journal.

I arrived at least eight months ago. Probably nine. Nine months.

Sitting between them, I find the strength to share a thought that's been haunting me for weeks. "If...if things had been different, if I hadn't miscarried, I would be holding my baby right now."

"I know." Leo shifts closer, his breath stirring my hair. "And that child would have been loved and fiercely protected by Kody and me."

Kody drapes an arm around my shoulders, leaning in. "We've been through hell. Can't get much worse, right?"

"Whatever happens tomorrow, we face it together." Leo glances at the plane that waits in the field. "We survived these hills. We survived Denver. We can survive anything."

I hope he's right.

Starvation has really left a cruel mark on me, ravaging my figure and my self-worth until both are unrecognizable. The woman who stares back at me in the mirror is a stranger, her features sharpened by necessity, her body whittled down to the bare essentials.

I don't like her, this bony, sick version of myself. I

don't want anything to do with this new *normal.*

Each glimpse of my nude form chips away at the little self-confidence I've managed to cling to, leaving me feeling vulnerable and unattractive.

Feeling ugly has a way of killing a girl's libido. So does fear and worry and calorie-deficient exhaustion.

The guys don't have this problem. They're always hard, always horny, always in the mood. And despite their weight loss, they've retained their chiseled, otherworldly beauty. It's unfair.

We sleep together every night, our bodies entwined tightly. But the second a hand touches between my skeletal legs, I go frigid.

They sense it and never pressure me. We talk about it. They love me and reassure me. They constantly tell me I'm beautiful. Every day. All the time. Too often.

I know why they do it.

They want me to be happy.

That just makes me feel worse.

I might be depressed.

It helps to talk to them. I draw strength from their words, from their steadfast love. "I know I've been struggling lately. But spending every day with you guys, it's given me something—two very important somethings—to hold onto."

"If Wolf were here..." Leo stares up at the stars. "He'd have something outlandish and inappropriate to say in response to that."

If I listen hard enough, I can hear his dry laughter in the chambers of the night. "Did he ever tell you the fairy tale about the lion, the bear, and the drag queen?"

They shake their heads, their expressions carved in permanent loss.

"Oh." My heart constricts. "It's just...it was something he shared the day I arrived. It made no sense at the time, but now…"

I fall quiet, searching for him in the starlit skies.

"Now you have to tell us." Leo squeezes my hand.

"I wouldn't do it justice. No one tells a story like he did. I can't."

"Try." Kody kisses my shoulder.

"I'll cry." My breath trembles beneath the weight of the eyes pressing against me on both sides, waiting.

Dammit.

"Okay." I clear my throat. "So there's a drag queen with a grand plan to hit up Disney World, but she won't go without her pets—the lion and the bear."

Leo groans. "I hate it already."

"Just wait." I pull his hand onto my lap. "When she breaks the news that they're heading to the Magic Kingdom, the lion gets all dramatic, declaring that they're all going to die. The bear's just there for a good time, asking if there will be vodka because, apparently, that's his thing."

Kody grunts.

"The queen assures him that Disney has everything. But the lion claims that vodka isn't allowed and tries to bail on the adventure. The queen's not having it. She decides to sneak the vodka in, which wins the bear over. So they head out on their quest but immediately hit a roadblock—a literal cliff standing between them and the Disney dream." My vision fills with tears. "That's when the lion announces he can't fly. Meanwhile, the bear's a mess, spilling vodka everywhere. And the queen, in a fit of defiance, says…"

My voice breaks, the sadness overwhelming.

Kody catches my tears as they slide down my face. "What did the queen say?"

"Fuck it. Let's jump." I swallow a rising sob. "But

they don't. In his story, no one jumps off the cliff."

"Come here." Leo pulls me onto his lap and holds my face against his neck.

"I didn't understand what he was trying to tell me. When I asked, he said the point is that lions can't fly, bears are drunks, and..." My face crumples. "The Magic Kingdom will forever be without its queen."

"Goddammit, Wolf." Leo sucks in a harsh breath and leans back, taking me with him. "Fuck."

It hurts. It hurts so fucking much.

Tears stream down my face as the story hits home, too heavy to bear.

Disney World.

Such a simple dream for a tragically broken man.

A dream that feels obtainable now.

"He should be here." I drag my sleeve across my wet cheeks, my sniffles seething into anger. "There were so many signs. They were all there—in his stories, his sarcasm, his games. Remember when he pressed us for our red flags? When it was his turn to share, he said his red flag was that he could say his red flag with a blank face. I mean...*Jesus.* That was it, right there. He literally told us he was waving a red flag."

"Frankie..." Kody exchanges a look with Leo.

"He was screaming for help, and I ignored him."

"Stop." Leo grips my chin, forcing my eyes to his. "With a heart like yours, you will always feel like you didn't do enough. But you did. You did everything you could, and now you need to stop. Stop punishing yourself for the decisions he made. None of us is to blame." He releases me, his jaw stiff. "He was wrong about a lot of things. We survived the winter, and tomorrow, we're leaving this behind. We're taking only the important parts with us—each other. We'll start fresh, build a new life where the shadows of this evil place can't reach."

"And we'll remember," Kody says quietly, "not the hardships, but the moments of peace and the origin story of the three of us."

We sit in contemplative silence, lost in a poignant sense of closure, cuddled in the calm before the storm of our escape.

Tonight, we'll sleep one last time in the hills of shivers and shadows, where I made a bargain with the devil, killed the monster, lost my Wolf, died in a lake, and fell in love twice.

Tomorrow, we'll attempt our most dangerous journey yet.

Tomorrow, the lion will fly.

frankie

TWENTY-EIGHT

This is it, the moment we've dreamed of and dreaded for months.

With a woozy stomach of nerves, I press my spine against the airplane seat and concentrate on breathing.

Kody kneels before me, fixing the harness over my shoulders and smoothing the straps with a sweetness unexpected of someone so manly and feral.

His eyes lift to mine, those dark, gooey centers swirling with concern, before they return to his task.

He checks the buckle. Clicks it into place. Tightens the straps, but not too tight. As if he's handling something precious, something irreplaceable.

"I'm not a child." I grip his hand, halting his fussing.

"Hush, woman." He twists his wrist and captures my fingers, lifting them to his teeth.

"Don't you do it."

He bites down. Hard.

I yelp through a laugh. "You're the child."

"Hold still."

He leans back, making minor adjustments and giving the harness a visual inspection, his gaze lingering.

Not in a sexual way.

This is more than a safety precaution for him. It's a ritual, a way to express his care and say what words cannot—that, with all the looming uncertainties, ensuring my protection is something within his control.

I also think that immersing himself in preparation distracts him from the fear.

He put me in the third seat behind his. No doubt the safest seat. The crate of supplies is locked down behind Leo's chair. A deliberate arrangement to balance our weight perfectly across the aircraft.

Of course, it wouldn't be Leo if he wasn't doing another inspection of the plane, examining every inch before takeoff.

Their meticulousness shines through in every action—calculations of payload, corrections for wind direction, vigilant checks for signs of inclement weather.

As the sun breaks the horizon, bathing us in light, the skies stretch out without a cloud or snowflake in sight.

"Perfect day to fly." I hold Kody's gorgeous face in my hands, stroking the clean-shaven skin.

"If Wolf were here, he would say *perfect day to die.*"

"Yep. Then he would take a drag from his cigarette, pause for effect, and follow up with *put that in your pipe and smoke it.*"

We share a sad smile.

"We're not dying today." He cups my jaw, matching my pose. "We'll make it. We have to."

"I believe you."

The crunch of Leo's footsteps draws our attention beyond the cargo door.

Rather than approaching, he strides across the field, a shovel in one hand and determination in his strides. With a practiced eye, he identifies a spot, rolls aside a large rock, and begins to dig into the icy, barren ground.

"What's he doing now?" I crane my neck, trying to get a better look.

"No idea."

The sound of metal hitting frozen earth echoes back at us.

We watch in silence as he uncovers a clear plastic bag, its contents obscured by slush and mud. With unhurried patience, he coaxes it from the earth, cradles it in his arms, and makes his way back.

"What the hell?" I glance at Kody.

He shrugs and moves to the front seat, making room for his brother.

Leo climbs into the cargo hold and stows the shovel and bag in the crate. As he starts to close the lid, the contents become heartbreakingly clear.

Bones and blueberries...frozen in ice.

I shiver with memories of the night I spilled those contents on the dinner table. Not my finest moment. It was a reckless temper tantrum with unimaginable consequences.

My gaze flies to Kody's hand, to the jagged red scar that mars the top, a match to the one on his palm.

The marks of kin punishment.

"I thought..." My voice cracks. "Wolf returned the bones to the fire pit."

"Not all of them." Crouched before me, Leo wipes

his muddy hands on his thighs. "That night...things started changing for me. For all of us."

"What do you mean?"

"You helped me." Kody opens his scarred palm, pressing against the healed wound with his thumb. "When you stitched me, lines were drawn, and you stood stubbornly on our side."

"That night, you said we could escape. We only needed to learn how to fly the plane." Leo touches a knuckle beneath my chin. "You were so adamant about it, demanding that I consider it. So I did." He turns back to the crate, sealing the lid. "I took some of the bones before Wolf returned them. Kept them close." He nods at the field. "Because, for the first time in my life, I had hope."

"You kept them...my mother..." Kody regards Leo, his expression unreadable. "So we could bring her with us."

"Yeah."

Kody's mother. Maybe Wolf's mother, too. But not Leo's. She wasn't in the fire pit.

She was buried alive.

As their gazes hold, I feel their connection, their uncanny exchange of unspoken words, in the achiest corners of my soul.

But Leo doesn't let the heavy mood linger.

"Shall we make our ascent?" He swings the cargo door shut, latches the lock, and looks at us expectantly.

Everything essential for our journey, or our survival beyond it, is packed in the crate beside me. The flight manual, survival gear, fur pelts, outerwear, medical supplies, firearms, and ammunition for whatever conditions await us. We also have my journal and personal documents from Sitka, the DNA samples, driver's licenses, thumb drive, mementos of Wolf, and a bag of bones—everything that will tell our story...if we don't survive to tell it ourselves.

The only thing we don't have is food.

I really hope that's not what kills us in the end.

"Cleared for departure." I grip the edges of my seat and try not to throw up.

In a blink, Leo is kneeling before me, his hands around mine, prying them free.

He flattens my palms to his chest and floats closer, his lips parting mine in a slow, distracting kiss.

Against my mouth, he murmurs, "When we faced down that blizzard, and you wanted to search the cave, do you remember what you said?"

"Put some damn trust in me." I lift a hand to brush a strand of hair from his face.

Unlike Kody, he didn't shave off his beard. He trimmed it short and neat, which pairs so well with his tangled, braided hair. He doesn't give a damn how civilized people perceive him when he barrels out of the Arctic looking like a Viking.

"I trust you." I give his beard a tug. "Let's get the fuck out of here."

A flash of teeth in a gorgeously rugged face. Then he swoops in with a parting kiss before pulling away to strap himself into the pilot seat.

"I triple-checked everything." He flicks switches and levers on the instrumental panel. "The plane's ready. We're ready."

With only two wired headsets, it makes sense for Leo and Kody to wear them. I'll be dependent on my eyes to know what's going on. I hope I can read lips.

Maybe it'll be better if I don't.

I trust Leo's newfound knowledge and confidence in handling the aircraft on the ground. But in the air?

He's never made a turn, adjusted altitude, or dodged a mountain peak at ten thousand feet.

The cold sensation of fear trickles down my spine.

He's got this.

Kody twists to look at me, his deeply brown, savage-soul eyes commanding my attention with their alpha intensity. They hold a world of untold pain, battles fought, and a depth and rawness that's not just seen but felt.

When he looks at me like that, I shut up and listen. It's a look that promises protection and fierce loyalty, yet there's a hint of tenderness that he reserves only for me.

"We're leaving a lot behind." He cocks his head. "But we can always come back."

"Oh, God." I grimace.

"Too soon?"

I nod, swallowing the lump in my throat.

My gaze drifts to the cabin—the shelter that was my prison for nine months. Its walls have witnessed our lowest moments, our fight for survival against Denver, wolf attacks, hypothermia, starvation, and grief.

Kody's gravelly voice draws me back. "We're not just fleeing from death. We're chasing life. Remember that."

"You're right." My heart hammers so fiercely I'm convinced he can hear it.

"Kody." Leo tosses him a headset. "You can close your eyes or grab the *oh shit* handle. Lady's choice."

"Where's the *oh shit* handle?" He looks around.

"We don't have one. Better grab your dick...if you can find it."

"He's a goddamn comedian," he mumbles and shoves on the earphones.

"Frankie." Leo shifts, finding my eyes over his

shoulder. "I love you."

"I'll say it back when we land. Deal?"

"Deal." He returns to the instrument panel. "Here's to no crash landings, expectedly or unexpectedly."

The engine roars to life, a sound that's both terrifying and exhilarating.

As Leo pushes off, guiding the plane away from the only home they've ever known, a tear escapes me, trailing down my cheek.

"Goodbye," I whisper to it.

Hard to hear anything over the whirring turboprop, but Leo looks focused, his hands steady on the controls as we begin our taxi, the cabin receding into the distance.

Shallow, rapid breaths escape me, my anxiety mounting with the plane's acceleration. The uneven terrain of the runway causes our vibrating metal cage to buck and kick like a wild, unbroken stallion under the command of an untested pilot. Each jolt sends a shockwave through the aircraft, gripping me in a chokehold.

The relentless, overwhelming noise makes it impossible to share fears or words of encouragement. They don't need my distractions anyway.

I'll just sit back here like a good girl and try not to wet myself. No biggie.

Outside, the Arctic expanse scrolls by like a long dream, giving way to a blur of motion. The rush of speed presses against my lurching stomach, shoving it into my spine.

Without turning around, Kody reaches behind his seat, his hand extended.

I grab it, squeezing the life out of his calloused fingers.

Then, the moment of lift—a sudden lightness, a breath held collectively.

The plane slants, the climb fraught with violent shaking. Every dip and sway feels like a hand trying to slap us back to the ground. But Leo holds it steady, propelling us higher with an upward hunger that brings surreal weightlessness.

The aircraft wobbles, flirting with the earth once more before he pulls it up hard and wins the fight against gravity.

The world tilts and shifts outside the window, marked by the turbulence that tests the strength of my bladder. But holy fuck, we're airborne.

We're flying. Truly flying.

Kody bellows a victorious shout and releases my hand to twist in his seat and check on me.

A grin sparkles in his eyes and stretches from cheek to cheek, completely free from its constraints. It's a moment of transcendence.

As we gain altitude, the plane levels out, and the Arctic becomes a sprawling mural of white snow and blue skies, standing witness to our escape.

For the first time, I dare to breathe.

The fear remains, humming beneath the roar of the engine, but it's tinged with a whisper of freedom.

"Love you," I mouth to Kody.

He mouths it back and returns to Leo, talking to him through the headset. I can't hear their voices. There's only the deafening din of the engine and propeller that swallows every thought but one.

We're finally leaving.

As we reach a cruising altitude that Leo seems to navigate with unexpected ease, my heart remains a prisoner to every creak and murmur of the plane. With each passing minute, as the ground falls farther and farther away, my fears shift from the dangers of takeoff to the myriad of catastrophes that could still lie ahead.

Every revved hum, subtle vibration, and wobbly tilt drives my pulse into the danger zone. What if the engine fails or a piece of the wing falls off or we run out of fuel?

And the landing...

Will we find an airstrip? Or will Leo have to land in a field, on a highway, or in a valley of mountains?

I can't shake the bundle of nerves tightly wound inside me.

From my seat, I steal glances at Leo's profile, finding comfort in his indomitable focus, the deliberate movements of his hands, and the confidence in his posture. Even as my fears try to shove me into hysterics, he inhabits the role of pilot as if he were born into it.

He and Kody are in constant communication through their headsets, sharing information and strategies that I'm painfully excluded from. I try to read their lips, to glean some hint of what's being said, but the task is impossible.

Frustrated, I turn my gaze to the window, to the vast emptiness below us.

After thirty minutes of steady flying, the landscape hasn't changed, underscoring how remote Hoss truly is, how far removed from the world we've been, and the incredible distance we're attempting to cover.

Even so, a part of me dares to hope that the worst of our struggles are behind us.

An hour into our flight, high in the sky with the world stretching infinitely below, the terrain begins a slow transformation. The stark, white hills gradually give way to patches of thawing ground.

Beyond my window, hints of green start to puncture

the monotonous white, a tentative resurgence of vegetation. Birds dot the skies. Sparse at first. Then they grow denser. Indications that we're leaving the barrenness of the Arctic Circle behind.

As the plane flies southward, dipping lower, the view sharpens into a breathtaking mosaic of green.

Kody and Leo go still, their heads turning in every direction.

Trees. Thousands of them, rippling in an endless sea of emerald waves, their tips dusted with the golden light of the morning sun.

The alpine forest, punctuated by the occasional clearing and winding rivers that gleam like veins of liquid silver, is a stark contrast to the ice and snow Leo and Kody have known their entire lives.

They've never seen a tree outside of a movie screen and the glossy pages of their books.

Kody shifts toward the side window, his nose practically pressed against it, his breath fogging the glass as he absorbs the view. His eyes, wide with wonder, dart from point to point, trying to soak in every detail.

Leo doesn't let the sights steal his concentration. But there's a softness in his gaze, a grin pulling at the corner of his mouth.

Kody leans toward Leo, pointing and talking, and Leo nods, his smile growing brighter.

A vicarious thrill flutters through me, chasing away some of the nerves. I can't wait to experience more with them, to show them everything they've missed.

Just watching them, seeing the world through their eyes, fills me with an emotion I can't quite name.

Turning toward me, Kody makes his eyes go wide and drops his jaw, wordlessly communicating his reaction to the views.

I bite my lip, laughing at his playfulness. Then I blow him a kiss, which he catches before shifting back to the front.

Time, from my seat by the window, becomes a fluid thing, stretching and unfolding like the expanse of uninterrupted splendor below us.

Vibrant canopies of trees ripple in the unseen breeze, uninterrupted by roads, buildings, or any marks of human existence. There are no other planes in sight, no trails of civilization. The world here is raw and unspoiled, a secret kept in isolation.

Kody and Leo, now quiet, share my rapt attention as the shadow of our small plane skims across the wild, untamed beauty of Interior Alaska.

Miles and miles of unpopulated land float by, lulling me into a state of contemplation. The sheer scale and serenity of it all solidifies my belief that Hoss is in the Brooks Range.

If that's true, we should be approaching Fairbanks soon.

Leo doesn't have a manual for the radio equipment. He thinks it has a line-of-sight range. Depending on the antenna and atmospheric conditions, he'll probably see signs of human life on the horizon before he can communicate with anyone. But I notice him constantly checking the frequency bands.

Reaching forward, I tap Kody on the shoulder. When he twists toward me, I point at my wrist.

His brow wrinkles, and he removes his headset, shouting, "What?"

I could totally kick his ass in a game of charades. I mean, of course, he doesn't understand my gesture. He's never worn a watch.

"Time?" I yell, motioning at the cockpit. "How

long?"

He checks the clock on the instrument panel and holds up two fingers, shouting.

The roar of the engine snatches his voice away, but I got my answer and give him a thumbs up.

We've been airborne for two hours.

Instead of turning forward, his gaze stays with me, pulling me in.

He stares and stares, letting time burn between us, incinerating me. He should be taking in all the majestic views. I want to tell him he's missing it.

But he continues to sit with me, twisted in his seat, his eyes glinting like arctic snow in the sunlight.

I know that look. It says *you're so fucking pretty* and *I want to sink my teeth in you.*

The air in the cabin sprints from my lungs as I stare back.

I can't see his muscles anymore, but I know how they shift and move when he's healthy. I know how fucking sexy he looks when he swings an ax and shoots a crossbow and stalks me across the tundra under the northern lights.

I know he'd rather look at me than at any other view in the world. I don't know what I did to deserve that level of admiration and love, but I respond in kind. This thing we have means as much to me as it does to him.

As our gazes intertwine, I sense a shift in the atmosphere.

A shift that has nothing to do with our eye contact.

My instincts rear, scenting something's off. Kody feels it, too, and slips his headset back on, swiveling forward.

Leo's shoulders stiffen, a subtle change. His hands, previously steady on the controls, make urgent adjustments, each movement precise yet tense.

Glancing over, Kody's eyes flick rapidly between the instruments and the window, a crease forming in his profile.

I follow his gaze, trying to see what he sees.

What is it? What's wrong?

Nothing beeps or lights up in the cockpit, but silent alarms blare in my head.

Kody stiffens as he leans forward, as if bracing against an invisible force. His profile hardens with a quiet intensity, a mirror to Leo's focused determination.

My boots tap against the floor, a nervous rhythm I'm entirely aware of. The suspense is killing me.

Leo's glances outside become more frequent, his eyes scanning the horizon with a vigilance that makes my heart career off the rails. His lips separate, accommodating the fluctuation in his breathing, and I know something is terribly wrong.

I'm about to unlatch my seat harness and climb into the cockpit when Kody finally glances back at me, his complexion pale as he points at the windshield.

From my seat back here, I can't see shit.

Then I do.

The skies, so clear just moments ago, start to change.

Clouds gather. From the west, from the south, a darkness creeps in.

An ominous front rolls over the horizon, charged with flashing electricity and advancing at an unnatural speed.

It's a goddamn ambush.

frankie

TWENTY-NINE

My heart sinks as the world turns black before our eyes.

The weather was on our side when we took off, lulling us into a false sense of security, a belief that maybe, just this once, luck was on our side.

I should've fucking known better.

It's as if the storm was lying in wait, biding its time until we were far enough from Hoss, too committed to our course to turn back without risking the fuel we conserved for this flight.

Without radar, weather forecasts, or communication with the outside world, we took a risk on the clear skies.

We couldn't have known.

Don't freak out. It's just a storm.

I've flown in all kinds of weather—lightning, fog, heavy snow, and rain—and survived.

With an experienced pilot.

Fuck, we need to land.

Now.

Kody and Leo are already on it, leaning toward their windows, their eyes searching the wilderness.

The forest beneath us forms a lush, verdant carpet in every direction, so dense that no patch of earth shows through. The treetops sway gently in the breeze, a deceptive calm that belies what's coming.

Finding a suitable place to touch down grows more improbable by the second. The tightly packed spruces and uneven ground offer no openings for an emergency landing. None of the rare clearings are large enough, flat enough, or free of obstacles.

Even if we could land, then what? We have no food, and this is the Alaskan bush, still below freezing this time of year. That storm, hidden behind a deceptive curtain of dark clouds, will hit in a monstrous swirl of snow and ice. How would we hunt for food in those conditions?

"Can we go faster? Fairbanks should be close!" My shout bounces off their headsets, unheard.

I continue to watch the passing landscape, hoping to glimpse a bare patch, a riverbank, or even a lake that might offer a potential landing spot. But the reality is a continuous, unyielding forest.

My breaths sharpen into bursting gasps. With each ruthless dip, each unexpected drop, a silent scream builds in my throat.

Leo gives up on finding a clearing and tries to veer us away from the encroaching threat, reversing our path.

Kody twists to look at me, his face drained of color. No words needed. The plane is already shuddering, caught in the clutches of advancing winds.

I give him a tight nod, trying to assure him.

I'm okay. We're okay.

It'll be bumpy and terrifying. I'll probably throw up. But we'll get through this.

When he turns back to Leo, I grip the armrests, burying my fingernails into the vibrating metal, as if I can somehow anchor myself, keep the plane steady through sheer will. But the truth is evident in every violent, jarring tremor.

We're not in control.

The storm's rapid assault and raw power feed on the air, growing larger and more ferocious with each passing minute. Too soon, it bears down on us, gripping our little aircraft and shaking it back and forth.

Every bump shoves my stomach to my throat. The dips are the worst, when my heart stops, suspended in free fall, before the plane catches itself, only to be thrown into another breathless descent.

The instrument panel comes alive with flashing lights and warnings. I don't understand all the gauges and dials, but I recognize the urgency in their behavior.

The altimeter needle bounces as if in panic, reflecting our rapid ascents and descents. Other lights flicker—a blaring red that screams danger.

Leo glances at them and tightens his grip on the controls.

"You can do this!" Encouragement pours from me, even if it's a one-sided conversation. "Talk to him, Kody!"

The bond between them, their unspoken language, will keep him focused. Their lips are moving, communicating. They're working together. Not panicking.

Unlike me.

Panic sets my heart ablaze. Every muscle in my

body tenses, ready for the slightest jolt, but when the jolts come, I'm not ready. I scream, my voice raw with emotion.

The world beyond the window sweeps by in a blur of wind and gray clouds.

How can Leo see anything?

He can't.

I close my eyes against it, trying to find some semblance of peace in the darkness behind my lids, but the relentless motion of the plane, being smacked and tossed by the storm, won't let me escape.

Then I hear it.

The pelt of ice against the steel body, hitting us in vicious waves.

I open my eyes to a whiteout, sudden and complete, erasing the line between sky and earth with no end in sight.

The cockpit illuminates with the erratic dance of lights flashing across the instrument panel.

Leo battles against the torrential sleet, his efforts to outrun it carved in the set of his jaw. But the late winter blizzard fights back, its whipping winds dragging us downward at stomach-sinking speeds.

"Watch the trees!" I can't see them, but I know they're there. "Go higher! Higher! Oh, God, please, don't crash! Don't crash! Don't crash!"

Terror explodes from me, my shouts tumbling into the chaos, unable to influence the outcome.

A buzzer sounds, a harsh, grating screech that pierces the air, signaling an emergency within the plane's many systems.

Leo adjusts knobs and switches with a reflex that attests to his deep dive into the manuals and crash course in aviation.

I'm scared. So fucking sick with fear that every

shiver hits my nerves like a pickax.

But through it all, Leo's composure remains tightly controlled. His jaw is clenched, the muscles in his neck taut with the effort. His hands grip the controls with the steadiness of an experienced pilot.

He hides his fear well, trying to shield us from it, but I see his gaze darting to the instrument panel and the brief flickers of doubt crossing his face.

I should've told him I love him rather than holding it back until we land. What if I'm never able to say it to him again?

As I brace against another jolt, I swallow hard, repeatedly trying to moisten my dry throat and keep the tears at bay.

Leo's fighting not just for his life but for all of ours. Piloting a plane without training is a monumental undertaking in perfect conditions. But this?

This is fucking inconceivable.

In the dim, flickering light of the cockpit, amid the mayhem of alarms and warnings, his resolve is exquisite, his ferocious profile a mask of calm concentration.

Kody, hidden by the seat, reaches back, his hand finding mine. Our fingers entwine, and the plane plunges again.

"We're going to crash," I whisper, my blood violently pumping, rushing to my heart.

I feel the strain on the aircraft, the way it fights against the wind's merciless push and pull. The tension in the cabin thickens into a cloud of held breaths and unsaid prayers.

I can't see the ground, but I feel it, the trees rushing up to meet us, their branches clawing at our underbelly, cleaving away vital parts as we fall.

Tears stream down my face, the terror overwhelming as I squeeze Kody's hand and scream.

Impact.

Metal explodes in sound and fury, the bending of steel, the rending of trees. The plane shudders, breaking apart, each jolt a hammer blow, sharp and deadly.

As the cockpit rips away, taking my entire world with it, something strikes my head.

Blinding pain.

Sudden silence.

The terror yields to darkness.

monty

THIRTY

After two months of combing the Alaskan tundra for my unhinged brother, a Turbo Beaver, a hydroelectric log cabin, or anything that might lead me to Frankie, I'm hollowed out.

I would be in the skies right now, flying over the next grid, but a major fucking winter storm stands in my way. The deadly blizzard is moving across the Interior to the hills north and east of Fairbanks.

Not even I can fly in that.

So I'm grounded in Anchorage until it passes, a prisoner in my hotel suite, surrounded by luxury and consumed by restlessness.

I pace worn tracks into the plush carpet, my gaze frequently drawn to the expansive windows. The postcard views of downtown Anchorage, Cook Inlet, and the Chugach Mountains are buried under snow, offering no solace.

My mind races, haunted by unanswered questions and gnawing fear.

The revelation that Denver still breathes after three decades is a torment on its own. But the possibility that my wife has fallen into his twisted, depraved hands? That she could've given birth to my child while at the mercy of such malevolence?

It's more than I can bear.

It guts me with talons of pure, paralyzing dread. It's an agony that eclipses all others, a horror so visceral it permeates my every waking moment and preys upon my rare attempts to sleep.

Nights are the worst. The darkness amplifies my fears, turning the shadows into ghosts of my soulless brother. I lie awake, staring at the ceiling, envisioning nightmare scenarios that leave my heart racing and my body slick with a cold sweat.

Sleep, if it claims me, is fractured and fraught with visions of Frankie's fear, her pain, her calling out for me in a place where I can't reach her.

The dawn brings no relief, only the harsh light of day and the return to a reality where she's still missing.

She was one to two months pregnant when she took that test the morning of her disappearance.

Nine months ago.

Wilson, my head investigator outside of Alaska, checked every birth center in the country for patients matching Frankie's description.

Another dead end.

I'm a shell of myself, driven only by the singular obsession to find her, to bring her back to the safety of my arms.

Food has lost all taste, becoming a chore that I force down, if I remember to eat at all.

Work, once my domain of ambition and power, is

now a distant, meaningless endeavor. My desk is piled with tasks left untouched, emails unanswered, calls unreturned.

Doesn't matter. News of my brother's crimes spread far and wide, dragging my name through his filth.

I shut it all out.

My world has narrowed to one purpose, and every minute is consumed with the search.

I pore over maps, cross off grids, chase down leads, interrogate sources, anything that might bring me a step closer to Frankie.

Every instinct screams that Denver's the linchpin in her disappearance. Maybe Kaya's, too.

But I don't have proof.

The bank account he set up for Alvis Duncan is untraceable. Just like my father's offshore accounts.

Without solid evidence, like the location of that goddamn cabin, my hands are tied.

Winter in the Arctic Circle is brutal. On days when the pilots of my search parties won't fly, claiming the risk is too great, the weather too unpredictable, I turn to my own plane and fly alone, battling the elements and continuing the operation.

Using what we learned from Alvis Duncan, we narrowed the search to the region between Whittier and the North Slope Borough. That's two hundred thousand square miles of wild, sprawling wilderness.

We're looking for a needle in an area that's larger than the entire state of California.

The constant raging storms make the effort infuriatingly more challenging.

Like today.

Where the search parties see a blizzard with insurmountable risk, I see a day slipping away, another day without Frankie.

Waiting is not an option.

Yet here I am, doing exactly that, because not even the most experienced pilots can fly in this storm.

I turn back to my maps, the marked-up pages spread across the table. My eyes ache from strain, my body tense from constant stress, leaving me frayed at the edges, operating on a razor-thin margin between determination and despair.

"Where are you, my beautiful girl?"

With each sweep of the land, each grid I mark off, I feel a step closer to finding her, to unraveling the mystery that has decimated my life.

She's out there, somewhere, and I'll move heaven and hell to find her.

A sudden knock on the door shatters the monotonous thrum of my thoughts.

I find Sirena on the other side, her appearance a rare interruption to the solitude I've cloistered myself in.

She stands in the hallway, her phone clutched tightly, and her back stiff as a board. The usual glimmer in her eye, the one that hints at crafty flirtation, is gone.

"Monty." Her voice trembles slightly. "I just got word of a plane crash. A small turboprop outside of Fairbanks."

A chill, colder than the blizzard's breath, creeps down my spine and hardens my stomach. I know, even before she continues, this news is going to hurt me.

She pushes inside, closes the door, and turns.

"It's a Turbo Beaver." Chin raised, she sets her wary gaze on mine. "Three passengers. They're being transported to a hospital here in Anchorage right now. No one will confirm if they survived or who they are."

Her words clot the air, dense with a gravity that

demands my response.

But I can't move. Can't speak.

Carved in shock and disbelief, I'm a motionless statue as my mind grapples with the possibility that Denver was on that plane.

And the other two passengers…

They could be mine.

My wife and child.

I struggle to breathe, each inhalation a war against the suffocating horror.

"All adults?" My voice breaks, sounding foreign to my ears. "Is there an infant among them?"

"I don't know." Her expression softens. "I have asked those questions and more. The instant I have answers, I'll—"

"Get them now!" I stab a finger at her, pulse sprinting. "Make calls. Demand information. Learn everything you can." My volume explodes with intensity. "I need their identities yesterday!"

She's cultivated a network of contacts and resources over the years as a private investigator. Police officers, hospital staff, aviation authorities, people who respect her tenacity and trust her discretion. Hell, maybe she seduces the sensitive information out of them. I don't fucking care.

I just need answers.

If Denver was on that plane, if fate steered his path here, I hope—deep in my black, guilt-ridden soul—that he survived.

Not for salvation, not for redemption, but for retribution.

The thought of confronting him, of being the arbiter of his demise, ignites a blood-thirsty hunger within me. I want to look into his cold, depraved eyes and kill him myself. Slowly. Painfully. Permanently.

But beneath the rage and vengeance lurks a terrible dread. If Frankie was on that plane with him, my worst fears would be realized.

If she's been in his possession for nine months, the damage will be greater than any injury sustained from a plane crash in a blizzard.

If she survived at all.

"I'm on it." Sirena nods, her expression grave. "I mean, I've already made calls. But I'll call again. We can head to the hospital as soon as we know something."

Fuck that. I'm already gathering my coat, keys in hand before she finishes the last word.

"What are you doing?" She tracks me with wide eyes. "Monty, you can't. Have you seen the roads out there? And the hospital has strict policies about sharing patient information."

"If they have my wife and child, they'll tell me any goddamn thing I want."

The blizzard outside, the treacherous roads, the uncertainty of what I'm walking into—none of it matters. My mind is laser-focused on the hospital, on the survivors of that crash, and on the slim chance I'll see my wife for the first time in nine months.

As I stride to the door, the stark ring of a phone cuts through the heavy air of the suite. Sirena answers with a calm that no longer fits in my world.

I watch her, every fiber of my being strung tight, trying to read the unfolding conversation from the subtle shifts in her professional demeanor. When she asks if an infant was among the passengers, my heart lurches.

As she listens, her composure begins to fracture, her face paling with each word she hears.

"Are you sure?" she asks, her voice a thread of

sound in the harrowing silence. Then a nod. "Thank you."

She disconnects the call and turns to face me.

"One of the victims is a woman." Hesitantly, she steps closer. "A small redheaded woman."

The room tilts, shifting beneath my feet as I hang on one word. "Victims…"

"Passenger." She rushes forward, gripping my arm. "Not victim. I don't know—"

"Did your contact say *victim*?"

"I…I think so, but that doesn't mean anything. Don't jump to conclusions. I don't have any information on the woman's condition. We don't even know if it's her. She just arrived at the hospital with the other two passengers."

My heart seizes, caught between the jaws of hope and dread. "Who are the other passengers?"

"Adults. Both male. That's all I know."

It can't be her. The universe wouldn't be so cruel.

But I know it is.

A small redheaded women in a Turbo Beaver outside of Fairbanks.

My wife was in that crash.

The urgency that propels me into the hallway is no longer a need for answers. It's a race against time, against the unfathomable prospect of a world dimmed by her absence.

As I stride toward the elevator, haunting images seize my mind. Frankie, lying crumpled and lifeless in the wreckage of a plane. Her bright red hair splayed against the cold, twisted metal. Her face serene yet void of the life and ferocity that defined her.

No, she can't be gone. The very notion is the anathema to every shred of hope that surges through my veins, to the love that's been the cornerstone of my existence since the moment she walked into my life.

She's alive. She has to be. The thought of her not breathing, not smiling, not existing alongside me, shatters something fundamental within me. My love for her refuses to flicker and die. That love convinces me beyond reason, beyond evidence, that she still draws breath.

She's alive because my soul refuses to accept any other reality. I cling to this belief as I have clung to nothing else in my life.

The denial that prevents me from losing my fucking mind is also the fuel that drives me forward, through the blizzard and into the hospital toward whatever truth awaits.

She's alive. I will not accept any outcome where she isn't by my side.

THIRTY-ONE

I float in a haze, swimming without my body, untethered and directionless.

Panic bubbles at the edges, a rising static in a sea of feelings and sounds. The beeping, rustling of fabric, distant murmuring of voices—everything fizzes dully, every thought fragmented.

None of it makes sense. My mind struggles to latch onto something, anything familiar.

Where am I?

A short, high tone pierces through the fog, an electronic noise, accompanied by the whirs and hums of machinery.

My eyelids, heavy as lead, resist at first, then relent, parting to a world awash in sterile white and harsh fluorescent lights.

And piercing blue eyes.

Wolf's eyes.

They hover inches away, heartbreakingly familiar and intimate, so damn beautiful.

I gasp, blinking, confused and overwhelmed. My arm lifts awkwardly, connected to tubes, as I try to touch his face.

No.

Not Wolf's face.

These eyes are older, sharper, creased with maturity, shadowed with worry, and glaring with intensity.

It's the glare that dawns recognition.

"Monty?" The name feels foreign on my tongue, a keepsake from a life that was taken from me.

The last time I saw him, we were fighting.

No...wait. The last time I saw him, he was a man on a video screen, thrusting inside another woman.

The sting of that betrayal, that terrible pain, floods back with a vengeance, warring with the physical agony that flares in my body.

"Frankie. Thank fucking God." He lowers his head to mine, sighing against my lips. "You're safe now."

Machines buzz around me, the purpose of every beep and alarm clear to my trained ear.

I'm in a hospital.

I was in an accident.

A plane crash.

Leo and Kody.

Panic seizes me, my breath quickening, sending the heart monitor into a frenzy of beeps.

"Where are they?" I try to sit up, forcing him back as I frantically scan my surroundings.

Familiarity seeps through the cracks of my confusion.

The unmistakable, muted color of the walls, the layout of the room, the arrangement of medical equipment, the placement of the door, the bathroom, and the window with views of the cityscape framed by distant mountains—it all clicks into place.

This is where I did my residency program, where I spent years training, learning, and growing.

This is the hospital that shaped me as a nurse.

I'm in Anchorage.

And Leo and Kody aren't here.

Visions of the crash flash before my eyes, vivid and gutting. The screeching, the breaking, the cockpit ripping away. Each memory is a blade, cutting me open and spilling raw terror down my cheeks.

A cold sweat breaks across my skin. Icy dread seeps into my bones.

I can't be alone in this survival. I can't.

"Shh. Please, don't cry. Everything will be okay." He softly kisses the tears from my cheeks. "I've been searching for you...for so long." His voice cracks with rare emotion. "I thought I lost you."

So strange, that shattered, unguarded expression on his cruel face. It stirs a whirlpool of conflicting feelings within me. Betrayal and love, pain and nostalgia, they swirl together, indistinguishable from one another.

"Leo and Kody," I gasp out, my concern for them overpowering everything else. "They were with me. Are they...?"

A muscle twitches in his jaw, and his hand finds mine, a touch that's both familiar and alien. "You crashed outside of Fairbanks, not far from a busy hunting lodge. The guests saw the plane go down and had a helicopter on the premises. They were able to transport you and the other two passengers to Anchorage in record time. The others are unconscious but alive." He nods at the door. "Just down the hall."

Relief swamps me.

They're alive.

We survived.

We fucking did it.

We actually fucking escaped.

"I never stopped looking, Frankie. Not for a moment." His eyes search mine, seeking forgiveness, understanding, a bridge to a past I have no interest in rediscovering. "I made so many mistakes, but finding you, making sure you're safe, has been my only focus."

He rolls his bottom lip between his teeth while working that jaw. There are questions he wants to ask, things he doesn't know or understand. My miscarriage, his brother, my traveling companions, the past nine months—there's so much to unpack.

Right now, all that matters is that Leo and Kody are here, alone in a new world, and I need to be at their sides when they wake.

"They're unconscious? Any life-threatening injuries?" My head pounds as I push away the blankets and try to slide off the bed. "I need to get to them."

The room spins, and I grab the bed railing for support.

"You're not going anywhere." He lifts my bare legs, tucks them back in, and directs his eyes to my head. "Do you remember what happened?"

I reach up and prod at the bandage covering my entire skull. "How long have I been here?"

"A few hours. You have a head injury. Concussion." His Adam's apple bobs. "Lacerations and contusions all over your body from your broken seat, flying debris, and impacts with the interior of the aircraft."

"What about Leo and Kody?"

Impatience, anger, and something else flash in his eyes. "You know better than anyone that the hospital doesn't provide patient information to non-family members."

Monty *is* their family.

Maybe he doesn't know.

Or maybe he's still keeping secrets, pretending to be someone else.

He never told me he had siblings. Never *warned* me he had a raping, kidnapping, pedophile brother.

Why hasn't he asked me who Leo and Kody are or why I was with them? It's as if he's deliberately avoiding the topic.

Do I even know this man?

Married or not, we're strangers with the same last name, and that name isn't even real.

He said he was searching for me. Does that mean he knows I was kidnapped?

He knows something.

Do I think he was involved in Denver's evil bargains? No. Jesus, I can't fathom that. But he may have been privy to it, and that's a level of fucked-up I can't process right now.

I don't trust him.

But I do know one thing. If Monty wants something, he gets it.

"You're telling me..." I narrow my eyes. "You let a little privacy act stop you from acquiring information? The Monty I knew would've pressured and plied everyone here until he found out who his wife was traveling with."

He lowers to the edge of my bed, studying me. "I overheard the nurses talking about them. They sustained injuries, but they aren't life-threatening."

"Spinal injuries?"

"Nothing serious. That's all I know. I didn't even

know their names until you just told me."

I briefly close my eyes, savoring that confirmation.

"Do you remember what happened?" he asks again, coaxing my gaze back to him.

"A lot has happened, and I remember every goddamn second of it."

I'm not the same person I was nine months ago, and I'm not the only one who's changed.

The man sitting before me looks startlingly different. He's the Monty I remember but older, sadder, and brutally worn down. He looks fucking exhausted.

His face, once so chiseled, smoothly shaved, and distinguished, now bears the shadows of unkempt stubble and sleepless nights. The wrinkles around his eyes are deeper, more pronounced, as if each day without me added another layer of age.

Those eyes are still hard and cutting, but they now hold a depth of sorrow and regret so profound it hurts to look at him.

They're the eyes of a man who faced the very real possibility of never seeing his wife again.

He's lost weight, not to the dangerous degree that I have, but his suit hangs off his shoulders, oversized and crumpled, as though he's been wearing it for days on end, perhaps even sleeping in it.

He doesn't look like a man who's been out on the town, fucking every woman in Alaska.

He looks broken.

I've been searching for you...for so long.

I have so many questions I don't even know where to begin.

Despite his deterioration, there's a resilience in his bearing, the same focused, unwavering determination that made his global consulting firm so successful. He's not a man who gives up, no matter the cost to his physical and mental health.

He's been ruthlessly punishing himself for a long time, and it's unsettling to see it so clearly in his haggard appearance.

I harbor deep-seated anger for him, but I feel a pang of guilt for the pain he's endured, a swell of love for the man I married, a man who evidently never stopped looking for me.

I've always been weak where he's concerned. But I can't afford to be that way now.

"Can you forgive me?" He braces his hands on either side of my head, ensnaring me with his gaze.

"What are your sins, Montgomery Strakh?"

He doesn't react to his real name on my lips. Doesn't blink or breathe. Then slowly, stunningly, a sound rises in his throat. A deep, guttural sound of pain.

Pressing his lips in a tight line, he strangles the sob, swallows it down, and stares at me with a staggering cloud of agony and rage pulsing in his eyes.

I shiver. "Do you know who Leo and Kody are?"

He shakes his head, hands fisting in my pillow, his eyes never leaving mine.

"Denver took them when they were children. Held them captive all these years." I lower my voice, a soft murmur against the wall of tension between us. "He took me, too."

My heart clenches at the thought of them, my feral protectors. Are they awake? Looking for me? Needing me? How badly are they hurt?

The heart monitor accelerates, a frantic tempo that signals my spiraling fear.

"I'm so fucking sorry." He blinks rapidly, trying to ward off the unthinkable.

But it's there in his eyes.

A sheen of wetness.

Numbness spreads through me, dulling my senses to everything but the sight of Monty's vulnerability.

I've never seen him cry.

He doesn't make a sound. Doesn't try to hide it. His face lowers to mine as if he can't fight the pull.

I still don't trust him, but as his fingers twist in my hair, and our foreheads connect, I hold still and give him this moment.

A shudder runs through him.

"Breathe." I touch his bristly, rock-hard jaw. "With me. In, out, in, out."

He loosens a minty breath against my mouth, smothering me in his dark, rich, familiar scent.

A flurry of sound drifts in from the hallway as he draws in the next breath.

Then, in a blur of violent motion, he's gone as someone yanks him from the bed and hurls him across the room.

frankie

THIRTY-TWO

My heart stops as a wild, bare-chested man lunges at Monty like an animal, raining down fists with primal ferocity.

The room explodes in chaos as medical staff and security converge on the scene, obscuring my view.

Desperation shoves me upward. I attempt to stand, only to be ensnared by the IV line entwined in my blankets. I try again, and a rush of nausea hits me sideways, blotting my vision.

Fuck!

A nurse is on me in a heartbeat, guiding me back down.

"You guys are stirring up quite the commotion." She gently unravels the tangle of tubes that bind me. "With all those reporters outside and police everywhere..."

I tune her out, trying to track the raging man amid the pandemonium.

"Leo!" I scream into the din of shouting and scuffing shoes.

It has to be him. No one else embodies that raw, untamed fury.

Through the mesh of bodies, I catch glimpses of him, but not as the man I saw just hours ago.

Swathed in bandages from head to toe, he's a vicious, snarling creature wrapped in white tape and wrath, no longer attacking Monty but lashing out at anyone approaching.

"Leave him alone." I angle around the nurse. "Don't corner him like that."

Oh, God, I ache for him, for the misunderstanding and fear that sent him over the edge.

"Frankie, please lie down." The nurse urges me back onto the pillows.

"You don't understand. He's never been around people. Let me talk to him."

Where's Monty? I can't see him in the fray.

Security guards and uniformed police form a barricade around Leo, pressing closer and closer to him, ignoring my shouts.

More people swarm the room, led by a figure who sends my heart into a gallop.

Shirtless and covered in bandages, he swings his head toward me. His face is swollen beyond recognition, but I know those black bear eyes, the protruding bones in his too-thin body, and every scar on his back.

The instant he spots me, he limps forward, bypassing the commotion and scanning me up and down for injuries.

I shake my head, pointing at the crowd before he reaches me.

His gaze flicks to Leo, who just sent another guard

sprawling, then back to me.

"Help him." I gesture again. "Talk him down."

He hesitates, torn between erasing our distance and dealing with his brother.

"Please." I direct a worried glance at the frenzy.

He gives me another thorough once-over and angrily bares his teeth before turning away.

As he squeezes into the crush, Monty shoves his way out.

He reaches me in three strides, wearing the aftermath of Leo's punches across his face. Blood runs from multiple gashes, and one of his eyes is already swelling.

"I'm sorry. Leo is…I'll explain later." I grip his arm. "Please, you need to make everyone leave. Kody can handle Leo. He can calm him down."

My plea churns between us, thick with the promise of answers if he does this for me.

Skepticism blackens his expression, the doubt evident even through the blood. But he's hungry for explanations, just as I am.

With a scowl, he pivots toward the mayhem.

His influence is undeniable, his authority grounded in clout, money, and sheer force of will. The moment he sets his fingers between his lips and releases a sharp whistle, the room shifts.

"Clear out." His voice booms, swiveling every head in his direction. "I'm not pressing charges. No one is in danger. Everyone, leave now."

The guards hesitate.

"I said now!" He roars.

They jump. Some of them exchange looks. But eventually, they comply, their departure a reluctant retreat.

To the nursing staff, his tone allows no dispute. "Give us a minute."

As the room empties, I catch his stare.

"Thank you." Reaching for a box of tissues, I hold it out.

"There's a lot to discuss, Frankie." He takes a few tissues and clears the blood from his eyes.

"I know."

"In private only." He leans down, voice low. "Reporters are everywhere. Your reappearance made national news. Anyone in this hospital can sell your story to the highest bidder. Don't say a damn thing when people are around, including the nursing staff, unless you want it twisted and publicized. Understand?"

National news? Why? Because I married America's favorite billionaire playboy, Monty Novak?

My stomach sinks. "Got it."

Before we left Hoss, I advised Leo and Kody to keep their mouths shut and refuse to answer questions about themselves or anything else until we have an attorney present. Not knowing where we would land or how it would unfold, they agreed that we would wait until we could evaluate the situation together.

The door closes behind the last nurse, sealing us in with a charged silence.

Across the room, Kody grips Leo in an unbreakable embrace, whispering at his ear.

This must be the first time they've seen each other since the crash. Even from this distance, I feel the complex emotions of their reunion and survival thrumming in the air around them.

Their injuries appear miraculously superficial, a small mercy in the wake of such a violent crash. I'm desperate to see their charts, to understand exactly what they're dealing with. But at first glance, it looks like their heads, faces, and necks received heavy lacerations. Probably from broken glass and trees.

A shiver travels down my spine, the reality of what we survived chilling me anew.

Kody's limp implies a break or sprain. They're both wearing the pants they put on this morning. I imagine them grabbing those on their way out of their rooms to find me.

Leo's beard appears to be gone beneath the bandages. His head is wrapped, too. It'll break my heart if his hair was removed.

They should both be in their beds, but I'm so fucking grateful they found me. We can't be separated, especially not now as they adjust to their new life.

As they pull apart and start toward me, Kody's gaze lands on Monty, who stares at him with a look of recognition, or perhaps confusion, shining in his eyes.

Leo's expression mirrors his brother's as they both fixate on Monty with an intensity that makes me uneasy.

"What?" I tense.

"Wolf." Kody rubs at the bandage on his breastbone. "He looks like Wolf."

A vise tightens around my chest, making it hard to breathe.

Monty stiffens. "What did you say?"

"Do you know that name?" I ask.

"It was…" Monty straightens, tugging at the cuffs of his shirt. "That was my nickname when I was a kid."

My thoughts scatter, and I share a look with Leo and Kody.

Wolfson.

Wolf's son.

"Do you know Gretchen Stolz?" I manage to choke out.

Monty's reaction is immediate, his face draining of color. "How do you know that name?"

Oh, God. He knows Wolf's mother.

How did I not see it before? Maybe because the similarities weren't there. I mean, the same eye color, yes. But Wolf's hair was shaggy and messy, framing a gaunt face that looked nothing like the Monty I knew.

The Monty who stares at me now, however...

This resemblance is new.

Monty has changed. He's lost so much weight it thinned out his face and narrowed his entire frame, altering his appearance into Wolf's likeness.

He no longer looks polished and rigid. He has this whole beaten-down, strung-out, emo vibe that wasn't there before. His jaw is scruffy. His eyes are haunted, dark with torment and shadows. He looks so sad. So broken.

Like Wolf.

Tears blur my vision, the implication cleaving my gut like Gretchen's knife.

Monty is Wolf's father?

He didn't want kids. He didn't want *our* child. But he had a child with that raping bitch, Gretchen?

The questions crash over me, each one more painful than the last.

"Helena Weiss?" Leo growls his mother's name. "Do you know her?"

"No." Creases appear on Monty's bleeding face.

Kody limps forward, watching him closely. "Kaya Knowles."

Monty staggers backward as if physically struck. "How?" His expression collapses with startling pain. "How do you know her?" His eyes dart between us, landing on Kody with a dawning comprehension.

"Kaya was my mother," Kody says coldly.

"No..." Monty collapses in a nearby chair. "Was?"

"She died when I was two."

Monty knew Kaya, possibly even loved her, given the horror limning his features.

Does that mean he fathered Kody, too?

So many connections forged in blood and shrouded in secrets, and Monty's at the center of it. I don't know which way is up or what truth to believe.

Everything spins around me, hitting me in waves of dizziness and making me wobble on the bed. But Leo and Kody are there, wrapping me up in their strong, safe arms.

The steel frame of my bed groans as Kody climbs in with me, adjusting my legs to rest over his lap.

Leo stands beside us, arms crossed and knuckles bleeding.

We all need medical attention.

"Where is Denver?" Monty lifts his head, his eyes burning as he takes in the three of us.

Leo and Kody stiffen.

"We'll answer your questions." I close my eyes and focus through the reeling bouts of vertigo. "But I have some demands first."

"I'm listening."

"I want to see their medical charts."

"You can't even open your eyes, Frankie. You need rest."

I turn my neck, squinting at him. "I want their medical charts. And I will not be separated from Leo and Kody again. If we're staying the night here—"

"You're staying the night," Monty confirms.

"I want them transferred in here with me."

His jaw turns to stone. Oh, he doesn't like that one bit.

Too bad.

"I want a lawyer." I meet his furious gaze. "Not one of yours. I want someone who isn't connected to you. A neutral party who will represent Kody, Leo, and me."

"Frankie…"

"I'm not finished." I pull in a steadying breath. "I assume detectives are working this case? I saw uniformed police officers here. I want one present when we talk."

"My investigator—"

"Someone who doesn't work for you."

"Everyone works for me." He stands, pushing back his shoulders, his posture unbending.

He's seconds from yanking me away from Leo and Kody. They notice it, too, leaning forward and bracing for a fight.

Every scorned cell in my body wants to tell him I know about his affairs. But I must wait for a lawyer before we start hashing things out. I'm afraid I'll let my emotions get the best of me and inadvertently say too much.

Like the fact that I murdered his brother.

"I don't know what's going on here." Monty eyes my lovers, his nostrils flaring. When he returns to me, his expression softens. "I can only assume that the three of you escaped something unimaginable. I can't begin to fathom what you've suffered. The thought is fucking killing me inside. I don't want to know, but I need to know. I need every fucking detail. I'm here to help you, Frankie, in every capacity. You can trust me."

Trust, once given freely, was crushed over the past nine months by revelations too monumental to grasp.

My need for truth, for clarity, overshadows his need

to help me.

The path forward with Monty is uncertain. He's too entangled in this, and I hate to admit it, but I need his power and money to smooth the transition for Leo and Kody.

But one thing is clear. Leo, Kody, and I must navigate it with eyes wide open, no matter what truths await us.

"Don't ask for her trust." Leo glares at him. "Your brother kidnapped her."

"He kidnapped all of us." I look into Monty's eyes, so similar to Wolf's. "A brother I didn't know you had."

"There's a damn good reason I didn't tell you. But I'll tell you now. I'll tell you everything."

"Yeah, you will. But before we tell you anything, you will see to my demands."

"Frankie." His stance hardens, a wall of muscle against the siege of his own rage. "I'm not the bad guy."

"What would you do in her position?" Leo tilts his bandaged head. "How would you advise her if you weren't emotionally invested?"

Monty holds his stare, gritting his teeth. Then he releases a sharp breath. "I'll make it happen."

Leo strides to the door and opens it, wordlessly evicting Monty from the room.

Making him leave feels cruel. I loved him once when I thought he was a good man. Part of me still loves him. But it's darkened by rage.

Because he's not innocent. I saw the recording of him cheating. He hurt me far worse than I could ever hurt him.

Silence overtakes him as he flicks his gaze between us, his expression impenetrable.

When it lands on me, I stare right back, dizzy and

exhausted, every inch of me hurting.

Maybe he sees that because instead of fighting me, his shoulders drop, and he strides from the room.

The second the hospital room door closes, it opens again.

"Go away!" I shout before the intruder comes into view.

A young male nurse rounds the corner, glowering at me before whipping his head toward Kody. "Sir, I need you to get off her bed and return to your room. Hospital policy doesn't allow—"

"Any minute now, your manager will give you a change of plans." Frankie clutches Kody's wrist as if he intends to go somewhere. "Leo and Kody will stay in this room with me until we leave."

"This is a private room for one patient." The male steps toward Kody and abruptly stops at the sound of his threatening growl. "We can't accommodate your request."

"I did my residency here and know that this is the

largest room in the hospital. Speak to Monty Novak about the new arrangements."

He perks up at the mention of Monty's name, which is really fucking irritating.

"I need to check your fluids." He steps toward her.

"I already checked everything." She waves a hand at the equipment. "All good here."

He hesitates like he wants to say more.

I point at the door. "Give us five goddamn minutes alone, for fuck's sake!"

"Leo..." She sighs and offers the nurse an exasperated grimace. "Look, we've been through some shit and survived injuries far worse than this. We're not going to die in the next few minutes. Please, can you just give us a moment alone?"

The man shoots another glare in my direction. "I'll find Mr. Novak."

"Thank you," Frankie says.

When the door clicks shut behind him, gravity realigns, pulling us irresistibly toward one another. Without speaking, Frankie, Kody, and I collide in a tangle of bodies on her bed, our tightly wound embrace a convergence of relief, love, and quiet fears that have been riding us since takeoff.

"We made it," I breathe into our huddle.

"We really did." Her arms squeeze around us, her strength surprising given everything she's endured.

"Against every goddamn odd." Kody's grunt carries the weight of the world.

Or maybe just the weight of *our* world since we're piled on top of him.

We rearrange into a more comfortable position on the small bed, clinging to one another with Frankie between us.

She kisses us, and we kiss her back, taking turns at

her mouth, licking and tasting her lips.

My hands move of their own volition, tracing the contours of her ribs, the slope of his shoulders, seeking the tactile proof that this is real, that they're here with me.

Long red hair slides between my fingers, softer than I remember. Her arms and waist, thinner than I remember. My palm skims across Kody's back, feeling the solid reality of him and tracing the scars that knit unspeakable memories.

Every inch of them, warm and alive under my touch, reassures me more than words ever could.

We're here, together, wrapped in bandages like mummies, resurrected in Anchorage where she did her residency.

It all feels surreal, surrounded by the constant buzz of machinery and the steady flow of people just beyond the door.

My life in the tundra didn't prepare me for this—the incessant noise, the glaring lights, the smell of chemicals mingling with a hundred other scents I can't name.

The most jarring part, though, isn't the sensory overload. It's the touching. People here, especially the nurses, don't think twice about laying hands on me. From the second I woke in this strange place, they've been poking, prodding, and directing me with a familiarity that sets my skin on edge.

I'm not used to being touched by strangers.

In the wild, physical contact means one of three things—a sign of trust, a form of abuse, or a precursor to battle.

Here, it's routine and clinical. It's meant to heal, but it feels invasive, a reminder of how far I am from the world I know.

But none of that matters, not really. My focus, my only concern, is Frankie and Kody. Seeing them here, hurt but alive, is a consolation that's hard to put into words.

I'm gentle when I brush the gauze that covers their heads, the texture rough and grounding beneath my fingertips, dispelling the fear that this might all be an elaborate dream from which I'll awaken back in Hoss.

We're battered to hell with concussions, a mess of cuts and bruises decorating our skin, and severe malnutrition. I'm glad she asked to see our charts. I didn't even know that was a thing.

My attention jumps to Kody. He was limping earlier, favoring one leg over the other.

"What's wrong with you?" I lock onto his gaze.

"Knee hurts."

"Let me see it." She tries to sit up.

"No." He catches her by the throat, holding her down. "It's fine."

"Kody."

"Frankie."

She grits her teeth. "Did they X-ray it?"

"I wouldn't let them." He caresses the lines of her neck. "I needed to get to you guys."

I understand that. The need to find one another, to see with our own eyes that we're all okay, it's a force more compelling than any pain.

When they had me separated, tethered to an IV and a bed, the walls felt like a cage. So I did what Kody did. I tore out the IV, ignored the protests of nurses, and went searching.

Through the network of hallways, past rooms filled with strangers, everything amplified. The squeak of shoes on plastic floors. The distant cries of pain. The unintelligible announcements over the speakers. Everything here is disorienting, all these new sounds and sights, the throngs of people everywhere.

When I found Frankie's room and saw a man leaning over her, I snapped. The sight of his face near hers—kissing her, hurting her, or trying to take her—it lit a fuse I couldn't snuff out.

"Did you kiss him?" My voice drops to a low growl, barely contained.

"No, Leo." Flipping to her back to look at me, she tucks a hand against my neck. "He was crying, and I was just...trying not to be an asshole."

It's irrational, the surge of jealousy and protectiveness thrashing through me, but I can't stop the words from crashing out. "You're not getting back together with him."

Her gaze hardens. "It never even crossed my mind."

"He knew Gretchen and...my mother." A shadow passes over Kody's face, clouding his features like a veiled moon. "Monty is my father. Wolf's and mine."

"We don't know that." Her expression falls, looking horrified.

"He's not what I expected. Nothing like Denver." He absently picks at the tape on his arm. "He wears his emotions out in the open. He's...kind of a mess."

"That's new." A frown tugs at the corners of her mouth. "When I met him, he was super uptight, cocky, and always in control. I guess he still is, but he's changed in the past nine months. I mean, that was the first time I've ever seen him cry."

I scoff, not even trying to hide my distrust. "Shedding a few tears doesn't make him trustworthy. He lied to you, cheated on you, and let you get kidnapped by his own damn brother."

"He wasn't involved in the kidnapping."

"Are you sure?"

"Yes."

"Do you have proof?"

"It's a feeling in my gut."

I don't know if she's right. My instincts tell me not to trust him. "He should've been there to protect you."

"We can argue about this, Leo, but it doesn't change the fact that we need him."

"No, we fucking don't."

She huffs and looks at Kody.

"He thinks you belong to him." A vein pulses in his forehead.

"I don't care what he thinks." Her chest rises with a deep breath. "Here's the reality. We have no money, nowhere to live, no way to pay for all these medical bills, no jobs. You two don't have IDs, birth records, or proof of citizenship to get jobs, and let's not forget..." She lowers her voice to a whisper. "I killed Denver."

"It was self-defense." I feel my face heating, my temper flaring.

"Was it? He was in a cage, and I murdered him in cold-blood."

"He was holding you captive."

"From his cage? This isn't an open-and-shut case. I did what I had to do, but I'll have to prove that."

"That's why we're getting a lawyer."

"One of the many reasons. Oh, and we'll need money for that, too. I have some savings, a little bit stashed away, if it's still there. But it's not enough." Her shoulders slump, the bruises darkening around her eyes.

Is she hurting as badly as I am under all the bandages? I feel like I've been trampled by a thousand angry moose.

"Come here." I carefully gather her against my chest and share a look with Kody.

He needs rest, too. We all do.

"I know Monty made some unforgivable mistakes." She lifts her arm, letting Kody untangle her IV tubes. "But we might need his help. He's the most powerful man in the state of Alaska. He can make most, if not all our problems disappear with the snap of his fingers. And, whether we like it or not, he's the only family we have left."

I catch myself chewing the inside of my cheek, using pain as a distraction from the turmoil roiling inside me.

I'm not afraid of Montgomery Strakh or her history with him. Fear doesn't enter the equation. It's not about being fearless, either. It's about what matters. Frankie and Kody, they're my world. Everything else—the unfamiliarity, the discomfort, the rules of society—it's just background noise. I would navigate worse, endure anything, to make sure they're safe.

I guess that means I'll endure her ex.

She trails a finger along the old wound on my abdomen. "Did the medical staff ask about your scars?"

"Yeah." I rest my chin on her head. "They asked a lot of questions. I didn't tell them shit."

"Same." Kody yawns.

I wonder how he's doing with all this. When uncomfortable, he tends to withdraw into himself, making it difficult to read his thoughts.

Monty might be his father. That's enough to take in alone without all the bright lights, loud noises, and people.

How am I related to them? Monty claims he didn't know my mother.

Someone drew my blood, so the hospital has my DNA. With access to medical technology, Kody and I can finally confirm Denver's allegations of our blood relation.

"This is just a transition period." I pull back enough to look at them, to see the determination and love reflected back at me. "We have a whole new life to start."

"Together." She gives me a tired half-smile. "With or without Monty's help, that doesn't change."

Kody's right about Monty. The man stares at her with an unnerving sense of ownership. That's going to be a problem.

"We'll have to figure out how to deal with him." My eyes connect with Kody's. "On our terms. We protect each other, first and foremost."

Kody cocks his head. "Someone's coming."

"Okay, let them examine you, take X-rays, and do whatever else needs to be done." She reaches for both our hands. "But don't tell them anything about Hoss until we talk to the lawyer."

I slide out of the bed, and Kody stands beside me, forming a united front as the door swings open.

kodiak

THIRTY-FOUR

People flood the hospital room, pushing two additional beds into the already cramped space, screeching the wheels across the floor. Nurses, a blur of scrubs and focused expressions, follow close behind, orchestrating the transformation.

Leo intervenes, demanding that Frankie's bed goes in between ours. Of course, he's right, but they argue with him for a few minutes before giving in.

The buzz of conversations, ringing machines, and artificial air blowing from the vents merges into a dissonance that I struggle to filter.

As the room changes and settles into its new configuration, I instinctively keep Frankie in my line of sight, ensuring her safety against the unknowns that swarm around us.

Among those unknowns, Monty stands out. Expensively dressed in his suit with a phone pressed to his ear, he commands everything and everyone with an authority that grates on me.

His eyes constantly find and linger on Frankie, loaded with a proprietary claim that tenses my battered body. I've never been comfortable with the idea of ownership when it comes to people, and seeing it so blatantly displayed on his busted face makes me want to add more bruises.

I lean against the wall closest to her, shifting the weight off my throbbing knee. I already miss the silence and stillness of snow-covered landscapes and the quiet company of the northern lights.

The continuous fucking noise, nonstop movement of humans, confinement of small rooms, and the antiseptic chill in the air goes against nature itself.

My senses are honed for the subtleties of the wilderness, not this barrage of stimuli.

An older female nurse approaches Leo, her hands quick and practiced as she prepares the machines, directs him to his bed, and offers him a large cloth with arm holes, similar to the one Frankie wears. Must be a standard protocol in the bustle of medical procedures, because she gives me one, too.

"There's a bathroom." She gestures at the attached room. "Please, change in there and return to your beds."

Leo's response is quintessentially him—direct, unapologetic, and devoid of self-consciousness—as he sheds his pants in one smooth motion and sits naked on his bed.

I cough, stifling my amusement as I remove my own pants and tie the strange garment around my hips like a towel.

"Kody." Frankie motions me toward her bed with laughter in her eyes. "Like this."

She repositions the gown to cover my front half

while leaving my backside exposed.

What the fuck?

"My way makes more sense." I lift the corner of her blanket and peer beneath it. "Is your ass hanging out, too?"

Monty charges forward, shooting me a murderous glare as he extends his phone to Frankie. "I have a call for you."

I widen my stance and ball my hands into fists. If the old man wants to brawl, I'll gladly wipe the floor with him.

Reading my thoughts, she rests a hand against my abs and takes the call.

"Hello?" Her demeanor instantly lightens. "Hey, Rhett." Her head tilts as she listens, and a soft smile blooms on her face. "Thank you. Yeah, that would be great." Then her eyes widen. "Yes, of course, I want my job back. I'll be in touch after all this is...well, after a period of adjustment. Thank you again."

She hands the phone back to Monty, thanking him, too.

The tension in my chest constricts.

Monty's role in returning this normalcy to her life puts her in his debt. That doesn't sit well.

Leo, now wearing a gown like me, extends his arm as the nurse reinserts the IV. A scowl twists the bandages covering his face, his glare fixed on Monty.

Yeah, he doesn't like the man, either.

"That was Rhett, my manager in Sitka." Frankie looks between Leo and me through the traffic of busy nurses. "He connected us with his attorney. Her name is Melanie Stokes, and she resides here in Anchorage. She's on her way to the hospital now."

That's good news. Securing a lawyer, someone who

can decipher the legal complexities ahead, offers a glimpse of stability. It's a load off our shoulders.

But as she thanks Monty again, that relief is tainted with a bitterness I can't shake. He helped her get a lawyer by calling someone I assume she trusts—her boss at the hospital.

My gratitude toward him is overshadowed by an ingrained distrust. His brother made my life a living hell. His infidelity hurt her so deeply that she considered jumping off the cliff. And the way he handled her pregnancy?

Fuck that guy.

It's a contradiction that gnaws at me, this reliance on someone I'm inclined to feed to the wolves.

A young blonde nurse approaches, trying to direct me to my bed. I give her a growl, but this one doesn't scare easily. She anchors her hands on her hips, wearing a withering scowl.

"Kody..." Frankie stares at the discoloration in my knee. "You need to get off that leg."

I'm not interested in leaving her side, even if my bed is only a few feet away.

"Stick me." I hold my arm out at the nurse. "I'm not moving from this spot."

"Just do it." Frankie nods to the reluctant woman. "He needs the fluids and electrolytes, and he's not going to let it happen any other way."

"I understand that you want to be close to her." The nurse makes a face at the arrangement of three beds. "But for your safety, it's important that you're in a stable and secure position when I insert the IV."

"You won't change his mind." Frankie inches up the front of my gown, revealing the scar left by lethal fangs. "A wolf attacked him, and I gave him a direct transfusion on a kitchen table. Trust me, he can handle an IV while standing up."

The nurse gawks at my chewed-up thigh, blinks a few times, and gathers her supplies without another word.

While she sticks the IV in my arm, another woman enters the room. This one wears a buttoned shirt and pants, marking her as someone outside the nursing staff.

"Mr. Novak instructed that we give you these." Her voice is neutral, businesslike, as she extends two folders to Frankie. "Medical charts for Leo and Kody. We don't have their full names since they refused to provide those." She glances at Leo and me and returns to Frankie. "I hope you'll convince them to share their health history and other personal details."

Our refusal to cooperate brings a grim satisfaction. It's a small rebellion, a way of clinging to the last vestiges of our privacy in a world that seems hellbent on stripping it away.

Yet, as I glance at the folders, reality cuts through the defiance. This is serious. Those charts represent our presence in this foreign system, a footprint that's currently nonexistent.

The problem is we don't know our identities, birth dates, addresses, emergency contacts, genetic diseases...I don't know the answers to most of the questions they asked me when I woke.

"I'll see what I can do." Frankie flips open the folders, scanning the contents with an experienced eye.

"Thank you." Monty dismisses the woman without looking at her.

He's staring at me.

As the nurse finishes my IV and steps away, I lock onto those arctic blue eyes and hate how much he looks like my brother.

That's what Wolf would've looked like in twenty-five years.

A static charge agitates the short distance between us. Separated by Frankie's bed, we're in a standoff, a battle of mutual suspicion. I read the distrust in his eyes as clearly as if he's shouting it. It rivals my own.

The air thickens with unvoiced questions and assumptions. His gaze sharpens and digs like he's trying to peel back the layers of our survival story to find the truth. It's evident he's piecing together his own narrative, one where Frankie's heart no longer belongs to him.

Tension ripples from him in waves, holding the room in a tight grip. I can tell he's on the brink of voicing his suspicions, of asking the one question that's eating him alive.

Did Leo or I fuck Frankie?

Yeah, Montgomery Strakh, blood of my blood, kin of my kin. We've been inside her in every way possible, and she lives inside us. You may have fathered me and married Frankie, but she's with us now. Until forever.

Our eyes remain locked, a silent acknowledgment of the standoff. There's an understanding, however reluctant, that this confrontation must wait.

The room is too crowded, too full of ears straining to catch snippets of private conversations. This isn't the time or place for accusations and personal disclosures.

When we finally look away, the bristling tension doesn't dissipate. It merely recedes, lying in wait for a more opportune moment to surface.

Monty steps back, physically distancing himself, but the questions remain, hovering like Wolf's cigarette smoke.

He's going to fight for Frankie and try to salvage his

marriage. I feel the foreboding, the looming battle, and the implications it holds for all of us.

Despite the dread, there's a resolve within me. The medical evaluations will come to an end. The room will clear. The lawyer will arrive. The moment for open, unguarded discussion will present itself, and Leo and I will tell him exactly how it will be.

Until then, we exist in a limbo of waiting and wary observation.

"Kody needs an X-ray." Frankie hands the charts to my nurse and looks at me. "Other than your leg, concussion and malnutrition are the biggest concerns. They took blood when you both arrived. Those tests are in the works now."

She grabs her own medical chart from the holder on the footboard and quickly skims through it.

"You provided all my information?" She glances at Monty.

He nods, his expression unreadable.

I watch her closely, the tremble in her fingers as they trace the words on the page.

The hospital room feels colder, the beeping monitors more distant as she reads. "A gynecological test was performed when I arrived." Her whisper barely cuts through the heavy silence. Her eyes, wide and searching, flick over the words again, absorbing them. "Because...my known recent pregnancy."

The way she hesitates, it's like watching a snowflake caught on the cusp of an arctic wind, hovering briefly before being swept away.

Sitting behind Monty, Leo instantly senses she's upset. He starts to climb out of his bed, flexing his arms and pulling the IV tube taut, a predator about to break his chains to get to her.

I give him a sharp shake of my head and a commanding glare. This doesn't involve him or me.

He knows I'm right and stays in his bed, but his gaze remains ever vigilant.

"The tests came back..." With a courage that rips out my heart, Frankie slowly, painfully lifts her gaze to the man who demanded an abortion. "You know, then. That I lost our baby."

Monty's nod is heavy, burdened with a sorrow so shocking that it suffocates the room, wrapping us in a chilling fog. Why does he look so devastated?

"When? How?" He reaches for her hand.

She yanks it away before he makes contact and scans the crowded room. She can't discuss Denver or her captivity now.

Pain flashes across Monty's face. "We'll talk about that, too."

A private moment stretches between them, their connection a delicate thread fraying under their shared grief.

They created a baby together.

But Leo and I were there when she lost that baby and stood witness to her anguish in the aftermath. Hearing her speak of it now, seeing the memory resurface in her beautiful green eyes—it's a different kind of knowing. It's my pain now, and Leo's, irrevocably imprinted on our shared existence.

I want to reach out, to bridge the gap of cold, sterile air between us with a touch, a word, anything to ease her sorrow. But I'm frozen, caught in the burning glare of Leo's eyes, conscious of his need to comfort her, too. It's a visceral, wrenching thing, this impulse we have to protect her from the harshness of the world.

Monty's face contorts with guilt and empathy, his eyes glossed with unshed tears.

For a fleeting moment, I feel for the man. He's about to find out that he didn't lose just one child.

He lost two.

I swallow hard against the lump in my throat, aching for Wolf, for Frankie, for us.

A hush closes in, alloyed with the inadequacy of words. No platitudes can mend the chasm opened by loss. No assurances can bring back what was.

If Monty's assistance helps her heal and move forward, I'll swallow my pride and unease, one step, one breath, one heartbeat at a time.

"I met all your conditions but one." He waits until the nurse closest to us moves to the other side of the room. Then he whispers adamantly, "No cops. No detectives. They are required to report everything. If..." He searches her eyes, his voice barely audible. "If laws were broken, we need to tread carefully."

My mind reels. He doesn't know she killed Denver.

Obviously we escaped, so maybe he suspects it.

Or maybe he's involved in his own criminal activity.

Without giving anything away, Frankie meets his stare. "I wanted someone present to keep the peace, but we can proceed without that." Her gaze flicks to Leo and narrows. "No brawling. Not here. Not in public. Promise me."

He grinds his jaw back and forth, relaxes it, and tips his head in agreement.

I sense his vulnerability in the gesture, a rare concession from the complex man who is my brother. He's fiercely independent yet understanding of necessity, unbound by societal expectations yet willing to engage with them when it matters.

She turns to me with a different demand in her eyes.

No words needed. It's my job to keep him on a leash and prevent him from biting anyone who comes too close.

Lucky me.

"When you were seeing to my demands…" She rubs her bandaged head and peers at Monty from beneath her lashes. "Did you learn anything about the plane crash?"

"I did." He steps to the end of her bed and grips the footboard. "It was nothing short of miraculous how things unfolded. From what I've been told, your lives are owed to a combination of luck, quick reflexes, and crucial decision-making on behalf of the pilot." He looks directly at Leo. "How did you learn how to fly?"

Leo meets his stare squarely, giving him nothing.

"Fine." Monty's sigh punctuates the air. "The press has a lot of theories on why you were flying in a deadly blizzard, but I can only think of one reason. You had no choice. You were starving, that much is obvious. But I know it's far worse than that. I know you saw an opportunity to escape, and you took it."

His gaze sweeps over us, sharp and probing, looking for confirmation.

We're a fortress, our faces void of any sign that might betray our thoughts or feelings.

We can't trust him.

His jaw flexes, and he clears his throat. "You crashed near a luxury hunting lodge. When the plane tore apart in the trees, the cockpit landed in a small lake on the property. The water cushioned the fall, saving your lives." He pauses, glancing at Leo and me, letting that sink in. Or maybe to collect his thoughts before continuing. "Frankie." He shifts his attention to where she lies, a softness creeping into his voice. "Your seat broke away from the rest of the plane. Somehow you stayed harnessed in it. That seat...it acted like a buffer, absorbing the brunt of the impact. It shielded your vital organs from severe damage."

"Damn." Her eyes connect with mine, and she shakes her head with a trembling smile. "How many times have you saved my life now?"

I strapped her in and triple-checked that harness but... "Leo was the one behind the controls. He wins this round."

When I look at him, our eyes hold a conversation of their own, sharing the disbelief that we survived something so catastrophic. I don't remember the cockpit tearing away or falling into the lake. I blacked out the instant the trees stabbed through the windshield and smacked me across the face.

It's a lot to absorb, knowing how close we came to a different ending and how fate or luck or sheer happenstance intervened on our behalf.

But we made it.

Frankie follows up with a dozen questions, but Monty doesn't have details beyond what he shared.

The nurses continue to maneuver around us, touching, adjusting, and instructing with authority born of routine. I've never felt more out of my element.

The instinct to stand, to place myself between Frankie and any perceived threat, is a constant hum beneath my skin. But I recognize the necessity of their actions, the importance of their role in our recovery.

It's a precarious balance between my primal urge to guard her with my body and the understanding that, here, protection comes in the form of IVs, monitors, and the skilled hands of medical professionals.

But let's be clear. I don't have to like it.

The constant prodding, the sanitized environment,

the way everyone seems to move with purpose without understanding—it's unsettling.

The dynamics may have shifted, the landscape altered beyond recognition, but the core of who I am, what I stand for, remains unshaken.

As for Monty, he'll just have to adjust to us.

While the Arctic might be behind us, the strength it forged within us is very much alive.

kodiak

THIRTY-FIVE

With our beds aligned together and the nurses' tasks complete, the room finally settles. I take a deep breath.

The overstimulation remains with every invading sound and scent, but so does my determination. I will adapt. I will learn. And above all, I will protect Frankie and Leo against anyone or anything that threatens them.

Our bubble of calm barely lasts a minute before a new nurse enters, clipboard in hand, a wheelchair preceding her.

"Time for your X-ray, Kody." Her tone brooks no argument. Neither does the security guard standing at her side.

Apparently, the entire medical staff has been warned about Leo's temper and our noncompliance with procedures.

Worry fills Frankie's eyes. I can see the cogs turning

as she strategizes a way to tag along and coddle me through the ordeal.

"Your ass isn't leaving this bed, woman." I lift her hand to my mouth, kissing her soft fingers and inhaling the sweet scent from her skin. Then I turn to Monty Novak. "You're coming with me."

The decision isn't up for debate. I can't leave him here with Leo. The possibility of a repeat brawl while I'm not here to intervene is unacceptable.

And it's not just about my brother. Leaving Monty with Frankie, even with Leo protecting her, feels wrong on every level. My trust only extends so far.

I expect Monty to argue, but he's already striding to the door.

That doesn't bode well.

Leo catches my eye, an unspoken understanding passing between us. He won't let anything happen to our girl.

"Behave," I growl.

The asshole smirks.

The nurse hangs my IV fluid bags on a pole with wheels and guides it and me toward the door.

My knee protests immediately, a sharp stab of pain that buckles through me like lightning. The hot, searing sensation reminds me of the crash, sharp and violent.

I grit my teeth and limp through it.

Until the nurse spins the wheelchair into my path.

Yeah, right.

Grunting, I grab the IV pole, push past her, and step into the hall, my senses on edge, vigilant and prepared.

Monty must've chased off the security guard. He stands alone, hands in his pockets, watching me with a strange expression.

But my focus isn't on him. It's on Frankie, the room I'm leaving behind, and the silent promise I make to return as quickly as I can.

As I follow Monty down the corridor, I'm acutely aware of the cold air on my exposed ass and the nurse's footsteps hurrying after me.

"Kody." The nurse wheels that damn chair into my path again. "If your leg is broken—"

"It'll still be broken if I sit in that thing." I motion her forward. "Lead the way."

I have no idea where I'm going.

"Radiology." Monty points at a sign and rounds the next corner, following the nurse.

Another corridor stretches before me, a bland, impersonal space that seems miles away from the room where my entire world waits.

Limping along, I concentrate on each step. The pain in my knee is insistent, a constant echo of the crash. But it's just one more thing on the long list of discomforts I'm pushing through.

The harsh lights, the buzzing voices and machinery, the unnatural smells, it's all an overwhelming assault on my already frayed nerves.

Then there's the silent shadow beside me.

He could be my father, not just the man who married Frankie and the brother of my enemy, but a link to my existence.

When we turn into another hallway, he pauses, looking at the ceiling, his eyes darting around as if searching for something.

The nurse continues on, unaware of our stop.

Without warning, he grips my arm and the IV pole and steers me into an alcove, hidden from the prying eyes of passersby and, more importantly, away from the hospital's ever-watchful cameras.

If I wanted to fight him, I would lay his ass out. But

curiosity gets the best of me.

He senses my cooperation and quickly releases my arm. His face remains close, inches from mine.

We're the same height. Same build. He's lost weight, like me. When I saw him in that video, he had muscle mass, an impressively honed physique. Like I once did.

We have the same black hair, same bone structure, same resting scowl, strong nose, and stern brow. But my eyes are my mother's. I don't remember her, but Denver always mentioned it. He called them *dark, soulful eyes*. It still makes me shudder.

Monty sizes me up in the same manner I measure him, examining my features as shadows of emotion dart across his.

Does he see Kaya or himself when he looks at me?

The air shifts, spiking with tension, right before he asks, "Did you fuck my wife?"

A silent alarm rings through my mind. I desperately want to ignore it and hit him with the truth.

Instead, I fire back, "Did you fuck my mother?"

I don't expect an answer, but the accusation seems to suck the life out of him.

He deflates, takes a step back, and chokes, "No."

"You and I share blood. That much is certain. If you're not my father—"

"I'm not." Sudden anger flashes in his eyes. "That would be impossible." His denial is firm, vehement. "I loved Kaya. We grew up together, but she was too young...I never touched her. Christ, you look so much like her. Your mannerisms, the way you carry yourself, your eyes..." His hands clench and unclench at his sides, betraying the frustration and disbelief simmering beneath his composed exterior. "I haven't seen her in twenty-five years. How old are you?"

"Twenty-five."

"If we're related, it's because Denver is your father. He was obsessed with Kaya since she was...very young." His words cut through the tension, a confession that lays bare the disgusting nature of Denver's evil.

"How young?"

He pauses, swallows. "It started when she was eight."

Horror wraps cold fingers around my throat, squeezing tight.

He's not just telling me that Denver molested my eight-year-old mother. He's testing my reaction to see if I was a victim of the same abuse.

I open my mouth—to confirm or distract, I'm not sure—when I'm abruptly cut short.

"There you are." The nurse, oblivious to the turmoil she's interrupting, appears at the entrance to the alcove. "Radiology is just a few doors down."

She beckons, her gesture insistent, pulling me back toward the task at hand, the X-ray that feels inconsequential in the emotional storm Monty and I are weathering.

As I follow her, casting a glance back at him, the questions and what-ifs pound in my head. But for now, they'll have to wait.

She leads me into a lifeless, echoing chamber, where the walls are too white, the lights too bright, and there's a hum in the air that sets my teeth on edge.

The X-ray machine looms over me, a giant of steel and technology that buzzes with unseen energy. It's intimidating, this behemoth that can peer through flesh and bone. Makes me stand a little straighter under its gaze.

While the technician adjusts my leg for the images,

Monty lingers in the waiting area, watching me through the doorway with his penetrating, blue eyes.

He claims he's not my father, and my gut believes him.

But is he right about Denver?

I took you because I hated you. Hated you with every breath. Until I couldn't. Until I loved you most of all.

I'm desperate to know more about my mother and her relationship with Monty and Denver.

The technician's instructions to *hold still* and *breathe normally* float in the background of my swirling thoughts.

Kaya grew up with Denver and Monty.

On Kodiak Island.

My namesake.

I want to know everything, and the only person who holds the answers is the man who intends to take away my world.

Frankie.

The yearning to return to her side, to see her safe, torments me relentlessly as the machine whirs and clicks.

Throughout the procedure, I can't stop thinking about how far removed this is from anything I've ever known.

Back home, healing was a matter of patience, a splash of vodka, maybe some makeshift stitches— primitive but effective. Here, technology takes the lead, offering efficient and utterly incomprehensible solutions.

Despite the cold, impersonal nature of the machine and the room, I'm profoundly grateful. This strange, whirring contraption represents a chance at healing properly, at ensuring that my leg won't keep me from protecting and providing for Frankie.

Stepping out of radiology, the clinical hum of the hospital envelopes me once more.

"I told the nurse I would walk you back." Monty slips his hands into his pockets, his face devoid of emotion. "I would offer assistance with your leg, but you strike me as someone who would rather throttle me than accept my help."

"You don't know me."

"That goes both ways." He leads the way back to the room.

As we navigate the corridors, I feel the itch of watchful stares. It's subtle at first, the fleeting glances from strangers. Then I start to notice a pattern. Females, in particular, let their eyes linger just a moment longer than necessary, their gazes trailing over me with an intensity that heats my skin.

Some men glance my way, too, but their looks are quick, dismissive, unlike the women whose eyes seem to ask for something in those extra seconds.

Monty catches the edge of unease in my limping stride, the slight furrow of my brow perhaps giving me away.

"You'll get used to it," he says, his tone light.

I shoot him a look, puzzled, feeling like I've stumbled into one of Wolf's games where the rules make sense to everyone but me.

He exhales a hint of resignation. "You're a good-looking man. Women appreciate that." He pauses, peering at me as if to gauge my reaction. "Attractiveness runs in the family. It's a blessing and a curse."

Is that why you cheated on your wife?

My mouth tightens, physically holding back the question.

A blessing and a curse? The concept that a man's appearance could influence interactions to such a degree is baffling. Survival depends on strength, resilience, and the depth of one's character, not the symmetry of one's face or the cut of their physique.

"Doesn't help that your ass is hanging out. This way." He veers right, entering another corridor.

I glance back, and sure enough, the females trailing a few feet behind aim disarming smiles at my backside.

As we continue our walk back to the safety of our hospital room, I ponder the idea that women—strangers—would find something appreciable in my appearance.

This is a shared experience among the men in our family?

Monty's casual acceptance of these social norms and silent judgments bugs the piss out of me.

I refocus on returning to Frankie, to the familiarity of her scent.

His observations continue as we weave through hallways. "You're severely malnourished."

"I hadn't noticed. Thanks for the heads up."

"I don't know what happened that left the three of you starving..." The undercurrent of concern in his voice swiftly gives way to a different kind of forewarning. "As you return to health and get your strength back, the attention from female admirers will only get worse. You'll have your pick of any woman you want. Comes with the genes."

He says it matter-of-factly as if commenting on the darkness of polar night, like it's just another inescapable fact of nature.

There's a huge disconnect between his perception of what's important and mine. Yes, the past few months have chiseled away my physical form, the evidence of our survival beaten into the very ligaments and bones of my body. But the prospect of female admirers or the so-called pick of any woman feels utterly inconsequential against what we've endured.

Besides, I don't want my pick of women. I only want Frankie.

As I limp along the corridor, trying to ignore the fiery pain in my leg, Monty unexpectedly stops. Not to corner me again. He pivots toward an elderly woman who leans against a walker and stares at her slippers.

"Are you lost?" He offers his arm for support.

She takes it, petting his sleeve. "I...I don't know. My family should be here. I can't find them."

"I'm sure they're on their way. Is this your room?" He points at the open doorway beside her.

"Ellen." A nurse rushes over. "What are you doing out of your room?" She looks up at Monty and gasps. "I'm so sorry, Mr. Novak. Let me..."

"I have her." He guides Ellen with patience and a gentle smile into her room, murmuring something in her ear that makes her laugh, blush, and swat at his shoulder. "Shush. You'll make my heart stop, young man."

I hang back as he helps her settle onto her bed and exchanges words with the nurse.

Then he returns to the hall, breezing past me like nothing happened.

"What was that about?" A low fire burns in my leg as I catch up with him.

"What do you mean?"

"Why did you help that woman? Do you know her?"

"Jesus." He stops abruptly, scrutinizing me, peering too closely. "Denver really did a number on you."

Standing under the harsh lights and his intense

glare, I feel exposed, transparent, stripped of the defenses I've built up over years. I hold impossibly still, knowing that any movement can reveal too much.

He couldn't possibly know what Denver did to me.

If he knows, that means he did nothing to stop it.

My spine prickles with long-buried anger, every instinct screaming for me to lash out and reestablish the boundaries that his gaze threatens to dismantle.

"I don't know the details, but I know you've endured a terrible evil." He loosens a sharp breath. "I can't express how fucking sorry I am for that."

The isolation I once found comforting now leaves me ill-prepared for the invasive nature of this conversation.

I want to return to Frankie and Leo, to the security of what's familiar. But I stand my ground, unwilling to let his probing dictate my reactions.

Defiance builds within me as our gazes hold, my expression blank, shielding the essence of who I am from his too-perceptive study.

He finally breaks the connection, moving on from whatever judgment he formed about me.

"I helped that woman because no one should feel lost or alone." He resumes down the corridor, leaving me staring after him.

Fuck me.

What am I supposed to do with that?

I trail behind him in tense silence for the remainder of the short distance.

Just before we reach our room, he turns to me, his gaze earnest. "I've made mistakes. Hell knows I'm not perfect. But I'm not *him.*"

As we step back into the room, I wonder, however cautiously, if there's more to Montgomery Strakh than the cheating douchebag billionaire in that video.

I push open the door to the hospital room, unsettled by the conversation with Kody. His defiance, the guarded look in his familiar eyes, and the unknowns about his father open a fissure of conflicting emotions inside me.

Amid my anger and guilt lurks an aching sense of responsibility for these two men.

Two feral, overprotective men who spent nine months with my wife in an isolated cabin.

My imagination of their time together is a vicious twisting of sex and perversion. If I don't keep that shit locked down, my jealousy will destroy any chance I have at winning her back.

As Kody follows me in, Frankie's gaze instantly touches him, checking on him as she speaks to a woman I don't recognize.

She doesn't acknowledge me at all.

Kody limps over to his savage, hot-tempered

companion with the mismatched eyes. With preternatural focus, they watch the ongoing conversation between Frankie and the woman.

Frankie.

She's really here.

A fresh surge of relief overwhelms me, seeing her in the flesh, not a figment of my cruel imagination, but real and safe and alive.

I ache to go to her, hold her, make love to her. But she won't allow it. Not even a touch of my hand on hers.

Our connection is broken. Lost. I did that when I rejected our baby. And my brother did it when he took her.

With that thought comes the worst kind of horror, the most profound pain, knowing that the woman I love more than life itself was abducted, starved, tormented, and worse—so much worse—by an evil I failed to vanquish.

As I take in her emaciated, bandaged, tortured body, I imagine her cries muffled by Denver's filthy hand. Her pleas for mercy falling on his dispassionate ears. Her ferocity pitted against his unspeakable depravity. The helplessness of it, the brutal unfairness, as he hurt her over and over, night after night, month after month.

The vividness of my imaginings is a landscape of agony, painted in the stark hues of sexual abuse and terror, that Frankie, my beautiful wife, was forced to traverse. The thought of her suffering is unbearable. It's a gutting, disfiguring blade in the marrow of my bones that I will never truly fathom nor escape.

Wherever he is now, I'm about to find out. Because the woman speaking to Frankie, with her designer skirt suit and blonde hair twisted neatly atop her head, must be Melanie Stokes.

The lawyer we've been waiting for.

If Denver is still breathing, he won't be for long.

The horror of what Frankie must have endured, the brutal hell she faced—it feeds something monstrous inside me, a ruthless beast I struggle to contain. I'm a pulsing, simmering, ticking time bomb of rage, vying for dominance, tearing at the seams of the composure I fight so hard to maintain.

Just a bit longer.

I'll have my answers and, hopefully, Denver's location. Then I'm going hunting.

The woman types on her phone as she speaks with Frankie. Their voices are hushed, but I hear something about a crate, thumb drive, and journal.

I make a mental note to follow up on that.

Frankie falls quiet, and the woman peeks in my direction, her expression filled with an understanding that goes beyond professional courtesy.

I have a good feeling about her.

"You must be Monty." She extends a slender hand. "I'm Melanie Stokes. I'll be representing Frankie, Kody, and Leo."

"Thank you for arriving so quickly."

"No problem." She gives Kody the same greeting and adds, "You haven't missed much. Leo and Frankie signed a retainer. I'll need your signature as well. And they gave me a brief overview, highlighting your biggest concerns and needs. The scrapbook will help us catch up while the three of you get rest." She glances at her phone, makes a pleased sound, and turns back to Frankie. "My assistant is retrieving the things we discussed as we speak. The book will be here shortly." Her tone softens. "You've had a day. When you're ready to dig into the details of your story, I'll come back."

I stiffen, fighting against a storm of impatience. I won't sleep until I learn what happened and what these two men mean to my wife.

Bruises darken Frankie's eyes as she shares a wordless conversation with Leo and Kody. They rally around her like some sort of tight-knit trio.

Like they're in a relationship.

I'm so twisted up I want to roar and break shit until I can't feel a fucking thing. But my composure holds, a fragile veneer over the chaos and violence thrashing inside me.

Standing quietly on the sidelines, I assume the role of stoic businessman, estranged husband, and brother betrayed.

Beneath it all, I'm just a man fighting to right the wrongs of the past and protect the woman I love from the fallout of choices made by me and my fucked-up family.

"If you don't mind..." Frankie pushes back her shoulders and looks at Melanie. "None of us will sleep until we have this conversation. We want to do it now."

"I understand." Melanie removes a laptop from her satchel. "I'll sit over there, record the conversation, take some notes, and only intervene when needed."

Frankie thanks her. Melanie quietly shuts the door, sealing us in a tomb of tension and expectation, and finds her seat near the entrance.

Kody navigates the room with a pronounced limp and his IV pole. Pausing at Frankie's bed, he adjusts her pillows and ensures her comfort, his movements gentle and deliberate, before reclining on his own bed.

Impossible to miss the bond between them.

Between all three of them.

In their eye contact, in every subtle interaction, there's a connection that transcends sexual intimacy.

She looks at them in a way that she's never looked at me.

It makes my pulse race out of control. My muscles tense. My hands shake. A shiver crashes down my spine as shadows rise around me.

I know what this is.

It's the chill that creeps in before the storm, the haunting whisper in the void, the dark ink seeping through the veins of existence. It's pure, unchained, ravenous, soul-shaking fear, ravaging the edges of my sanity.

Frankie is here, in this room.

But she's out of reach.

She's lost to me.

Because she's with them.

I remain on my feet, spinning in a black hole of violence and misery, unbeknown to them, in the settling calm of the room.

"You should sit for this, Monty." Frankie's voice, though soft, cuts through my breakdown.

I don't move, don't speak.

"Fine. Before we begin..." She directs her gaze to Kody, then Leo, before returning to me. "I want to declare a moratorium on physical altercations. I'm too fucking tired to deal with temper tantrums. Stay in your beds. Keep your hands to yourselves. And Monty..." Her gaze pulls me in. "You really should sit."

The pallor of her skin and the way she braces herself against the pillows Kody just arranged ignite profound concern in me. She's a striking portrait of strength carved from the trials of survival, but she's visibly drained.

The Frankie I know always pushed herself too hard, too far. It's a trait I both admire and fear for, knowing the price she's paying with her health. The fact that she needs to lay down such ground rules, to forestall violence in what should be a place of healing, highlights the depth of her fatigue.

My chest aches for her, reaffirming my resolve to protect her, to alleviate her burdens in any way I can. "Let's postpone this."

"Nope. We're all adults. Despite how hard this conversation will be for us, I know we can have a peaceful, honest discussion."

The instinct to overrule her and demand she rest hardens my stomach. But for now, I keep my mouth shut.

"Are we still married?" She lifts her chin.

The question snaps my head back. "Yes."

"You didn't file for a divorce?"

"Fuck, no. I told you, Frankie. I never stopped looking for you."

"How many women have there been since I was taken?"

I freeze, rooted to the floor, eyes locked on hers.

This is not how I intended for this to play out. Not in a room full of strangers with my back against the wall. I knew I would tell her today, but Jesus Christ, not right out of the fucking gate.

My defenses bristle. Everything clenches. I pace to the window, searching for the right words, but there are no right words. Nothing will soften this.

I turn back to her, finding her beautiful, pained eyes. "I thought you left me."

"How many women?" she asks again.

"One."

"Her name?"

"Aubrey."

She blinks, expressionless, not a sliver of surprise in

her body language.

She knew.

How did she fucking know?

"How long has the infidelity been going on?" She sits taller. "Were you ever faithful to me?"

The accusation slams into my chest and knocks the wind out of me.

Infidelity.

The term feels misplaced as she levels it against me, her eyes alight with conviction.

"It was one time." I draw a steadying breath. "One time too many. I regretted it instantly, but I won't make excuses for it."

"Don't fucking lie to me." She bends forward, jabbing a shaky finger in my direction. "You were unfaithful long before I was kidnapped."

"No, I fucking was *not.* Why would you think such an outlandish thing?"

"I saw a video of you with Aubrey. In your office in Sitka. You fucked her on your desk."

"How...?" This can't be real. I'm spiraling into a dark abyss, the horror pulling me into its depths. "What video?"

"Denver recorded you. He said there are more videos. More affairs. He had cameras in your office and all over our house for two years. You've been cheating on me for years."

Cameras? For two years?

A cold chill snakes through me. "He put cameras in our fucking house?"

"Yes. But right now, we're discussing your infidelity."

"You believe him? About these alleged affairs?"

"I saw the video."

"One video. There can only be one, because that was the *only* time. I swear on my life, Frankie."

Her pain is a seething, quaking entity in the room, one I wish I could banish with a word or a gesture.

Leo and Kody, sitting on either side of her, form a battalion of condemnation. Their eyes blaze with accusation as I scramble for footing in the quicksand of their collective judgment.

Near the door, Melanie is relaxed yet attentive, a silent observer of the unfolding drama as she types on her laptop.

This is my goddamn penance.

"Why?" Frankie's jaw sets, her eyes glistening. "Why did you fuck her?"

"I was trying to forget you."

"Did you succeed?"

"No." I surrender to the weight of my guilt and slump into the chair near the foot of her bed. "It happened six weeks after you vanished. I thought you quit me because of my godawful reaction to the pregnancy. I was so fucking hurt and angry. Angry with you. Furious with myself. I needed to move forward, move on, and I tried. Aubrey was there, an invitation that I accepted. It lasted all of five minutes—"

"Seven."

"What?"

"You fucked her for seven minutes." She touches her quivering lips and averts her eyes. "I'm ashamed of how many times I watched that video."

Goddammit.

Fucking hell.

Fuck, fuck, fuck!

My hands clench. My molars grind. My fucking regret punches through the roof.

I wish we didn't have an audience. I wish I could

pull her into my arms and kiss her beautiful, trembling mouth. If she cries, I won't be able to stop myself from climbing into that bed with her.

"I don't remember those seven minutes." No matter how true, the words sound hollow, even to my ears, drowned out by doubt that fills the room. "I only remember the shame that followed. The guilt. The misery. It made me feel wretched, not better. I never did it again. You have to believe me."

The tension crackles, a live wire in the cramped hospital room.

"How can we believe anything you say?" Leo leans forward, snarling, "You kept your entire family a secret from her."

Kody's silence is equally indicting, his stare sparking with unspoken censure.

"I've made mistakes, but not this." My defense falls on deaf ears, tangled in a thicket of disgust. "Denver is a psychopath. He fed you lies to turn you against me. But he couldn't provide proof of infidelity beyond that video because...It. Does. Not. Exist."

The space between us widens with each uttered denial, an insurmountable mountain of mistrust.

Frankie's gaze is the hardest to meet.

"I don't trust you," she whispers, her features stark with a sorrow that guts me. "But you're right. His lies, his manipulations, his lack of evidence...there's a lot to untangle."

Like the other two men in this room.

Denver and Kaya must be their biological parents. Their names alone, Leo and Kody, eerily correlate to Port Lions on Kodiak Island, where Denver and Kaya met and grew up.

Leo said his mother was Helena Weiss, but that

name doesn't exist in my memories.

My running theory is...When my parents died, Denver abducted Kaya, hid her on the Turbo Beaver, kept her in the off-grid cabin, and produced two sons with her.

Leo and Kody.

Strangers to me. But not to my wife.

After everything she's been through, I didn't want to jump in with this line of questioning.

I should start with Gretchen, Frankie's abduction, and the cabin's location.

Where is my fucking brother?

But the room is already pressurized with drama. Now that my affair has been aired out, and my character has been measured, judged, and deemed unworthy, I need to know.

How faithful has Frankie been to me?

I steel myself and ask her the one thing that's been burning in my throat since the moment Leo punched me. "How long have you been fucking them?"

It's not a question but an admission of my deepest fear laid bare in the sterilized light of the hospital room.

Leo meets my gaze, unflinching. "She was faithful to you, her heart untouchable, her loyalty inexorable. Until she watched you fuck another woman."

"It broke me." Frankie stares at her lap, blinking rapidly, fighting back tears. "I wanted to die."

I did that. I put that pain inside her.

Leo tenses as if fighting the impulse to go to her. "If she hadn't been shown that video, she would've loved you and remained devoted to you through every horrendous thing she endured in the hills. Even after your betrayal, she waited."

"How long?" The tremor in my voice exposes the storm brewing inside me. "How long have you been fucking her?"

"Five months." He holds my glare with a confronting confidence that doesn't waver. There's no apology in his tone, no hesitation. Just the raw, unvarnished truth. "I've been in love with her much longer than that."

Leo's words hit like shrapnel, scattering shards of heartbreak and jealousy through my wasted soul.

Five months.

The span of time echoes in my head, a haunting refrain of shared moments, bonds formed, and a betrayal that cuts deeper than my seven minutes with Aubrey.

"You think that gives you some claim to her?" Fire and venom seethe through my veins, dredged from the depths of my hell.

"No." Leo sets his shoulders, his unusual, bicolored eyes never leaving mine. "I don't own her. She owns me."

I hate that response.

I *despise* it.

It's a challenge, a declaration of reciprocated love delivered with a boldness that wounds me.

My heart fractures in totality.

I've lost her, the love of my life, the epicenter of my universe.

She sits amidst the blizzard of tension, her stunning presence a calm anchor in the swirling chaos. Her eyes, windows to the grief and tenderness inside her, move among the three of us with compassion I don't deserve. But maybe they do.

She loves them. That much is clear. Their shared trauma in my brother's clutches cemented bonds that I have no hope of rivaling.

Yet, when her gaze gravitates to mine, there's a flicker of something there, something that speaks to the intimate history, love, and happiness we created in our marriage. It's not trust—not yet—but it's not indifference, either. It's a caring that survives betrayal and tragedy, because that's the kind of person she is.

She cares, even when she shouldn't.

It gives me the strength to turn my attention to the dark, quiet force in the room.

Kaya's son.

His presence is a storm cloud on the horizon, silent, ominous, and looming.

How long have you been fucking my wife?

I don't need to voice it. He's perceptive as fuck.

"Two months," he says softly, but it's deafening in its clarity.

His eyes, dark and fathomless, lock onto mine with an intensity that makes my scalp crawl. There's a lethal stillness about him, his posture relaxed yet poised as if a breath away from action. Like a hunter. A predator.

It's in that deadly stare that I find another answer. The love Kody harbors for Frankie is a shadowed thing, deep and perhaps more dangerous for its silence.

As I sit here, with my head in my hands, grappling

with the magnitude of what's unfolding, I'm caught in the crossfire of losing Frankie to not one but two men.

How does that even work? Does she intend to carry on with both of them? Has she thought through any of this?

She's not thinking. She's banging two virile, attractive men half my age.

Jealousy, a dark and gnarling creature, takes root in my stomach, its tendrils wrapping around my balls with a vice-like grip.

As I thrash in a sea of rage and inconsolable heartache, watching the remnants of my life with Frankie slip through my fingers, a sucking, gut-wrenching sadness settles over me.

I'm tempted to surrender to it, to let it have me.

Then I think about the past nine months and how her absence haunted every aspect of my existence—the empty space on her side of the bed, the silence in our home where her voice should've been, the hollow part of my chest where my heart used to reside.

I can't return to that. I won't.

Giving up, giving in, is simply not in my nature. Not when it comes to her. Not ever.

Winning her back, I know, won't be a matter of grand gestures or eloquent words. The path to earning her trust will be paved with sacrifice, vulnerability, honesty.

And revenge.

I rise to my feet and ask the room, "Where's Denver?"

Frankie looks at Melanie.

Ah.

My intelligent wife remembers the attorney's role here. Even as we deal with our private drama, she hasn't lost sight of the legal realities of her missing-person case.

Melanie shakes her head.

Fuck.

That can't be good.

"I don't trust you, Monty." Frankie pulls in a breath, her chest rising. "I know you're grieving and carrying a massive amount of guilt. I'm not blind. But we have some hard truths to discuss, some terrible things to share. We need to set aside our emotions from the previous conversation and focus on the next thing."

It's this strength, this indomitable spirit, that once drew me to her and now, more than ever, underscores what I've lost. And what I'm determined to regain.

"You never told me about Denver's existence." She tips her head. "You changed your name. Never told me that, either. So we don't know if or how you're involved in our abductions."

"I'm not."

"I'm speaking." She shoots me a stern glare with tired eyes. "Before we tell you anything about Denver, you need to give us something. Explain the secrecy. Convince us of your innocence."

I've been on trial since the moment I walked in here.

If I want to earn back her trust, I'll have to open myself up, show her the vulnerabilities I've kept hidden behind walls of pride and pretense since the day I met her.

She deserves to see the real me, flaws and all, to decide for herself if the man I've become is someone she can love again.

"I'll start at the beginning." Slipping my damp hands into my pockets, I pace at the foot of her bed. "I told you my parents were Russian oligarchs. But I didn't tell you they fled to America in fear for their lives."

I walk through the history of my family, explaining their legacy of shadow and wealth, my father's construction company, and how he used it as a cover for our family's vast, illicit fortunes in offshore accounts.

"The cabin." Leo shares a look with Frankie and Kody, confirming my suspicion about what they've been living in.

If only I knew *where.*

"The cabin…" I rub the tense muscles in my nape. "A few months ago, in my search for Frankie, I found blueprints hidden in a wall in my childhood home. Blueprints for an off-grid, two-story log cabin. No location. But I'm certain my father was the architect and funded the project, and Denver designed a hydroelectric generator for it. Was that built as well?"

Leo nods, his expression grim.

"When my parents fled Russia, they constructed an estate in Port Lions on Kodiak Island. That's where Denver and I grew up." I meet Kody's eyes. "And Kaya Knowles. Her mother was our live-in maid."

I wear a path on the floor as I give voice to my painful memories of Kaya, describing the crush that Denver and I had on her, the rivalry, the age differences, and my father's threats to stay away.

"Denver molested her when she was eight." I pause, raking a hand through my hair. "He was ten. Too young to be held accountable. But what he did to her…"

I look at Kody, silently questioning.

A sharp shake of his head indicates he doesn't want to know.

I release a sigh of relief.

The details are too horrifying to fathom. And sodomizing Kaya Knowles with a blunt object was only the beginning of Denver's reign of terror.

"He went on to molest other children on the island, tying them up in the many caves on our expansive property, tormenting them, and…" My breathing becomes heavy and labored. I scrape a hand over my mouth. "By the time he was eighteen, he was hunting and sexually assaulting children beyond the island in nearby coastal towns."

"How did he not get caught?" Frankie's voice trembles into fragmented whispers. "Did you know he was—?"

"No. Christ, I was a child myself through most of it. I'm only a year older than Denver. My parents kept this from me and paid off the families of the victims. But Kaya…she had no family." I step to Kody's bed, grip the footboard for support, and meet his dark gaze. "Kaya's mother died of a heart condition around the time the abuse started. I don't have proof, but knowing what I know now about the lengths my father went to protect Denver, I think Kaya's mother refused to be paid off like the other families."

"Your father killed her." Kody's jaw clenches.

"He had assassins on his payroll." I drum my fingers on the bed rail. "After she died, my father adopted Kaya into our family and raised her like his own. I went away to college, but when I was nineteen, I came home for winter break. Kaya was sixteen at the time. We stole some of my father's wine and sneaked to the beach to drink it, as kids do. That's when she told me." A swallow sticks in my throat. "Denver abused her for years without my knowledge. When she became too old for his tastes, he went on to abuse others. She reported all of it to my father, and he handled it the way he handled everything—hush money, blackmail, and when all else fails, he called in a hitman."

In the charged silence that follows, Melanie's presence is a reminder of the legal nightmare I'll be facing in the days and months ahead.

I should have my own attorneys present to protect my ass, but I'm risking it. I'm risking it all because nothing matters but my wife.

"I couldn't face Denver. Couldn't look at him." My stomach buckles with the memory. "But I confronted my father that night."

I tell them every incriminating detail about my involvement—the conversation between my father and me, my demands to imprison Denver, my father's fears of the media exposure, of being found and killed by his enemies, and my directive to have it dealt with the old-fashioned oligarch way. Quietly and lethally.

"I remained in the room when my father made the call to have him eliminated. I wouldn't leave until I heard the words that hired the hitman and sealed my brother's fate. Then, like a coward, I fled. I returned to university the next day, knowing I would never see my brother again, knowing he would be killed for his crimes because I forced my father's hand. For thirty years, I thought he was dead. I carried that blame."

"No one in this room blames you for wanting him dead." Frankie's voice is steady, but there's something in her tone, an undercurrent of secrets too grim for daylight.

"Do you blame me for not telling you about him?"

"Jury is still out on that. Did you suspect what he was doing growing up?"

"No. Never. Denver is charming, intelligent, never violent, never killed animals or anything like that. By age eighteen, he was a genius engineer with a promising future. My parents adored him. Favored him."

"A textbook psychopath." Her eyes thin. "Your father loved him so much that he canceled that hit on his life?"

"Yes. I made that gutting discovery three months ago while searching for you."

I summarize the past nine months, my efforts to find her, the secrets I unearthed in my childhood home, the blueprints, the flight logs, and the man who helped Denver for twenty years. Alvis Duncan.

For the next hour, I lay out my assumptions about what happened—my father forcing Denver into isolation in an off-grid cabin somewhere, the flight logs that tracked his comings and goings, and the plane crash that killed my parents.

"I think Denver tampered with their plane." I take a calming breath. "I don't have proof, but the motivation is there. He didn't want their supervision."

"Your parents died twenty-five years ago." Leo braces his elbows on his knees, studying me. "I arrived at that cabin with my mother twenty-seven years ago."

"He must've sneaked you onto the plane. All of you. Alvis Duncan said he hauled—"

"Crates." Her head dips forward, chin resting on her chest, as if the strength to keep it lifted has ebbed away. "Coffin-sized crates. That's how he transported me."

My stomach sinks, the blood draining from my face. "Frankie..."

"There is so much I need to tell you." She rubs at the shadows circling her eyes. "Difficult things."

"It can wait." It pains me to say it. My need for answers beats relentlessly against my ribcage. "You were in a plane crash today. You have a concussion, and you're about to fall over."

Ignoring me, she directs her eyes at Melanie. "Is it here?"

"Yes." Melanie straightens, her tone professional. "It is sensitive evidence. Handing it over goes against counsel wishes."

"I trust him with this. His involvement and relationship with us outweigh everything else."

"Very well." Melanie rises from the chair and steps into the hall.

She returns just as quickly with a book in her hands, its cover worn and edges frayed.

Frankie accepts it, her fingers tracing the rough, cracked texture of the spine.

"We have already removed the DNA samples from the pages." Melanie returns to her seat. "When you're finished, we need it back immediately."

"Okay." Frankie bites her lip, her gaze intertwining with mine. "Everything that happened over the past nine months is here. I logged it all in this diary."

A diary? That must be the journal that Melanie mentioned earlier.

Do I want to read about Frankie's time in that cabin with Denver?

Yeah, I fucking do. It'll make me want to burn down the world. I'll devour every goddamn detail with a lit match in my hand.

"I journaled my thoughts, feelings, assumptions, secrets, every ugly, terrible event that occurred, as well as the history of those who came before me." Frankie caresses the book's cover, which bears the marks of a survivor, from the staining of snowmelt to the patches worn from constant use. "I trust you with this information. But Monty, there are things you need to hear from us before you read it."

As the air in the room tightens, the door swings open, and a nurse chooses that moment to breeze in.

Oblivious to the tension, she focuses solely on the machines that beep and blink beside each bed.

The timing couldn't be more intrusive. We glare at her as she moves from one bed to the next, doing routine checks.

Leo and Kody exchange glances, a silent consensus building, rife with impatience. Yet none of us voices our frustration, recognizing the necessity of her tasks.

She finally completes her rounds and makes her exit, the door clicking shut behind her.

Frankie's weary gaze finds mine.

She kept a diary, an account of her ordeal.

That she would entrust me with her innermost experiences, despite everything, signals a bridge, however fragile, being rebuilt between us.

As quickly as relief washes over me, unease seeps into its place. The thought of what that journal contains, the *ugly, terrible events* and secrets laid bare on its pages, fills me with visceral fear. It's not just the anticipation of confronting the horrors she faced, but the apprehension of learning about what can only be the darkest chapters of Denver's evil.

The bandages on her head, the rawboned condition of her body, the heavy-lidded look in her eyes—all of it amplifies my concern about the tolls the past nine months have taken.

"Frankie." My heart pounds a thunderous echo. "I'm grateful that you trust me with this. With your story. Whatever you need me to know, whatever you want to tell me…I'm here. I'll listen."

Nodding slowly, she blinks rapidly, presses her fingers against her mouth, and looks at Leo as if trying not to cry.

He slides out of his bed and goes to her, dragging his IV pole with him.

My hackles bristle as he perches beside her legs and laces their fingers together.

Then his gaze lands on mine. "Twenty-three years ago, Denver buried my mother alive for trying to escape. That same year, he abducted Kaya and her two-year-old son, Kody."

I stop breathing.

"Two weeks after we arrived," Kody growls, "my mother committed suicide. I used to curse her for abandoning me, but after everything I learned today, I understand."

Kaya.

Sweet, gentle Kaya…

Abused.

Destroyed.

Lost to a monster.

Christ.

Fucking God.

I lower into the chair because I know there's more coming. I can feel it siphoning all the air.

"That was a busy year for Denver." Leo works his jaw. "When Kaya died, he brought another woman to the cabin. This one was pregnant, and her name was Gretchen Stolz."

Pregnant.

"No." Numbness swamps me. Disbelief clouds my mind. "It can't be."

"Are you sure?" Leo crosses his arms. "Twenty-three years ago, were you not fucking Gretchen Stolz?"

I need a goddamn minute to process this.

Standing, I pace to the window. It's dark outside. Snow swirls. I see nothing.

I rest my fingertips against the cold glass, gathering myself, bracing against the shadows of the past.

"Gretchen...was a regrettable mistake." My breath shakes as I turn and face the room. "She was after my money. I was young. Twenty-five and naive. My parents had just died a year prior. I was dealing with that, managing their fortune while my company was blowing up with overwhelming success. I didn't realize Gretchen's motivations until it was too late. Until she tried to trap me with a pregnancy."

I fall into Frankie's horrified gaze. Before we married, I alluded to women trying to trap me but never gave her names or details.

"I demanded she terminate the pregnancy, and I set up the appointment." The confession spills from me, echoing the cruel demand I gave nine months ago.

Frankie battles the tears brimming in her eyes, her body trembling to suppress the sob that nonetheless breaks through. A sound that lacerates my soul.

The impulse to rush to her, to offer whatever cold comfort my touch can provide, propels me forward.

"Finish the story." Leo positions himself like a bodyguard, his stance a physical barrier, his silent message loud and clear.

There are lines I can't cross and wounds I can't heal.

He's not fucking around. My face still throbs from the beating he gave me earlier.

I can hold my own in a fistfight. I have a terrible temper. Though I rarely resort to violence against others.

Fighting him to get to Frankie won't help anyone. But I can give her the raw, shameful truth.

"I'm terrified of children, Frankie. Given Denver's sickness and my...my preference for younger women, I developed a phobia."

"Explain your preference for younger women." Leo's eyes blaze.

"I had a crush on Kaya when she was too young. My *wife* is twenty years younger than me. This is a hereditary disease."

"No, it's not." Frankie sniffs, wiping her eyes. "I understand your fears, Monty, but unless you're molesting underage—"

"Never." I seethe.

"You don't have a disease," she says with conviction. "You love *women*, not little girls."

"I love *you*." My declaration triggers a storm of aggression in the room. I ignore the growling males and focus on her. "Will you tell me about your pregnancy?"

"It was short." She nudges Leo toward the head of her bed so she has a direct view of me, where I stand near her feet. "Denver took me from our house."

My blood chills. "He took you on your boat?"

"Yeah."

In a monotone voice, she lays out the abduction—the encounter in our bedroom, the rope bindings, the tranquilizers, the transfer to his yacht, then to the Turbo Beaver, the arrival at the cabin, and her immediate attempt to escape on the snow machine, which led to the miscarriage.

She was alone through all of it, through the pain, the fear, the loss, and the entire time she thought I didn't want the baby. Because that's what I told her. That's what I believed at the time.

How fucking wrong I was.

How fucking cold and cruel.

She should hate me. How can she even look at me?

"What happened with Gretchen?" Leo flexes his hands.

"She went to that appointment. I dropped her off. She refused to let me go in. We broke up that day. She only cared about my wealth. When I refused to marry her, she returned to Iowa, where she grew up."

"Denver brought that bitch to the cabin." Leo flares his nostrils. "I was seven and helped deliver her baby. Denver named him Wolfson."

My heart plummets to my stomach as a weighty dread floods my circulation.

Wolfson.

My son.

He's not here.

I have a son, and he's not fucking here.

The silence is a roar, the darkness a blanket too heavy to lift.

"Where...?" I step forward. "Where is he? Did you leave him behind?"

A strangled noise escapes Leo's throat. "He committed suicide four months ago."

Four months ago.

Shock strikes like lightning. My breath staggers.

He was an adult, a twenty-three-year-old man, who spent his entire life with a child molester.

A chilling gale of horror howls through me, stripping away the warmth of my sanity and burying me in the dark with the cold, rotting bones of my failures.

Frankie pulls her knees to her chest and loses her fight with her tears. The agony shattering in her sob is a torment all its own.

"I'm sorry." Ringing peals in my ears. "I didn't know." My lungs collapse. "I'm so fucking sorry." I slam a hand down on the footboard, sending a sharp crack through the air, as I roar, "Where is Denver?"

Lifting her damp eyes, she holds my stare. "I killed him four months ago. I shot him and beat him with a pipe."

Standing there, frozen in abhorrence and thwarted by Leo's protective guardianship, the full measure of her trauma crashes over me.

I can't avenge the nine months she suffered. I can't bring back our baby or Wolfson. I can't comfort her with my body. The divide between us is more than physical space. It's a gulf of hurt and betrayal with a long road to redemption, if such a path exists at all.

Her tears mark the map of my failings, a painful yet necessary confrontation with the consequences of my actions.

If I had stayed home that day, I could've prevented Denver from taking her.

If I had stayed in Port Lions and confronted Denver like a man, if I had killed him myself, I could've prevented him from taking all of them, including my son.

Wolfson.

"Growing up, Denver called me Wolf." My voice is hollow, numb. "The nickname stuck until the night I ordered his death. My parents disowned me, and I disowned them. I severed ties, changed my name, and started a new life. I never wanted to look back." I look forward, directly to Frankie. "I'm sorry I kept this from you."

"I understand. I hate it. But I do understand, Monty." Her features are marred by fatigue, her eyes bloodshot and glistening with tears as she attempts to continue the conversation. "There's one more thing we need to tell you before you read my journal."

"You're done." Kody steps in, the protective edge in his tone leaving no room for protest as he takes the book from her.

As Leo tucks her into bed, every bone in my body

aches with helplessness.

The plane crash that could have claimed her life is written all over her face. Her eyes, so darkly shadowed with pain and exhaustion, flutter in a struggle to remain open. Her strength is fading fast.

Kody steps forward and extends his hand toward me, the journal held between his fingers. I reach for it, but he tightens his grip as if parting with it requires monumental effort.

I get it. This is more than just handing over sensitive information. It's an act of trust, a bridge being tentatively extended.

Our eyes lock, fraught with everything that transpired and all that remains unsaid. His gaze hardens with challenge, demanding me to honor the faith he's placing in me by entrusting me with their personal, tragic experiences.

Slowly and with great deliberateness, he loosens his hold on the journal, allowing it to pass into my hands.

The book's physical weight doesn't compare to its emotional heft. I'm not just holding a collection of pages. I'm holding a piece of Frankie's soul and, with it, a key to understanding the ties that bind her to Leo and Kody.

I crack it open, and the pages greet me with the intimacy of her handwriting. The ink bleeds into the paper in some places, indicating the rawness in her strokes.

Her notes and thoughts spill across the pages without order or pattern. Headers tally the days. Some entries are meticulous, others hurried, but all pulsate with the life force of a woman who stared down oblivion and chose to document her journey through hell and back.

This isn't merely a narrative to be read. With each

page turned, I will be there with her, experiencing her strength, suffering, and courage.

I set it on the table, carefully tucking it into the folds of my discarded jacket.

"The last thing you should hear," Kody says, pulling my attention to him. "Denver claimed we're all blood-related. Leo, Wolf, me, him, you."

I glance at Leo, unsure how he fits in. "I'm listening."

"On his dying breath, he told us that you are his brother. That was the first confession. Except he said you have two brothers. His words were to the effect of...you ripped away his life, so he ripped away all of yours. The way he revealed it implied he took more than Frankie and your unborn baby."

The notion that Denver, in his final moments, sought to justify his actions through such a twisted declaration of lies is fucking vile.

Two brothers? Where does he come up with this shit? What's his motivation?

"If he took more than Frankie and the baby..." My mind spins. "He must mean Wolfson."

"I assume. But he never told us Wolf was your son. We pieced that together today."

"I don't have another brother." I steal another peek at Leo. "Will you both be willing to do a DNA test?"

"I'm already working on that." Melanie's gaze darts over us, not missing a beat. "Frankie has DNA samples for everyone at the cabin."

"One more thing," Kody continues. "Denver's final words were a riddle, which led us to the missing flight manual. That's how Leo learned to fly."

"From a flight manual?"

"Yeah." Kody's eyes gleam. "With that hidden

manual was a thumb drive."

"What was on it?"

"Don't know. When Denver died, he left us without food or power for four months. He deliberately skipped the last supply run and shut off the generator in his attempt to control us."

That's why they risked the flight today. Given their severe malnutrition, they were out of time. All of it illuminates the depth of Denver's spiral into madness, painting a picture of the purest form of evil. Calculating. Soulless. Sinister for his own selfish reasons.

"I have the thumb drive," Melanie says. "My team confirmed that the data on it survived the cold and the crash."

I meet Kody's eyes. "It may hold answers."

"Or more riddles."

"Monty." Frankie's whisper arrests my breath. "Come here."

Kody stands resolute, a barrier to the distance I ache to erase. Then, reluctantly, he lets me pass.

As I approach, the world narrows to the space between me and my wife, every step landing with a significance that tightens my chest.

She extends her hand, a gesture so simple yet so laden with meaning. The instant my fingers enclose hers, I'm consumed by the warmth of her touch.

"You're going to read some painfully graphic things in my journal." Her eyes hold mine. "Including a hate letter I wrote to you. I'm sorry about that. I don't want to hurt you, but I think you need to know...all of it. It explains how Denver controlled us, his demise, our escape, and every single day in between. I could filter it for you—"

"I don't want it filtered."

"Okay. Good. Because I would rather not relive most of it." She glances at Leo and Kody. "None of us wants to relive it."

The words dangle like daggers, heavy with pain and death.

Before I can respond, I see the fatigue crashing over her like a relentless wave and the tears that begin to spill from her eyes.

Goddammit.

Ignoring the animalistic growl behind me, I lean in and embrace her dangerously thin frame.

As she cries, I hold her tighter, despite the snarls, the tension, and the eyes burning into my back.

Her tears, warm and wet, seep through my shirt. But they're tears of relief, of release.

There's a long road ahead, with many more tears, but I'll be with her, kissing away every single one.

frankie

THIRTY-NINE

Two days later, Leo pokes at a bowl of fluorescent green Jell-O and grimaces. "It wobbles."

For a man who didn't eat an actual meal for months, he sure does bitch about hospital food.

With the IVs gone and the nurses' routine checks less frequent, we're moving around the room and coveting our alone time.

Melanie Stokes has been in and out often, repeatedly going over our story and keeping the detectives at bay. We'll have to answer their questions eventually.

We received our treatment plans, and I'm taking a fresh supply of birth control pills. Now we're just waiting on paperwork and final assessments. I expect we'll be released from the hospital tomorrow morning.

My heart quickens at the thought of *what's next?*

We haven't seen or heard from Monty since he left

with my journal two days ago. Melanie said he returned the book to her yesterday, but she refused to comment on his appearance other than to reassure us he'll be here when we're discharged.

New clothes arrived last night. Expensive casual outfits in all our sizes, delivered by a personal shopper.

Typical Monty. Always taking care of me.

And now them.

But who's taking care of him?

He'll turn up after he's processed everything, and when he does, he'll have demands. I'm bracing for it.

I wrote some heavy shit in that scrapbook, including the bargain I made with Denver and the two harrowing weeks I longed for death while in his bed.

There are dozens of pages dedicated to Wolf and his soulful art, Gothic beauty, dark humor, and my bottomless grief after he died.

I also detailed all my intimate experiences with Leo and Kody, leaving nothing to the imagination. It was cathartic and beautiful, and whenever I needed to be reminded of the good moments, however few and far between, I revisited those entries.

I could've removed those pages from the journal and saved Monty that pain. But I'm unapologetic about my relationship with these two men.

The next time I see Monty, he'll look at me with new eyes. He'll see how much I've changed. I need him to see it, to understand.

Our marriage is over.

I'm with Leo and Kody.

Regardless of how he feels about me after reading the journal, I want him to have a relationship with Leo and Kody. They're his only family.

Sitting beside me on my bed, Kody tackles his meal with the fervor of a grizzly that just emerged from hibernation.

His leg, though free of fractures, bears painful friction burns caused by a violent impact with the interior surface of the plane. The angry red discoloration of second-degree burns is a constant source of discomfort. The healing process will demand patience and meticulous care to prevent infection and aid in skin regeneration.

In matters of our mental health, a clinical social worker sat with us to assess, diagnose, and provide counseling for the trauma resulting from our plane crash.

The crash is just a surface wound atop layers of deeper, more persistent scars left by our time in Hoss.

We told the counselor nothing.

No one outside our trusted circle knows about the evil we endured. Monty and Melanie have worked behind the scenes, letting everyone believe we got lost in the Arctic and nearly starved. The details connecting us to Denver Strakh remain guarded until we have a course of action.

In truth, we have years of therapy ahead of us. Who knows how we'll pay for it? Financially, we're adrift, with no immediate plan to draw upon. Monty's wealth is a possibility, but I can't entertain that. After everything revealed in my journal and the complexities of my relationship with Leo and Kody, turning to him for financial support is unthinkable.

As for our physical health, it'll take time to come back from the brink of starvation, but I'm noticing small changes in Leo and Kody. Hydration has returned color to their cheeks, and solid food is already rebuilding their strength.

I lectured them on the importance of nutrition in

their healing, highlighting how proteins, vitamins, and even the much-maligned carbohydrates play a role in repairing their bodies.

They know this. But the hospital food, a far cry from the organic, unprocessed fare of the Arctic Circle, elicits a range of reactions from them.

"This isn't food." Leo stabs the green cube of Jell-O with a fork. "It's river slime."

"It's gelatin." I already devoured mine.

"Is that a plant?"

"No. It's derived from animal bones and skin."

"Bullshit. I've never seen an animal this color." He pushes it away. "Hard pass."

Given their extensive education in Hoss, they know so much about so many things. So it takes me by surprise whenever they don't understand ordinary concepts.

Like Jell-O.

"Kody ate his." I motion at Kody's empty tray.

"No, he didn't."

I look again. His gelatin is gone. When our eyes engage, his expression empties, expertly concealing any trace of his thoughts.

"What did you do?" I twist, scanning around the bed until my gaze lands on the waste basket and the glow of green gelatin within. "How quickly we go from starving to throwing away food."

"Leo's right." Kody scowls. "That's not food."

"Eat it." I point at Leo, assuming my sternest nurse glare.

"I'd rather eat *you.*"

A spark of heat ignites in my belly.

The bandages that encircled his head are gone. His beard, that was so much a part of him in the Arctic, is also gone, exposing the chiseled cut of his jaw.

Thank God he didn't lose his gorgeous hair to wounds or stitches. The contusions along the top of his head necessitated shaving small patches, but I took care of that. Yesterday, I braided those thick shoulder-length locks back into the Viking style that suits him so well, ensuring the shaved spots are cleverly hidden.

He takes a cautious bite of the Jell-O. "Fucking weird." Another bite and his eyebrows slowly lift. "It's...not terrible."

As he voraciously shovels in the rest, his mouth widens in a surly, reluctant smile that's so inherently Leo.

My God, he's beautiful.

Those eyes, the striking blue and captivating gold, sparkle with renewed energy. Two days of IV fluids and food have worked wonders, filling out the gauntness that hollowed his features. Despite his complaints about the hospital's culinary offerings, he hasn't stopped eating since we were admitted.

In my periphery, Kody reaches for the waste basket, going after the Jell-O he discarded.

"Don't even think about it." I grab the bin before he reaches inside it.

"It fell into a paper cup."

"The cup is garbage. We don't eat garbage."

"The cup had clean water in it."

"And now it's below the rim."

"Why does that matter?"

"If it's below the rim, it's garbage."

"What if the garbage was above the rim?"

"Then the three-second rule applies."

He stares at me. "It's like talking to Wolf."

"Wolf would agree with me on this."

Wolf would've also known what Jell-O is because

he was a sponge when it came to pop culture and irrelevant information.

Kody snatches the waste bin away and holds it out of reach of my grabby hands while shoving a huge paw inside it.

"Fine. Go ahead." I turn away. "Just don't expect to kiss me with your garbage lips."

The sound of the waste bin hitting the floor makes me smile.

In the next breath, his arms band around me and toss me onto my back on the bed. His body lowers, pinning me beneath his heat.

Bruises and gashes from the crash crisscross his face. But rather than detract from his appearance, they add to his dangerous allure and rugged handsomeness.

His dark hair, hinting at his Inuit heritage, falls just a touch too long in a way that's stylishly sexy and rebelliously messy. It frames his sculpted features, every sharp angle carved with hardship and silent strength. Freshly shaved, that square jawline accentuates the plush curve of his lips, a contrast to the usual stubble that adds mystery to his imposing, misunderstood demeanor.

But, like Leo, it's his eyes that always draw me in. Broody, yes, but beautifully so. They guard his emotions while penetrating mine. There's something about his presence, a quiet magnetism that commands attention without demanding it.

His gaze darkens, and high-voltage currents arc between us, charged with too many weeks without sex.

"Your mouth is distracting," he says thickly, darkly, oh-so gravelly. "Give it to me."

This man knows his mind and heart and chooses when to share them as surely as he chooses when to capture my breath.

I'm already straining my neck to reach him. The instant our lips touch, he kisses me with the full brunt of his pent-up arousal. No preamble. No exploration. He consumes me with every intention of deleting my hesitancy and replacing it with his essence, his flavor, his hunger.

Kody, in all his moody, hot-as-fuck glory, isn't just a pleasure to look at. He's a brick wall of gentle strength, and I'm reminded of that as he rocks his hips and crushes me into the bed.

His hands sweep over my body, turning me on as his tongue seduces my mouth. My legs fall open, and for a mindless moment, I almost forget where we are.

Almost.

"We can't do this."

"You've been saying that for a month." His eyes scorch. "You're fucking gorgeous, woman."

Feeling unattractive has been an ongoing and uncomfortable reality, but when I looked in the mirror this morning, I didn't see the starved, half-dead woman who's been staring back at me for weeks. I saw a woman who survived hell, a fighter ready to chase her forever with the men she madly, desperately loves.

After two days of nutrients and medical care, I feel stronger, rested, and ready to reclaim the sense of self that starvation and survival stripped away.

I have a long way to go to get my sexy back, but right now, I would love nothing more than to have wild, filthy, celebratory, survivor sex with Leo and Kody.

Except the timing is terrible. We're in a hospital room, and anyone can walk in.

Then again, timing has never been on our side, always overshadowed by more pressing concerns like freezing, starving, grieving, hiking, solving riddles, fighting wolves and bears, and conquering a psychopath.

But amid all of it, we made time. In the darkest winter, we found one another in the stolen moments and fell in love.

If we don't take advantage of this moment now, we may not have another for a while. We don't know where we're going, where we'll live, how we'll support ourselves. The struggle is never-ending.

Letting this reprieve slip through our fingers, losing it to whatever comes next, that's not us.

We need this.

Leo's presence, just a few feet away, adds another layer of conviction. His stillness is no less charged with vibrating desire. The wordless understanding in his posture and cautious readiness in his eyes confess his deep love for me.

He expects me to stop this, and he won't utter a complaint, no matter how badly he wants it.

"How's your leg?" I grip Kody's flexing, denim-clad ass.

"Leg is fine. But my cock..." He grinds the hard, heavy beast against my pelvis. "It fucking aches."

"We need to be quick." I find Leo's smoldering eyes.

"I'll guard the door." He rises from the bed, drawing my gaze to the swollen bulge trapped behind the zipper of his jeans.

Watching me have sex sets him on fire. By the time Kody finishes, Leo will be in a frenzy of need.

He leans against the door and crosses his arm, ready to watch and wait his turn.

One of these days, I'm going to convince them to fuck me together. Double-penetration would be a first for all of us. But I need to work them up to that. Kody is still skittish about anal.

I peer up at him, and the burnish of lust in his eyes wings butterflies beneath my skin. The affection that binds us is a vibrant, fluttering energy that pulls our mouths together in a language our souls instinctively understand.

His tongue seeks mine, licking me with a love so deep, so raw and honest, it engages every cell in my body.

He grabs my hips and wrenches down my pants. We shove aside clothes, caress and grope bare skin, and through it all, never break the kiss.

Our lips slide together. Our tongues dance. When he fits the plump head of his cock against my opening, we combust.

I'm dripping wet. He's hard as steel. We groan in chorus as he slowly pushes inside.

His eyes glow and swirl like the northern lights, completely black, heavy with arousal, and deep as the polar night.

"Fuck, you feel good." His throaty growl rumbles through me, each word searing as he pumps his hips. "So fucking warm and tight. Let me in. Take my cock."

I widen my legs and open for him, letting him fill me and stretch me and take anything he wants. He kisses me harder, grunting as he sinks deeper, snarling as I squeeze my inner muscles.

"I love you." I wrap my arms around his sinewy back and throw myself into the kiss, swishing my tongue with his, riding his thrusts, and tumbling toward that blissful edge.

His delicious, masculine taste makes me wild, and I lift my hips, reaching, climbing, pushing him deeper.

He tears his mouth away and buries his teeth in my shoulder, fucking me faster, panting against my skin.

A guttural curse yanks my attention toward the door.

Leo stands against it with his legs braced apart, his zipper open, and his hand working his stiff cock. Those beautiful, unmatched eyes collide with mine.

The space between us inflames, setting every nerve ending on fire.

"Make her come, Kody." He drops his head back against the door, fucking his fist. "Hurry."

My pussy clenches.

Kody kisses a trail along my neck and licks my bottom lip. "We're going to have a great fucking life together."

"I can't wait."

"Now be a good girl and come for me."

My entire body trembles at the husky rumble of *good girl* on his delicious tongue.

I stab my hands in his hair and draw that tongue into my mouth as he fucks me like a man on a mission to ruin me, worship me, and make me whole again.

A growl reverberates in his chest. Fresh heat gathers between my legs. I float in a fog of skin-tingling, mind-numbing kinetic energy.

"Now." His hands twist in my hair on the pillow. His pace slows, and his strokes hit just right. "Come with me."

Our eyes lock, and the orgasm comes at me from every direction, crashing into sharp spasms and electrocuting me in shimmery, powerful waves.

He buries his face in my neck, muffling his roar, as he jerks and twitches through his release.

When he comes up for air, his hooded eyes land on mine, glittering with a Kodiak smile. "I love you, too."

Relaxed and tingly, I kiss his lips, drifting in a happy haze of delirium.

He slips out of me, the silky heat of his cock trailing wetness along my thigh. He tucks himself away and lifts me into his arms.

"Your leg." I wriggle to get down, which earns me a swat on the ass.

"Shh." He brushes his nose through my hair, smelling me as he carries me to Leo and nods at the bathroom. "Take her in there, just in case."

Leo takes me from Kody's arms and pivots, stepping into the small private restroom.

He sets me on the counter, shuts the door, and turns on the shower.

Kody managed to strip everything off me except my t-shirt. Leo relieves me of that as the sound of spraying water fills the room.

Then he steps back, letting his gaze crawl up and down my naked body while ignoring the erection jutting from his open zipper.

My thighs quiver against the sexual tension that crackles the air.

A smirk twists his savage lips, and he leans in and licks my earlobe. "You're so fucking hot."

I reach down and latch my fingers around his thick, veiny cock. "You're one to talk."

My hand traces the rippling washboard of his abs and granite hardness of his muscled ass. He's a Viking god.

"I missed you," he breathes against my lips, parting them with his warm tongue. "Missed you so fucking much."

This kiss is gentle, loving, and just as ruinous. The heat of his mouth melds with mine, fusing us together, burning us alive.

"Want to take my time with you." He pushes down

his jeans and takes his place between my legs. "But I can't. Not this time. I'm not going to restrain myself."

"Leo?" I stroke his girthy length, making it leak all over my hand.

"Yeah, love?" He groans, spearing his fingers into my cunt, into the wetness of Kody's come.

"I missed you, too." I rock my hips, riding those long, curling digits. "I should've told you on the plane instead of waiting until we landed. I love you."

"You tell me every time you look at me." He eats at my lips. "I see it in your eyes. I'm the luckiest fucking man alive." He leans back, watching his fingers glide in and out of me. "Look how pretty this pussy is."

His touch is a brand between my legs, a decadent heat swirling through Kody's mess. He scoops some of it out and holds it up to my mouth.

I open, holding out my tongue, and he pushes his wet fingers past my lips.

"Goddamn, Frankie..." He grips his cock with his free hand, rubbing it as I suck on his fingers. "Fuck!"

His restraint snaps. He clutches my waist with both hands, pulls me to the edge of the counter, and impales me on his cock.

I'm so fucking wet that he slides right in, groaning, pistoning his hips, and palming my breasts as we kiss.

The shower continues running, filling the space with steam and drowning out our moans.

"Need to fuck you every day." He plows into me, releases a shuddering breath, and grips the base of my skull, bringing our foreheads together. "Multiple times a day. Never going to stop."

He watches where we're joined, sinking into me with long, deep strokes in an achingly soft rhythm.

"Not gonna last, love." Panting, shaking, he baptizes me in tenderness as he fiercely stares into my eyes.

"Come on my cock."

The gentle, spiraling sensations of his thrusts send me into a tailspin. Wetness gushes between my legs. Heat lashes through my core. I cry out, coming, drenching him with my orgasm.

He crashes his mouth against mine, growling as he fucks me, clutching my throat, finding his release, and filling my body with a hot wash of wetness.

"Fucking love you." He sucks on my swollen lips and slides his hands over my breasts, shooting a million tiny prickles across my skin, making me thirsty for more.

"I'm so proud of you." I cup his sculpted face, running my thumbs along the harsh angles. "You put so much work into learning to fly that plane. You saved us, Leo. You gave us a future, a real chance at forever. You're going to have your airport someday, and you'll be a great instructor. You'll be great at anything you do."

"I want to be great with you."

"You already are."

leonid

FORTY

A restless itch squirms beneath my skin as I sit at the window beside Kody, mechanically winding spaghetti around my fork.

Only a few hours ago, I burned off some of this energy in the bathroom with Frankie. But it's slowly creeping back, this need for movement and fresh air and purpose.

I need to get out of this cramped hospital room.

Frankie says it will be tomorrow.

I glance at the bathroom door that blocks my view of her, the sound of the shower running softly from within.

Another source of my agitation—not being able to see her.

After a bit of maneuvering, Kody and I positioned the too-small plastic chairs near the window, creating a makeshift dining area. Trays of spaghetti balance on our laps.

We angled the chairs to face each other, making conversation easier. The position provides a view beyond the window. But more importantly, it gives us a clear line of sight to the door leading into the hall and the one to the bathroom.

The threats against Frankie are different here, less tangible than wolves and blizzards and empty pantries, but no less real in the potential harm they could bring to her.

"This is supposed to be meat." Kody looks offended as he swallows a meatball.

The concept of pasta with tomatoes, herbs, and ground caribou isn't foreign to us. We ate it on rare occasions in Hoss.

But this?

I choke down the last bite on my plate, noting its lack of connection to the environment from which it came. What is the animal in these meatballs? I can't taste the wilderness, the flavors of the creature's diet, or the freshness of the kill.

"It's artificial." I stack our empty trays, setting them aside. "Everything is artificial here."

We stare out the window, watching the city of Anchorage unfold at a blurring pace. People move about their day with urgency. Cars weave through the streets in a continuous flow, the headlights cutting through the falling snow. The nonstop activity is daunting and thrilling.

"We'll get used to it." He rests an elbow on the windowsill, taking it all in with a determined glint in his eyes.

City life. It's right there, so damn close, whispering promises of adventure and new beginnings. With every passing second, my excitement grows for the world beyond these walls.

Distant mountain peaks dusted with snow loom over bustling city streets. Outlines of buildings congregate in clumps, capturing the late afternoon light and throwing shadows across the urban landscape.

Even through the glass, the sounds filter in—a distant siren, the muted hum of traffic, the occasional burst of laughter from the sidewalk below—so different from the stillness of Hoss.

If I close my eyes, I can imagine the scent of food from nearby restaurants, the exhaust from cars and, if the wind is just right, a faint hint of the sea.

"Is it what you thought it would be?" I stare at a world we've only seen in movies and books.

"Everyone appears safe and at ease. But it feels like we're standing on snow-covered ice, thin and cracking beneath our feet, with darkness waiting below."

"A cynical perspective." I glance at him. "This isn't Hoss."

He grunts. "This room feels like a prison. I'm ready to get out there and find out what we've been missing." Our eyes lock. "What are your thoughts about living in Sitka?"

"Frankie has a job waiting for her there." I shrug. "It makes sense. Is one city better than another? You want to make vodka, and I want to fly planes. Does it matter where we do it?"

"Monty is in Sitka." A deep growl vibrates in his chest. "He looks at her like she's still his wife."

"She is...on paper. But things have changed. She's with us. Are you questioning that?"

"Fuck no."

"Official closure between her and Monty will happen. Until then, I'm not threatened by their marriage status. Are you?"

"No, but she's adamant about him helping us transition." Frustration lowers his voice. "I don't see that divorce happening anytime soon."

It's a precarious balance.

Over the past nine months, his love for her hasn't waned. In every look, every gesture, his devotion is fucking glaring. And it's not just her he shows concern for.

Kody and I are dressed in the nicest clothes we've ever worn in our crisp button-down shirts, dark denim jeans, and leather boots, with every thread in perfect condition, free from holes and signs of wear.

I haven't felt this clean or put together...ever. And it was all purchased by him.

His willingness to assist us, to ease our integration into the world, suggests kindness.

Or ulterior motives.

Denver's generosity was never without strings.

"Maybe he'll rescind his help now that he's read her journal." I grit my teeth. "I hate this, relying on him for anything. But I also know we can't give her everything she needs right now."

We don't have jobs or money, and the thought of her going hungry again is out of the question.

"She's *our* responsibility." He frowns at the window. "It should be us providing for her, protecting her." He meets my gaze. "We'll make our way and build something for ourselves, for her. But for now, if he continues to help us keep her safe and fed, then...we swallow our pride."

It's a bitter pill.

"This is just temporary." His eyes shift to the bathroom door. "She loves *us*. Remember that."

Our unbreakable bond has carried us this far. I

don't even know where to begin to establish work and earn money, but we'll figure it out. Someday, the reliance on Monty will be a distant memory.

In the meantime, I can't shake the feeling of being caught in a web of manipulation and hidden agendas, each thread pulling in a different direction.

Frankie's explicit writings about her sexual relationship with Kody and me will undoubtedly enrage him. As much as I'm wary of the influence he might wield, I also worry about his jealousy and what kind of man that can twist him into.

"Let's just wait and see how things unfold," I say, even as the uncertainty of it all sits heavily on my chest.

As we turn back to the window, we're interrupted by a rap of knuckles on the door.

The hospital staff don't knock.

We're out of our chairs before the door creaks open.

Shoes click against the floor as an unfamiliar woman strides in.

A stunning woman.

As her gaze sweeps over us, my skin heats and tightens.

There's something about her that commands immediate attention. A dangerous allure. It's in the way she appraises us, in the confidence distilled into each step, each lingering look as she floats closer, swaying her hips.

I don't think Kody is breathing. He shifts, trying to mask an involuntary response.

"Hey there. I'm Sirena Fisher." Her smile suggests she's no stranger to the effect she has on men. "You must be Leo and Kody."

Her blue eyes lock with ours in turn as she extends a slender hand, an invitation to touch her golden skin.

We just stare at her, neither of us moving.

Other than Frankie, our experience with such overt displays of attraction and sensuality is nonexistent.

The hospital has been a parade of faces, many of them kind and pretty in their own right, but none have struck us quite like this woman. Her beauty is undeniable, unsettling in its potency.

She reminds me of Gretchen, only softer, seemingly less sinister.

After a beat of awkwardness, she retracts her hand, resting it on her ample chest. "I lead the investigative team working for Monty Novak."

"What do you want?" My snarl ricochets through the room, aggressive and unwelcoming.

Her smile widens. "I wanted to introduce myself to the two *feral* men who have caused quite a stir in this town. The gossip appears to be true."

My muscles instinctively tense under her invasive gaze. "What gossip?"

Long, black hair cascades over her shoulders and curves between her breasts like a dark river cutting through a gorge.

I tear my eyes away, only to find my brother staring at the same thing.

"Word on the street is that two insanely attractive, ferocious men barely escaped the Alaskan bush with their lives." A sparkle dances in her eyes. "Understatement of the year." She fans herself. "As for the ferocious part...well, the bruises on Monty's face attest to that. Evidently, living off the land turns men into..." Her tongue darts out, wetting her lips. "Real men."

She winks unapologetically as if seduction is her nature, her very essence.

I know Kody and I are different. We're shaped by

the raw, unforgiving, lawless wilderness. It'll take us time to adapt to this world with its unfamiliar rules.

As Frankie's absence in the shower stretches on, I grapple with how to deal with this woman. She doesn't appear to be a threat. But I sense she came here for more than to satisfy her curiosity.

"Whatever this is…" I cross my arms. "We're not interested."

"Don't worry, I'm here strictly on professional grounds. Though, I must admit, working with you both will be a delicious bonus."

leonid

FORTY-ONE

"Working with us?" I exchange a quick glance with Kody, unsure where this is headed.

"There's an ongoing investigation that I need your help with." Sirena's gaze sweeps the room, pausing momentarily on the closed bathroom door. "I would like to meet Frankie and have a quick conversation with her as well."

I step into her line of sight, blocking her access to the door. "If this has to do with the plane crash..."

"No, it's—"

The bathroom door opens.

Frankie steps out, towel-drying her hair, and I'm caught in a moment of breathless wonder.

The rippling wet glow of her hair captures the very essence of fire, each strand alive with its own flame.

Her eyes widen at the new presence in the room. Vibrant green eyes that have seen and experienced things that would make most people curl up and die.

As she steps forward, squaring up the other woman, I'm struck by the undeniable truth of it.

Frankie isn't just beautiful. She's fire incarnate. In her light, everything and everyone pales in comparison.

Sirena can't hold a match to her.

"Sirena Fisher." The woman shakes Frankie's hand and smiles. "I was just getting to know your gorgeous companions."

Again, Sirena's eyes linger too long on Kody and me, inviting a silent conversation in the spaces between words.

"Is that right?" Frankie sets the towel aside and arches an accusing brow at us, her cheeks flushed from the shower.

Why do I feel a stab of guilt? I don't know the rules here, especially not the rules of women.

"I work for your husband." Sirena leans against the edge of a nearby table.

I sense a shift in Frankie's demeanor, the straightening of her stance, the tiny lift of her chin, and the hard glint in her eyes as she stares at the other woman, probing, assessing, distrusting.

"Are you fucking him?" Her tone is cool and direct, demanding honesty.

The inquiry catches me off guard. Why would she care if Sirena is fucking her ex? Is she jealous?

Jealousy implies unresolved feelings.

Anger spikes through me.

Beside me, Kody might snap his molars from how hard he grinds his jaw.

"Forgive me." Frankie backs down. "I've been away from society too long. I don't usually attack people I just met."

"You attack them *after* you get to know them?"

"Exactly."

"Good to know." Sirena grins and dips her head, meeting Frankie's much shorter height. "The answer is no. I haven't been intimate with your husband."

There's more she's not saying. I can feel it.

I watch the exchange closely, trying to parse Frankie's motivations. When she glances at Kody and me, her expression holds a depth of emotion I can't quite decipher. A trace of relief maybe? But it's shadowed by lingering skepticism.

"When you disappeared," Sirena says, "Monty hired the investigative firm I work for. I have been at his side for nine months and know every detail of the case except the contents of your journal." She hardens her voice. "Whatever he read in that book affected him deeply."

"You saw him?" Frankie clasps her hands against her stomach, trying to hide her tremor.

"Yes. He destroyed his hotel suite, punched the hotel manager, and has been, needless to say...unapproachable." Her eyes thin. "Piecing together what I know about Denver Strakh, I can't fathom what the three of you have survived. But Monty knows. He lived it through your words. I saw the trauma in his eyes this morning. You showed him a darkness that will forever stain his soul, and he chose not to look away."

Frankie's chin trembles as she nods.

"He's smoothing over the mess he made at the hotel." Sirena pushes off the table and paces to the window. "When he shows up here, I imagine he'll have everything put back to order, including his composure. But he's not okay."

"You care about him."

"Very much. But my affection for him is not

reciprocated." Pursing her lips, she peers at Frankie through a thick veil of lashes. "I propositioned your husband over and over for months. There isn't a man I can't get, but Monty is impenetrable. He thought you left him. He was heartbreakingly lonely, and I still couldn't seal the deal. Not even for a night. He is infuriatingly smitten with you."

Shadows cling to Frankie's furious glare, fed by the dark fire in her eyes. "Why are you telling me this?"

"Before I agreed to work with him, I investigated him. I know he had an affair with his office manager six weeks after you left, and he let her go immediately after the indiscretion. I pegged him as a cheater and expected him to pursue me. Most men do." When she smiles, it's tight around the corners. "I assumed a lot of things about him, and most of them were wrong. That never happens. In my profession, I've encountered every shade of character. Clients hire me to investigate other clients. Everyone is suspicious. Over the years, I learned to read people, and let's just say...very few surprise me." She pulls in a breath. "I'm telling you this because I see what's going on here." Her eyes dart over Kody and me. "They're beautiful and protective. Can't say I blame you."

"You don't know us," I growl.

"Perhaps." Sirena returns to Frankie. "But I do know that Monty will burn down the world for you. I watched him do it for months. His company, his life, his health—he scorched it all to the ground in his search for you. If you let him go, it will destroy him. There will be nothing left. He's a good man, and those are so hard to find."

"Are you finished?" Frankie crosses her arms.

"Don't be angry with me. I wanted to clear the air because..." She fingers her long hair. "I'll be sticking around for a while." She turns to me and Kody. "Monty tasked me with finding his son."

My breath dies. Kody goes still, and Frankie presses a hand to her throat.

"He said Wolfson fell into a gorge." Sirena's expression softens. "His body was never recovered. That's all I know. He said I should ask you for the details...when you're ready to give them."

The lawyer confirmed that Wolf's things were salvaged from the plane crash. The hard case protected his saxophone, and Frankie had packed his drawings and other keepsakes in dry bags. Everything survived.

Except him.

"We don't know the cabin's location." My heart hammers. "But we can describe the landscape, the river..."

"And you can go with me when I begin the search." She holds up her hands. "I know. It's too much, too soon. That's okay. I'm working on another investigation for him in the meantime."

"What other investigation?" Frankie tilts her head.

"Oh, just some things he found on Kodiak Island. I'll let Monty tell you about that."

"Tell her about what?" Monty enters the room with a stride that exudes authority, his finely tailored suit and imposing scowl eclipsing the bruises I left on his face.

"I was just explaining the depth of my loyalty and dedication to you." She winks at him.

He hisses through his teeth and jabs a finger at the door.

"That's my cue to leave." Her eyes gleam as she swivels back to us. "I look forward to working with you two." To Frankie, she says, "It's a pleasure to finally put a face to the name that's haunted me for months. You're just as lovely as I expected."

Frankie pinches her lips, her gaze writhing with distrust.

"Alrighty then." She sashays past Monty, wriggling her fingers at him. "I'll be in touch, handsome."

When the door closes behind her, Monty searches Frankie's face. "Did she upset you?"

"No." She steals a look at Kody, then turns her scrutiny to me, sifting through our expressions for something. "Your investigator is a beautiful woman."

She says this to Monty while still looking at Kody and me. Her fingers twitch at her sides, and a brief flicker of possessiveness crosses her features. A quick glance away, followed by a deep breath, reveals her struggle.

She thinks Kody and I are interested in that woman?

The thought makes me want to bend her over my knee.

Sirena might command attention with charm and a pretty face, but Frankie...she commands the soul.

Her beauty stands alone, an inner strength that radiates from within her, making her presence felt in every room she enters. Sirena has no hope of rivaling that.

"Yes." Monty squares his shoulders, his eye contact stern. "She's beautiful. Denying it would be ridiculous. But it has no bearing on the investigative work she provides. I tasked her with finding..." A shadow darkens his composed features. "Wolfson."

"I know." She steps forward, leaving a few feet between them. "You read the journal? All of it?"

"Yes." He sweeps past her and strides to the window with deliberate, measured steps, each one broadcasting his control.

I recognize the action, the need to pace, the attempt to conceal the chaos within. I do the same damn thing right before my temper blows.

Adjusting my position, I put myself between him and Frankie. Kody edges closer, too.

"You destroyed your hotel room?" She steps to my side, gripping my forearm with both hands.

"Sirena has a big mouth." He faces us, occupying his space without fidgeting or shifting, exuding a sense of belonging and confidence. "I'm...*angry.*" His voice carries a calm, cold tone, indicative of a man who knows how to fake it. "That doesn't begin to describe what I'm feeling. But if you expect me to walk away from this, from *us,* you're out of your mind."

"You can fuck off with that right now." Heat fumes from my lungs. "I'll gladly help you fuck off, but you'll be squatting to piss when I'm done."

"Leo..." She digs her nails into my arm.

Monty ignores me. "I never let go of you, Frankie. Not even when I thought you quit me." A quiet, guttural sound cracks his voice. "I didn't let go. I tried once and failed. A useless attempt that I'll regret for the rest of my life. Your reaction to seeing that video of me, the agonizing words you wrote about it, I'll never stop relieving the pain I caused you."

A shudder grips her, and she closes her eyes.

I seethe, hating this conversation. But if Frankie taught me anything, it's the importance of honesty and communication, so I'll bear this, goddammit, and be the silent support that she needs.

Kody is frozen beside me, an unmoving statue.

"I want to ask you to leave so I can talk to my wife alone." Monty looks at Kody and me, enraging me with the *wife* reference. "I want to hate you for touching her. I want to beat your fucking faces until they're unrecognizable. But I'm not going to do any of those things." He stands taller. "You were there for her when I wasn't. You were there when she needed me the most. So when the thought of you fucking her creeps into my head like a goddamn cancer, I hear her words on those pages, her pain and fear and loneliness, and I'm grateful she had you."

A sharp burn ignites in my chest.

He steps closer, pinning his keen Wolfson eyes on me. "But if you ever threaten her or hurt her the way you did in those initial weeks, I will fucking gut you."

A shiver runs down my spine. "I was wrong, and she made sure I wouldn't forget it."

"I know," he rasps with a rough shake of his head. "I won't forget it, either."

I glance at her, at the flush crawling up her throat. She wrote about that day in the workshop? When she demanded I grovel and beg for forgiveness after I had my fingers inside her?

She meets my eyes and presses her lips together.

I really want to redden her fucking ass.

"I know your hatred of me is justified." Monty clasps his hands behind his back, radiating chilling confidence as his gaze connects with hers. "I'm sorry. I'm sorry for—"

"Monty, don't—"

"—the hurtful things I said about pregnancy ruining your body and demanding you choose between your job and our child. I was desperate to give you any reason but the truth. I'm sorry. I'm sorry for every second you spent in the cabin, for every ounce of pain my actions and inactions caused you. I should've stayed home the day of our fight. I should've done a lot of things differently. I'm prepared to right my wrongs, heal your broken heart, and grovel, beg, and fight to win you back."

She gasps. "Monty, no, I'm—"

"Don't say anything. Just...let me help you." He lifts his determined gaze to me and Kody. "All of you."

Her shoulders slump. This is what she wants, and he's offering it in the palm of his hand.

"I don't trust you." Kody steps forward.

"If you did, I would question how you survived my brother." Monty draws a slow breath. "I realize that to earn back her trust, I must also earn yours."

My brows furrow, and a sharp pang resounds in my chest. I hate him for betraying her. But that betrayal cracked her open enough to love me and my brothers.

Everything is shifting, tilting in the wrong direction.

The door opens, and Melanie strides in. "Oh good, you're all here."

"This conversation isn't over," Monty says under his breath.

No, it's not fucking over. But Frankie doesn't need a battle. She needs respect and space to make her own choices. Monty's declaration feels like an imposition.

My protective instincts, tightly coiled, will explode if he oversteps. Kody's black glare at Monty carries the same silent warning.

We'll ensure Monty understands the boundaries, that his stance won't change how we—along with Frankie—will decide the future.

"Are you ready to get out of here?" Melanie pauses beside us, her blonde hair twisted in a knot at her nape. "The doctors are releasing you today."

My pulse races, a frantic drumbeat in my ears.

Monty removes his phone and types on the screen.

"I have a security team on standby."

"Okay, good." Melanie nods, turning to us. "I reviewed the contents of the thumb drive. Before you make any decisions about where to go, you need to review the information on that drive. Monty can transport you to my office in Anchorage. It's private, comfortable, and, above all, secure. Sound good?"

"What is on the thumb drive?" Kody growls.

"DNA paternity and maternity tests." She sets her shoulders. "They checked out. The information proves the biological parents for you two and Wolfson."

"Oh, God." Frankie grips my hand.

"Is that all?" I ask.

"No. There's more. Including a video of Denver Strakh addressed to all of you."

frankie

FORTY-TWO

Squeezed into the back seat of a sleek sedan beside Kody, I choke on the tension crammed in such a small space.

Monty, Leo, and Kody in one car.

Their DNA results.

Denver's video.

The temperature of my blood is negative degrees. I can't feel my face.

Monty navigates the snowy streets of Anchorage with practiced ease while Leo, positioned in the passenger seat beside him, drums his fingers against his knee.

No one speaks.

Through the windows, Anchorage stretches out alongside us, flickering with lights and shadows that trace the rhythm of the city.

Kody takes up most of the back seat, filling it with

his muted yet powerful presence. His dark eyes flick from one landmark to the next, absorbing every detail of the unfamiliar environment.

Leo, on the other hand, is more openly restless. The rhythmic tapping of his fingers betrays a nervous energy or perhaps excitement. His attention flits between the city outside and the interior of the car.

They're both out of their element, propelled from a world of snow and silence into the bustling, noisy reality of city life. I can feel the effort it takes for them to process everything.

As for Monty, it's strange to see him behind the wheel. Where are his chauffeurs and personal assistants who do everything for him?

Sirena said he scorched his life to the ground during his search for me. Is that what this is?

His voice cuts through the silence, directed at Leo. "If you're cold, you can adjust the temperature." He points at the panel of dials.

Leo leans forward, his interest piqued as he studies the controls. "How does it work?" His finger hovers over the array of options.

"This dial controls the temperature. Turning it to the right makes it warmer, to the left, cooler. And these buttons operate the fan speed and direction of the air."

Leo nods and shifts his attention to the instrument cluster. "What about those?"

Monty turns onto the next street and launches into an overview of the speedometer, fuel gauge, engine temperature, oil pressure, and battery.

I nudge Kody, and he bends into me, sniffing my hair. When he makes a purring sound against my scalp, I melt.

There's my feral man.

"It's like a cockpit." Leo's gaze moves from one dial

to the next.

"In a way." Monty eyes him, his brows knitting before he returns to the road ahead. "Just a lot simpler to operate than a plane or helicopter. You'll get the hang of it."

The exchange, simple as it is, eases some of the awkward tension.

Monty's eyes meet mine in the rearview mirror with a frequency that feels comforting and disconcerting.

Each glance carries a thousand pounds of worry, particularly about what we'll discover on the thumb drive. But there's something else, too. His concern for what remains unsaid between us, for the state of my feelings toward him. I sense his fear that my heart is forever lost to him.

It complicates everything.

Sitting here, sandwiched between Kody and the door, I tense against the turmoil. Monty's recent vulnerability, the raw openness he displayed by baring his heart, is not something I would have ever expected from him. It was an act so unlike the Monty I knew. It shook me.

But the truth is, along that hellish road between the pregnancy test and the sex tape, I fell out of love with him.

If Leo and Kody weren't here, would I give Monty a second chance?

I have no fucking clue. But this battle between my heart and my head is a mess I can't afford to untangle right now. Not when there are more pressing matters like the imminent meeting at the office and the revelations awaiting us on the thumb drive.

Monty's gaze in the mirror finds me again, a silent question lingering in his eyes.

I offer a small, reassuring smile, a gesture meant to ease his worry, even if I can't fully assuage my own.

For now, I must shelve my feelings and compartmentalize the confusion and conflict. There will be time later to sort through it.

"How's your leg?" I run a hand over Kody's knee.

"Stop asking, woman." He grimaces.

God forbid he admits it hurts.

Stubborn man.

Before we left, I applied a medicated cream prescribed by the doctors. He's not limping as much, but I suspect that every small movement feels like fire.

As the car moves through the snowy streets of Anchorage, I force myself to look out the window, to let the passing scenery distract me from the chaos within. Survival has always been about prioritizing, and this is no different.

There's more pain ahead, and I don't know if I'm ready for it.

Monty guides the car into a parking spot within a dimly lit garage, the tires squeaking against concrete. As we disembark, the chill of the enclosed space wraps around us.

Monty leads the way to a set of elevators, his stride confident and familiar with the path.

"Have you been here before?" I ask.

"Yes." He presses the call button. "I personally returned your journal to Melanie."

"Oh." I peer at him. "It's strange...I mean, you usually have people doing things for you."

"A lot has changed, Frankie."

As the wait for the elevator stretches out, I sense a shift in Leo and Kody. They exchange brief, uncertain glances.

The urge to hug and comfort them through every

new sight and sound twitches through me. But they don't want that.

They don't need it.

They survived the Arctic Circle, for fuck's sake.

When the doors finally slide open with a soft chime, Monty steps in without hesitation. Leo follows, a hint of reluctance in his movement. He stands just inside the elevator, his body rigid, eyes scanning the interior as if assessing a strange new territory.

Kody hesitates at the threshold before stepping in beside Leo, his expression tight.

Give them space, Frankie. They need room to grow and adjust.

As the doors close, sealing us in, Kody's hand grips the rail tightly, his knuckles whitening.

Leo keeps his gaze fixed on the numbers above the door, watching them change with an intensity that makes me smile.

Their reactions to the ascent, the subtle vibration underfoot, and the sensation of movement unconnected to any visible change in the environment seem to fascinate and unsettle them.

Neither of them speaks, but their body language communicates their disquiet. The elevator's gentle hum and the smooth glide upward are everyday experiences for most. But for them, it must be overwhelming.

Their wide-eyed, alert stances hint at a readiness to face whatever comes. But there's an underlying curiosity, a desire to understand this new aspect of the world they've stepped into.

I love this for them.

I love that I get to experience their new freedom.

When the elevator reaches the top floor and the doors open, Leo steps out first with an exhale of relief.

Kody follows, his posture relaxing as he wanders into the expansive hallway.

Monty seems oblivious to their discomfort, or perhaps he's chosen to ignore it, focused on leading us to our destination.

The soft hum of the city behind sealed windows follows us to the door at the end of the hall. As it swings open, Melanie greets us with a practiced smile, her presence immediately grounding, despite the undercurrent of dread.

The vibe in the air reminds me of the uncomfortable silence at a funeral. No one knows how to handle the heaviness of so many choking emotions.

"Welcome." Melanie steps aside to allow us entrance. "Please, come in and make yourselves comfortable."

Her gesture sweeps us into a private room designed to take the edge off formal meetings. A plush couch beckons invitingly, flanked by multiple chairs, all arranged to face a large TV mounted on the wall.

As we file in, Melanie nods at the wet bar nestled in an alcove. "Can I get anyone something to drink?"

Kody and Leo exchange a look before Leo says, "Vodka for us."

"Bourbon for Frankie and me." Monty lowers into a chair and straightens his suit jacket.

Leo stiffens. "You assume to still know her?"

Monty pauses, his eyes shifting to Leo, glinting with something. "You're right," he concedes, turning back to me with a more open posture. "What would you like, Frankie?"

The room holds its breath.

"Bourbon." I hold his stare, giving him this small victory.

His nod, subtle but meaningful, signals his effort to

respect and recalibrate the changing dynamics between us.

Melanie steps away to procure the drinks as Kody and Leo join me on the couch, bracketing me.

My stomach knots, and my hands grow damp. I rub them on my jeans. "I'm nervous."

Leo grips my fingers, pulling them onto his lap.

Monty turns to me, his expression softening. "I know this is hard, and it's okay to be nervous. But remember, you're incredibly strong. You've shown that time and time again."

"Thank you." I tip into his beautiful blue eyes and before I get lost there, I quickly look away.

"Here we are." Melanie distributes the drinks and lowers into the other chair. "I've reviewed the files on the thumb drive and watched the video. There's nothing graphic, but given everything this man has put you through, I know it won't be easy to watch. It's...disturbing."

My throat dries, and I take a sip of the bourbon, savoring the heat, the flavor.

"If you're ready," Melanie says, "I think we should start with the DNA results." At our nods, she removes a stack of papers from a folder on the coffee table. "I printed these documents off the files on the thumb drive. Denver had all the tests run through the same company. He provided the DNA samples to the company, and we matched them to the samples you provided. Everything has been checked and double-checked. It's all accurate. You can read through the results, or I can just tell you."

"Just tell us." Leo drains his vodka and sets the empty glass aside. "Start with Wolf since we know that one."

Bees swarm my stomach.

"Wolfson Strakh." Melanie places a paper on the table, turning it to face us. "He is the biological son of Gretchen Stolz and Montgomery Loshad Strakh."

For a heartbeat, Monty is utterly still. Then, slowly, the initial shock gives way, and the hand, which had been resting on his knee, clenches into a fist as if in an attempt to grasp the enormity of this confirmation.

"You would've loved him." My heart aches. "He was so smart and talented and funny."

"You wrote a lot about him." Monty swallows. "But I would love to hear more stories."

"Of course." I squeeze the circulation out of Leo's hand, and he squeezes right back.

Kody stares at the paper on the table, reading and rereading the test results.

I glance at it, too, my gaze catching on the father's name. "Montgomery Loshad Strakh?" I find Monty's hard eyes. "That's your given name?"

"Yeah."

"Do mine next." Kody shifts to the edge of the seat, his muscles taut.

I hold out my free hand, and he grabs it, linking the three of us together.

"Kodiak Strakh." Melanie's voice hangs in the weighted silence. "You are the biological son of Kaya Knowles and Rurik Strakh. This also confirms that Monty and Denver are your half-brothers."

The room becomes a vacuum of stunned silence, every sound sucked away, leaving only the echo of Melanie's words.

My stomach drops as the revelation sinks in.

"Did you know?" Kody's gaze slams into Monty, raging with shock and confusion. "Did your father rape my mother?"

"Kody..." Monty shakes his head, looking horrified. "No. I had no idea. My father took her in, treated her like a daughter..." He chokes. "Oh, God. I didn't know. How did I not fucking know? She was young. Only twenty-one. And my father...It must be a sickness. It's in the family. This...this runs in the fucking family."

This is a hereditary disease.

"Monty, no." I lean over Kody's lap, capturing Monty's attention. "You are not your father. You are not them. Do you hear me?"

Ignoring me, he stares at Kody, his expression fraught with turmoil. "I'm sorry. If I'd known my father touched Kaya in that way, I would've killed him myself..." His eyes widen. "Fuck. Denver did it. He killed him. He found out about Kaya and tampered with Rurik's plane."

"He says as much in the video." Melanie nods.

Leo's brows furrow in pain for Kody as he reaches across me and clutches Kody's arm, gripping hard in silent support.

Kody is Monty's half-brother.

And Denver's half-brother.

When Denver told us there was a third brother, he could've told Kody right then, to his face, that Kody was that brother. Instead, he tossed him a riddle because he couldn't say it. The fucking coward. He raped his own goddamn brother and couldn't admit it, not even on his last breath.

I shake at the thought of it. I shake so hard that Leo pulls me against his side and strokes my hair.

"I'm okay." I measure my breaths. "Just really fucking mad."

"Me, too." Leo looks at Melanie. "Let's get this over with."

The room seems to contract around us as Melanie places the final paper on the table. "Leonid Strakh. You are the biological son of Tia Langston and Denver Yastreb Strakh."

"What?" Monty jumps from the chair and grabs the paper, scanning the results.

"Tia Langston?" Leo releases me, standing, too. "My mother is Helena Weiss."

Denver is Leo's father. I don't think that has hit Leo yet.

Denver raped his own biological son.

My insides lurch. I'm going to be sick.

"Tia Langston." Monty gulps down the last of his bourbon and paces through the room. "Her father was Paul Langston, our groundskeeper. He lived in a guest house on our property on Kodiak Island." He groans. "He died in a car accident when Tia was young. Christ, she was..."

"Fifteen," Melanie says and turns to Leo. "She was fifteen when she gave birth to you in Fairbanks. She named you Brennan. Brennan Langston."

"Who is Helena Weiss?" I pinch the bridge of my nose. I'm so confused.

"Tia Langston changed her name to Helena Weiss." Melanie tucks a loose lock of hair into her bun. "Denver explains it in the video, and we fact-checked it. I can walk you through the details or—"

"Let's watch the fucking video." Leo eases back into the couch with a casual sprawl, as if the identity of his father hasn't phased him in the slightest.

I see through the facade. His entire foundation has been violently and irreparably rocked.

"Leo." I tuck myself into his side and rest my head on his pounding chest. "It's okay not to be okay about this. I'm here."

"I know." He grinds his teeth.

Kody's arm stretches behind me along the back of the couch, his hand landing on Leo's nape.

My mind spins as I redefine our relationships and dynamics.

Monty and Kody are half-brothers.

Leo and Wolf are cousins.

Monty and Kody are Leo's uncles.

Kody is four years younger than Leo, and he is Leo's uncle.

I don't even want to contemplate Denver's relationship with them. I'll dwell on that later when I'm ready to have a good cry.

Monty returns to his chair, his nostrils flaring. "Play the video."

"Before we jump into it..." Melanie powers on the TV screen. "There were a few other documents on the thumb drive. One was a digital copy of the flight manual with an instructional training guide on flying the Turbo Beaver. The other was a step-by-step operational handbook on the hydroelectric generator."

"Of course, there was," Kody snarls.

"Psycho fucking prick." Leo runs a shaky hand through my hair.

I release a sad breath. "He included the instructions because, in his sick, fucked-up way, he wanted you to survive."

"I wish he were alive right now so I could tell him how I feel about that." Leo scowls at Melanie. "Anything else? Like bank account information or a last will and testament?"

"No, I'm afraid not."

My heart sinks.

With that, Melanie returns to her chair and presses

play.

The room darkens, the focus shifting to the screen where the video comes to life.

There, displayed with disarming familiarity, is Denver, lounging with the ease of an arrogant monster, wearing the smile that makes me quake with murderous rage.

But my heart stops at the sight of the couch he occupies, a piece of furniture deeply embedded in my memories.

I handpicked it when Monty and I got married.

It's the very couch in the main room of the house I shared with Monty in Sitka.

frankie

FORTY-THREE

My ears ring. My entire body shudders.

That couch and those surroundings are part of a world I shared with Monty, a world that now feels like a distant dream.

A dream that Denver violated.

Seeing him there, in a setting so personal and intimate, tunnels ice through my veins.

I glance at Monty, wondering if he feels the invasion as viscerally as I do.

His face is a stone wall, his gaze fixed on the screen, but I sense his tension. His eyes, a barometer of his temper, flash with the fury building beneath his composure.

"Where is that?" Leo leans forward.

"In our fucking house." Monty flexes his hands.

"He didn't record this the night he abducted me. It's daylight outside." I point to the window on the video.

Kody drains his vodka and grips my thigh.

Denver starts to speak, his voice filling the room. "*I've lived to bury my desires and see my dreams corrode with rust. Now all that's left are fruitless fires that burn my empty heart to dust.*"

"More riddles." Kody's breathing changes, becomes more pronounced.

Denver sprawls on my couch, arms stretched across the seat back, the very embodiment of a psychopath.

His smile is all charm, sweetly warm, yet the coldness in his eyes is chilling. "If you're watching this, it means I shuffled off this mortal coil and entrusted one of my sons with my riddle. Who was it, I wonder? Which of my boys did I deem smart enough to solve the puzzle and retrieve the thumb drive? Which one was worthy enough to share my legacy?"

"The fuck?" Kody shifts restlessly, fighting to stay anchored to the sofa.

"Technically..." I clutch Kody's hand. "He gave the riddle to me."

Monty's gaze remains glued to the screen. He hasn't seen Denver in thirty years. I can't fathom what he's feeling right now.

"I have a story to tell and not much time." Denver glances around the room—the space I shared with Monty. "When I reached the tender age of eighteen, my coldblooded brother—Wolf, the name I fondly bestowed upon him in our youth—had our father commission my execution. A twist of fate spared me when I confessed to my father that same week that I would be a father. I got sweet, little Tia Langston pregnant, and that revelation stayed my father's hand. He had just finished building a safe house in the hills of the Arctic Circle using my hydroelectric design to power it. My punishment? A life exiled within that desolate cabin, erased from the world I knew. My survival hinged on sporadic flights to Whittier, supply runs facilitated by a man known as Alvis Duncan. My father gave me a Turbo Beaver, which was logged and supervised. Then he had Tia Langston's parents killed, changed her name, and moved her to an unknown location. Make no mistake. Rurik's intentions were never rooted in affection for Tia or me. It was the bloodline he sought to preserve—his son and now his grandson, the continuation of our lineage."

A war drum thunders in my chest.

Leo doesn't move or blink. No one does.

On the screen, Denver twists his lips. "Unbeknown to my father, my efforts to locate Tia had borne fruit. I discovered her in Fairbanks, where she brought my son into the world, only to vanish again, emerging in California under the guise of Helena Weiss." His smile is a grimace of twisted satisfaction. "No matter. My persistence paid off. I reclaimed what was mine when my son was three. I named him Leonid in homage to Port Lions—the cradle of his mother's and my fateful encounter. But those first two years were rough. Whenever my nosy parents visited the cabin, I had to tie up poor Tia and Leo far away from the property and rid the rooms of their existence. My parents couldn't know that I had brought them home with me in crates."

"Melanie, can we pause it for a moment?" I ask, my voice calmer than I feel.

The video halts, freezing Denver's smirk.

Turning to Leo, I search his bloodshot eyes. "Do you remember visits from Denver's parents? Anything about him tying up you and your mother away from the cabin?"

"It's all a blur." He grips his nape. "There were times when things didn't make sense. Moments of fear, of hiding, but it's like trying to grasp smoke. I remember...fear. And confusion. But specific visits? It's hard to say."

"My parents died when you were five." Monty braces his elbows on his spread knees and stares at his clasped hands. "It's possible, with all the trauma you endured, your brain buried it as a way to protect..."

His words trail off as he tries to make sense of it. They're all struggling, and it breaks my heart.

At my nod, Melanie resumes the video.

"During one of my father's visits without my mother, he revealed that Kaya was with child, *his* child." Denver cocks his head at the camera. "My disillusionment was profound. The irony that Rurik and Montgomery conspired against my life for my adoration of Kaya, only for Rurik to sully her with his seed. What an unfortunate situation. Unfortunate for him. On his next visit to check up on me, we met in Whittier during my supply run. A subtle manipulation of his aircraft's mechanics sealed his fate. As for my mother, she was collateral damage, a mere shadow that never imprinted upon me."

"God, just shut up already." My stomach hurts just looking at him.

"In the wake of my father's demise," Denver muses, "I had more freedom. His goons still lingered, collecting flight logs and living out their contracts. Unfortunately, I never determined how many contracts were in play or how long they were hired to supervise me. Some were hitmen, contracted to execute me on sight if I broke my father's rules after he died. I had to learn to bend those rules and sneak around them. I won't bore you with details on how I tracked Tia Langston to California, shadowed Montgomery's promiscuous activities, and hunted down Kaya while being watched by my father's goons. Maybe I had another plane. Maybe I had a protege to sow confusion. Maybe it's merely a matter of my superior intellect." His gray eyes glimmer. "Since my father hid Kaya's location from me, it took two years to find her. By the time I was twenty-five, the world was my chessboard, and I, the grandmaster, orchestrated the fates of pawns and kings alike. And Tia..." He makes a tsking sound. "Poor, irrational Tia tied me to my bed. So I buried her alive."

Leo's hand jerks in my grip.

"Want to pause it?" I ask.

His head gives a sharp shake.

"In that pivotal year, the pieces of my chessboard aligned." Denver leans back on the couch and props a socked foot on his knee. "I located Kaya. My father, ever the architect of isolation, hid her outside a northern coastal village. Completely alone. Lost to the world. Much in the way he isolated me. Kaya gave birth in solitude, undocumented, and named the child after our beloved Kodiak Island. I would've left them there. But my brother ordered my death, and my father brought another brother into the world. So I intended to use Kaya and that child to hurt Montgomery. Killing Montgomery would've been a mercy. My long-term plan was to slowly strip away everyone from his life and banish them to the shadows that have become my realm. A balancing of scales. Unfortunately, Kaya didn't last. She was too soft. Too weak. And Kodiak? I hated him for existing, for being my father's son. Then I raised him. He became more important than vengeance. He became *mine*."

The air feels colder, the devil's presence emanating from the past. I shiver, reminding myself repeatedly that he's no longer alive, that he can't hurt us anymore.

Monty tightens his jaw, fighting his emotions through controlled, deliberate breaths. His eyes harden into chips of ice as he aims his frosty, seething anger at the screen, at Denver's smug expression.

A shadow hovers over Kody's features, and the muscles in Leo's arms haven't stopped flexing.

Denver's smile flashes on the screen. "I monitored Montgomery's endless parade of women, biding my time, waiting for fate to present herself. And then there was Gretchen. She let Monty believe the pregnancy was terminated, left the clinic with his child intact, and fled to Iowa to hide her deceit. It was I who orchestrated her return, guided Wolfson into the world, named him, and claimed him as my own creation." The light catches in his eyes, a spark of mirth in the grim narrative. "Oh, the tales I could divulge. You must be frothing with questions. How did I locate Gretchen from my secluded cabin? Why did I allow her to fuck Leo? Why didn't I interfere when eight-year-old Wolfson killed her? I'll leave it for you to unravel. But I'll confess this. When she died, we were all relieved. Gretchen was not the fate I had so patiently anticipated. Neither was Jasmine nor Alyssa. Devoid of ties to Montgomery, they were nonentities, mere pawns in a game my boys refused to play. Then, a few years ago, the stars finally aligned. The perfect pawn to play with my boys and the fate that would destroy Montgomery once and for all presented herself." Leaning closer, he stares directly into the camera. "Frankie, *my whole life has been pledged to this meeting with you.*"

"Stop the video," Monty's command cuts through the chilling narrative, firm and resolute. He surges from the chair and positions himself between the screen and me, as if to shield me from the venom spilling from Denver's lips.

The screen freezes.

My insides coil. Nausea rises. I'm on the brink, teetering between fleeing from this room and forcing myself to see it through to the bitter end.

The clip's timeline looms at the bottom of the screen. We're approaching the finale, and knowing Denver, he saved the worst for last.

Monty stares at his phone, typing something on the screen.

Kody's hand finds mine, his grip reassuring, his voice guttural. "We've made it this far. We need to know the rest."

Leo nods, his mismatched eyes stark. "It's the only way to understand, to see the full scope of what he planned."

Monty looks up from his phone, his eyes softening as they connect with mine. "If you need a moment, we can take a break. But I agree with Kody and Leo. We need to see this through." He holds up his phone. "Denver used two quotes in this video. The first line when he opened and the last line we just paused on. I recognized them because they're in a book I found hidden in the wall in my childhood home. A book of Pushkin's poems. Sirena is getting the book analyzed. I don't know what any of this means, but Denver put those quotes in the video on purpose."

"To send us on another scavenger hunt." Leo's jaw clicks.

I draw a deep breath, bolstered by the arms around me and Monty's penetrating gaze. "Let's finish it."

After a collective nod, Melanie resumes the video. We brace ourselves as the screen flickers back to life, and Denver's madness unfurls.

"Ah, Frankie Trevis, my enchantingly vicious

butterfly. Six weeks ago, I freed you from this island and introduced you to my boys." Denver sweeps his arms through the air to embrace the expanse of Monty's opulent living room. "Today, I returned to Sitka to check on my murderous brother, expecting to find him engaged in his usual whoring. He didn't disappoint. Only one affair, modest by his standards. But one is sufficient to sway your affections toward my boys." His voice drops to a chilling cadence. "I'm making this recording to serve two purposes. Firstly, I will eventually die, and should my boys rise to the occasion, proving themselves deserving, they shall inherit the riddle that leads them to this video and all the answers they seek. Secondly, consider this a warning. The legacy I leave is twined with peril as much as promise."

My hands shake. My chest aches. I try to focus on breathing—deep, even breaths—hoping to quell the panic.

"The first time I laid eyes on you, Frankie, was in a hospital," Denver purrs. "But it was long before Monty entered your life. I happened upon you during your residency days in Anchorage. You sparked something in me then, but my plate was too full to pursue you properly. For years, I watched you though, tracked your journey to Sitka."

"He never told me that," I whisper.

He leans back, a calculated casualness to his posture. "Your meeting with Montgomery wasn't serendipitous. I orchestrated that." He winks, turning my lungs to ice. "And now, if you're watching this, you've found the plane's instructions and are poised to reenter the world I saved you from." His next words slither through the room like a serpent. "Remember, with civilization comes danger. Not all admirers are as upfront as I was. There's another, lurking, yearning for you in a way far darker than my own affection." His voice turns somber, deadly serious. "Mark my words, they are meant to guide and to forewarn. Look around you. Is your admirer there now? Watching? You were safe with me in the hills. Out here, no hills can save you." His gaze sweeps the room as if he could see through the walls, through time itself. "I could reveal the identity of this lethal hunter, but such answers must be earned. So I leave you with the riddle that may save your life. Not all wounds bleed. Not all scars show. Some live beneath bones, cold and alone. In the chambers of frost, pain is my art. I'm the silent ache, the shadow that lingers, the present from your past, the knife in your heart. Who am I?"

The video ends abruptly, leaving a haunting silence in its wake.

"No." My heart pounds fiercely, his razored words scraping at my mind. "No, no, no! Why can't he just leave us alone? Even from the grave, he torments us."

Kody pulls me onto his lap, holding me against his chest. He's so quiet, so still, his thoughts undoubtedly racing through the implications of what we've just heard.

"This is bullshit." Leo can't contain his fury as he bursts from the couch and paces back and forth. "He just wants us to live in fear. He can't accept anything else."

Monty remains the epitome of composure, but his eyes are sharp, analytical. He's already moving past the shock, thinking several steps ahead. "We have to consider every possibility. Denver was many things, not least of which was cunning. We can't dismiss this as mere posthumous theatrics."

"It's another game." I shake my head, partly in disbelief, partly in an attempt to clear the fog of fear. "He wants us to be scared, to jump at shadows. He can't stand the thought of us living freely, without him pulling the strings."

Monty's gaze meets mine, unyielding. "Whether it's a game or not, we can't afford to take chances. Frankie, you know what he was capable of. We all do." He turns to address Kody and Leo. "Since you two are new to this world, the situation is even more dangerous. You can't protect her when you don't even understand your surroundings. You need time, a safe place to adjust." He lifts his chin, his gaze unshakable. "You're coming to Sitka, to my island, all of you. There's a guest house there, separate from the main residence but close enough for safety. I'll install a new security system, hire a security team. It's remote, private. It'll give you both the space to adapt and transition, and it'll keep Frankie safe while we scour this video, figure out what the riddle means, and how deep Denver's plans go."

Leo stops pacing, the cords in his neck strung tight. Kody remains silent, his expression unreadable, but the slight nod indicates his agreement, albeit begrudging.

Moving to Monty's island, returning to a place steeped in memories and complicated emotions...it's a terrible idea.

But the logic is undeniable. We need safety, time, and resources—things only Monty can provide right now.

Fuck.

"All right." I slide off Kody's lap and gulp down the rest of my bourbon. "We'll go to Sitka. We'll take this time to heal, to learn, and to prepare. But Monty..." I'm caught in his direct gaze. "I'm not going there as your wife. And we're not your dependents."

Monty nods, a trace of relief in his expression. "We're family."

The story continues with:
HEART OF FROST AND SCARS
RISE OF INK AND SMOKE (Spin-off)

OTHER BOOKS BY PAM GODWIN

LOVE TRIANGLE ROMANCE
TANGLED LIES TRILOGY
One is a Promise
Two is a Lie
Three is a War

DARK ROMANCE / ANTIHEROES
DELIVER SERIES
Deliver #1
Vanquish #2
Disclaim #3
Devastate #4
Take #5
Manipulate #6
Unshackle #7
Dominate #8
Complicate #9

DARK COWBOY ROMANCE
TRAILS OF SIN
Knotted #1
Buckled #2
Booted #3

DARK PARANORMAL ROMANCE
TRILOGY OF EVE
Heart of Eve
Dead of Eve #1
Blood of Eve #2
Dawn of Eve #3

DARK HISTORICAL PIRATE ROMANCE
King of Libertines
Sea of Ruin

STUDENT-TEACHER / PRIEST
Lessons In Sin

STUDENT-TEACHER ROMANCE
Dark Notes

ROCK-STAR DARK ROMANCE
Beneath the Burn

BILLIONAIRE REVENGE
Dirty Ties

OLDER WOMAN/YOUNGER MAN
Incentive

New York Times, Wall Street Journal, and *USA Today* bestselling author, Pam Godwin, lives in the Midwest with her husband, cats, retired greyhounds, and an old, foul-mouthed parrot. She traveled the world for seven years, attended three universities, married the vocalist of her favorite rock band, and retired from her quantitative analyst career in 2014 to write full-time.

Her interests veer toward the unconventional: bourbon, full-body tattoos, and tragic villains. Equally peculiar are her aversions to sleeping, eating meat, and dolls with blinking eyes.

EMAIL: pamgodwinauthor@gmail.com